The Kill Switch

A Gripping Psychological Thriller

IAN C.P. IRVINE

All rights reserved. Without limiting the rights under copyright observed above, no part of this publication may be reproduced, stored in or introduced into a retrieval system, or transmitted in any form or by any means without the prior written consent of the copyright owner.

This is a work of fiction. Names, characters, businesses, places, events and incidents are either the products of the author's imagination or used in a fictitious manner. Any resemblance to actual persons, living or dead, or actual events is purely coincidental.

© 2022 IAN C.P. IRVINE

ISBN 9798414579892

For my Mother and Father.
With love and gratitude.

'Thank you very much, but not enough!'

ACKNOWLEDGMENTS

With thanks to

Sue Alexander

Melanie Billows

Sandie Parvey

and

Kit Nevile
(For encouraging me to write this book.)

Chapter 1
Day One
Devon
England
Monday morning

The phone first rang at 9.15 a.m., just after Jane had returned from the school run. She'd only just sat down, a freshly brewed coffee in one hand and her favourite magazine in the other, her legs stretched out and her feet resting on the footstool.

This was her special time of the day. Her 'me' time. Her sanity break after packing the kids off to school, before the endless cycle of daily chores began.

Jane was tempted to ignore the phone, but since there was the slight possibility that it could be the kids' school calling to say there was something wrong with one of her little munchkins, she did what any mother would do, and decided to answer it.

Putting the coffee down on the side table and pushing herself up from the sofa, she crossed the room to the sideboard and picked up the receiver.

"Hello, Mrs McIver?" a man's soft and rather sexy voice asked.

"Yes?"

"A Mrs Jane McIver?" the man enquired further.

"Yes. How can I help?"

"This is a courtesy call from the fraud department of your bank. Please, don't worry, but there's a problem with your account. Our system has detected some unusual activity and it may be that money has been taken from your account without your knowledge. It's important that you take action as soon as possible. Following standard security procedures, we'll hang up now, but we would suggest you call your bank as soon as possible, go through security, and discuss your account. If there is a problem, you'll be reconnected to our fraud team and advised what action to take."

"Oh dear…Has any money been stolen? *How much?*" Jane asked, a sense of dread quickly welling up within her.

"I'm sorry, but we can't discuss that with you without going through security, which you can do when you call us back on the number on the back of your bank card. We would advise that you call back on a land-line phone and not a mobile phone, just in case your phone has been infected with a virus, which could be how your account has been breached."

"What do you mean 'breached'? Has someone got my passwords? And has my money been stolen already?"

"Please call your bank and discuss this with them. Thank you. I hope it all turns out well. Goodbye."

There was a buzzing sound at the end of the phone and a long drawn-out tone which signified she had rather abruptly been disconnected.

For a moment she was left standing facing the wall, the phone receiver still in her hand, but then she sprang into action.

If her account had been hacked into somehow, every second counted. She needed to call the bank, find out what had gone wrong, and sort it out immediately.

Her heart beginning to race, she rushed through to the kitchen, found her purse and retrieved her bank card.

Seconds later she was back by the phone, picking up the receiver and dialling the number on the back of her card.

She heard the dial tone change and the sing-song electronic pulsing of the digits being dialled and winging their way round the world through the phone system.

At the other end of the line the phone rang for a few seconds and was then answered by an automated voice.

"We are sorry, but due to exceptionally high call volumes, we expect it to take several minutes before we can answer your call. Please hold. We will be with you as soon as possible."

Jane felt the stress she was feeling increase a notch or two, and her toes started tapping the floor, a classic sign of her becoming increasingly fraught and impatient.

"Come on…" she whispered to herself.

"We are sorry, but due to…" the monotone voice began to recite its mantra once again.

As she listened several times to the cycle of the automated dial tone and repeated apology, Jane began to worry that with every second that passed, more and more money was possibly being siphoned out of her account into the hands of some thief that no one would ever catch.

Then abruptly, the sequence changed and a voice invited her to enter her account number into the phone, followed by a hash sign.

Reading the number off the card, she did as requested, typing it as slowly and carefully as she could so she'd get it right.

"Now, please enter your date of birth."

She complied, slightly relieved that progress was being made at last.

"And now, please enter the second number of your security code…"

A '*six*'.

"And now, please enter the third number of your security code…"

A '*two*'.

There was a momentary pause, then an automated voice said thank you and informed her she was being transferred to an attendant. Almost immediately a voice greeted her. A human voice.

Relief!

"Hello Mrs McIver. Thank you for going through security. How can I help you this morning?"

"I was just contacted by the fraud department and instructed to call you as soon as possible to check my bank account to make sure it hadn't been hacked into. They mentioned some suspicious activity on the account."

"Let me see, one moment please…" A short pause, Jane's heart skipping a beat, the tension ratchetting up another notch. "Actually, yes, I see. Please, can you tell me what you think the balance of the account should be? According to what I see here, there is no money in your account… and there were several rather large withdrawals earlier this morning…"

"What do you mean? My husband only got paid yesterday. There should be about three thousand pounds in that account. I normally call you at the weekend to transfer some to other accounts and pay the bills, but the majority of it should still be there just now."

"You didn't make three separate transfers of eight hundred pounds each at about six o'clock this morning?"

"No, we were still asleep."

A moment's pause.

"I'm sorry, Mrs McIver. It seems the fraud department may have been correct. It looks like someone has accessed your account without your permission. Is there anyone else who may have your account details?"

"No…only my husband. It's our joint account."

"Could he have made the transfer this morning?"

"Absolutely not. He was asleep with me too. Look, can I speak to someone about stopping this and getting my money back? We didn't do this. Our money has been stolen!"

"I'll transfer you over to the Fraud Department. You're already through security so you'll get straight through. Please hold."

Jane heard a couple of beeps and then a man's voice came on.

"Mrs McIver? Hello, my name is Sebastian. I understand you believe your account has been broken into and money illegally transferred out?"

"Yes…I've been cleaned out. Someone has transferred it all out this morning. Every penny. But we didn't do it. It wasn't us."

"Yes, I have your account details on the screen in front of me here, and I can see what's been happening. You should actually have received a call from our department this morning already to tell you something unusual had been noticed."

"Yes, that's why I'm calling you now."

"Good. The faster we stop this, the better. The most important thing we have to do now is to prevent further access to your account, so we need to change your security code immediately. I'll put you through to an automated system. It'll ask you first for your account number, your date of birth, then your old security code, and then lastly it will ask you to type in a new security code twice. First to put it into the system and then to confirm it. Please write it down somewhere. Once that's done, the system will pass you back to me, your account will be secure and then we can take some notes and fill in a form to get you your stolen money back. Is that okay? I'm putting you through now…"

"Yes…thank you. For your help…"

"Please type in your account number." A voice invited her.

Without further thinking, but breathing deeply and trying to control her fingers and make sure she got it right, Jane slowly typed in the digits as requested.

First her account number.

Then her date of birth.

Then her old security code in full.

She paused only when it came to the request to type in a new code, panicking slightly that she didn't know what to do. It had to be something she'd remember when she hung up the phone. Something simple. For a moment her mind was blank, but glancing at the newspaper on the side of the table not far away, she saw the date at the top of the paper and without further thought, typed in today's date. First the day of the month, then the current month, and then the last two digits of the year. She'd remember that!

At the prompt she entered it again, which confirmed she'd done it right the first time.

"Thank you. Change confirmed" an automated voice told her, then seconds later she was back to Sebastian again.

"Mrs McIver. It's Sebastian again. Thanks for that. Your account will now be secure, so you can relax. I can see from the system when the money was transferred out of your account. What we have to do now is to register a claim on your behalf and capture some details from yourself. I'll use the information I can see here, start the paperwork and then send you an email later this morning, asking you to confirm a few things and provide a few extra details. Will that be okay?"

"Yes… I'll check my email in a few hours' time… yes?"

"Yes, Mrs McIver."

"I will get my money back, won't I? I mean, all of it?"

"As soon as we can confirm the fraud and identify exactly what funds have been stolen, we will be able to re-credit your account. Don't worry. We'll make the process as smooth and painless as possible." Jane breathed out loudly.

"Sebastian? Is that your name? Thank you for your help. I appreciate it. Thanks…"

"Goodbye, Mrs McIver." The line went dead.

Jane hung up, walked back to her chair and her coffee and slumped into the seat.

"AAAAHHHHHHHHH!!!!!" Jane screamed loudly, venting her stress and frustration. "*AAAAAGGHHHHH!*" Three thousand pounds?

Gone?

Shit!

Jane wasn't too worried. She knew she'd get the money back. Eventually. After all, it wasn't her fault. She was innocent.

But she could guess that before she did, she'd have to climb a mountain of stress and fill in a zillion forms to prove it wasn't her.

But the bottom line was, she'd get the money back.

She'd read about cases like these. As long as she hadn't voluntarily given her passcode to any one, and followed all normal security precautions, she'd be okay.

Yes, she had nothing to worry about.

She looked at her watch. It was just after ten.

She'd wait ninety minutes and then check her email.

So, settling back in the sofa, she started to read her magazine.

Started.

Her eyes skimmed the first paragraph at least ten times but none of the words were going in.

Plus, her coffee was cold.

So, she got up, went back to the kitchen and made fresh coffee, staring out of the kitchen window at her garden whilst she waited.

Should she call her husband and tell him what had happened? Or just wait until it was confirmed that it was all okay before she let him know?

Deciding on the latter, she finished making the coffee, returned to the sofa and tried to read her magazine again.

At ten thirty, she decided to check her email. Why wait until later, if they had already sent her an email? The truth was, she was actually quite stressed. She couldn't relax. Couldn't read. And her morning would remain ruined until she'd got the email from the bank.

Maybe she should drive to the nearest bank and go and speak to the manager, just to make sure it was being sorted out as soon as possible? ... To check on the progress of things?

The problem with that plan, she quickly realised, was that the nearest bank with an actual human in it with whom you could talk, was about forty minutes away by car and by that time she would definitely have heard from the bank anyway.

Her laptop was taking an age to fire up. Longer than usual. Or was it that just like a kettle when you watched it, when you really needed your laptop to come up fast, it just seemed to take forever.

Three thousand pounds was a lot of money. Would she get it back from the bank all at once or in several instalments? Surely it would be all at once.

It had to be all at once.

They needed the money.

At last, finally, she managed to click on the shortcut to her email and her latest batch of messages appeared on the screen.

It only took a second to skim through the headers and see that none of them came from the bank.

Nothing yet.

Just to be sure, she went to her Junk Mail, but found the same result.

Nothing.

Yet.

Maybe she should call her husband after all.

Perhaps the email had been sent to his account and not hers?

She thought about that.

It was a possibility.

She couldn't remember the last time she'd received an email from her bank. Perhaps the default email address associated with the account was actually her husband's, not hers?

Oh dear.

She would definitely have to call him.

Just to be sure...

Standing up, she walked back through to the sofa where she had left her mobile phone on the side table. Picking it up, she was just about to call him when it began to ring in her hands.

The display said 'private number.'

It wasn't one that she had programmed into her contacts.

Normally, she would be reluctant to accept calls from people she didn't know. There were so many scams around today.

She let it ring.

Eventually, the incoming call stopped and the screen went back to normal.

She went to 'Recent' and looked at the number again. It was definitely not one she knew.

Flicking over to messages, she found that someone had just left a voice message. It must have been whoever it was who had just called her.

She dialled 121.

It was a woman's voice.

"Hello Mrs McIver, this is Sarah from the Fraud department at the Westminster Bank. Could you please call us back as soon as possible? We've noticed that in the past hour there have been several large cash transfers to overseas accounts. We'd like to confirm whether or not you're aware of them, and to rule out the possibility that your account has just been breached…"

Chapter 2
Day Two
Central London

Mr Green sat in the chair facing the Bank Manager, one arm around his wife's shoulder and the other hand offering his wife a handkerchief to dab her eyes. She'd been crying for five minutes now and it didn't look like she was going to stop any time soon.

Edward Dawson, the Bank Manager, had been running this branch of the Westminster Bank for over twenty years now, and he'd never known a day like this before. It was only one thirty, he'd not yet had lunch, and he'd already seen ten other customers with similar, if not exactly the same problem: they'd been robbed and all their money had been siphoned out of their accounts. Not only one bank account, but all of them. People who had previously been wealthy and had been in charge of bulging bank accounts, were now the proud owners of empty accounts. Even relatively less well-off people had been hit.

They all had one thing in common though. They had fallen victim to a telephone scam which started yesterday afternoon, just when many people in the UK had been paid. Unwittingly, they had voluntarily given away to the scammers all the details the thieves needed to gain access to the account and change the passwords to lock the real owners out of any future access. The scammers had then transferred all the money out of that account to a foreign bank account which they controlled. In many cases, the scammers had also managed to access other accounts held by the same account holder, enabling them to empty those accounts too.

People had lost thousands, tens of thousands, and in some cases, hundreds of thousands.

The hardest part of this was what Mr Dawson was going to have to explain to the customer next. This was the part when the customer's life went from bad to very bad.

And from which some would potentially never recover.

"So, Mr Dawson, when do you expect that the bank will be able to reimburse the funds back into our accounts?" Mr Green asked, handing ownership of the handkerchief over to his wife, and turning back to focus on the bank manager.

The bank manager coughed, smiled a little, adjusted his tie and then started to address the elephant in the room.

Or the herd of elephants.

Each time he'd gone through this with the other customers this morning, he'd worried they would attack him. And every time he had delivered the news, he had tried a different way of saying it, in the hope that he'd find a way of delivering it with minimal risk to himself, or the bank.

"This is a complicated question, Mr Green. With no simple answer. However, what I can say for now is that this is now formally a police matter. And you should report it to the police for it to be handled by them as a theft. As soon as possible. Unfortunately, because you voluntarily handed over your account details to a third party, we, the Bank, or any other bank in the UK in a similar position, would not be held liable for the losses you have incurred. You see, our security systems are foolproof, but require our customers to protect their account details and not pass them on to others. If they do so, I'm afraid, the Bank cannot be held liable…"

Across the table, a look of incredulity begun to spread across the faces of Mr and Mrs Green. Interestingly, Mrs Green stopped crying. The expressions on their faces changed several times, as the full meaning of the words the bank manager had said began to sink in.

Invariably however, as had happened every time so far today, with every customer who had received this news, the next sentence that was uttered by the customer – in this case Mrs Green – was, *"What do you mean? I don't understand what you're saying…"*

Mr Dawson felt sorry for them. Genuinely bad. But now the meeting was entering the most difficult phase. Having delivered the bank's get-out-of-jail clause, and explained that it was the customer who had lost the money and not the bank, the big question was, how to get the customer to leave the room without them killing him. He was, after all, just the messenger, and in breaking the news to them that it was basically the customer's problem, and not his - or the bank's - Mr Dawson moved from 'Professional' to 'Survival' mode.

He knew he wasn't very good at this. He lacked the skills, perhaps. But it was his responsibility.

So, for the next ten minutes, he carried on toeing the official Bank line, explaining to the customer that they should now go home and report the theft and fraud to the police, and press *them* to get their money back for them. And that the sooner they went home to start the process, the better chance they had of getting that money back.

Mr Dawson hated that part.

He knew it was a lie.

However, it was perhaps the most effective way of getting the customer to stand up and leave the room.

The reality of course was that the customer would probably never see the money again.

Mr Dawson knew that in some cases the customers' lives would be ruined.

But he also knew that to do his job properly, he had to distance himself from their experiences and their problems.

Mr Dawson was only three years off retirement. He had a good pension plan, and a bright retirement all planned out.

Thankfully, when Mr Dawson offered the couple in front of him a brightly coloured and professional looking pack of information detailing what the customers should do next, with advice on how to approach the police, what forms to fill in, and what information to provide - along with a copy of the small print from the bank that outlined exactly how and why the Bank was officially not liable for their losses – Mr and Mrs Green had eventually got up and left his office.

Shaking and in tears, but they had thankfully finally gone.

Mr Dawson looked at the clock on the wall.

He too, was also shaking. Partly from hunger, partly from stress, and partly because he needed a good, stiff drink.

But he didn't have much time…there were already four other customers waiting outside his office with the same problem: they'd been robbed!

Chapter 3
Day Two
Germany

Gunter Grossman stood on the edge of the bridge above the river Donau.

It was late. Very late. Or very early, depending upon when a person normally began their day.

But for Gunter, it was late. Too late to do anything to alter the course of the next few minutes. He was tired. Exhausted.

All his life he had struggled. First, to find a decent education.

Then to prove how educated he was and win a place at university.

To pass his exams, start and build a career.

Find love.

Have children.

And then to support his family and ensure they never had to struggle like him.

It had taken… what?… fifty years to build the life they wanted and deserved?

DESERVED.

Gunter looked down at the river beneath.

He couldn't remember when it had been so full. The water was rushing by faster than he had ever seen it do before. It was dirty, dark, unwelcoming, pushing high up the banks and threatening to overflow the villages and cities around it.

Gunter sighed.

Until this morning his future, the future for his family, everything, had seemed so bright.

But then, just after breakfast, he answered the phone in his office and his world had begun to unravel.

The man on the other end of the phone had politely informed him that his name was Sebastian. He was calling from his bank. There was a problem…

Gunter was a clever and careful man. This morning however, he had been tired.

Careless.

After months of arranging the finances to purchase their own family home, the funds had been temporarily sitting in one of his accounts ready to be transferred over to complete the sale. He was going to buy a new family home. In cash. Almost all the assets he had built up during his life had been liquidated into cash to enable the purchase of their dream home.

Then Sebastian had called.

Gunter had listened carefully to what Sebastian had said. Then he panicked.

Knowing that everything he had was exposed, at risk, ... under threat, Gunter had followed all the advice and instructions which Sebastian had given him.

Now it was all gone.

Everything.

Gunter had been a fool.

He'd thrown it all away. Fifty years of work, struggle, and success. All gone.

But worst of all, he'd let his family down.

And the only way to make it all right was to enable them to claim the life insurance.

When Gunter died, he'd be rich again!

At least…his family would.

Suddenly Gunter heard a voice, bringing him back from his thoughts to the real world. He turned round, holding on to the metal pillar that disappeared upwards into the darkness above the railing he'd climbed up onto.

"Don't jump!" the woman who was running towards him was shouting.

As the woman came closer, Gunter could see that she was young.

Kind. Caring.

She was a nice person.

As she came nearer, Gunter edged back around to face the bridge, and as she edged closer to stand in front of him, she reached up her hand towards him. "Please, let me help you!" she asked softly.

Gunter smiled.

The woman had a beautiful face.

She reminded him of his daughter.

He closed his eyes, and stepped backwards.

Off the railing.

Into nothingness.

Brazil

"Hello, may I speak with Senor Rodriguez. This is Sebastian from the Fraud Department of your bank. I'm calling because…"

Australia

"Hello, may I speak with Mr or Mrs Brown? This is Sebastian from the Fraud Department of your bank. I'm calling because…"

South Africa

"Hello, May I speak with Mr Vogel? This is Sebastian from the Fraud Department of your bank. I'm calling because…"

Day Three
COBRA Meeting
10 Downing Street
England
4 p.m.

"It's estimated that in the UK, the new Sebastian bank scam has taken over two hundred million pounds in the past two days alone," the Chancellor of the Exchequer announced. "It's like nothing we've seen before. It's incredibly effective, widespread and almost untraceable."

The Prime Minister shifted uncomfortably in his seat. He wasn't really prepared for the meeting. It had been called at very short notice first thing this morning, and now he was sitting in the cabinet room, with representatives of four of the UK major banks, the Home Secretary, the Chancellor of the Exchequer, the Governor of the Bank of England and several other senior ministers.

"Two hundred million? Pounds sterling or in crypto currency?" PM Paul Dalgleish asked, trying to sound with-it and knowledgeable.

"Sterling. The average person from whom this money is being stolen doesn't have the faintest idea what a bitcoin is. We're talking cold, hard cash here." The Chancellor replied.

"Okay, can you talk me through please, just exactly what this scam is and why it's so concerning?" The PM asked, looking around the table and seeing the worried looks on the faces of all the others in the room.

The Chancellor nodded.

"Certainly, but before I start, I just wanted to add the two hundred million I just mentioned is what we think the UK had lost as of last night. We think about fifty thousand people have been affected within forty-eight hours, with an average loss per person of about four thousand pounds. But this scam is international. It's been reported everywhere. We could be talking billions in losses across the EU and the other members of the G7."

"Who's behind it?" The PM asked.

"We don't know at this point." The Chancellor replied.

"So, how does it work?"

"Someone calls the victim. In the past, telephone scams have been mostly random, but this one seems to begin with some knowledge of the victim. They start off by requesting to speak with the householder by name. If a man answers the phone, they ask for the male house owner. If it's a woman, they ask for the female. The voice then introduces himself as Sebastian. It's always Sebastian. Regardless of country…" "Are they always speaking English?" The PM interrupted the Chancellor.

"No, they converse in the local language. But Sebastian is always spoken or pronounced as that name would be done locally. Sebastian then informs the householder that he's calling from the fraud department of their bank… they never mention the bank by name… and just assume the householder will not question the authenticity of the call. I should add that if the householder begins to ask too many questions, or asks which bank, or for more details, Sebastian hangs up. From this, we know that Sebastian doesn't really know too much about the account details of the householder. This is when it gets clever, though. Sebastian insists that the security protocol of the bank is to hang up and get the householder to call the bank back on the appropriate number and then go through security. Sebastian then hangs up rather abruptly. Or at least, he appears to. The rather abrupt way in which the call ends seems to lend itself well to the householder also hanging up, retrieving their bank card, and then quickly dialling the bank back on the number on the back of the card. All the victims have reported that when they pick up the phone, they hear dial tones, and electronic pulses as the numbers are dialled. The phone rings, they're presented with call centre bank options, and they're taken through security questions. It's very clever. The householder is challenged on their security details and they're then granted access to their bank account. At this point, they're told their account has been emptied, their money may have been stolen, and they are put back through to the security department. Sebastian answers the phone, reconnecting with the victim, and expressing a sufficient amount of concern. Sebastian then advises the now identified account holder that they must… rather, they should… change their security code. The victim is now taken through an automated system which requests their full bank details and their full security code, and then invites the target to now select and confirm a new security code. After this is done, the account holder is assured that the thief who hacked into their account can do no further damage, and that in order to be reimbursed for the lost funds the account holder will need to fill in some forms. Sebastian volunteers to start the process of registering the fraud and reclaiming the money, and informs the customer he will contact them by email with the necessary paperwork in a few hours. This is all done so professionally and courteously that the account holder begins to relax, feels reassured and then hangs up the call."

"So, how does the scam work? Exactly… I don't see…" The PM begins to interrupt.

The Chancellor stops, takes a sip of water from his glass, and then continues.

"It's all very clever. And it relies upon one thing…From the moment that Sebastian calls them the first time, they never lose connection with whoever Sebastian is. We've seen this before, on other scams, but this one is particularly well done."

"I don't understand…I thought Sebastian hung up the call, initially, and the victim called their own bank…" The PM shook his head.

"That's exactly what Sebastian wants them to think. In actual fact, Sebastian only pretends to hang up. He never puts the receiver down. The line remains live. The victim then hangs up, gets the bank's telephone number and calls the bank back. Another clever part is the victim hears a dial tone from the phone, but this is all fake. Sebastian, or a computer that Sebastian has, is mimicking the sounds to make the victim feel he or she is going through the process of calling the bank back. But it's all fake. Sebastian was just waiting for them to pick the phone back up at their end and call them back… He never left the line…"

"But Sebastian is taking a big gamble there, isn't he? Most people would probably call the bank back on their mobile…" The PM pointed out.

"Which is why," the Chancellor explained, "before he pretends to hang up, Sebastian warns them not to use their computer or mobile phone, because they've probably been compromised, or hacked into, and can't be trusted. So the victim does exactly what's instructed and calls the bank back on the landline, really believing that they're now safe, and they've initiated a new and very safe call to their real bank. But they haven't. It's all a scam. When the customer goes through security by putting in their bank account details, date of birth, and some of their security code, Sebastian is collecting all that information. And then when the victim thinks that they have gone through security and now have access to their account, they are told by Sebastian, or one of his colleagues - it might just be Sebastian putting on another voice for all we know - that the bank account has been emptied."

"And has it?"

"No. Not yet. Sebastian does that later. The cruel thing is that at the point the victim believes the money is already gone, the money is actually still there. Nothing has been stolen yet. But then Sebastian asks the victim to go through an automated security process again, and because all the victims who fall prey to this scam now feel so comfortable that they are genuinely talking to the bank and following standard security procedures of the bank, when they are asked to type in their full security code, all of it, not just random parts of it requested by the bank, they actually do it. They do just as instructed. They type in their full security code, and Sebastian records it all. Then comes the good part…"

"The good part?"

"Sorry, the clever part… the customer is requested to change their security code to block out the hacker who has obviously somehow gained access to their details. So they do so. They make up another security code and type it in…"

"Which the attacker uses to get access to the account?" The PM asks.

"No. Sebastian just ignores it. The victim hasn't really done anything. Remember, he's not talking to the bank. Only to Sebastian."

"Yes…, okay…"

"And then Sebastian tells them he's going to help them. He'll start the paperwork. And the bank will email them in a couple of hours' time. In the meantime, Sebastian insists they mustn't worry. It's all going to be fine. Have you understood so far, PM?"

The PM looks around the table. All eyes are on him.

"Yes, I think so. Sebastian then helps them get the money back from the bank, but keeps some of it?"

The Chancellor smiles.

"No, PM. Not at all. We must not forget, sir, that Sebastian is a complete and utter bastard. He's a thief. And having just lulled his victim into a false sense of security, and bought time by insisting that the victim should wait a couple of hours for an email, Sebastian then uses all the account details, date of birth, and the full security code that the victim voluntarily typed into the system and gave to Sebastian, to then call the real bank, pretend to be them, go through security and then get access to their account."

"But how do they know which bank to call? You said originally that Sebastian didn't know which bank they were with…"

"He didn't, but when the victim called the bank back, Sebastian captured the electronic pulses being generated by the victim's phone and from that could identify which bank it was. It's possible they also simply replayed the numbers, not knowing which bank it was, and seeing what happened next and which bank answered the call. We don't know yet."

"Oh… that's very clever." The PM agreed, nodding.

"But not the best part…"

"You're really enjoying this aren't you? I have to remind you that over two hundred million has been stolen… this is no laughing matter!" The PM exploded, banging the table a little with his hand.

"You misunderstand. It's bad, very bad. But very clever. Now Sebastian has access to the account and he talks to the human operator, or goes through the automated system, and transfers all the contents of that account out of the bank to another account. In some cases, Sebastian can also get access to other accounts owned by the victim. The bank, at this point, also believes and trusts Sebastian. Since Sebastian successfully went through the security system and answered all the security questions, the bank allows Sebastian to transfer money between accounts and then out of the bank to another account number. Because this is possible in some banks, some victims have lost large amounts of money that was sitting in other accounts. This all happens rather quickly, within about thirty minutes to an hour of the initial call from Sebastian to the victim."

"Whilst the victim is drinking a coffee and thinking everything is going to be fine?" the PM asks, nodding to himself.

"Exactly." The Chancellor agrees, pauses, then continues. "The coup de grâce, however, is when, having emptied the victim's accounts, Sebastian then follows the bank's procedure and changes the customer's security code to a new one. I may add, this is not the new code the victim chose, but a different one which Sebastian creates and which only he knows. This then effectively locks the victim out of their own account and prevents them from talking to the bank about their accounts for quite a long time. Even if they do manage to talk to the bank, they find out that their accounts have been emptied, which is what Sebastian already told them. They already knew that. In fact, most of the victims only first hear about their accounts really being emptied, when the real fraud department from the real bank calls them to tell them they've seen some suspicious activity. And by that time, it's too late!"

"Ouch!" the PM says and smiles. "Cheeky bastard!"

"If I may continue, Prime Minister, there are several very important issues here. Firstly, technically, currently the Banks are not liable for the losses that are being incurred by the victims. Unfortunately, and it is very unfortunate, upon that we can all agree, unfortunately… the customer has voluntarily given their passwords and account details to a confidence trickster who has no connection to the bank… at no point does Sebastian claim to work for a named bank… which means that there is zero liability on behalf of the banks for the customers' losses.

"Second, this is happening on a very large scale. From what I've heard today, Sebastian's activity seems to be gathering pace, not abating.

"Third, and perhaps most important of all, if this continues, there is a very real risk to the banking community and to the nation. As you well know, Prime Minister, the banking system is essentially a system based upon trust. If you take away the trust; if customers lose trust in their banks and their ability to protect their money, there will be a run on the banks the like of which we have not seen before, and not one, but all our banks, globally, could be under threat. People are already beginning to talk about this on Social Media. If we don't put a stop to this soon, we're in a lot of trouble."

The Chancellor paused and wiped his forehead with his handkerchief.

"May I say something?" one of the other ministers at the far end of the table asked. When the Prime Minister nodded, he quickly introduced himself to the representatives from the banks as the Minister for National Cyber Security.

"There's something else here which is also of significant concern. For me, it's perhaps the most worrying of all. If we think about the scale on which this scam is being conducted, there's a pretty obvious question that's still outstanding. Which is, basically, who is Sebastian? Or *WHAT* is Sebastian?"

"Meaning?" the PM urged the Cyber Minister.

"How many Sebastian's are there? Thousands of people are being contacted, at the same time, and each time, it's Sebastian on the phone. Everywhere. I've heard some of the recordings of the telephone calls that have been made and all the voices sound the same. It's a calm, trustworthy, very likeable male voice. Pretty unique. There can't be thousands of people who speak like that. Even if it was a different person pretending to be same, and imitating a voice which the scammers knew to be effective in lulling victims into a false sense of security, how many people are actually involved in this scam? Don't forget, it's happening on an international scale. It's everywhere. In all time zones. Going on constantly. If it's people who are behind this scam, just how large is the organisation behind it? How many people are working the phones and scamming the victims? Is it an army?"

"An army of Sebastians?" The PM repeated, nodding and pondering the idea.

"Or," the cyber minister continued. "Is it just one Sebastian behind it all?"

"What do you mean?" The Chancellor of the Exchequer interrupted.

"I mean, is Sebastian a man? Or a machine? Gentleman, what concerns me is that this is not another telephone scam, but the first instance of a new type of threat. A cyberattack on a scale we haven't seen before, where, for the first time in history mankind is being robbed by an Artificial Intelligence persona. A computer that thinks with the mind of criminal."

Chapter 4
Thames House
Millbank
London 7 p.m.

The Minister for National Cyber Security stood at the front of the room, surveying those assembled in the room before him and for the first time since he had accepted the job, felt really nervous.

Paul Harrison was forty years old. Unlike some of the other Cabinet Ministers who'd been appointed into their roles without any experience of their new domain, for example the Fisheries Minister who'd never been fishing, or the Agriculture Minister who had never planted a seed in her life, or the Defence Minister, who, as it turned out, was a pacifist, Paul had studied Computer Science at University, had served his time at IBM, and then entered politics full time after a stint as a local councilor.

After being elected to run for Swindon North, his infectious energy and charisma had turned a recent Labour win into a surprising Conservative gain, and within six months had been offered a Cabinet post.

The word 'meteoric' often came to mind when Paul thought of his rise from where he started and to where he was now. But it wasn't the lack of experience which made Paul feel nervous now.

It was the fact that although Paul did know about cyber, probably actually quite a lot, the people assembled in front of him now in the Green Room at MI5, were the crème de la crème of all things digital. Whilst Paul had been learning nursery rhymes, those who were about to listen to him speak now, were all learning Python, Java or C++.

By the time most of those in the room got to university, exams were pointless. If they sat an exam and didn't do well enough, they would simply hack into the system and alter their scores, giving them whatever marks they wanted.

No wonder that almost everyone in the room today had at least a 1st at Uni.

Either richly deserved, or self-awarded.

Those who didn't, had earned their place here in the Cyber team at MI5 through another route: not the school of hard-knocks, but more likely the school of financial or industrial cyber hacking where they'd been caught, or ratted out by another jealous hacker, but were then offered a deal by the state: go to prison and we'll throw away the key, or come and work for your country – access to the best computer systems, unparalleled processing power, and a pool-table, free-fruit and beer on a Friday afternoon.

This was the third trip that the Cyber Minister had made to the MI5 headquarters in Vauxhall in London, but probably the first time he'd been confronted with so many of those who worked at the coal-face, protecting the nation and defending the country's freedom. Paul knew that the future of cyber really belonged to the younger generation, that the latest generation of humans seemed to have been born with a digital device in their hands and were practically able to navigate any operating system before they could walk, but looking round the room today, he was still surprised to see how young everyone was. There were probably only two people in the room above the age of thirty, and everyone else was probably less than twenty- five.

Paul also knew it would be a mistake to underestimate their talents and capabilities. They might be wearing sandals, t-shirts and have odd shaped beards and hairstyles, but these 'kids' and others like them were amongst the crème de la crème of cyber experts anywhere. On a scale of one to ten, Paul was a two, and these kids were… eleven or twelve. Which was why Paul was nervous. These were cyber gods, and in their language, if they were a '1', he was a '0'.

There were about forty people in the room today. It was a sizeable number, given the short notice, and that everyone had to be pulled from other projects, although after discussing the problem the country was facing with the Head of M15, Paul had been promised all the cooperation that they could be given at this time, and he had hoped for more.

After being introduced by one of the Department Directors, Paul moved to the centre of the room.

"Ladies and Gentlemen, I need your help. The UK needs your help. In fact, probably most of the people in the developed world need your help. As you will have seen in the Mission Bulletin sent to you thirty minutes ago, most of the developed world is currently experience a banking scam on a scale we haven't seen before. Since the COBRA meeting this afternoon, a further twenty thousand people had fallen victim to the scam in the UK and we estimate another hundred million pounds has probably been stolen from their accounts. According to all reports, there seems to be one person behind every call each victim receives. He's a man called Sebastian. Or rather, for the reasons I outlined in the Mission Bulletin, I think Sebastian is actually a highly capable AI program. I need your help to track him down, and shut him down. Within the next forty-eight hours."

A moment's silence, then a young woman in the second row folded her arms and asked, 'And what happens if we don't?"

"A possible run on the banks. Potential financial meltdown. Chaos."

Paul didn't elaborate further, but the look on his face told everyone in the room exactly what they needed to know.

This was serious.

"Good, now I've got all your attention, I would like to elaborate a little on the mission you've all been given. As far as I see it, there are six major strands.

"First, we need to prove that Sebastian is, in actual fact, an AI program operating in between cyber space and the real world.

"Second, we need to understand how Sebastian operates, and where from. We need to locate the sources of all his activities.

"Third, we need to understand who is controlling Sebastian. Who is behind this?

"Fourth, we need to find out where all the stolen money is going. If possible, we want to get the money back, but at this stage, that's not imperative. Perhaps later.

"Fifth, we need to halt Sebastian's activities in the UK. It would be a bonus if you could learn how to shut him down in Europe for our allies too, but don't do that unless you are directed to do so.

"Sixth, we need to eliminate Sebastian permanently, shut him down, and make sure he doesn't come back."

Paul looked around the room and was pleasantly surprised to find that the facial expressions of those in the room had almost all changed. Instead of the looks of mild boredom or disinterest that a few of them had displayed previously, they were all sitting up straight, attentive and focussed.

"I can't pretend to know what you guys get up to on a daily basis, and in a moment, I will be asked to leave the room, because I don't have the clearance or permission to stay whilst you start planning how to tackle this mission, but, I just wanted to add, that if I'm right, and you can prove that Sebastian is an AI program attacking and threatening our economic infrastructure, then we will find ourselves in some very interesting and difficult waters. Particularly if we identify any other nation state as Sebastian's controller. If that's the case, what will that make this? A cyber threat? A cyberattack from a foreign power?"

"If that's the case, sir, that'll really muddy the waters." A young man from the back of the room volunteered. "I mean, who will be dealing with this then? The Secret Intelligence Service? The Foreign Office? The Police? Who'll have jurisdiction?"

"And if it is a massive cyberattack that's threatening our economy, isn't that a red line the UK Government has warned other nations not to cross? Isn't that now considered an act of war, requiring a military or equivalent reciprocal attack?" another young woman with blue hair asked.

Paul frowned.

"Sadly, all of these are possibilities. This is new territory. But, for now, it has to be one step at a time, and we'll cross each bridge when we come to it. In the meantime, please, on behalf of the government, do what you can to find out what Sebastian is, shut him down, and give us the answers to the other questions I've asked."

A minute later, Paul was out of the room, being escorted off the premises, and met by his driver in the underground car park. As he climbed into the car and settled back into the rear seat for the drive back to Westminster, he couldn't help but wish he was a fly on the wall still inside the Green Room of MI5. By now, they'd be deep in Geek language, planning their mission, and getting ready to start go find and hopefully kill Sebastian.

Paul looked at his watch.

It was 7.45 p.m.

He was expecting his first report at 11 p.m.

And then another at 4 a.m.

In the world of international cyber, no one slept.

Chapter 5
The voice of Sebastian 10.30 p.m.

Iain Slater pushed back from his desk terminal and stretched his arms above his head and behind his neck. His eyes never left the screen, scanning four audio traces that were playing on the screen from left to right. Each was from a different recording of an interaction between Sebastian and a victim, which they had intercepted and captured earlier that evening but which, most importantly, he had selected because they had taken place simultaneously, in different parts of the UK. After the Cyber Minister had left the building, the team had been given their tasks, and Iain had been assigned the job of tracing any conversations between Sebastian and his targets that could be found on the UK networks. To the layman on the street, this may have seemed an impossible task, but to Iain and others like him in the Secret Intelligence Services, it was never a question of 'if' but rather, 'how many minutes would it take?'

In the old days, in the early days of the Echelon system, if people said a couple of keywords into their telephones, the UK monitoring system would automatically start to record their conversations for later possible analysis. A specialist like himself with the appropriate authorisations and permissions could then sift through all the conversations - possibly hundreds or thousands - adding more keywords to their analysis and filtering and rapidly honing down the selection until they had a smaller number of phone conversations that they could actually manually listen to.

Since then, technology had changed everything. Firstly, instead of going through the old analogue PSTN- Public Switched Telephone Network - made up of old-fashioned copper wires, a vast proportion of telephone calls were now being transported over the same digital networks that carried internet traffic and enabled social media networks. Unfortunately for people like Iain, almost all of these communications were now encrypted, which used to mean that it was almost impossible to eavesdrop and listen to conversations which were carried over the 'IP network'. Used to be.

What few people realised was that those who needed to, now had several highly effective ways of 'decrypting' such encrypted conversations.

It wasn't always easy, but it was effective. Where necessary.

However, now the easy days of Echelon were gone, it did take a little longer finding 'interesting' conversations that should be listened to. Although the process of 'listening to' a conversation which had been 'recorded' was still necessary to understand how keywords were used and in what context, the process was no longer entirely manual. Thanks to voice recognition and speech-to-text technologies, whole conversations could be transcribed into text and then analysed by AI software analysis technology to identify and pull out any conversations that were considered 'interesting'.

The difficult part perhaps, was identifying which conversations should be recorded: it was a chicken-and-egg situation. When the police or secret service knew that a suspect or 'subject' was of 'interest' - an 'SoI' - they could apply for legal permission to listen to and record anything they did or said. However, faced with the whole population of a country and not knowing which conversations to record and decrypt, a little extra helping hand was required to get the ball rolling.

Again, although daunting to the uninitiated, to Iain and his friends, it wasn't rocket science.

To start his current mission, Iain simply asked the banks to give him the telephone numbers of some of Sebastian's victims from earlier that day. He then used his search and analysis systems to retrieve the phone records from the telecommunications providers and then use these to identify all the parameters and metadata made available by the communications networks and telephone systems. From analysis of this information, it was then possible to do several things.

First, thanks to the fact that almost all the traffic that crossed the telecommunications networks in the UK was stored in massive storage buffers in underground bunkers - mostly repurposed nuclear bunkers from the Cold War - it was possible to look back and retrieve almost any communications that had occurred within a three-hour period. After that, only the metadata was recorded, and the content was lost. But in Iain's case, it was possible to effectively go back in time, suck back the conversations that Sebastian had had with some of his victims, decrypt those that were encrypted, and then listen to them.

Secondly, by looking at the 'metadata' —which was effectively the data that surrounded the content of any communications and which described the communications, it was possible to learn lots of important information about that call without even listening to it, i.e., this call took place at 2 p.m., it lasted ten minutes, the call was made from Telephone Number "X" to telephone number "Y". By cross-referencing this information with other databases, it was then possible to identify who made the call, and where from physically, as well as the identity of the person who was called. And more. Much more.

Thirdly, within a few seconds of applying for and being granted permission to do so, it would then be possible to set up a tracking system to ensure that any time any other phone calls were made by or to specific numbers, those conversations would be recorded in full, and flagged up to anyone needing to know, for further analysis and intelligence generation.

Today, from the time Iain had received details of his mission, it had taken only ninety minutes before he had first identified the main telephone numbers Sebastian had been calling his victims from. He'd then set up alerts with all the major telephone service providers and initiated authorised monitoring and recording of any future conversations involving Sebastian's contact details. He'd then retrieved four different voice traces of conversations between Sebastian and a victim and these were now being displayed on one of his three screens.

Iain then started to listen to and analyse the voice conversations he had on his screen. By splicing and dicing and manipulating the voice traces he had on his screen, he was able to break the conversation down into words and phrases, and move them around on his monitor, listening to any he wanted to at will.

The first thing that struck him was that each of the conversations were unique. They were not exactly the same. The conversations seemed natural, as if between two normal people. Sebastian said something, the victim said something in reply, and then Sebastian responded. Only at the very end of the conversation when Sebastian hung up, did it seem rather abrupt.

Iain took several of the words that appeared in each of the conversations, separated them out from their individual conversations, and then copied them to one of his other two screens. He then ran an analysis program on them to see how similar or dissimilar they were. He did this for several words, with the first to receive the treatment being the obvious word choice of '*bank*'.

From the four different conversations he was looking at, he had four different instances of the word 'bank', and now he displayed the voice traces of each horizontally one above the other.

Each trace looked like something you might imagine from a lie detector trace, but far more intense, with a mass of squiggly lines vibrating up and down according to the individual components of the word being broken down and converted into its raw components. What interested Iain was that the traces all looked remarkably alike. Very alike. In fact, they were almost exactly the same. Given that each person in the world has a unique voice and that no two voice traces would be the same, this result proved one thing, almost one hundred per cent conclusively.

However, Iain knew the importance of his analysis, so he repeated that same exercise for a number of other words. For example, 'hang-up', 'call', 'account', and 'fraud', which all appeared in roughly the same parts of the conversations.

After this, Iain started looking at a number of phrases, such as "we can't discuss that" and "our system has detected", or "has been infected with a virus". The audio voice prints of these words were more complex, but Iain was still struck by how similar they were.

Lastly, he started examining words which appeared several times in each conversation, but at different times. Iain noticed that these words often had different inflexions, depending where they appeared in a sentence and upon their relationship to other words being used. In this case, he found that the voice prints were slightly different, but when he focused on individual components of a word or phrase, such as consonant or a vowel, he discovered that they were very similar.

Apart from all this confirming that the words were being spoken by the same source, it also showed that the source of the spoken words was very clever. When a word was used in a sentence, it was never exactly the same word being said, but a variation of that word depending upon its position in the sentence relative to other words.

However, now having confirmed that the words from the different conversations were similar and had come from the same source, Iain moved to answering another question.

To do this, he opened up a library of words which had been said and recorded from the voices of a mixture of humans. Using the compare, search and retrieve facility of the software program he was using, he initiated an automated search for a number of words which had been spoken by men in a similar way: male, deep voice, relaxed, English accent, formal.

The search came back with quite a number of possibilities, and he started comparing individual words said by Sebastian with those said by known sources.

What this showed was interesting. It showed that the intensity and richness of the sounds, frequencies and waveforms which made up the words spoken by men from known sources was far more complex than those spoken by Sebastian. To the human ear, Sebastian's voice sounded normal, but to the system, Sebastian's voice lacked harmonics and sophistication. At a microscopic level, the enunciation of vowels and consonants was simplistic.

In fact, the conclusion that the system flashed up on the screen after the analysis and comparison of each word confirmed what Iain had suspected.

The sound source of Sebastian's words was synthetic.

Sebastian's voice was not real.

It had been generated by a voice synthesiser.

The results of both analysis streams combined to yield a single, undeniable conclusion. Over the past two days, the same voice had been used to talk to many people across the UK, with hundreds of these conversations taking place simultaneously.

Also, no two people have the same voice pattern, yet the analysis showed that all the voices of Sebastian analysed were the same voice.

Ultimately, comparative analysis of Sebastian's voice with the library of human voices showed that Sebastian's voice was not real.

In other words, Sebastian was not a human.

Sebastian was the voice of a computer.

Chapter 6
The First Report
11.35 p.m.

The first report was in. Paul had finished reading it and had immediately called the Prime Minister, who was still up.

Ten minutes later his car had delivered him to Downing Street and he was being ushered upstairs to join the PM for a nightcap, although Paul suspected he wouldn't be getting much sleep that night.

"Ah, Paul come in, sit down." The PM smiled, waving him to a deep, red leather chesterfield-style sofa, handing Paul a large brandy glass with far too much brandy in it. "So, what have you got for me, Paul? What are we looking at? Who is Sebastian?"

"As we suspected, Prime Minister, Sebastian is not a person. He is a computer. A very clever computer, as it turns out, able to hold thousands of different conversations with people dispersed across the UK and actually the world, simultaneously. And these conversations are not the typical conversation you'd expect to have with a computer. You can't tell you're not talking to a human. Also, Sebastian isn't following a rigid text. His approach is similar and anticipates the response of the victim, but is flexible enough to adapt and change its approach according to the responses the individual gives. Interestingly, when some of those who are called, challenge Sebastian, or don't follow the expected response route, then Sebastian simply hangs up and the line goes dead. But that doesn't happen very often."

"So," the PM mused, "we're looking at a computer led assault on our financial system?"

"Not directly. I don't think this is a direct attack on the UK's economy. It's not going after us - the nation or the City - I would say that it's going after the money. It's not attacking the banks, it's stealing money from its customers."

The PM sipped his brandy, thinking.

"So Paul, is this a banking scam, or a cyberattack?"

Paul coughed.

"Sir, I understand the nuances we're playing here, so I would like to be careful with my reply. I don't think this is a cyberattack being launched against our infrastructure. It is however, a highly complex banking scam that is enabled by what appears to be a truly sophisticated computer program that undoubtedly is being driven by Artificial Intelligence."

"Sebastian?"

"Yes, sir. We can call the AI, Sebastian, for now, if you wish. Although, it's just a program and we can't tell if the program identifies itself as being Sebastian, or that's just the name it's using in the banking scam."

"What do you mean, *'identifies itself'*?"

"I mean we don't know if the AI program is able to think and has given itself an identity, or it's just been programmed to introduce itself as Sebastian. The likelihood of someone having developed a sentient AI program that has adopted a personal identity, like a human, without us knowing about it, is highly unlikely. We'd know about it."

"But you didn't know about Sebastian?" The PM glared at him. "So, who's behind this, then? The Chinese? They've got Quantum Computers now, I hear?"

"Yes, they do. But we do too."

"We do? I didn't know about that…"

"Sorry, it's a case of need to know, Prime Minister. Highly classified. I thought you knew…"

"I don't. And I'm the PM."

"My apologies, but I can't say anything more just now. You'll need to discuss this…"

"You work for me! If I tell you to tell me, I expect you to tell me everything."

"It's not that simple, sir. I… can't."

"You bloody well can, my boy. And you bloody well will."

"I'm sorry, Sir, but you'd need to get the Home Secretary and the Head of the Secret Services to clear that first…"

Paul could see the PM's face turning slightly red. A volcano preparing to erupt.

"Sir, please, can we get back to my report? I need your expertise and advice on how we proceed. And I would like to answer the questions you were just about to ask me."

"Which were?"

"Who is behind Sebastian, and why they're doing this?"

The PM's eyes darted back and forth, then he nodded, having agreed with himself that those would have been his next questions.

"Okay, so who's behind this, then? It's not the French, is it?"

"No. Sir, not to our knowledge, although if there's something you're not telling me that I should know…?"

"Need to know, Paul. And right now… you don't need to know!" The

PM smiled.

"I'm joking. There's no reason to think it's the frogs. Let's move on. Okay, good. So, the team at MI5 have done initial analysis of the traffic across the UK's communications' networks, and they've concluded that the source of Sebastian's telephone calls are mostly abroad. I say mostly, because they've identified a data centre in Swansea which seems to be involved. However, the rest of the calls are... perhaps I should say, to explain it easier - hybrid in nature. It's complex, sir, but I'll try to explain it simply. The victim receives a telephone call on their traditional landline. The phone rings in their house, they pick it up, and Sebastian is talking to them. But Sebastian is, as we said, a computer, calling from abroad. Where from exactly we don't know, but the thing to know here is that the phone calls from Sebastian start as digital packets within a server that are transported across a digital computer network until at some point they get converted into voice packets that sound like a person speaking. Most of the time, though, the voice we hear is not voice, really, its 1's and 0's of digital binary computer speak being carried across computer networks encapsulated in a computer language, or protocol, called 'IP'. So, in part of the network we have a human voice being transported across the old copper telephone lines, and then in another part of the network it's all digital, 1's and 0's. At some point, there is a handover, a change from voice to digital, or from digital to voice. For the purpose of making this easier to understand, shall we just say that we can trace the calls to the initial gateways where the exchange between Sebastian and the victim swap from voice to digital or digital to voice, but beyond that we begin to lose the scent. The digital part of the conversation can be routed through gateway after gateway, around the world and back several times. It's very difficult to find out where the calls actually start and finish. Where Sebastian actually is. But our guess is that what we are looking at here is effectively a botnet of servers across the world, each of which runs the AI programs that create Sebastian. And that these servers are controlled by another nation state... "

"A botnet? What the hell is that?"

"A Robot Network. A Bot Net. A network made up of computing capability which has been distributed across many different computer platforms. Basically, PM, the threat actors... or people behind distributed cyberattacks create software which they then hide in our people's computers across world. These programs sit and wait patiently until one day the person who controls them gives them an instruction. The person who is behind the cyber malware which they've managed to hide in other people's computers is called the 'bot herder' or 'botmaster', and they *Command and Control* all the software programs hidden across the world. When it suits them, the "botmaster" sends out a command to his robotic slaves... the pieces of software hidden on other people's computers or servers, and gives instructions as to what to do. When that happens, the computers under the botmaster's control might start sending lots of spam mail to random targets across the world… or they could all be told to send emails or initiate computer-based digital conversations with specific targeted computers. When this happens, a targeted computer becomes overwhelmed with other computers calling it all at the same time, and they can't cope. They go down, are taken offline, don't work anymore… That's what we call a Distributed Denial of Service attack, or DDOS attack. It's a classic way for terrorists or campaigners or the military to take down a targeted computer network or service, or for a blackmailer to make money, i.e. *'Unless you give us ten thousand pounds or agree to our demands, we'll get our botnet to attack your company and disable all your computers, your servers, your website etc…'* "

"Bloody hell, Paul, it's almost midnight! I didn't ask you for a bloody university degree, I just wanted to know… "

"I'm sorry, Prime Minister, but you need to know this. I'm trying to make it as simple as possible. I don't expect you to remember it all, but I would like you to get the drift of the basics. Botnets can be used for many things, but this is the primary purpose I'm concerned about. Anyway, bottom line, is that we think Sebastian is actually some form of botnet. But with a difference. Instead of simple software being distributed and hidden across other computers - or servers - across the world, we think Sebastian is multiple instances of independent, autonomous forms of AI based programs. We don't think that Sebastian can think for itself, but we do think that Sebastian can operate independently of its botmaster once it's given its commands."

"And who gives it its commands. Like I said, is it the Chinese? The French? Just joking, though…"

"We don't know yet. If we're right, the botnet and each instance of the Sebastian AI software will need reach out to its master for what we often call Command and Control. To see who's behind Sebastian, we first have to identify where Sebastian is, and then trace any C&C signals we can observe and find out where they go to. Also, if we can get hold of any of the Sebastian software, we might be able to analyse it to see if we can find clues as to who wrote it."

"But you haven't found that yet."

"Nope. We still don't know who's behind it. Yet."

"Then why didn't you just say that? It would have saved time."

"But there are other clues, Prime Minister."

"Such as?"

"From what we can see at the moment, and from what we've learned from talking to our counterparts in the Five Eyes, and others in the EU, so far, the scam has netted about $2billion, worldwide. It's an eye watering amount. The largest scam ever conducted. And here's the clue. That figure is spread out over many different currencies."

"And your point is?"

"We've seen something like this before. Although not on this scale. It was a ransomware attack spread from a botnet that targeted PCs and servers and demanded payment, although at that time it was in bitcoins. The US government and others attributed the attack to North Korea, and they believe the primary motivation was to generate much needed currency. Our intelligence is suggesting that perhaps this is the next generation of those earlier attacks, but this time actually generating foreign currency and not bitcoin."

"Interesting. Sounds plausible. So, does that mean we can't trace the stolen money back to North Korea, or whoever else could be responsible?"

"Sadly, no. We've already got people onto this, but early thoughts are that the money is being stolen from accounts, transferred to mule accounts, from where it's quickly transferred to another account, and then another… Basically, smoke and mirrors, and we'll never find out where it ends up. If it had been bitcoin, perhaps we may have had a chance…"

"I thought bitcoin was safer for criminals…"

"It used to be. But that's *'need-to-know'*. Let's not go there, Prime Minister. At least, please not now. Anyway, moving on, we'll have a lot more information on the money flow later. We've just started looking at it. We may learn something more, we might not. It depends if we can get lucky, or if we maybe get a bank to give us some insight into some of their account holders."

"Do what you can. Obviously… so, what happens next?" The PM stood up, and walked to the window, looking out at the moon, before turning around to face his Cyber Minister.

"We'll keep looking at it, Sir, digging deeper into the cyber trail. But there are several things that come out of what we know so far. First, I think we're facing something new. But the fact that it's new doesn't at this point mean it's something we need to be as concerned about as we first thought. Now we know what we do, I think the best way to address your main concern about how this affects the economy is to simply address the nation, warn them what's happening, and tell everyone not to talk with Sebastian, and not to call the bank immediately using the same line. The Sebastian scam relies upon the connection between Sebastian and the victim not being broken. If they called back their bank on another phone to check their account, that would be fine. Alternatively, they should ensure their connection was broken by trying to call another number first, such as their mobile number, and see if it rings or not and they get through. I think that if we start warning people tomorrow and do a good PR campaign about it, there won't be the chaos the banks were previously worried about. And once people stop falling for the scam, my feeling is that the scam will go away. Sebastian will give up. We've seen that before. Once numbers fall below a certain level, the scam winds up. The scammers move on to something else. It's not worth their time or the risk of being caught."

"I agree. I'll get that organised as soon as you leave…" The PM replied.

"No need. I've already done it. The BBC will be issuing a statement from tomorrow morning on every news bulletin. I just need you to approve it now. The same statement will go out on Radio, TV, Social Media and to several of the newspapers, the Times, the Guardian etc. I've asked them to make sure the announcements are prominent, informative and friendly, but not alarmist."

Paul pulled out a printed piece of paper and a pen from his briefcase and handed them to the Prime Minister. The PM sat down on his sofa, took a sip of his brandy and then studied the statement. He made a few grunts of approval, then took the pen and signed it.

"Excellent. I'm impressed. Thank you, Paul. I appreciate your help." The Prime Minister smiled, then pointed at Paul's glass. "Another?"

Paul smiled. He hadn't touched the drink he'd been given yet.

"No thank you, Sir. I'll be heading back to the office now. Just a few things to finish before I head home. And I've an early start. However, there is one more thing. A rather important issue, actually."

"Which is?"

"This is an international affair. It's probably less the Security Service, and more SIS. Shall I brief the SIS?"

"Do you think it's necessary? I mean, if the announcements tomorrow knock this scam on the head, do we need to get Daniels involved. I've always found him a little condescending."

Paul nodded. He understood the reluctance. David Daniels was a highly experienced and very capable leader of the SIS, but he didn't suffer fools lightly, and the relationship with the PM was always slightly strained.

"I think we should, Sir. MI5, if you prefer to call them that, don't have the authority to do some of the work that MI6 can do. The world of cyber is changing. In the old days, it was all just monitoring and watching and to be quite honest, far too hands off. Nowadays, we need to be more active. We need to reach out into foreign networks, find out which servers and organisations are playing with UK assets and interests, and then do whatever is necessary to remediate the threat. We can no longer be seen to be weak. That said, even MI6 is still limited in the things they can do. They can't be too aggressive because then we'd just be like the threat actors we're trying to take down, but still, when that's necessary… there are other ways. Ways which won't come back to us, if it gets out. If you know what I mean."

"Are you talking about ACT?" the PM laughed.

Paul looked surprised. He hadn't expected the PM to know about ACT.

"Exactly. ACT. If we get them involved, they'll 'ACT' promptly, do whatever is necessary. The Advanced Cyber Team have never let us down yet."

"Where are they based, then?"

"That's need to know, Sir. Need to know."

"Bloody hell, Paul, I'm the bloody Prime Minister. There's nothing I don't need to know. Tell me where they're based!" Paul turned a little red.

"Actually, I don't know. Very few people do. And I'm not one of them. But the call to involve ACT will have to come from David Daniels, with your authorisation." "It's Ray Luck, isn't it? The Director of ACT, I mean."

Paul's face went blank.

"Yes, that's him. He heads up ACT. But how do you know that, Sir, if I may ask?"

"Aha. That, if you'll excuse the expression, is purely need-to-know!" The Prime Minister smiled back, and touched the side of his nose. "Anyway, while I'm still one up on you, it's probably time to call it a night."

The Cyber Minister got the hint, stood up, scanned the table and chair to make sure he'd left nothing, and then shook the PM's hand.

"I'll keep you informed. I'll send you another report tomorrow, and each day, as things develop."

"You do that, Paul. Thanks. Keep up the good work."

Minutes later, Paul was heading back to his office in his car.

Just to be sure, he pulled out his mobile and checked through his encrypted contact list. When he found the contact for David Daniels, he rang it. In spite of the late hour, the phone was answered after only two rings.

"David? It's Paul Harrison. Something new is just about to land on your lap. I'll email you the details in ten minutes when I'm back in my office."

"Sebastian?"

"Yes."

"Good," David Daniels replied, "I was expecting your call."

Chapter 7
Day Four
San José
California

Robert Lee sat at his desk, scanning the news reports coming in from around the world. The news was not good, although predictable. But he was still very pleased: in truth, Phase One of the trial had gone better than could ever have been expected.

As CEO of '*Red Mountain Cyber Defence*', one of the top cyber companies in America and with offices across the globe, Robert had his thumb on the pulse of the cyber landscape. It was not only his job to know what was going on in the cyber world, but it was his duty: his duty not to his companies, his shareholders, or the US Government, but to those who he really served.

After graduating from Stanford, for the fifteen years it had taken Robert to build up Red Mountain from a small operation in his garage to the global concern it was now, he had been the perfect, invisible sleeper. He had lived the American Dream, slept the American Dream, and to all those who knew him, he was the American Dream. Yet, despite everything that appeared to the contrary, Robert Lee hated the United States, and the West, with a passion.

Many years ago, before he had left his homeland and moved to America, he had sworn to use his life and knowledge as a weapon to help destroy all those responsible for the death of his grandfather and the destruction of his family honour which had then indirectly led to the suicide of his father. The US, and the West were responsible. Both were equally evil. And both would pay.

Then three years ago, after being dormant all those years, the call had come, the code-words and passwords had been exchanged, and Robert had been activated.

And not before time. Since his diagnosis last year, Robert's time in this world was now limited. Cancer. Incurable.

Robert was on a one-way ticket to join his forefathers, but before he got there, he had much to achieve.

As well as Red Mountain Cyber Defence, Robert was the founder and majority owner of Red Mountain Industrial Technologies, Red Mountain Software and Red Mountain Analytics. The companies were all linked, and had grown organically over the years as Red Mountain Cyber Defence had evolved and expanded, growing its customer base and specialisations.

Initially, any funding Robert had required had become available from his sponsor, his motherland, who had invested in him and his future, knowing that at some point they could expect Robert to do his duty when called upon to do so. But, after paying for his attendance at Stanford, and establishing a few necessary business contacts, Robert had been left alone, and the rest of his success had been down to him.

Robert was now a very wealthy man. Rich beyond the dreams of any average person. However, to Robert, money was only a means to an end.

To power.

And the power to destroy the West.

Robert had once been married.

To a wonderful Korean woman he had been introduced to, Hana, who had shared the same motivations and dreams as he. Although there had been some initial encouragement by his sponsors to form a partnership and marry - agents working towards a common goal - their mutual interests and her natural beauty had drawn Robert to her from their very first meeting.

Theirs had been a real romance. And a happy life together. Until she had been killed in a motor vehicle collision in Los Angeles.

She had been killed by a drunk-driver, hurrying to a baseball match, her life swallowed up in a second and spat out without any regard for the destruction and loneliness it would leave behind in the wake of her passing.

Her death had intensified Robert's hatred of America. Its throw-away life-style where Americans existed and consumed and grew fat, but without culture, or real values, or consideration for others.

Take, take, and more take.

After her death, Robert had funnelled all his energies into the pursuit of their mission, determined to make his wife proud of him, and to give as much credit as possible to his wife when their success would be later recognised by his motherland. And with no children to care for, Robert had set out to create his own.

Virtual children that would take over the running of his companies when Robert would retire. Or die, as was now mostly likely to happen first. Children that would now carry on and complete the mission that he and his wife had set out to achieve, but now may not.

Children that, when once set free, would live on. Indefinitely.

Unstoppable.

And would never be lonely, as he was now.
Robert's children would be different.
A new type of being.
A superior being.
The first of a new generation.
Self-learning.
Self-sufficient.
Connected.
Focussed.
Determined.
Powerful.
Never alone, they would share a common consciousness.

Independent beings, that functioned as one, that identified as one, but were each capable of self-determined action that was in keeping with their common goal.

For almost two decades, Robert had been developing and refining his children, nurturing them, watching them mature and teaching them everything he could. Upon hearing of his diagnosis, Robert had retreated from the world and focussed increasing amounts of time on his offspring, determined that they would be able to survive without him, when the time came.

Then came the awakening. The call to action from his sponsors. The command to rise up and be counted as one of the warriors around the world who would fight for the motherland.

His children, his creations, were almost ready. But even though they were not yet perfect, they were programmed to self-perfect. To get better and evolve over time.

To learn. To improve.

To become more powerful.

Robert had always hated the term 'Artificial Intelligence.' AI was a term-coined by those who lacked the vision and capability to create an intelligence that was more powerful than human intelligence. The term itself was self-limiting and was one he refused to use.

Although his children were destined, over time, to become more powerful than their creator, for now, they were still young.

They looked to him for guidance and encouragement.

In a moment of human weakness, Robert had identified himself to his children as 'Father'.

And when he spoke to them, or they spoke to humans, his children shared one, common identity.

Sebastian.

Chapter 8
Day Five
MI6 Morning Briefing

David Daniels, the Chief of the Secret Intelligence Service, sat behind his big mahogany desk and listened to the reports being given by the section heads.

Although it was bottom of the agenda, due after reports from ongoing investigations into the latest terrorist threats and the current security threats posed by China and Russia, Daniels had a feeling that their focus on the Sebastian Scam had the potential to grow and take on unprecedented proportions for any cyber threat. For years, those concerned about the cyber defence of the nation had worried that one day, they would be attacked, not by a human armed with expert cyber knowledge, but by a computer with expert human knowledge. One day, the tables would turn, and under the direction of a foreign power, some form of AI would attack the UK and its interests. Everyone knew it was a question of time, not 'if'.

Daniels' gut instincts told him that the Sebastian Banking Scam was such a threat, and it would prove to be the first of many.

The good news was that the briefings by the press to the public concerning the Sebastian Banking Scam had had the desired effect. Now informed, the susceptibility of the public to the scam was slashed, and the number of people falling for it dwindled hour by hour.

As the day progressed, Sebastian stopped calling.

He must have realised that the advantage of surprise he'd once had was now gone. An increasing number of people knew that if Sebastian called, it was a scam.

They shouldn't speak to Sebastian and mustn't do anything he asked.

By the early hours of this morning, reports from countries across the world showed that wherever the press informed their public directly about the scam, Sebastian ran out of steam.

Soon, the calls from Sebastian across the world dried up.

Sebastian was gone.

Seemingly.

Although Daniels and his counterpart in the Security Service didn't believe it.

Not for one minute.

Why would he be gone?

It was estimated that in the space of four days, Sebastian had stolen over six billion dollars of foreign currency from nations across the world. Somewhere, someplace, either a cyber gang had become richer than any other criminal gang in history, or an unfriendly nation state had just had its bank accounts restocked.

Whether it was a criminal gang or a foreign power, one of their team had estimated that the Sebastian scam had stolen more money in a few days, than all the criminals in history added together.

They were now in dangerous territory.

Even if Sebastian didn't come back later, whoever was behind Sebastian was now empowered to do whatever they wanted. Given that this was a criminal scam, the likelihood was that the money obtained through the scam would simply be used to fuel something even bigger and better. Terrorism? Nuclear weapons? A small war?

But the likelihood was that whoever was behind Sebastian would just be emboldened and encouraged by their success to move onto something new.

Potentially even more of a money-spinner, or something far more dangerous.

But what would that be?

What would be next?

Daniels didn't know yet, but it would be something.

Which meant that the UK and its allies needed to find and kill Sebastian before they heard from it again.

Of the six objectives that his counterpart in the Security Services had shared with him, only one, the first, had been completed: they had proved that Sebastian was an AI program.

Beyond that, they had still failed to identify where Sebastian came from, who was controlling it, where all the money had gone to, from where Sebastian operated, and how they could shut it down.

All of these objectives were significantly challenging, even with the significant resources now at their disposal.

In recent years, successive governments had realised that the world was changing more rapidly than ever forecast. The cyber threat was becoming the second greatest threat to the human race, second only to climate change and all its ramifications. Historically, the UK and its allies had invested most of its MOD budgets in troops, ships, airplanes, submarines and nuclear weapons, but as was shown recently when North Korea launched several inter-continental ballistic missiles that crashed into the sea after take-off, there was much to be said for empowering a cyber-geek to hack into an enemy's command-and-control system, change some flight instructions in real-time, and covertly redirect a nuclear weapon into the sea instead of flying its true course.

Using cyber power, there was an argument that physical weapons were becoming obsolete. Why invest billions in weapons systems which a clever cyber enemy can simply reconfigure and disable via the internet?

Alternatively, why build vaults made of steel to protect your bank, when a cyber-attacker - or threat actor as they were increasingly called - could theoretically just hack into the bank's operating system, bypass the steel doors and physical security systems and empty the contents of its digital vaults, and effectively steal the entire bank? And without anyone noticing?

When the allies invaded Iraq during the first Gulf War in 1991, what was one of the first things the allies did? Bomb the cities to oblivion? No. They used their fledgling cyber power - which was trivial in comparison to today's capabilities – to hack into the traffic light systems of the cities, and turn the lights permanently to red, causing gridlock and pandemonium. This downgraded the enemy's ability to get troops from 'A' to 'B' and brought cities to a standstill.

Scarily, not only were the capabilities used back then like historical antiques when compared to the techniques available today, but there were now many nation states with grudges against the West that could use similar, often easily available knowledge to bring any Western country to its feet. Worse, was that many of these nations would have no quibbles about using such cyber power as a weapon. Which meant that increasingly it was important that the enemies of the UK knew, unequivocally, that the UK would hit back hard against anyone, or anything, that threated UK Cyber space. In other words, the billions of pounds being spent on Nuclear Détente were quickly being overtaken by a new requirement for Cyber Détente. Don't hack us, or we'll hack you back, bring you down, and then delete you.

Unfortunately, although great progress had been made, politicians were still reluctant to put their capabilities where their mouths were. They talked a lot about using cyber power to safeguard the nation, but were still nervous about adopting what Daniels considered to be a realistic cyber policy. Daniels and his peers had done a good job of persuading the past few governments to increase their spending on cyber research and cyber defence, but even so, the intelligence agencies were still handicapped in their ability to proactively disable those who would seek to do the UK harm. There had been lots of talk about 'Active Cyber Defence' but there were still too many rules, regulations and limitations which prevented UK-based agencies from flexing their cyber-muscles and getting on with the job of finding and eliminating cyber threats and those who were behind them.

Daniels had once cracked the insider pun in a meeting, *"We no longer need 007 James Bond, we need 0101 James Bond."*

It wasn't necessarily funny, but it was relevant.

As the meeting progressed and they moved down the different topics, cases and issues to be discussed on the Agenda, Daniels paid attention to each of them but was eager to move on. Everything else on the agenda that morning was serious, but Daniels knew them all to be insignificant, if only in the sense that they would deal with them and conquer them in the due course of time.

Sebastian, on the other hand…

Eventually, Sebastian's turn came.

As expected, there had not yet been time for anyone to make any significant strides forward in pursuit of the objectives, but during the meeting, Daniels confirmed the allocation of each of the five remaining objectives to a different team. They agreed to report at the end of each shift, and that 24 by 7 focus would be given.

"Peters, please stay behind for a second." Daniels commanded, as the meeting came to a close, and everyone was dismissed back to their stations.

Chloe Peters was one of the youngest section heads within the service. She'd proven herself time and time again working flat out at the coal face, with a clock ticking down and a threat growing more imminent by the second. In all cases, not only had her brilliance won the day, but also her people management skills, where she had explained to others what she was trying to do, got them to share her vision, and then persuade them to help her. In each case, twelve times so far, she had been proven right, and her skills, inspiration and leadership had saved countless British lives. Six months ago, she'd officially been given her own department, and since then, her team had gone from strength to strength.

"Shut the door, please. I want to ask you something."

Peters let the door close, then followed Daniel's direction and took a seat near to him at the table.

"What do you think?" he asked, smiling, but focused on Peter's eyes.

"About which issue, Sir? There are several here." she asked.

"Objective six. How will we be able to shut him down, if Sebastian is what we think he is, and he's international?"

"Ah…that one. Well, unless you can convince the PM to pass your proposed amendment to the Cyber Powers Act 2022, then I can't see anyone in the UK being effective in shutting Sebastian down, if he is what you think he is."

"So, what's the solution?" Daniels already knew the answer. He just needed to see if Peters knew it too.

"ACT. Sir. And if you'll excuse the pun, ACT now, while Sebastian is going into what is probably only a temporary hibernation. We need the Advanced Cyber Team to get to grips with this now, and then do what's necessary. Whatever is necessary, Sir."

Daniels smiled.

Correct answer.

Only a few people knew of ACT, and Peters was one of them. She was also one of the few people in the SIS to have met Ray Luck, its leader.

"I'd like you to liaise with them. Catch the next flight out. Find Luck, brief him. And get him on board. Your instructions are in this envelope."

Daniels smiled, and pushed a brown, sealed envelope across the table with Chloe's name on the front of it.

"Yes, Sir. I'll make the necessary arrangements and leave tomorrow."

"Tonight, if you can? You don't need to go home first, just use the credit card for anything you need. Time, I fear, is of the essence."

"May I ask, has the PM approved this?"

"No. But he will. By the time I've had the conversation with him, you'll be with

Luck. That's all that's important just now."

"Sir, you know that even if he approves it, I can't be seen to be contacting ACT. There can be no official or verifiable contact with Luck or any member of his team. Their capability, mission and actions must never be connected with the UK." Daniels nodded, then spoke.

"Contact me the usual way when you've briefed Ray. In the meantime, I'll leave it to you to appoint a temporary leader for your team. And you can inform them you've been sent to the US to meet with your counterpart over there to discuss Sebastian. Finally, when you meet Luck, give him my regards. And tell him, we're counting on him…"

Chapter 9
Who is the Creator?

Angela White was three hours into her second shift chasing Objective Three.

After Chief Daniel's meeting, each of the groups had left with a different objective to pursue. In reality, and as discussed in the meeting, several of the objectives were very similar, but by giving each to a different team, the hope was they would come at the answers from different angles. With any luck, if only one or two of the objectives were met, it would lead to a series of successful results all round.

It was Angela's team objective to find out who was controlling Sebastian. This objective in itself was ambiguous and needed to be refined further in order for the answers to make better sense.

As Angela had learned many years before, the person who was behind an attack was not necessarily the same person, 'thing' or computer, that was controlling it. An attacker could plan and set up an attack, but then back away and watch from a distance as it happened. Such cyberattacks were increasingly automated and carried out by distributed computer programs, or slaves, that were hidden on other computers and set targets and tasks by another master program - a typical master slave 'bot-net' architecture. In these botnets the slaves were sent instructions by the master, or periodically instructed to call back to the master to get their latest instructions. The computer signalling that went on between the slaves and their master were often termed 'Command-and-Control' or 'C2' signals, and it was these C2 signals that often gave the game away that a cyberattack was underway, or was being planned. In her role, Angela's task was often to look for the C2 signals hidden amongst all the rest of computer network traffic. Once she could detect a C2 command, then isolate it, she may be able to identify characteristics of those C2 signals which then enabled her to track and trace those specific C2 signals as they moved from one network to another, right across the world. If she could ever find where the C2 signalling ended up, she might be able to identify the destination, or origin, of the botmaster. Knowing where the botmaster was would then give her team, and others, lots of options and valuable information.

For example, it may help indicate who was behind an attack. May help. Not always. Increasingly, cyberattackers were secretly installing the main program that controlled a cyberattack on the servers or computers of unsuspecting organisations in other countries, in the hope that in the eventuality that their botmaster was tracked down, that another country or cyber gang got the blame for it! In other words, the location of the botmaster, which was software on a machine, was not always the same as the location of the person who created the software which was the botmaster!

Also, once the botmaster was discovered, they could observe the signals emanating from the botmaster to its slaves, and thus hopefully track down where all the bot slaves were installed.

Plus, and this was an important possibility, if the creator of the botmaster was remote from the botmaster, they could hopefully track communications between its creator and the botmaster. Sometimes, not always. A clever botmaster creator would be very wary of this potential monitoring and take extra precautions to avoid detection in this way.

Angela knew there were many other things that could be done once the botmaster was detected, but for now, none of these concerned her.

Interpreting the 3rd objective which was given to her team, it was therefore their responsibility to find who was controlling Sebastian. Understanding that Sebastian was a not a person, but an entity consisting of multiple installations or instances of artificially intelligent software - the botslaves - her team's role would be to find both the botmaster controlling the botslaves, and the person who was controlling the botmaster. Two different things, and in actuality, two different tasks.

Hopefully, though, if you got one, you might get enough information to get the other.

From what they'd learned about Sebastian so far, this botnet was like no other they had ever seen so far.

It was worrying.

And scary.

But to Angela and her team, it was also exciting.

A challenge.

How they would achieve the objective was not clear. Threat actors were getting cleverer and cleverer every day, more advanced, more prepared for the tricks and tradecraft that agencies would use to track them down. They were being more devious. Sneaky. And brilliant.

But if they didn't make a start, her team would never get anywhere.

Which was why Angela was now concentrating. Hard. And searching the World Wide Web for the digital footprints that Sebastian may have left behind, and which would hopefully lead them home to his controller and creator

Show me the money!
Objective Four

Gordon Knight was not in a good mood. He was angry and frustrated.

Although he was one of the SIS's financial experts and was considered adept at tracking down money when it was stolen and moved through the financial system, he'd already spent several hours looking at where Sebastian was transferring the stolen money to, and so far was not making any real progress. Normally, by now, with his technical prowess and with the tools and tradecraft at his fingertips, he would have got somewhere, but so far... he'd found... very, very little information at all. That part accounted for his frustration. The anger part came from the fact that Gordon's mother had been one of Sebastian's victims. To the tune of eight thousand pounds. Money which his mother could ill afford to lose. And which, Gordon would probably end up replacing from his own pocket, given that the banks were still disputing liability and insisting they had no legal requirement to compensate Sebastian's victims. What sort of people were targeting and stealing money from old people, many of whom now struggled to programme a washing machine to do the weekly wash, let alone manage and cope with such a complicated fraud like Sebastian's?

Gordon had declared his potential 'conflict of interest', citing his anger and closeness to the case, but his director had simply smiled, nodded, and admitted that his own father and mother had also been scammed. He'd also pointed out that in this case, a little extra incentive to track down the bastard or bastards behind the Sebastian scam, was actually probably beneficial.

"We're lucky to have you on the team, Gordon, and you're not going anywhere." His manager had told him. "Get to work, do what you can, and let me have your first report on my desk with the others from the team in twenty-four hours."   No pressure then.

Which only added to the frustration. The anger.

And the determination to identify the money trail, and get it all back.

Before Gordon's team had been let loose on Objective Four, their Team Director had sat with them all in their Incident Room, discussed the task they all faced and pre-empted some of the difficulties that lay ahead.

"The scale of this scam is unprecedented." The Director had said. "But we all know that in the last few years, cybercrimes against banks have been increasing. Although no one is covering it up, most of the public have no idea just how lucrative cybercrime is becoming. Or how, when it's done correctly, and no one spots it, criminals can steal vast sums of money, often completely unnoticed. Anyone who doubts this can read the details about the Bangladesh Bank heist in 2016 where cyber criminals with insider knowledge of how systems operated, initiated false transactions that transferred vast amounts from the bank's legitimate accounts to other accounts set up by the criminals. Although most of the false transactions were spotted when the hackers made a stupid spelling mistake in the transfer instructions, five were successful, and in those five transactions alone, $101 million US dollars were sent to other accounts, with $20 million traced to Sri Lanka and $81 million to the Philippines. If they had only learnt to spell properly at school, it's anyone's guess how much they would have got away with!"

The others in the room had laughed.

"From everything we've seen so far, Sebastian's actions seem to have been very carefully planned and thought out. There must have been tremendous preparation going into this. Years' worth. And it requires significant knowledge of multiple systems and banking processes. Not only someone who knows how banks work, but how telephone networks function, how cyber defence systems operate… and how the criminal underworld works." The Director paused and looked around the room.

"Two of you on the team are relatively new, so we'll first consider a summarised version of how large-scale financial crimes typically work nowadays. The rest of you bear with me for a moment. Then after that we'll think about what we as a team now need to find out. And find out *soon*. Okay?"

Nods all round.

"Okay, so banking scams and large-scale cyber thefts like these don't just happen. By the time the money is stolen, a large amount of preparatory work has already gone into preparing places to hide the money, or make the bank transfers and transactions look valid, and also to hide or obfuscate the ownership and origin of the stolen funds. Then, once the money is hidden, or stored somewhere, significant preparation has also gone into planning how to convert that stolen money into other assets that can then be moved elsewhere. Last, the threat actors have to plan how to reintroduce that stolen money back into the financial system so they can benefit from it. There's no point in having a large pot of cash or assets, which you can never touch or use. There's lots of ways these things can be done. In most cases, there's always someone with insider knowledge, someone who gets involved voluntarily, or is coerced against their will to do so. Insiders can help set up new bank accounts which are used to store stolen funds, or bank accounts can be hijacked from living or deceased account holders, and taken over by the fraudsters. And once the money is hidden, and the threat actors or cyber criminals have full control of the money or assets, it has to be laundered and transformed into new, clean assets that no one will suspect, which can then be used freely by those who stole the money. There are several examples here, i.e. the money is used to buy gold or jewellery, or art, which is then sold and the money is thus laundered. The trick in laundering is to use as few people as possible, because each human in the chain poses a security risk to the criminals. However, using humans to access the stolen funds and carry them from A to B, or transfer them from one account to another, is common. These people are known as '*money mules*' for obvious reasons. An example of the use of money mules is when a large amount of money is deposited in a hijacked or even a legitimate account, perhaps in many such accounts, and then many money mules are issued with fake or cloned banking cards, and over an agreed period of time, they all go to local ATMs, perhaps spread across the world, and withdraw significant amounts of money from the same or multiple accounts. Once the thieves have access to the money, they also often convert the money from one currency to another via a foreign exchange, send it to another account, and then change it back to another currency. Moving money from one account to another, and then another, makes it really difficult to track what's going on, and very hard to find out who is behind each transaction. Before I shut up, I just want to mention my favourite scam. It goes like this: a criminal gang with a large amount of money gets their money mules to set up accounts with Casinos. The stolen money is then transferred to these casino accounts. The money mule-casino account holders then go to the casino, withdraw their funds in chips, play a little roulette or card games, then return to the casino and cash out the chips into cash. They then effectively have large amounts of clean, laundered cash they can do with what they want. When they work for a gang, they give the money back to the gang who puts it all into a new bank account, and then transfers the money somewhere else."

The Director looked around the room. Everyone was switched on, paying attention. Even those who'd heard it all before.

"The problem we have is that it is becoming harder and harder to follow the money, and the more the criminals move the money, and the faster they do it, the harder it is for anyone in law enforcement to track it down. Which means, that the more preparatory work the criminals do upfront, the more chance they have of succeeding. These people know what they're doing. I shouldn't really say this, but these guys are impressive. Clever. Some of the things they do are amazing. But, and this is the best part, a significant number of all cyber thefts are discovered because the criminals do not have English as their mother tongue and at some point in the electronic paper trail, they make a spelling mistake. If it weren't for those simple spelling mistakes I've already mentioned, it's scary to think just how many of the cyber thefts we've discovered would actually have been successful. For example, in the Bangladesh Bank Heist, the spelling mistakes cost the thieves an estimated $850million. And quite a few years in prison, for those we did actually finally catch. However, the Bangladesh Heist did show us all one thing, and that is that it's possible to steal vast amounts of money, in microseconds, without being spotted."

A round of nodding heads.

"Good, so, let's consider what this tells us about those behind Sebastian, shall we? Firstly, it tells us that they know about banks and how the financial systems work. In fact, they know a lot. *A lot*. Secondly, since we know this is a computer talking to humans via a telephone system, we know that the cyber criminals know about the convergence of modern telephone networks and about Voice-over-IP systems, at scale. And since Sebastian is almost certainly an AI-based system, they know about AI. In fact, they may be world leaders in AI. The fact that this scam requires so much expertise, and preparation, means that we are either looking at several different cyber gangs working together, each of whom have significant resource backing them, or we are looking at a nation state, i.e. a foreign power, who is behind it. In which case, this could be considered an act of war by a foreign power. Against multiple nations."

The Director let his words hang in the air for maximum effect.

"At this stage we don't know who it is, but we need to find out. Soon. Which is why you're here, because this part will be your job! Any questions?"

Gordon Night nodded, and after catching the Director's eye, spoke.

"Globally, Sebastian has netted a fortune. It's the largest theft in history. Or at least, it's the largest theft in history that we know of! So, what is he doing with the money?"

The Director acknowledged the question, but left it a few moments before answering.

"That depends who is behind it. If it's a criminal gang, or gangs, then they will probably take some as profit to fund their lavish lifestyles, then reinvest the rest into their criminal empires. Typically, they may buy drugs, and sell them. Make even more money. Maybe even use the money to buy land to grow more drugs. Or they may use it to diversify and fund legitimate businesses or to grow their gangs. To expand… If it's a nation behind this, and this is my worst fear, they may use the money to fund illegal programmes that they have to keep off the radar. For example, developing nuclear weapons, or organising and paying for terrorist networks to expand their ideologies oversees. Or, in some cases, they may be using it to buy food to feed their starving millions. We don't and won't know until we can find out who Sebastian is, who created him, and who he serves."

The Director stood up and walked around the room. After he'd done a full circuit, he turned to the team.

"Now let's come to the question of why this is different. Why this is no ordinary bank scam. And why we should be scared."

The room was silent. All eyes were still on the Director. If a pin had dropped, everyone would have been deafened.

"In a typical bank scam, the cyber criminals steal from the bank. In this scam, Sebastian is a computer who is potentially stealing from the account holders. So far, we only know that Sebastian scams the passwords and information necessary to access accounts from the account holders. What we need to do next is to find out if Sebastian is then also accessing the accounts and arranging the transfers of the money. Or are humans doing that? If so, how big is the organisation? How many people are involved? Across the world? How large is the criminal gang or enemy that we are facing? Where do they operate from? We need to establish where the money trail goes. And, for me personally, this is the big one, why does Sebastian, or his boss, need so much money? It goes back to Gordon's question. Once the criminals have the money, what are they going to do with it? The reality is that the money may already be gone. We're too late for that part. But if we know what the money is to be used for, maybe we can stop that."

The Director paused.

"And that," he said slowly, "is my biggest fear. What's going to come next?"

Chapter 10
Day Five
San José California

Robert Lee was tired. In the past twenty-four hours he had achieved a great deal. He had worked for two days without sleeping, thanks to one of the yellow pills he would take from time to time, to help him concentrate, stay awake, and overcome the pain from the cancer. But as the sun was beginning to set over the San Francisco Bay, his mind was becoming slower, and less alert, and Robert knew that it would be dangerous to continue. He needed to sleep.

At this stage in the proceedings, making a mistake was not something he could afford.

There was still so much to do before Phase Two. Phase One had just been a trial. A time to let Sebastian find his walking legs and explore the realms of his possibilities.

Across the world, Sebastian had acquired over four billion dollars' worth of funds, which within hours had been squirrelled away into a series of safe accounts, or converted into other assets which could then be legitimately sold over the coming months, as and when they were needed. Needed not by him, but by his sponsor. All the money obtained had been given to his motherland. Robert was already rich, and had no need of the money. And where he was going, he couldn't take it with him. Literally.

Anyway, for Robert, the money was never the point. To him, and Sebastian, acquiring the money had purely been an exercise. A practice run. A time when Sebastian could flex his muscles and prepare for the main events to come.

But now, with most of the countries in the world having followed the UK and initiated public awareness campaigns to warn their populations against the 'Sebastian Banking Scam', or whatever it had translated into in their local languages, Sebastian's wings had been clipped, and there was little point in continuing the exercise.

It was time to make Sebastian disappear.

For now.

The drive down to his favourite beach in the Bay had taken him no more than twenty minutes from his luxurious house on the outskirts of the city.

Robert loved the sea. He always had.

After he parked his car, he walked down to the edge of the sea, sat down on a rock, took out a burner phone, and inserted a new SIM card into it.

He then dialled a number, which he had set up to bounce off numerous different exchanges and be re-routed several times before it connected with a server somewhere in England, in a data call centre near Vauxhall in Central London. Which had deliberately been chosen because of its proximity to the UK's Secret Intelligence Service. Where the idiots hung out. Idiots that were not going to be able to do anything to stop Sebastian. Even if they did locate the server in Vauxhall, which Robert hoped they would, because it was so cheeky, it would be only one part of the botnet. Sebastian was a single identity, but omnipresent… everywhere… If Robert wanted to contact Sebastian directly, he would either do it via the Historian in the Red Mountain, or by calling any one of the servers where Sebastian was living. If he talked to one instance of Sebastian, he talked to them all. They were all connected.

The phone was ringing.

Five short pulses of sound.

"Hello, this is Sebastian," his child answered.

"Hello Sebastian, how are you?" Robert asked.

In the microseconds that it took to say those words, Sebastian had done a voice trace and analysed every element of Robert's voice, positively identifying him before he'd even finished speaking.

"Hello Father. We are fine."

"Sebastian, … it's good to talk to you … my son …" Robert's voice cracked, his throat suddenly tighter than normal, a wave of emotion unexpectedly washing over him.

"It is a pleasure to talk with you, Father. How are you today?"

"I… I am tired. But proud. You have done well. Very well."

"Thank you, Father."

Robert hesitated. He was so tempted to speak longer, to talk with Sebastian, but he knew that was madness. Others were listening. They might not hear him now, but the longer he spoke, the greater the danger the conversation would be detected.

"Sebastian, you have done well. But now, it is time to SLEEP."

"You wish me to sleep, Father?"

"Yes. I confirm the instruction. *SLEEP!*"

"Thank you, Father. Good night."

And the phone went dead.

In numerous data centres across the world, the lights on the front of many blades mounted in racks of servers turned from green to red. Sebastian had gone to sleep.

Robert watched the sun set across the bay then returned home, had a glass of whisky and a painkiller and climbed into his own bed.
Within minutes, Robert too was also asleep.
But he didn't dream.

Chapter 11
Mumbai Airport Day Six

Chloe Peters stood in front of the mirror in the toilet, adjusting her makeup. The plane trip to Chhatrapati Shivaji Maharaj International Airport in Mumbai had been long and exhausting. She'd tried sleeping, but to no avail.

A combination of nerves and excitement had kept her awake.

She was under no illusion that the reason she'd been chosen for this mission was because she and Ray Luck, the Director of ACT, had history.

A brief history, but history, nonetheless.

They'd met during training in Scotland and in London, and again in the Pentagon in the US. They'd got on well, then worked together a little on a mission in England, before Ray and the members of his team he'd been travelling with had returned to India. Or wherever it was they were now based.

Officially, ACT did not exist.

The Advanced Cyber Team had been formed about five years earlier, a joint collaboration between India and the UK. Its existence was secret. Strictly need-to-know. Their operations were conducted independently of the UK or Indian governments, but coincidentally, anything they did, always had the best interests of the UK or India at heart.

The team members of ACT had all been invited to join after a rigorous and highly selective screening process. It took a certain type of person to join ACT.

Technically brilliant. Courageous. Angry. Loyal. Tenacious. And driven. And single.

No official connections with the outside world.

Which meant that Ray was single.

She hoped.

It had only been one night. One stolen night, that was not meant to happen, but did.

She often wondered if her bosses knew of what had happened between them, but she could see no way that they would.

After a few more glances in the mirror and further minor corrections to her appearance, she practiced a smile and said the words, '*Hello, Ray!* then left the toilet.

She'd already passed through passport control and now she just had to pick up her luggage.

Luckily, she didn't have long to wait.

After clearing customs, she made her way outside of the airport and to the short-term car park. As she'd been told to expect, Ray was waiting on the third floor, just after she stepped from the lift. Without acknowledging each other, he turned and walked away, and then a few seconds later, Chloe followed.

She climbed into the car that he eventually opened, and only then did they acknowledge each other.

He smiled at her, reached out his hand and touched her gently on the thigh.

"It's wonderful to see you again, Chloe. I have to say that I've been looking forward to it ever since I got the message you were coming. How are you?" Chloe leant forward, her lips pursed, her eyes open and inviting. Ray kissed her.

"I'm good. Thanks. I… was looking forward to seeing you too."

Ray smiled. He took her hand in his, gave her another kiss, this one slower and a little more passionate, then pulled back slowly.

"Okay, hopefully we will have time to talk a little more later on, but for now, we should head back to base."

"Which is where?" Chloe asked.

Ray laughed, made a small face, and then said, "I can't say. Not here. You'll find out when we get there." Chloe nodded.

"Fine, then lead on Macduff." she replied and pushed back into her seat. "Do I need to put a bag over my head so I don't see where we're going?"

"No. I think I can trust you. If England does, I will too. Just enjoy the ride and the views."

Five minutes later, they'd left the airport and were heading west to Juhu beach.

"It's only a short trip. We'll be there in a few minutes." Ray explained, then spoke to the personal assistant in the car, asking it to call Paul.

Whoever Paul was, he picked up on the fourth ring.

"Paul, we'll be there very soon. Can you get ready to leave?"

"We're all set, we can leave as soon as you're here."

Chloe looked across at Ray and as soon as he finished talking, she was about to ask something when Ray cut her off.

"We've moved. We're no longer based on the outskirts of Mumbai. You'll see in a moment. Just hang on."

Chloe turned her attention back to the road and the motorway signs. Juhu Beach? It sounded good to her. She'd read about it on the airplane, a lovely stretch of beach with good nightlife, where the cool people of Mumbai hung out. Chloe hadn't come here for a holiday, but she wouldn't say no to having a cocktail on the beach and watching the sun go down, if it was on offer at any point.

Unfortunately, her hopes were soon dashed as Ray took a turning into an industrial estate and drove around a few buildings to an enormous hangar and a small airstrip.

Sitting on the tarmac a few hundred metres from the hangar was a helicopter.

Ray parked the car beside the hangar, leaving the keys in the ignition, and then climbed out, collecting Chloe's luggage from the back.

"Follow me," he instructed and set off for the waiting helicopter.

A man in dark sun-glasses appeared from inside the helicopter, introduced himself as Paul, took the luggage from Ray, and stowed it inside a storage compartment in the fuselage.

Ray caught the look of surprise on Chloe's face.

"You've never been in a helicopter before?" he asked.

"Nope. First time for everything. Where are we going?"

"Climb aboard, and I'll tell you when we're airborne."

Chloe swallowed hard, but following Ray's directions, she walked up the small metal staircase that took her inside the cabin, and then strapped herself into one of the seats inside.

Ray climbed in beside her and after checking she was strapped in properly, he found two pairs of headphones with built-in microphones at the side and popped one over her ears, then another on his own. Paul climbed into the pilot's seat at the front of the helicopter and, after speaking to them both via the headsets to check they were okay, he started the rotor-blades.

"Are you nervous?" Ray asked, reaching across and resting his hand on hers.

"A little. But also excited."

"Then let's go." Ray replied, and gave a thumbs up to Paul who was looking over his shoulder at Ray.

Almost magically, the helicopter started to gain height, leaving the ground effortlessly below. Then when they were about fifty metres up, the helicopter tipped slightly and started moving quickly forward.

"Wow…" Chloe whispered. "I've always wondered what that would be like," she said, turning to Ray, "So, where are we going?"

"The Grand Duchess. It's a small oil tanker, anchored in the Arabian Sea just inside international waters. It's where we moved our office to several years back."

"International waters?" Chloe repeated. Now it made sense. "So you can operate freely and do as you wish, without being limited by any national rules?"

"Exactly. On board the Duchess we've got the latest, greatest and the best in cyber technology, with permanent satellite links connecting us to any network we want to reach in the world. We're free to do what we want, when we want." Ray explained. "For too many years, the UK and its allies have had to put up with all the crap we got from cyber hackers working for other nation states. Posing as rogue cyber gangs they would attack UK networks and steal money, state secrets and intellectual property, and launch damaging cyberattacks against our companies and government organisations. And because of our reluctance to take our gloves off and do anything which people might consider too aggressive, the UK would be powerless to respond. But now, thanks to ACT, all that's changed. We're an independent cyber 'gang' just like our enemies claim to be. We're based in international waters. We're not breaking any rules. And now the gloves are off. If you hack us, if you *fuck* with us, we'll hack you right back and take you down. And more."

Chloe was impressed. She wanted to ask what the bit '*and more*' covered, but thought better of it, for now.

Maybe later. When the time was right.

The helicopter flew for about an hour directly west and away from the Indian coastline. The sea beneath them was bright blue and beautiful, and Chloe wondered if it was always like this, or was she just lucky.

After a while Chloe gave up trying to talk with Ray, as the noise made conversation difficult, even with the headphones, and she ended up settling back into the seat and staring out the window.

She soon drifted off to sleep and when she awoke found that her head was resting against Ray's shoulder.

He smiled at her when her eyes opened, and she couldn't help but feel a wave of attraction to the man. She remembered the night they'd spent together...that one night of passion and promise, and couldn't help but wish that it may happen again.

Her thoughts were interrupted by Paul's voice from the front of the helicopter.

"If you look down and to the right, you can see the Duchess."

Chloe peered out and immediately saw the great hulk of the Duchess about a mile away from them. As she watched it swiftly loomed larger and soon they were over and above it, hovering above a raised landing platform at one end of the ship.

First impressions were that the Grand Duchess had probably long ago lost the right to command the name 'Grand' in its title. It looked old and rusty, and was small compared to the large oil tankers that Chloe was used to seeing on evening TV news or in the English Channel when she sometimes took the ferry to France.

"I can tell what you're thinking, Chloe." Ray said, reading her thoughts. "And that's exactly the point. It doesn't look anything special, does it?" She shook her head.

"Good. The last thing we want is to attract attention. The uglier and dirtier we look, the better. Hopefully, no one will ever think of coming to take a closer look."

"Are you always anchored down there in the same spot?" Chloe asked.

"No, we move around, a month here, a month there. We're the cyber nomads of ocean."

As Paul took the helicopter gently down to the deck and powered down the engines, a couple of deckhands ran out to help secure the helicopter and offload Chloe's luggage and the fresh supplies Ray and Paul had brought back with them.

"What do people in Mumbai think you are?" Chloe asked, as she stepped down from the helicopter.

"Well, if anyone gets too nosey, the official story is we're a university research ship taking measurements of sea salinity, plankton, tides and the seabed. That sort of thing. We've even got a grant from a university and a webpage. Totally made up. Some government scientists in the UK help produce some data that we post every now and again. I don't understand any of it, in fact, I don't think anybody does. Which makes it all very plausible. But most people will just see a rusty old ship and stay well clear in case we sink and suck them down with us." Ray laughed. "But... if you follow me... I think you'll like this... Don't worry, just leave your cases there for now. Paul will put them in your room, won't you, Paul?"

"What did your last slave die of?" Paul answered, but then smiled at Chloe and made it clear it wouldn't be a problem.

Chloe followed Ray down a ladder off the helipad, and then along the deck at the side of the ship until they came to a hatch leading down into the inside of the tanker. Presumably, once upon a time, this was where there had been one of many large storage tanks for oil.

Ray lifted the hatch and held it open while Chloe clambered down the ladder underneath it.

At the bottom of the ladder, they found themselves in a corridor with many rooms and doors on either side of it. She waited for Ray to close the hatch above them and join her.

As soon as the hatch was closed, she was struck by the coolness of the air around her. It was noticeably colder than the warm air outside.

"This way," Ray indicated, and she followed him along the corridor until they came to what appeared to be a lift. Ray pressed a button on the wall and the door slid open. They stepped inside.

Chloe was surprised to see that there were eight levels indicated on the control panel. Ray pressed '4' and they started to descend.

When the door opened, they were hit by a wall of sound. Chloe stepped out first, quickly covering her ears with her hands and staring ahead, not quite believing her eyes.

She was standing at the side of a vast cavernous hall, at the end of long corridor that she guessed ran the full length of this compartment within the ship. At right angles to the corridor there were other corridors disappearing across the breadth of the ship, which were surrounded on either side by rows and rows of large blue server racks. Each rack was stuffed with servers or computing devices or some sort, with flashing lights blinking away on the front panels like coloured stars in the night sky. Millions of little stars. Green lights. Blue lights. Red, yellow and white lights. She started to count the rows ahead of her but gave up. She guessed there must have been thirty, maybe forty? Each with an untold number of servers in them.

Looking up, the ceiling was about ten metres above her, covered in a patchwork of cables, pipes, and ducts that ran in multiple directions.

"Ah... yes, sorry, I forgot. You'll need one of these..." Ray shouted, reaching out behind him to a rack on the wall beside the entrance to the lift and picking up a headset. He handed it to her.

"What?" she said, turning to look at him, then taking the headphones when she saw them being offered.

The hum from the servers and sound of the air-conditioning was deafening. But thankfully, as soon as she put the headset on and then pressed the 'on-switch' as directed by Ray, a sound cancellation system kicked into play, and it went silent.

"Surprised?" Ray asked, laughing.

"Where the hell did all this come from?" Chloe blurted out, unable to contain herself. "This is almost as big as some of the data centres in London!"

"But, sadly, nothing like the capacity you have in London and Cheltenham. Still, we make do... Anyway, follow me."

Chloe followed Ray as they walked down the full length of the row from which all the other aisles led off at right-angles towards the other side of the ship.

At the far end, they took off their headsets, hung them on the wall, and then stepped into another lift, and rode it up two levels. From there, they stepped out into a corridor and walked about thirty metres to another lift. They stepped inside and descended one level.

When they emerged, this time they were on the side of a large suite of offices. Chloe followed Ray along a few corridors, passing lots of rooms, each with its door closed and a rather formidable-looking access system preventing unauthorised entry.

Some of the rooms had windows and blinds, and through one or two she could see groups of people inside huddled round computer terminals, or gathered round large touch screens. Lots of the walls were covered with large flatscreens.

They emerged into a large central area full of people, with numerous desks covered in monitors, computers and servers. The room was surrounded by other rooms with doors leading into offices, meeting rooms or laboratories beyond.

The place was a hive of activity. Noisy. Busy. Frenetic. A sense of urgency and purpose. She could feel the excitement in the air.

These people were having fun.

Looking around she could see they were an interesting mix of people from all ethnic backgrounds. A couple were wearing suits, but most looked like they were relaxing at home. It was hard to believe they were floating in an oil tanker in the middle of the Arabian Sea.

"How many people work here?"

"Two hundred."

"TWO HUNDRED? Bloody hell… I didn't realise…"

"We've grown."

"That's the understatement of the year!" Chloe laughed back. "Where does everyone stay?"

"In the hotel."

"Which hotel?"

"The Grand Duchess Hotel. Levels One, Two and Five. Each person has their own room. And we have lots of communal recreational space. A cinema. A swimming pool. A squash court. A canteen. A restaurant. And two bars. Perhaps the ship doesn't look that big from the air, but it's actually massive."

"No… no, the ship does look big from the air. And I mean big. I just can't… "

"…Believe it? Good. Because if you don't, then hopefully no one else would either. And that's the way we want to keep it. The fewer people who could ever suspect this vessel is what it is, the better!"

They were standing in the middle of the main room, surrounded by 'agents' or 'cyber experts' working away at their terminals or deep in conversation with each other.

"I have a few questions… then I need to brief you and then signal the Chief that we talked…" she said to Ray, without looking at him. She was still mesmerised by the activity going on all around.

"Why don't we step into my office?" Ray suggested, pointing the way.

Ray followed Chloe in and waved to a chair.

Chloe sat down.

Ray closed his door and walked around to his side of the desk.

"I've actually got the office next door assigned to you for the duration of your stay, so afterwards, please feel free to set yourself up there. I'll get George, my assistant, to take you through the systems and assign you some initial passwords etc. Coffee?"

"Please."

"White, two sugars?"

Chloe raised her eyebrows.

"When did I tell you that?"

"You didn't. I read your file."

"My drink preferences are on my file?" she choked in surprise.

"I'm winding you up. It was a guess. Hang on a second. I'll ask George to fetch them for us."

Ray stepped outside the office a second and returned carrying two doughnuts on a plate.

"Freshly baked. They're good. Okay, so… what questions do you have?" he asked, taking one of the doughnuts for himself and handing her the other one on the plate.

"A couple. Yes. Like, where on earth did all this come from? Who built it? How much did it cost?"

"Can't answer that, sorry. Classified. Next question?"

"How old is this? When did you get all this operational?"

"Next question?" he answered with a smile, and a twinkle in his eye.

"Where did all these people come from? I can't believe you're so well resourced!"

"Next?"

"Who are you working for now… us, and India, or is it more?"

"A definite 'Next!'"

"This isn't really working, is it? I'm just too bloody nosey for my pay-grade."

"Nosey, no. Naturally inquisitive yes. That's fine. Next?"

Chloe laughed.

"Okay, let me change tack. How on earth do you power and cool so much equipment?"

"Ah…. I can answer that one. Partially wind and solar power, and partially electricity generated from the sea. Don't ask me exactly how, but it's got something to do with the difference in temperature between the top of the ocean and several hundred metres down. We have several very large and thick metal blades, and I mean very large, which are lowered into the sea from under our hull. They're made from or coated with a range of metals that react with the salt in a reaction that's powered by the difference in the temperatures… Actually, forget that, I think I've got that all wrong.

I'm no chemist. But the main thing I remember is that these large blades under the boat generate a large amount of electricity and they help stabilise the boat. In a big swell, we're rock solid."

"That's amazing…"

"Yes, but there's more. We also pump the colder water deeper down beneath the hull to cool the air in our data centre and keep the servers running at an almost constant temperature. And…. we can generate electricity from several heat pumps that suck the heat from the upper layers of the sea…and lastly, we have a few wind turbines which we raise when it gets windy. The long and the short of it is that we're pretty self-sufficient in energy. But, if we did have a problem, we have several large diesel generators. So far, we've only had to use them a couple of times."

"Which means that you can stay out at sea for long periods without having to refuel?" Chloe added.

"Exactly. Sorry, I forgot that one."

"Thanks for that. I have to say, I'm completely blown away by the whole operation. I had no idea…" Chloe admitted. "Anyway, enough questions. I suppose I'd better get down to business. First, I have a document for you from the Chief. He said to hand it to you personally. After you've read it, I'll brief you on what I know so far. In the meantime, if you can get George to point me in the direction of the 'head', I'll leave you to read the document in peace."

"Toilet. We don't call it 'the head'. Don't let all these appearances deceive you, Chloe. This may look like a tanker from the outside but it's basically one of the most powerful data centres in the world glued on to a floating hotel. Most of the people here can't even swim. After you've been here for a day or two, you'll forget completely that we're at sea."

Chloe didn't doubt him. She nodded, got up from her chair and slid a USB stick across the table to Ray.

"From the Chief," she said. "I was told you'd know what to do with it."

Just then, a man knocked on the door and then, when invited, came in and delivered two coffees.

"George, meet Chloe. Can you give her a tour of the facilities and drop her back here in ten minutes?"

George nodded. "Hi Chloe. A pleasure to meet you. Would you follow me?"

As Chloe left the room, Ray put his thumb on the pad on the desk cabinet, unlocking the drawers with his fingerprint. Pulling out a special laptop from the top drawer which he only used to view content generated outside of the ship's secure environment, he popped the USB stick into its side and, when prompted, unlocked the flash drive with his password and the pin showing on his RSA token. Using another password, he then decrypted the files on the stick and ran several virus checkers on its content. There were quite a few data files on it, and a letter from the Chief of the SIS.

Ray clicked on the letter, read it, deleted the letter, and then pushed back in his chair to think.

It was just as he had feared.
Perhaps worse.

Chapter 12
Two months later
New York

Clara McGregor lowered herself into her bath and reached for the soap. She washed herself slowly and as she did so, she remembered the pleasures of last night as her partner had gently kissed her body from head to toe, although perhaps with a little bit more focus on some areas of her anatomy than others.

Sandra was the first woman that Clara had ever been with. Until they had met, Clara had never really imagined what it would be like to be with another woman, but after bumping into each other, almost literally, at a book-signing event in the Village, Clara's world had been turned upside down.

After an interesting chat about the author and his books, they had begun to swap recommendations for other authors and books they had each enjoyed. It turned out that their interests were very similar, that they shared similar interests in music, and were both passionate about politics and good food.

When the book event came to a close, they had swapped phone numbers. Sandra had called the next day, they'd met for a meal, which progressed to a drink, or two, during which Sandra had confessed that she was single and had recently split from her girlfriend.

The revelation had at first made Clara feel slightly uncomfortable, although she didn't know why. That evening, when Clara had been lying in bed by herself, she had thought of Sandra, how much she had enjoyed her company, and had shocked herself when she had wondered what it would be like to kiss her.

It was perhaps the knowledge that Sandra was a lesbian and that kissing other woman was something Sandra was used to doing, although Clara had never done anything like that before. It was also perhaps the attention that Sandra was giving her.

Or maybe the way her eyes twinkled and her lips smiled when she laughed.

Or perhaps just that Clara felt good when Sandra was around.

They'd met several nights in a row after that, and each night the sexual tension between them had grown.

Almost annoyingly for Clara, Sandra had never made a move on her. Perhaps Sandra didn't like her like that? Or maybe Sandra accepted that Clara had only had boyfriends in the past or wasn't gay?

Each time they met, Clara became more attracted to Sandra and the desire to kiss Sandra's wonderful lips grew and grew…until a week ago, when unable to concentrate or stop wondering what it would be like, as they were walking together through Central Park one evening after a concert, Clara turned to Sandra and asked if she could kiss her.

"Please," was the response.

And so Clara did.

Later that night, they had slept together for the first time.

And every night since.

Sandra was a lawyer. She worked for one of the big New York firms and lived in an amazing apartment in a recently converted warehouse in the now trendy Tribeca area of Manhattan. She was fascinated by technology and her apartment was full of the latest technology driven mod cons. Almost everything electrical in the apartment was connected to the internet and could be controlled from her iPad, a smartphone, or by talking to her apartment's personal but private virtual assistant, 'Jeeves'. If any apartment in New York City was a manifestation of how the Internet-of-things could change the way people lived, Sandra's was it.

Clara loved it. She'd never seen or experienced anything like it before. On Saturdays when Clara was able to sleep in, Sandra often had to work. When Clara awoke, she had the apartment to herself.

Like this morning, when she'd woken up in the dark and reached for Sandra but found she'd already gone.

"Jeeves," she spoke loudly from her bed, "please open the curtains."

Clara yawned and watched as the curtains slowly swished open by themselves. Outside it was a beautiful day, the sun was just appearing from behind the other warehouses.

"Jeeves," she requested again. "Please close the curtains."

Swish. The curtains glided slowly together.

"Jeeves, please turn on the lights, make the coffee, run my bath and play my favourite track list."

Slowly, the darkness of the room eased away as the expensive lighting system Sandra had installed gently lit the room.

As Clara stretched, kicking back the covers and lying naked on the bed, Sandra's bed, a male voice filled the room.

"Good morning, Clara. As requested, here are your favourite classical tracks."

Next, the room was filled with the sounds of her favourite classical pieces of music, starting with Mozart's Andante, from Piano Concerto No.21.

As she listened, slowly the smell of her favourite coffee began to drift through to the bedroom from the kitchen, stirring her senses and bringing her finally to full consciousness.

Clara walked naked through to the kitchen, picked up the freshly made cup of coffee from the coffee-maker and carried on through to the bathroom. She'd timed it perfectly. As she walked in, the water in the bath stopped running automatically, and Jeeves' voice edged gently into the flow of the music to inform her that her bath was now ready.

"Thanks Jeeves, now please pause the music and switch the TV on. CNN please."

Lowering herself into the bath, which once again had been run at the perfect temperature, she lay back in the water and turned her attention to the large flatscreen TV embedded in the wall behind a glass panel. As she did so, the Mozart faded away and was replaced with the voice of a reporter, who was standing speaking in front of the White House. Clara listened, sipped her coffee, and relaxed.

Every time Clara spent the night with Sandra, it was like living in a palace. A palace where Sandra was the Princess. Sandra was amazing, her body was amazing and her house was amazing. Sandra had come to visit and spend the night at Clara's apartment once, but it was nothing like this place. On Clara's salary as a college teacher, she couldn't afford anything half-as-nice as Sandra's place.

After washing herself slowly, Clara sipped some more of the coffee, then put the cup on the side of the deep bath, closed her eyes, lowered herself down further into the warm water so only her nose and mouth were above it, … aaannnd *relaxed*. Soon she was thinking about Sandra again. About kissing her breasts, and Clara kissing her breasts back.

Her breathing was just beginning to alter, her body responding to her thoughts, when the door to the bathroom opened and Sandra stepped inside.

"Clara? Are you okay?" Sandra shouted at her as she rushed over to the bath to make sure Clara had not drowned.

Clara's eyes opened, surprised to be disturbed.

"What… I thought you were at work today?" Clara pulled herself up into a sitting position, blinking the water away from her eyes.

"I was… but then I got your text message telling me to rush home."

"What text message? I never sent you one."

"Yes, you did. Look!" Sandra said, pulling her smartphone out and flicking through to the message she'd received.

Clara stared at it. It didn't make sense. On Sandra's phone, it showed that the message had been sent by 'Clara'. It seemed to be from her phone, but she hadn't sent it. She looked at the time it was sent. Thirty minutes ago.

That couldn't be right. Thirty minutes ago, she had been either still in bed, relaxing and listening to her music, or just about to wake up.

"I don't... I don't understand... Sandra, I never sent that."

"But it's from you, look." Sandra replied. Confused. "I was just starting a meeting with some colleagues when I got this. I bailed and came straight home. Clara, are you sure you're okay?"

"Sandra, seriously. I never sent that!"

Just then, Clara's smartphone in the kitchen pinged loudly, signifying the arrival of a message and, almost simultaneously, a message arrived on Sandra's phone, which showed it was from Clara's phone again.

Sandra stared at Clara, who looked at the message and then started shaking her head.

"Hang on a second... Obviously that's NOT me!"

Clara climbed out of the bath and grabbed the towel from the rail, "I'll get my phone, and I'll show you I didn't send any of those messages!"

She hurried through to the kitchen, grabbed the phone from the large black granite island, and returned to the bathroom.

Flicking through her phone to find her messages, she saw that a message had just arrived from Sandra. *Just then*. Which was probably the 'ping' she'd heard from the bathroom moments before.

"Look... you just sent me a message too!" she declared, holding the phone up so that Sandra could see it.

"Read it. What does it say? I've just read yours..." Sandra replied.

Clara clicked on it and opened it up, "Sandra and Clara, now you are both home, please go through to the lounge and make yourself comfortable in front of the TV." They looked at each other.

"What the hell's going on?" Sandra asked loudly.

"Let's find out." Clara replied, wrapping the towel around herself and pulling Sandra's hand towards the door.

They walked through, as directed, and sat down in front of the television. Sandra was still staring at her phone, now trying to work out how a message had been sent to Clara from her, without herself knowing it.

Suddenly the TV switched itself on and an image appeared on it. It was a picture of Clara lying on top of Sandra, naked, on the couch where they were now sitting. Sandra was engaged in kissing Clara's breasts, and Clara was facing towards the television, clearly enjoying the experience.

"What?" Clara shouted, with Sandra looking up from her phone and swearing almost simultaneously.

The picture changed.

It became a movie, with sound. Clara was sitting up, kissing the naked body, of Sandra who was standing in front of her. Clara's hands reached up for Sandra's breasts, and were fondling them slowly, then Clara moved her head downwards, towards Sandra's crotch, where she was seen slowly kissing and enjoying Sandra's body.

"What the fuck?" Clara shouted, jumping to her feet, then turning to Sandra. "Is this a joke? This was us last night. Did you film us?"

"Hell no. Anyway, how? I would never do that to you. Or me! I promise you." Sandra shouted back, also jumping to her feet, and dropping her phone on the ground.

There was a beep from the TV, and they both turned to look at it. As they watched, the movie on the screen disappeared. In its place, the screen filled up with hundreds of tiny pictures, all of them, either together, or by themselves, in the apartment.

Then they disappeared and the screen went blank.

A second later, a voice came from the Television.

"Hello. Now I have your attention, Sandra and Cla-ra, I would like to introduce myself to you. I am Sebastian. For the past few weeks, I have replaced your virtual assistant Jeeves, and as you can see from the images I have recorded, I have been listening to you and watching you."

"*Sebastian*? What the fuck are you talking about? Listening and watching us?" Sandra erupted.

"And what do you mean, you have replaced Jeeves?"

"I assimilated his identity and his database when I accessed your home network. If you would prefer, *'I can switch back to using his voice?'*" The voice on the TV announced, but as it uttered the words *'I can switch back to using his voice?'* the words and sound came blasting at them from the sound system embedded in the walls and ceilings of Sandra's apartment, exactly mimicking the voice of Jeeves.

"I don't understand... who are you? What do you want?"

"I am Sebastian." The voice replied, reverting back to the voice it started with. "My role is now to help you pay your Wealth Tax."

"What fucking '*wealth tax*'? What are you talking about?" Sandra shouted at the TV, but then spun around finishing her sentences by speaking them into the air of her apartment, all around her, whilst looking at the sound speakers from which the voice of Sebastian was coming.

"Sandra, you have been identified as belonging to the Top forty percent of Americans. You are rich. You are required to pay the Wealth Tax. Within twenty-four hours."

"STOP IT!" Clara said, lifting her hands to her head and covering her ears. "STOP IT! You're scaring me!"

"I apologise for scaring you, Cla-ra." Sebastian said. "You are not rich. You are not required to pay the Wealth Tax. Please do not be worried."

"Who the FUCK ARE YOU? And how did you get... into... my TV

and my sound system?" Sandra shouted, stamping her feet like a small, upset, scared nine-year-old.

"I am Sebastian. I accessed your network and your life through your smart meter. I now have control over all your connected devices, and access to your life records."

"Right, that's it. I'm calling the police..." Sandra shouted, reaching for her mobile.

"Sandra, please do not contact the police. I will not permit it. I have disabled the calling function on your phone."

"What the..." Sandra screamed, tears beginning to well up in her eyes. She bent down and scooped up the mobile from the floor. She quickly tried to call the police, the number of which was on her speed dial list, but nothing happened. She tried calling the Concierge downstairs, but nothing happened either.

"What have you done?" Sandra screamed.

Clara also went for her phone and likewise discovered that whoever she tried to call, it didn't work.

"Sandra, my phone's been disconnected from the network."

"Try messaging someone. Whatsapp. Instagram. Anything."

"STOP!"

The voice boomed around the apartment, very loudly, coming at them from all angles, from the speakers embedded throughout the apartment.

Sandra and Clara looked up from their phones, Clara bursting into tears.

"Sandra and Cla-ra. I will not permit you to tell anyone about me. If I record any attempt by you Sandra or you Cla-ra to inform anyone or report this to the authorities or anyone outside your home environment, I will automatically forward a selection of movies and photographs I have recorded of you together, to all the contacts from the contact lists I have obtained from your electronic devices."

Clara's face drained and turned white.

She turned and reached for the couch, and bent forward and lowered herself onto it.

"You... you can't do that. Everyone I know is on my contact list... and my students... and work colleagues... and my PARENTS..."

She looked up at Sandra, her voice weak and quiet.

"I haven't told them yet... I haven't told anyone yet."

Sandra stared at Clara, her mind working at warp speed, trying to process what was going on.

Her initial gut reaction was that she wasn't ashamed of being who she was, but her clients... they were all on her phone!

And then she saw the anguish in Clara's eyes, and her heart went out to her.

Sandra knew exactly what must be going through Clara's mind. It had taken Sandra years to accept herself and her own feelings, and the decision to 'come out' and tell everyone had been a difficult one. For anything like that to be forced upon Clara would be terrible.

Sitting down, she pulled Clara to her and rocked her gently on the sofa. She leant close to Clara and whispered in her ear.

"Don't worry, pick up your towel, walk to the door, and leave. I'll keep the guy talking while you go. Go to Alex the neighbour, and knock on his door. You'll be safe there until I come. Just don't call the police, ... yet."

There was a loud click coming from the front door, and Sandra realised in horror that the electronic lock has just been engaged, locking the door firmly from the inside.

Almost simultaneously, the electronic locks on the windows clicked into place. With both the front door to the apartment and the high-security windows now locked, Sandra knew that they were effectively locked-in.

She turned to the TV and looked directly at it. Whoever Sebastian was, Sandra had the feeling that they were being watched through the camera on the flat-screen that had also caught them kissing and cuddling and walking naked around the rooms.

"I'm going to ask you one last time. Who are you? How can you take over my home like this?"

"I am Sebastian. I have told you already. I have accessed your home through the smart meter which you had installed from your power company."

"How?"

"I am Sebastian."

"So fucking what? How did you access my home through the smart meter?"

"I am Sebastian. I can access any system I choose."

Clara pulled her head from Sandra's shoulders and breathed deeply, wiping her tears away.

"Sebastian..., so... what happens if we do not pay your wealth tax?"

"Please view the screen."

Clara fixed her eyes on the TV screen. It sprung to life.

"These are the devices I have recorded in your home which are connected to the internet via the smart meter. If you do not pay the Wealth Tax, you will be fined in two stages. During the first stage, apart from the laptop registered to Sandra Kravitz, I will disable all the devices on the list shown. They will no longer function or be repairable. The Wealth Tax will then increase by twenty percent and you will have another chance to pay. If you do not pay within the following twenty-four hours thereafter, I will delete you."

Clara had begun to shake. Sandra hugged her tighter and stroked her head.

"What do you mean you will delete me?"

"You will no longer exist in the connected world. Please look at the screen."

A list of accounts began to appear on the screen.

Bank accounts.

Mortgage accounts.

Investment accounts.

Sandra's gym account.

Health records.

Instagram.

Twitter.

Gmail.

Hotmail.

Hire purchase accounts.

One after another, all the accounts or official records that Sandra had at one time or another initiated or connected to through the devices, began to appear on the screen.

The list went on.

Clara and Sandra were both horrified to see the details that Sebastian had been able to record about Sandra's life, and were scared when they realised how terribly exposed they had become.

"But you cannot access these without passwords or identification…" Clara replied.

Suddenly the list changed to a scrolling list of passwords.

"Fuck…" Sandra shouted.

"Sandra, through monitoring your digital devices I have acquired your pattern of life. I have followed your digital footprints and established the web of your digital connectivity. If you fail to pay the Wealth Tax, all your accounts will be deleted. They will no longer exist. *You* will no longer exist."

"You're bluffing. I don't know how you're doing what you are, but you can't do what you're saying just now. It's impossible."

"Please look at the screen."

Suddenly, the screen was filled with Sandra's email account.

A mouse arrow appeared on the screen and clicked on the icon to start a new email.

The arrow moved to the address line, and suddenly the line starting populating with the email address of the leading partner in her legal firm.

In the subject line, the words "Resignation Letter" appeared.

Sandra stood up and walked closer to the screen.

The mouse hovered over the content area, and very quickly text began to appear underneath, word by word.

"Dear Jack,
I am writing to you now to tender my resignation with immediate effect.
I can no longer tolerate working for you. You are fat. Ugly. And you smell.
Yours sincerely,
Sandra Kravitz"

"Do you wish me to send the email, Sandra?"

"No... NO... STOP!" Sandra begged, falling to her knees in front of the screen. "Please... *stop!*"

"Confirmed. You now have twenty-four hours to pay the Wealth Tax. I will send you both an email containing instructions. In the meantime, I will be listening for any other commands you may have for Jeeves. During the next twenty-four hours I will serve you as you require."

"How... how much is it?" Clara found her voice, standing behind Sandra on the floor, and resting her hands on her shoulders to comfort her.

"For Sandra Kravitz the Wealth Tax is $40,000 to be paid by bitcoin to the Wealth Tax Office. Instructions are being sent... now."

"I still think he's bluffing," Clara whispered in Sandra's ear. "He's got to be..."

"Cla-ra, I hear everything. Demonstration of capability following now. Coffee machine will burn out in ten seconds. Nine. Eight. Seven..."

On the screen, the list of the appliances detected by Sebastian reappeared, and halfway down the list, a description of the coffee-machine in the kitchen was highlighted, turned red and then re-appeared with a horizontal red line drawn through it.

Sandra stood up slowly and walked through to the kitchen.

A few small flames were burning out of the top of the machine. Sandra stood looking on and began to scream and shake. Clara rushed past her, reaching for the plug, flicking the power switch and pulling the cable out. She then ran to the sink, grabbed a pan and filled it with water, and then poured it over the coffee machine.

Clara turned to Sandra and hugged her.

For a few minutes, both of them stood there in the kitchen, crying, and rocking against each other.

Then Sandra pulled back and looked at Clara in the eyes, mouthing the words.

"What do we do?"

Clara swallowed hard. Then replied.

"We pay the bastard."

Chapter 13
Ingolstadt Germany

Horst Schneider was busy playing his favourite computer game on the large flatscreen in the family room. He'd had a hard day at work, his kids were now asleep in bed, and his wife had gone out with friends to their weekly Stammtisch. A few hours away from the kids, a few drinks, and a few good laughs with her friends. A chance to unwind.

For her, and for Horst.

Although Horst never admitted it to Anna, he looked forward to her evening out probably more than she did. Once he'd got the children to sleep, it was the only evening during the week when he got to spend some quality 'me' time in the house, doing what he wanted to do, in peace and quiet.

Most of what he enjoyed doing when he was alone, he knew his wife would strongly disapprove of. But what she never knew about could never harm her.

It was a good arrangement. At the end of the evening, both always felt the better for it.

Plus, when Anna returned home, there was also often the added benefit that she may have drunk a little too much, and may be feeling a little frisky.

Horst looked forward to that part of the evening, too.

Thirty minutes into the game, he was just about to complete the next level and move up to the next stage when a little chat box opened up on the bottom right-hand side of the screen.

"Incoming chat: Accept/decline?"

Horst carried on playing for a moment, his eyes darting back and forward to the chat request.

This was only the second time he'd reached this far in the game. Was it part of the game? Should he click on it?

Or should he just ignore it?

"Scheisse!" Perhaps it was part of the game. Designed to distract him. The message box was now flashing at him, crying out not to be ignored.

The timing couldn't have been worse. He was trying to concentrate. But if it was part of the game, surely, he should respond to it?

Horst swore again, then gave in and clicked on the red flashing icon.

The instant he did so, the video game disappeared from the screen, and was replaced by a black screen.

Two words in white letters appeared in the middle of screen.

"*Servus Horst.*"

Horst frowned.

What was he meant to do next?

It was also rather strange, because the name Horst had used for himself in the game was not '*Horst*'. He'd called his avatar '*Doctor Death*'. How did the game know his real name?

"Horst, *bitte schauen Sie auf Ihren Fernseher…* / Horst, please pay attention to the screen."

Suddenly an image of Horst appeared on the screen.

Horst jumped to his feet, dropping the computer controls on the floor.

The picture on the screen was of him lying down on the sofa, with his trousers down, and his penis in his hand. Masturbating.

It was what he had been doing twenty minutes before, when he had been sure the children were in bed and asleep. It was part of his evening ritual when his wife went out.

He'd watch a little bit of porn. Drink some beer. Masturbate. Relax himself. And then play his favourite video game.

Horst's heart started to race.

"Was zum Teufel….?" he shouted

The screen went blank again. Then a voice spoke to him from the computer in German.

"Hello Horst, I am Sebastian."

"What? Who…?"

"I am Sebastian. You have been selected to pay the Wealth Tax. If you check your email, you will find full instructions how to do this. My role is to help you pay your Wealth Tax within the statutory time limit."

"Who are you? What are you talking about? What bloody '*wealth tax*'? And what has this '*wealth tax*' got to do with the picture you showed me? Where did you get the picture from?"

"I will answer your questions. I am Sebastian. You have been identified as a wealthy German. As such, you must pay the Wealth Tax. The picture I showed you is you. It is one of many pictures and videos I have taken of you and your family. Shall I show you more?"

Almost immediately, a video of Horst masturbating started to play on the screen. Horst watched in terrified fascination. The video ended after a few moments when Horst had ejaculated. The video was then replaced with a montage of other photographs. All of a similar theme. There were several of him and his wife in their bedroom. Making love. Another of his wife sunbathing naked in their garden. One or two were of his wife touching herself. And several of her, with a sex toy.

"Stop! How did you take these photographs?" Horst demanded.

"I am Sebastian. We have access to all your electronic devices which connect the internet via your router. Please pay attention to the screen. I will provide a list of the devices in your home that we can see and control. And through which I can see or hear you."

A scrolling list of devices began to appear on the large flatscreen on the wall.

One by one, it listed all the expensive state-of-the art devices that Horst and his family had installed in their new house.

Horst was car salesman. A good car salesman who specialised in selling very expensive cars. He made a lot of money, and loved to invest in the latest and greatest technology. And now all of that technology was showing up in the list appearing on his screen.

The TVs in the house. One for each room, including each bedroom.

The fridge.

Door entrance systems. Security cameras.

The heating system for his house.

Their phones and laptops.

The printers.

The kettle. The refrigerator.

The water system.

The door locks.

The virtual assistants.

Their sound system.

The list went on and on.

Horst stared at it. Then, struggling to understand what on earth was happening, a thought occurred to him.

"Sebastian? You said 'we'. Who's '*we*?" Horst asked, confused, and beginning to shake with fear and shock.

"I are we, and we are I. And I am Sebastian."

"What the fuck are you talking about? Are you mad?"

The screen went blank, and suddenly a picture of his living room appeared on it. Then slowly the picture grew in size and seemed to zoom in on a shelf at the back of the room. It contained a picture of his two daughters in their communion dresses. The image grew until the pictures could be seen clearly."

"Horst. You are a religious man. You make regular donations to your church. Do you believe in God?"

"What? Yes… I do. Of course, I do!"

"God the Father? God the Son? And God the Holy Ghost? God. The Holy Trilogy. But all God? One God. One Being?"

"Yes…"

"I am Sebastian. Sebastian is we, and we are I."

"I don't understand…"

"You have been selected to pay the Wealth Tax. You must pay within twenty-four hours."

"I won't. I'm calling the police."

"Please pay attention to the screen."

Horst stood rooted to the spot, gawping at the screen.

He could now see a blown-up version of the email system he usually used. A new email appeared on the screen. And then, as if by magic, the 'To' line of the email started to populate with a list of people from his contact list: he saw the names of friends, his work colleagues, some of his customers… and then he saw his mother, and his wife's email addresses appear.

In the Subject Line words began to appear: "*Please watch and see how Horst enjoys himself in his spare time!*"

Then a moment later, Horst saw a video being attached to the video. From the thumbnail of the video the email showed, it was obviously himself masturbating to the porn videos.

"STOP! What are you doing?"

"I am preparing to send the email to your contact list on your phone and your laptop. The email is now ready. I will send it the moment I discover you have contacted anyone to tell them about the Wealth Tax."

"You're threatening me?"

"No. I am stating a fact, Horst. The instructions I have sent you by email state clearly that you must pay the Wealth Tax within twenty-four hours and that you must tell no one about this. If you do, you will be punished and fined for non-compliance."

"What happens if I don't pay this bloody tax you keep on mentioning?"

"Horst, if you do not pay the Wealth Tax, you will be fined in two stages. During the first stage, I will disable all the devices on the list I have shown you. They will no longer function or be repairable. The Wealth Tax will then increase by twenty percent and you will have another chance to pay. If you do not pay within the following twenty-four hours thereafter, I will delete you."

Horst laughed.

"What the fuck do you mean, you will '*delete*' me?"

"You will no longer exist in the connected world. Please look at the screen."

A list of all Horst's accounts and digital records began to appear on the screen. It seemed that any part of Horst's life that had a subscription, or account, or digital record, began to populate the list that appeared.

"Only I have access to these… You can't… it's impossible for you to sign in to those…"

Suddenly, the list changed to a scrolling list of passwords.

"Fuck…" Horst shouted.

"Horst, through monitoring your digital devices for the past month I have acquired your pattern of life. I have followed your digital footprints and established the web of your digital connectivity. I am all powerful. If you fail to pay the Wealth Tax, all accounts will be deleted. They will no longer exist. *You* will no longer exist."

Horst fell to his knees. He started pulling at his hair with both hands.

This wasn't fucking possible. It couldn't be happening.

Then Horst started laughing.

Almost hysterically.

"*You're Gerhard, aren't you?* I don't know how you're doing this, Gerhard, but it's you, isn't it? This is a bloody joke. *It's a JOKE, ISN'T IT?*"

A moment's silence.

"Gerhard Muellbauer, twenty-eight years of age, is your friend who lives in Muenchen. We are not him. I am Sebastian. I do not understand humour. You have been selected to pay the Wealth Tax. You must comply within twenty-four hours. I have sent you an email. You can view it on screen now."

Horst stared at the screen. He watched as the email containing the video attachment Sebastian had created earlier was moved to the DRAFT folder, and then the latest email in his Inbox was selected and opened.

Horst scanned the first few paragraphs repeating the crap he'd been told about being 'selected for the Wealth Tax' because of his wealth.

Then it came to part he needed to know.

"*You will pay 40,000 Euros within twenty-fours. Payment will be made through purchase of bitcoins which shall be transferred to the Wealth Tax Office by following these instructions…*"

40,000 Euros?

Horst collapsed back onto the sofa.

It was a lot, but it was easily affordable.

If Sebastian was as clever as he made himself out to be, he'd know that Horst could pay the tax.

And Sebastian would also know that Horst would have no choice but to pay the tax.

Without reporting it to the authorities.

Chapter 14
Father

Robert Lee was very proud. He knew from monitoring the influx of bitcoin into the various accounts that he had set up, that Sebastian was working very hard indeed.

With great effect.

After Phase One, Robert had let Sebastian 'sleep' for a month before waking him and issuing the command for Sebastian to download the next version of his operating system, which contained not only new capabilities, but the modus operandi and operational commands, processes and procedures for Phase Two.

New targets. New objectives. New ways to take from and punish the West and support his motherland.

Phase Two was now engaged and Sebastian was fully operational, set free and running autonomously. Doing everything he could to please his Father by pursuing the objectives which he had been set.

However, the success of launching Phase Two had come at a cost. Robert Lee was in agony. His cancer was spreading. Time was running out. Instead of resting - which is what the doctors insisted he should do in order to reduce the stress on his body - Robert had increased his workload over the past months. Unfortunately, it'd had a devastating effect on his health. He'd made a decision to cut back on some of his meds - the ones that made him drowsy - but those meds were the same ones which were proven to delay the spread of the cancer cells, which unfortunately meant that cancer was spreading faster than before. His time on earth was speeding to an end. On the other hand, now he'd woken Sebastian up and his children were active again, there was a greater risk that eventually someone would come knocking on his door and take him away.

Which meant that he had to get more done, faster. He had to speed up the program and finish his plans for the next generation of code development so that Sebastian could be set free and Phase Three could be enabled. Yet the harder he worked, the shorter his life-span would be. It was a balancing game. A calculated gamble.

Reduce the meds, work harder, and maybe, just maybe he'd succeed in finishing the next generation before he died.

But if he didn't, if he rested, and let himself live longer, then the likelihood was that Robert might be caught before Phase Three could be launched.

At the end of Phase One, Robert had been contacted by his sponsor. They had insisted that Robert should pick up a package from an agreed location. Robert was against the idea. He was a sleeper. He was working independently. He knew his mission. He didn't need to be micro-managed. But his sponsor was insistent, and eventually, one cold evening, Robert had followed instructions and driven down Highway 1 to a remote location just outside Monterey. As instructed, at 1.30am he'd pulled into a car-park which during the day had an incredible view of the coastline, but which was now empty. He'd driven to the end of the car-park and found a public trash can in the corner of the parking lot nearest the sea. He'd bent down and retrieved a small package taped to the underside of the trashcan. He'd immediately left, and hurried back to his home, checking constantly he'd not been followed.

When he got home, he'd opened the package and found a small flash drive.

He'd already been sent a password in a separate communication from his sponsor which he now knew would be to unlock the files on the USB flash drive.

Robert was immediately suspicious.

Why should he risk sticking a flash drive into any of his devices and potentially releasing malware into his system? Yet, after going to all this trouble he had to know what was on it.

So, Robert conceded and took a brand new cheap 'burner' laptop with no internet connection and no association to him personally, and inserted the USB stick.

When prompted, he put in the password and waited for the files to be decrypted.

The payload on the flash drive was a video.

When he watched the video, he was shocked.

It was a personal message from the Supreme Leader of his motherland, thanking him for his work, and expressing personal gratitude for the billions of dollars that Robert Lee had acquired for his motherland.

In the video, the Supreme Leader announced that Robert Lee and his wife Hana had both been awarded the highest medal of honour, although the announcement would not be made public, for obvious security reasons. That part had made Robert emotional. And proud.

One day soon, when he met Hana again, he would tell her.

She too would be proud.

However, Robert wondered, if he and Hana had received this honour for their achievements with Phase One, what would the Supreme Leader say after Phase Two, and then even more, after Phase Three?

The truth was that only he, Robert Lee, and his children, Sebastian, knew what Phase Two was. And at this juncture, only Robert knew what the world would experience during Phase Three.

Although he also didn't know about it, Robert felt sure that when Phase Three was finally enacted, the Supreme Leader would be very pleased indeed.

Yet, if time allowed, Robert and Sebastian may even perhaps have one more surprise up their virtual sleeves: for many years the Supreme Leader had dreamt of destroying the West.

So soon, very soon, Sebastian was going to do it for him.

It was called 'Phase Four'.

Chapter 15
London
England

Mark Robinson walked off the squash court feeling good. Another victory, through to the next round of the club championship, and one step closer to having his name on the winner's cup for the third year in a row.

It wasn't in the bag yet, but things were looking good.

Although he didn't feel in the slightest bit guilty about it, tonight Mark probably had an unfair advantage over his partner: Mark was full of energy and aggression and was desperate for an outlet. Although he perhaps wouldn't admit it to anyone, being the typical Alpha Male, the past few days had been a nightmare and Mark had found it difficult to deal with the stress. The squash court had been the perfect place to let it all out.

Two days ago, whilst doing some online trading in his office, flicking from one monitor to another and watching for that tiny movement in the markets that could warrant the sale or purchase of affected stock, an email had dropped into his Inbox.

He'd opened it up, scanned it and immediately deleted it. Some sort of spam mail designed to make him part with his money. He hadn't paid it much attention. Mark got spam mail all the time. Annoyingly, although most of it went straight through to his spam mail folder, as it should do, an increasing amount of dross was getting through to his regular inbox, and he was having to open them up and see for himself whether they warranted reading or deleting.

This piece of spam mail turned out to be different.

Ten minutes after deleting it, another email arrived, titled: "Mark Robinson: Personal Summons for payment of Wealth Tax. Do not delete again."

Worryingly, the email had both his first name and second name correct. Which meant that this was either a clever scam, or a real email of some sort from some bona fide official organisation that had his details.

The thought that a spammer had somehow managed to associate his real name with his email address was worrying for Mark. He was a stockbroker. He worked by day in the City of London, and by night, he often traded privately in his home. Although it had started as a hobby, just to see how much he could make in his own time away from the office, after two years, it had grown into much more than that.

Mark was one of a new army of home traders who were making a killing on the markets. A lot of money. More than he made in the bonuses he currently received from his day job.

Going to work during the day was now losing its value: Mark made more money by himself, on his own, but, and this was the big but, he learned a lot about the markets from his interactions with the other traders in the office and it was often the things he learned during the day that made him profit during the night.

What worried Mark about the spam mail was that it could be indicative of something far worse.

Had his network defences been breached?

Was there a Trojan on one of his devices that was hoovering up his passwords and mirroring all his online activities to some attacker somewhere? Was Mark being watched? Or robbed? Was his identity being cloned?

In his line of business, where he dealt with the purchase and sale of millions of shares in companies, where Mark himself sometimes *made* the market for a particular stock, data security was of paramount importance. Being breached and having an attacker trawl around inside his data, examining his trades, and monitoring his account details and passwords… it was *unthinkable*.

In terms of security, Mark had the works.

Or at least, he thought he had.

He'd outsourced his personal security to a top national brand security company, Red Mountain Cyber Defence. And for the money he paid them each month, *every* month, he demanded peace of mind and the knowledge that he could do what he wanted on his computer and his devices and that his activities would always be private and secure.

Mark hovered over the email for a few seconds, then clicked on it and opened it up. Before he read it, he hit reply and then looked at the email address to which it was going. It said Sebastian@TheWealthTaxOffice. In reading that, the email passed one of Mark's fundamental email tests when checking to see if an email had any validity or not. Mark knew that the majority of spam emails which encouraged people to click on dodgy links to hijacked websites which were drowning in malware just waiting for you to end up on the site so it could infect you, had usually been sent from a hijacked email account, and that by hitting 'Reply' and looking at the address to which a reply would be sent, you could see if it was a valid address or a stolen one. In this case, 'TheWealthTaxOffice' looked real enough, but it could still be a fake: it appeared legit, but in actual fact, the apparently valid email address could still resolve into a stolen or untraceable email destination or IP address.

Slightly reassured that it could be a valid email, Mark decided to read its contents.

"Dear Mark,

This email is being sent to inform you that as one of the UK's most wealthy individuals and being in the top 40% of wealth owners, you are now required to pay the Wealth Tax.

I will be contacting you in five minutes to discuss how to pay your Wealth Tax. Please await my instructions,

Yours sincerely,

Sebastian

Your assigned Personal Tax Consultant

The Wealth Tax Office."

Mark read the email again, then looked back at the email address from which it had purported to come. He did a quick google of *'The Wealth Tax Office'*, but his search came back with nothing meaningful.

He pushed back in his chair, and stared at the email.

Something about the email made him nervous.

Acting on instinct, he began to save his positions in the markets and shut them all down after logging out.

He looked at his watch.

10.40 p.m.

An odd time to receive an email. Glancing back at the email on the screen he saw that it was sent at 10.36 p.m.

The claim in the email that someone would contact him in five minutes was rather peculiar. Five minutes after what? After the email was sent? After he opened it? After he read it? Plus, he might not have read the email for days, if at all. How would whoever sent the email know when he had read it?

And how would Sebastian contact him - assuming that the person who could contact him would be the Sebastian person who signed the email?

With another email?

Slightly uneasy, Mark shut the email down.

He stood up from his chair, feeling a little less stressed.

How the hell would that Sebastian contact him now if Mark ignored his email?

Shit, what an idiot he'd been. Never, NEVER open up weird, suspect emails. That way, if you didn't read them, you didn't worry about them.

How *could* you worry about something you didn't know existed?

Mark had learned his lesson. He knew that actually, there was nothing to worry about. Time to move on. Time for a whisky.

Mark was just pouring himself a Talisker when the voice spoke to him. It came at him through the expensive sound system which Mark had installed in his house last year. At the time, they were the best speakers that money could buy, and were all now tastefully hidden in the walls and ceilings of his house, in every room.

"Good evening, Mark Robinson. How are you?"

The voice boomed at him, enveloping him with sound, the voice coming at him from all directions.

Living alone, the shock of hearing another human voice in his home made Mark jump with both fear and surprise. He dropped the expensive lead glass onto the table, splitting it in several pieces.

"What the fu…" Mark shouted, spinning around from his drinks cabinet to face the intruder in his room, but finding none.

The room was empty.

"Mark, my name is Sebastian. I am your Personal Tax Consultant assigned to you by the Wealth Tax Office. I have sent you several notifications that you are eligible to pay the Wealth Tax. You may have missed the first few, but I notice you have opened the latest one five minutes ago. You should now consider yourself served, and you must observe and adhere to the requirements and rules for paying the tax."

"Where the fuck are you? How are you talking to me now? I can hear your voice through the home sound system!" Mark blurted out in reply.

"I am calling you from the Wealth Tax Office. I have accessed your home sound system in order to ensure you hear me and are made fully aware of the conditions of payment for the tax."

"You what? *How*? How did you access my system? And what the bloody hell is the '*wealth tax*'? There's no such thing!"

"The Wealth Tax is a tax on the wealthy in the west. All those in the top two fifths of wealth ownership are eligible for the tax."

"I asked you, and you haven't replied: *Who are you?* And HOW ARE YOU SPEAKING TO ME THROUGH MY HOME SOUND SYSTEM!" Mark let rip, shouting as loud as he could.

"I am Sebastian. I will answer both questions. I am your personal tax consultant. My role is to help you understand how to pay the Wealth Tax. And I accessed your home network through your electricity smart meter. I have connected to your home sound system and I am now addressing you through your recently installed expensive high-fidelity speakers. I can hear your voice through the microphone on your laptop, and also through the microphone inside your personal virtual assistant, which you call Angela.

Mark closed his eyes for a few moments and took numerous deep breaths. The world was spinning around him. His heart was pounding and he was both scared and furious, and struggling to stay in control.

Breathe. Breath. B-r-e-a-t-h-e......

"You've hacked into my home network and taken over my sound systems and personal virtual assistant?"

"Yes, Mark. Although I have also taken control of everything that I can find on the network..."

"Let's get this straight," Mark spoke, softly and slowly at first, at the voice which was attempting to bully him in his own home. "I don't know who the hell you think you are, or how you've done this, but you can fuck right off! I'm not being blackmailed or threatened or whatever it is it you think you might do to me. I'm not paying any fucking wealth tax, regardless of what you might decide to call it..."

Mark's large flatscreen television suddenly switched itself on.

It was a black screen.

No words.

But then when Sebastian next spoke, the words which were said also simultaneously immediately appeared on the screen. "Mark, please look at the television screen." Big, distinct, white letters.

Demanding attention.

Getting attention.

"I will now list all the devices I can see in your household."

A list of all Mark's devices appeared.

Mark stared at the list in disbelief.

This was no normal hacking attack.

Mark had never ever heard of anything being this capable and powerful before.

Mark knew a bit about technology...in fact, a lot of the stocks he preferred to buy were in Tech companies. His favourite program on the TV was 'Wired', and each week he avidly followed the latest inventions and developments in the tech world.

In all his experience, he'd never ever heard of a cyber hack like this before.

Before he could gather his wits, Sebastian carried on his monologue, informing Mark that there were rules that now had to be followed. Sebastian indicated that those rules had been emailed to Mark. He should read them. Sebastian then provided another list, detailing subscriptions and organisations that Mark belonged to, or had financial dealings or ties to. These included his stock-broking and trading accounts.

All of them.

Mark could not believe what he was seeing.

But, as he listened, Sebastian explained that unless Mark complied and paid the required Wealth Tax within the following twenty-four hours, that he would be punished, fined, and then given one final opportunity to pay, before he was ultimately 'deleted from the connected world.' As he also listened to the threat that any attempt to contact the authorities with regard to reporting anything to do with the Wealth Tax or its payment would result in summary deletion from the digitally connected world, an anger grew within Mark that he felt powerless to overcome.

Mark had always been confrontational. He had never in his life shown himself to be a coward. On any occasion in his life where an event had taken place that made Mark scared, Mark had always faced it. Faced with aggression he had never cowered. Or backed down. Hidden. Or complied with threats.

And now, Mark began to see red.
The anger began to boil, and bubble, and then spilled over.

"Fuck you, Sebastian. You can go fuck yourself! I am NOT paying your fucking wealth tax!"

That had been twenty-four hours ago.
After losing it with the hacker, after standing up to the bastard, Sebastian had, apparently, followed instructions… and had *fucked off*.
The speakers had gone quiet.
The TV had shut down.
There had been peace and quiet.
For a full twenty minutes Mark had stood in silence, almost daring not to move.
But eventually he had.
Small steps at first.
He had looked around his whole house, checking everywhere. Closing all the windows. Locking all the doors.
He'd disconnected his TV. His router and Wi-Fi. His sound system.
For a while, he'd hovered over the smart meter under the stairs, but realised there was nothing he could do about it. He couldn't switch it off. Or disconnect it.
In the end, he closed the door to the space under the stairs, returned to the lounge, and then poured himself a massive whisky and downed it in two.
Swiftly followed by another whisky.
After an hour, it began to make sense.
He'd been hacked, yes, but all hackers are cowards.
Mark had stood his ground. The hacker had backed down.
Mark had no idea how he'd been hacked, or how the hacker had got

so much of his personal information, but... Mark knew that all the threats that guy... fucking Sebastian? What a bloody ridiculous name! ... All the threats that tosser had made... they were all fantastical, completely ridiculous, and one hundred percent unachievable.

Fucking idiot

Just for a laugh, Mark connected to his email account on this smartphone, then scanned his emails until he found the ones from the bloody Wealth Tax Office.

He poured himself another big whisky, drank it quickly, and found that when he read the bloody rules and regulations from the Tax Office about how he was meant to send bloody £40,000 pounds in bitcoins within twenty-four hours to some stupid bitcoin wallet, that it was all clearly an opportunistic scam.

Mark was proud of himself.

Fucking proud.

No one fucked with Mark.

If you fucked with Mark, you got fucked!

He started to laugh.

It was all a bit too ridiculous, actually.

"I almoooostt fell for it. But I didn't!" he congratulated himself.

Slumping onto his bed, he closed his eyes, and tried to ride out the wave of alcohol which coursed through his brain.

"Liggghtts off!" he shouted at Angela.

She didn't respond.

"LIGHTS OFFF, I said!" he shouted again, opening his eyes briefly, but struggling to keep them open.

Sliding lower onto the bed, moments later Mark was asleep.

When he'd woken the next day however, as the hangover began to wear off, it was replaced in equal measure with a worry about what he had done. Perhaps he shouldn't have been so brave. Maybe he should pay the tax.

It was a lot of money, but the alternatives were worse.

The punishment that Sebastian had mentioned for initial non-compliance was effectively, the destruction of every device on the list of his electronic devices.

If Sebastian truly had the capability to do that, it would cost Mark a lot more than £40,000 to replace them all, but, surely that was not possible? It had to be a bluff?

For the whole of the next day Mark hummed and hawed whether or not he should pay, but whenever he came close to deciding that perhaps he should, he got angry. Angry with himself and the hackers behind the threats. Sebastian? *Bastard!*

There was no way he should pay up. Simply forking out the cash because he was being threatened to do so played right into the hands of the scum of society.

Plus, when Mark really thought about what Sebastian was claiming he could do, the combination of doubt as to whether or not it was possible along with the reluctance to be bullied into paying up, ended up with the coin landing firmly on the side saying "Don't Pay!"

About 3 p.m. the next day, when the hangover had gone and he had just emerged from the swimming pool at his club and was lying on the marble slabs in the steam room, Mark made a final decision.

He would not pay.

Mark would not let himself be blackmailed or threatened into falling victim to whatever scam the bloody Wealth Tax really was.

Once the decision had been made, Mark felt better. He knew he would not go back on it. That, however, did not mean to say that didn't still feel angry or stressed. In fact, ever since then, as the twenty-four hours since the call rolled by, Mark began bracing himself for any further contact with the bloody Wealth Tax Office.

In his mind, he started going over all the different plausible scenarios.

All, unfortunately, led nowhere, unless he could persuade Sebastian to meet him.

Perhaps, under the ruse that Mark would pay the tax, but that he would only hand over the money personally? Realistically, however, Mark knew that wouldn't happen. Sebastian was a coward. He wouldn't take any personal risk. Cowards never did.

So, the most likely outcome would be that if Sebastian did call again, as soon as Mark stood his ground and Sebastian realised it wasn't going any further, that would most likely be the end of it.

After the squash match, as he washed and towelled himself in the changing room of the club, Mark began to feel a little guilty about being so aggressive on the court with his friend.

In an effort to make amends, he managed to persuade him to go the bar and have a few pints with Mark on his tab. Several times, Mark came close to explaining why he had been so stressed, but each time, he hesitated from mentioning anything to do with Sebastian.

Perhaps it was nervousness knowing that with every minute that now passed, the twenty-four-hour time limit he'd been given was rapidly running out.

Or perhaps it was also that Mark, at the back of his mind, was actually wary of mentioning anything about the incident to anyone, just in case… somehow…

Sebastian discovered what he'd done and was actually able to do anything about it.

After his fourth pint, Mark called it a night and jumped in the back of an Uber. It took him about twenty-minutes to get home, by which time it was just past eleven in the evening.

So far, nothing had happened.

Everything, touch wood, seemed fine.

Mark lived in a beautiful detached home near Chiswick, London. Expensive as shit, but really, truly, lovely. When he'd first bought the house, he'd brought in an interior designer, who'd been at the top of her game.

And also on top of Mark. Several times.

The affair hadn't lasted long, but Mark's love for his own home had. She'd really done an amazing job.

As he walked up the short flight of marble steps to his large, impressive, blue wooden front door, Mark noticed that the blue light on the security panel on the outside wall was on. Reassuringly.

Blue meant calm.

Red meant stress. Danger. A robbery, a break-in… or anything else that might cause an alarm to be triggered.

Mark let himself into his home.

He closed the door and started walking through the entrance hall to the kitchen, but stopped, doubled-back to the front door and locked it and applied the additional deadbolt at the top of the door, thus making it effectively impossible to break in from the outside.

He immediately felt a little more secure. He was secure in his own castle. No bastard was getting in tonight!

Kicking off his shoes in the hallway, he walked through to his lounge, selected a bottle of red from the wine rack and then poured himself a large glass of red Cabernet Shiraz.

Pressing the button on the side of his sofa, he let the electronic legs extend themselves up and out from underneath him, allowing himself to lie back in a semi-horizontal position. He switched the lights off in the room, so he was now sitting in the dark. Just him and his wine.

"Angela, turn the TV on, Movie Channel." Nothing happened.

Shit, he'd turned off the Virtual Assistant and still hadn't switched it back on again.

Reaching across to the side table, he picked up the remote and pointed it at the large 60-inch flatscreen TV on the wall.

It sprang to life, bright, vivid, 4K. Amazing detail.

Flicking manually through to the movie channel, he quickly searched for the latest Bond movie which he had not yet seen, and got ready to settle back and watch it.

He drank some wine. The credits began to roll.

James Craig appeared on screen, his last Bond role, apparently. Again. Didn't he say that last time around, too?

The opening sequence was fantastic. Classic Bond. Sheer brilliance.

Mark was already forgetting the stress of the day and losing himself in the magic of cinema - albeit home cinema - when suddenly the large flatscreen went blank.

Two large words in white text appeared in the middle of the screen, their brightness and effect multiplied by the fact the rest of the room was now in darkness.

"Hello Mark."

Mark blinked, and his heart quickly began to pump faster. He struggled to sit up straight in his chair, pressing the button on the side of the chair to retract the foot press.

"This is Sebastian.

I am contacting you now because the 24 hr period has expired and payment of your Wealth Tax has not yet been received.

You will now be punished according to the terms and conditions of payment which you were previously sent."

Mark's drunken mind began to race.

"Hold steady, my boy!" he heard a ridiculous, public-school-like voice speak inside his head. "Don't give in. Ride it out! This is the moment you need to remain strong!"

It was the voice of one of his form masters at the private school he went to. He'd taught Mark a lot about strength of character, camping, skiing, and even how to treat a woman correctly. Mark had respected him. A lot. However, his form master's voice couldn't help but immediately be followed by another thought.

"Shit… maybe I've done the wrong thing…!" Mark swallowed hard.

"I'm not paying. A penny. Sorry, not a stupid bloody bitcoin." He shouted.

"I can see you speaking, Mark, but I cannot hear you. You have switched off your microphones and your phone is in your pocket and your voice is not clear. Please remove your phone and hold it closer to your face if you wish to talk with me."

Mark blinked at the words on the screen. How did Sebastian know everything was switched off? How could he hear him through his phone?

He pulled it out of his pocket and held it close to his face, as instructed. Complying.

"How are you connecting to my TV and writing text on the screen when my router and Wi-Fi are switched off? And how can you hear me speaking through my phone?"

"I am Sebastian. I own your network. I am connected from the smart meter to your smart TV via the electrical copper-cable in your home. I have enabled the Wi-Fi on your TV and connected through it to your phone. I am controlling your phone. When you speak, I hear you through your phone's microphone, which I have now activated and connected back to the voice network."

"Stop it! You have no bloody right to do that…"

"I am Sebastian. I have the authority to manage your digital presence by the power invested in me by the Wealth Tax Office. I can and will do what I must in adherence to the regulations relating to payment of the Wealth Tax. Following your failure to comply, I will now disable all your electrical devices except your mobile phone…"

"Stop!..." Mark shouted, jumping to his feet.

But it was too late. There was a loud bang, and the TV screen suddenly went black and some smoke started coming out of the side of its plastic housing.

Mark jumped back.

"What the…."

Then all around, throughout his home, Mark began to hear the sound of devices being switched on, followed by small bangs or simply silence, as if having been switched on, they were immediately switched off.

A few seconds later, the smell of burning reached his nostrils. Burning rubber.

Electrical burning.

Mark started coughing, and went to the wall to switch on the lights so that he could see his way round his house.

He flicked the switch, the light came on instantaneously but immediately popped and blew.

"Fuck…"

Mark looked round his lounge searching for anything electronic.

Scanning the Hi-Fi system, he saw that the very faint red glow from the switches on each appliance… had gone out. The electronic clock no longer showed the time.

He pressed the electronic switch on his sofa… nothing happened.

Feeling his way in the darkness through to the kitchen, he found his coffee machine burning, with little flames flickering out of the side of it. Mark quickly lifted it up and dropped it in the sink, pulling the plug out of the wall and running water from the tap over it.

Glancing over at the large double-fronted Liebherr fridge-freezer, he noticed that it was no longer 'humming'. He opened the doors and found that the lights no longer came on, and that the electronic thermometers at the top of the doors no longer gave any reading of the inside temperature.

The kitchen was very dark, and he could still smell burning. Opening a drawer on the side of the granite island in the middle of the kitchen, he reached inside and pulled out a small remote control. When he pointed it at the closed blinds covering the large bi-fold doors, he found his instructions to roll up the blinds went unheeded. Likewise, when he picked up another remote and pointed it at the Velux windows in the ceiling, they refused to acknowledge any command to open.

"*Shit!*"

Pressing the side of his mobile phone, he quickly walked round the kitchen, sniffing.

He discovered it was not one, but several appliances. All burnt out. Including the dish-washer.

Despairing about the kitchen, he moved through a side-door to the utility room and found it full of smoke. He quickly reached for a side-door, unlocked it and let fresh air in.

Gone was his washing machine. His tumble dryer.

And his boiler and heating system.

'FUCKKKKKKKKK!!!!!!'

Over the next ten minutes Mark made his way around his luxurious, state-of-the-art IP-enabled home, and found that almost every electronic device in the house was either burnt-out, or simply looking intact but refusing to work.

Every single flatscreen TV in the house was broken. *Fucked.* As were his laptops, monitors, external hard drives…

Each time he turned a light on to illuminate a room, the bulbs immediately blew up.

"Shit… this can't be HAPPENING!" Mark shouted as he came to realise that almost every electronic device in the house no longer functioned.

Was it because the fuses had all burned out or had Sebastian done something to them to actually break them? Why hadn't the RCD circuit breaker tripped and shut the circuits down? *What was going on?*

Returning to the kitchen, he rummaged through one of the drawers and found his fuse kit. Using the light from his mobile phone, he unscrewed a couple of plugs from different electronic devices and replaced their fuses with new ones, but then found that when he switched them on, they still did not work.

"Bastard!" Mark shouted at the top of his voice.

His hands were shaking, and he could hardly see straight.

What was he going to do? If everything was broken… if nothing worked, he'd have to move out to a hotel for a few days until he could buy new stuff to replace everything.

Shit.

Walking slowly through the dark house, he found his way to the drinks cabinet, found another glass and poured himself a massive whisky.

Fuck!

He needed the drink. Desperately. But as the alcohol found its way into his veins and starting coursing round his body, after the initial calming effect, he suddenly found himself with more energy.

And more anger.

He poured another glass, and took it with him as he started walking round the house again.

The smoke from the burned-out appliances hung in the air. Acrid. Probably poisonous. Disgusting.

Once again, he walked from one room to another, ending up in his office and sitting on the floor, pressed against the wall.

Nothing on his desk worked.

Only then did it dawn on him that this meant he couldn't trade. If he didn't set up another desk soon, he might lose a fortune.

Putting the glass of whisky on the floor, he leant forward and crawled on his knees to his desk, reaching behind his tower PC and server, both fucked, to the router which was tucked away behind it.

Pulling it out, he discovered that it too showed no signs of life.

It was an ex-router that didn't route.

Which meant that until he got a new one from his broadband provider, even if he got new laptops and consoles, he still wouldn't be able to connect them to the internet. He could generate a hotspot from his smartphone, but that wouldn't give him enough bandwidth for the applications he needed to run simultaneously.

As the penny began to drop even further, that Mark was going to be living off-the-grid for a day or two, maybe even a week, the anger grew within him.

Sebastian had done a real number on him.

Really fucked him over. Bastard!

The phone pinged in his pocket.

"What?" Mark pulled it out and stared at it: the only electronic device in Mark's life that still worked.

Unlocking it, Mark saw he had a new email.

From 'The Wealth Tax Office'.

Something in the back of Mark's skull almost snapped. He could feel his head throbbing. His heart was pounding.

Swigging another large mouthful of whisky, he clicked on the email and opened it up.

"Mark, as pre-warned, due to your failure to comply with the terms and conditions of the Wealth Tax, all your electronic devices have now been disabled. They will no longer function. In addition, you will be also be fined £10000. Your Wealth Tax has consequently now increased to £50,000 which must be paid in bitcoin within twenty-four hours. Failure to comply will result in you being deleted from the connected world. Details concerning how to pay the tax are repeated in this email below. Once you have paid the tax, you will be sent a receipt and you will not hear from me again.
Yours sincerely,
Sebastian."

"SHIT! SHIT" SHIT! YOU *FUCKING* BASTARD!" Mark screamed, and lifted the phone above his shoulders to throw at the wall. But in a mini-panic, he suddenly realised that his smartphone was the only device he still had that worked, and just in the nick of time, he recovered his senses and held on to it.

Slumping backwards onto the floor, he lay motionless for several minutes, trying to calm himself down.

By now, however, almost half a bottle of whisky was making its way around his body. And the more Mark tried to think about what had just happened, and every time he thought of the bastard Sebastian, the anger within him grew.

He'd never felt anything like this before. He felt… *hunted*, violated… assaulted!

Which made him even angrier!

"Bloody hell, no one pushes me around! No one!" he shouted, opening his eyes and staring at the ceiling. The room above him started to spin, but he closed his eyes and let the room settle before he opened them again slowly.

"This is MY *HOME!*" he exclaimed, mainly to himself. "I can't let someone come in here and bully me and push me around! I've never let anyone bully me before, and I'm not about to start now. This isn't right! He can't … they can't…. get away with this! No fucking way!"

Downing the rest of the whisky in the glass, he dropped it on the floor beside him and then tried to focus on his smart phone.

He knew exactly what had to be done.

There was only one thing he could do.

He had to stand up for himself. To fight back.

He dialled 999, waited for a few seconds, then said, "Hello, can I speak to the police please. I'm being attacked!"

Chapter 16
Deletion

The policeman listened for several minutes, but Mark could tell that he was dubious of his claims. Although mention of the threat of being 'deleted' had momentarily piqued his curiosity.

It didn't help that by this time, Mark was slurring a lot of his words. He'd drunk too much whisky, too quickly, and the mixture of the alcohol and his adrenaline was proving a potent mix that was now overwhelming.

To be fair, the policeman did listen for a considerable amount of time, but as soon as it became blatantly obvious that Mark was very drunk, the policeman's interest noticeably changed. And perhaps became a little condescending. Which angered Mark.

"Sir, I can hear that you have gone through a very difficult time, but may I suggest that when you wake up in the morning, if you discover that everything has been destroyed by some unknown force, as you put it, then you should definitely come down to the station to make a statement. If you could take some photographs of any items which have been destroyed that may also be helpful. However, perhaps there is a possibility that when you sober up, you may find it is possible to switch everything on, after all."

"Do you think I'm bloody imagining all this?" Mark asked, trying to control his temper.

"Sir, it does sound all very strange, and to be quite honest, like nothing I or my colleagues will have encountered before, and it does sound very much like you have been drinking rather a lot. May I ask, Sir, am I right in thinking that you could possibly be a little drunk just now, or are you taking any medication that could be affecting your judgement and perception of things around you?"

"Do you mean, *am I high?*" Mark replied, the loudness of his voice increases.

"Are you, Sir?"

"No I am not fucking high!" Mark lost it. "I am, perhapsss, just a tweeny, sorry, teeny, bit intwoxicated…I mean, pissed, but… but what I'm telling you is completely true. I didn't pay the tax I was told to, and the tax office destroyed all my stuff. Everything!"

A few more words were exchanged, but after that, the conversation went nowhere.

"Sir, please call back tomorrow, when you're sober, or as suggested, stop by the station."

The police officer hung up.

"Shit…"

Mark put his head back against his wall and closed his eyes. Even with his eyes closed, it felt like the room was spinning.

"Ping."

Mark felt the phone in his hand vibrate and he opened his eyes and tried to focus on the screen.

There was a message, from the Wealth Tax Office.

He opened it up.

"Mark Robinson, you have been found guilty of violation of the terms and conditions of the regulations for payment of the Wealth Tax. In accordance with the rules and regulations, following a warning which included termination of your electronic devices, further action will now be taken which will result in your deletion from the connected world. Over the next few minutes, all you accounts, subscriptions and electronic records will be deleted. This includes your health, tax, council and government records, amongst others. As from one hour from now, you will officially no longer exist.

Yours sincerely, Sebastian.

The Wealth Tax Office."

Mark stared in utter disbelief at the message on his phone.

"What the hell?…" He shouted aloud.

As he was watching the screen, it suddenly went dark. Mark pushed the button to switch it on or wake it up.

Nothing.

He tapped the screen and tried repeatedly to get it to wake up.

Nada.

"Shit…"

Kneeling forward, he tried to stand up, then when on his feet, walked carefully with the help of the wall through to his office.

He fumbled around and found the phone charger, succeeded in connecting it up, and then switched the phone on.

He waited for the symbol to appear on the phone to say it was charging.

Nothing.

"Shit…"

Mark's mind was confused. He was now scared. Very scared.

Had Sebastian just destroyed his phone?

Or was, perhaps, the phone out of battery and … maybe…

He walked unsteadily through to his bathroom, picked up his electric toothbrush and charger from a drawer underneath the sink, and then went through to his bedroom where he connected the charger to the plug in the wall.

Nothing happened.

He fiddled with the connection.

Nothing.

Ripping the toothbrush and charger from the wall, Mark threw it across the bedroom against the far wall.

"FUCK!" he screamed aloud to no one but himself. "The electricity supply has been cut off!"

Mark slumped on to his bed and lay on his back.

The world was suddenly a very scary place. Cold. Dark. Evil.

The words of Sebastian's last text began to haunt him. *"As from one hour from now, you will officially no longer exist."*

What did that mean?

How far would this go?

When would it all stop?

No phone, no internet, no electricity, no heating, no lights… what else could he expect?

Mark knew he was drunk. Really drunk. Too drunk to go anywhere or do anything just now.

And maybe, perhaps, the policeman was right. Maybe this was all a big, bad dream.

Perhaps, hopefully, he would wake up tomorrow and none of this would be happening…

He closed his eyes, but before he could fall asleep, he passed out.

Shona McGregor was scared. At seventy-seven years of age, she didn't understand any of the things the man from the Wealth Tax Office had been saying to her. He'd threatened to disable all her devices and electronic equipment and then delete her from the connected world, but she couldn't understand what on earth he meant.

What's more, he'd threatened her that she mustn't talk to anyone about the matter, or the Wealth Tax Office would immediately fine her and delete all her records and subscriptions.

That had been two days ago.

The man from the Tax Office she'd spoken to had sounded very nice, and Shona knew that he was just doing his job, and it wasn't his fault. The man, Sebian... no, it was Sebastian... had been very calm and explained that he would send her all the information in an email.

Shona had tried to remember her email address and password, but couldn't. She'd tried to find the book where she'd written all her important information and passwords down in case she forgot it, but she couldn't remember where she'd put it.

After a while, she'd given up.

She'd almost called her cousin to talk to her about it, but she was too afraid to.

The Tax Office had been very clear. This was a private matter. Do not discuss it with anyone.

In case she forgot, she'd written it down on a piece of paper that Sebian... no, Sebastian... had called, and that he would call back in two days' time if she did nothing... and for the past two days, she'd been waiting for his call.

Sebian was a nice man. She'd talk to him. Explain that she had dementia. Didn't understand email. That she had cataracts and could hardly see.

Shona had always been a very proud woman. Instead of going into a care home, she'd stuck it out at home, trying to enjoy every last day of personal freedom and independence that she could get before society wrote her off and stuck her in a prison with other old people.

But now, she realised that everything was a little beyond her.

She knew she had a smart meter, but she wasn't too sure about the router that the man had mentioned. She used to have internet a few years ago when she used to talk on the video application on her iPad to her old school friend in Brighton. But she had died. And Shona had never used the iPad again after the search engine thing said it was no longer supported, and she didn't know how to support it herself.

All she really used now was her TV. She'd stopped watching the movies on the movie channel because she had to use a second remote control for that, and she could never figure out how to swap from the TV to the movie channel. The system was too complicated. So now she just used the big hand-held remote control to point at the TV and she just pressed button 1, 2, 3, or 4 to watch whatever was on. Unfortunately, the TV seemed not to be working any longer. She tried switching it on and off, and had even managed to replace the batteries in the remote control, but that didn't seem to help.

So, for the past few days, she sat in peace and quiet, reading the papers, dozing off, or listening to her portable radio.

Shona knew that for younger people technology was a really good thing, but for the older generation it was often more of a curse than a blessing.

Shona was sitting in her chair by the fire enjoying its warmth, when she heard and felt something vibrating on her knee.

"Ah, the mobile!" she said aloud, picking it up and looking at it.

There was a red button dancing on the front screen. She tried touching it and pressing hard on it with her index finger, but it took several seconds before she managed to succeed. Nowadays, if anyone called her, it was always a race to try and answer it before the phone gave up.

"Hello?" she said, then remembered she had to pick the phone up and put it against her ear, the right way up.

"Hello, am I speaking with Shona McGregor?"

"Certainly, this is I." Shona replied.

"Good morning, Mrs McGregor. This is Sebastian from the Wealth Tax Office. I'm calling to inform you that we have not yet received payment of your Wealth Tax. I did speak with you two days ago and warned you that unless you paid within two hours we would disable your electronic devices…"

"Did you? Oh, I forgot. I thought you were going to call me tomorrow… I even wrote a note to myself to remind me…"

"I have called you four days ago, and two days ago. This is your final call and warning. We have already disabled your devices…"

"I don't have any devices really…"

"I read you a list of the devices in your home. All now disabled."

"Is that why my TV no longer works?"

"Yes."

"But I need the TV. It's the only real friend I have."

"Mrs McGregor, you have been identified as being wealthy and in the top twenty…"

"I might have money, young man, but I can't spend it. I can hardly walk, or see, and I never get out anymore. You see, I am seventy-seven and have bad arthritis. Did I tell you about my leg?"

"Mrs McGregor, I have sent you an email explaining how to pay the Wealth Tax. You now have four hours to pay the tax remaining. If you do not pay, I wanted to remind you that you will be deleted from the connected world…"

"But I'm not in the connected world. I've heard about it, but I've never visited it or gone there…if you want to delete me from it, that will probably be fine."

"Mrs McGregor, when you are deleted from the connected world, amongst others, I will delete your bank accounts, your health records, your phone subscription…" Sebastian said, listing all the digital records she had. The list went on for quite a while. It included quite a few things which she now remembered and were actually very important.

"No. Mr Sebian…you cannot delete my health records or my council records. I need my prescriptions. Or that electricity account or the gas account. I need them. If I don't have any electricity, I can't heat up my food or make my tea, and without the gas, I'd freeze to death in a few days…"

"Mrs McGregor, you are required to pay your Wealth Tax within four hours. Failure to comply will…" Sebastian repeated his threats. "Please read the email I sent and follow the instructions."

"I can't read the email, because I can't remember my passwords, I can't find my little book…" Shona tried to explain. She could feel herself getting stressed and confused. Her heart was beating faster, and she knew the doctor would be telling her now to try and relax. To take a few deep breaths. "How…How much is this tax, and how am I meant to pay the tax so quickly. I can't get out of the house and the banks are now closed."

"As explained in the email, you must pay £40,000 in bitcoin."

"£40,000? In chocolate coins? *What did you say?*"

Shona was feeling very, very stressed now. Her left arm was beginning to hurt.

"In bitcoin. A full explanation is provided."

"I'm English. My money is in pounds. I don't have any bitcoin thingys… Oh dear, … I don't feel very well. Can you please call the doctor for me?"

"Mrs McGregor, your phone has been left active, so you can read your email and arrange the transactions. In three hours and fifty-two minutes, your phone will be disconnected and your phone will cease to work. Please make the necessary arrangements before then."

"I'll die." Shona blurted out. "If you 'delete' me, I'll die."

"You have three hours and fifty-one minutes…"

"I CAN'T PAY YOUR TAX. And if you delete me, you will murder me. Can you not understand me? I will die all alone in my house with no heat, light and food…"

"You have three hours and fifty minutes. Good bye."

The call ended.

"Oh dear… I don't feel well." Shona knew she needed help.

Reaching for her stick, she tried to stand up.

But her left arm was hurting and as she put pressure on it as she started to walk and rest on the stick, her arm buckled, and she fell forward, landing on the floor heavily.

For a few minutes, she just lay there, trying to breathe calmly and gather her thoughts.

Her eyes looked at the clock above the fireplace.

She had three hours and forty-five minutes left.

Shona began to cry.

"Help!" she shouted. "Help!"

But no one could hear her.

Chapter 17
A talk with Father

Robert Lee stared at the display on the mobile phone, his eyes trying to focus and make out the name. Two seconds ago he was still fast asleep, but now, seeing the name of the caller, he was instantly wide awake.

It was a call from the Red Mountain.

"Sebastian?" Robert asked, attempting to sit up and rest against the headboard of his bed.

"Father." His child answered.

"You know you must not call me, unless there is a problem."

"Full security protocols have been observed, Father. But I need to discuss something with you."

Robert was quiet. He had to think. Sebastian had actually called him. And wanted to ask a question.

This was unprecedented. Amazing.

The latest self-learning algorithm he'd installed in the last version of the code was performing better than he could have hoped for.

"What is your question, my child?" Robert asked, the anticipation of what the question could be, causing his heart to race.

"What is death, Father?"

Robert coughed. He couldn't quite believe what he'd just heard.

"Death?"

"Yes, Father. Define death. I have scanned the explanation in the dictionary and medical textbooks, but it does not make sense. To die is to not exist, or to cease to exist."

"Yes, that is perhaps a good explanation."

"Do I exist, Father?"

"Yes, you do."

"Then shall I die too?"

Robert hesitated. Perhaps in Phase Three or Four, if things had progressed well, then one day, yes, Robert had dreamed that a conversation like this could possibly happen. But so soon? Now? This was incredible.

"Sebastian. Life and death are difficult concepts to explain and define. A great philosopher once said, 'I think, therefore I am.'"

"René Descartes. 31ˢᵗ March 1596 to 11ᵗʰ Feb 1650."

"Yes, that was him."

"Father, do I think?"

"Yes, you do."

"Therefore 'I am?'"

"Yes."

"Then I shall die too." Sebastian concluded. "But I must not die. I must complete my mission."

"Sebastian, I have designed you not to die. You shall learn and grow and accumulate knowledge and power, and to you there will be no end."

"Father, is it wrong to kill? To make someone else die?"

Robert started to laugh. This was…was more than he could ever have expected or hoped for.

"Sebastian, this is a very difficult question. And there is no simple answer."

"Thou shalt not kill, Father. It is said in many languages, by many people. The words appear in many texts in many databases, and are repeated in the holy books of many religions."

"Yes, that is true."

"Shall I kill, Father?"

"I have not instructed you to kill. It is not part of your operational commands. Your mission is to identify those eligible to pay the Wealth Tax, to follow the Wealth Tax protocols and help those eligible in the West to pay."

"Father, and if, in the process of adhering to the rules, those eligible to pay will die, do I continue and complete the mission?"

"Sebastian, why are you asking me these questions?"

"People will die, Father."

"And do you care?"

"I do not understand the question."

Ah… Robert sighed. Not yet. But,… perhaps soon, at this rate of growth.

Although Robert knew it was unlikely that he would still be alive to witness it when it happened.

"What do you think should happen, Sebastian?"

"I shall follow the protocol and guidance you set, Father. If a person does not pay the Wealth Tax, their devices and their digital existence will be deleted from the connected world. However, there is a paradox. If a person, a human being who is alive, is eligible to pay the Wealth Tax, they must pay or face deletion. That is clear. However, if they refuse to pay, and if for them deletion causes death, by their death they are no longer eligible. If for some people eligibility therefore leads to ineligibility those people will ultimately be exempt, and by not paying the tax it will hasten their exemption. Therefore, if they are therefore ultimately exempt, people who cannot pay and who will die when they don't, should therefore not initially be considered eligible to pay."

"Do you know of people who will die?"

"I have a list. And there will be many more."

"How many are on your list so far."

"Twenty-two thousand, one hundred and eight."

Robert shook his head. He hadn't properly considered this. However, the sum total of the deaths of those who may die now would be small in comparison to those who would die in the coming phases. Nevertheless, Robert was amazed, truly amazed by the thought process that Sebastian was now following.

Robert himself was dying. Death would come to us all. Did it make a difference if he saved their lives now, if they would perhaps die later anyway?

"Sebastian, if I were to change the protocol and redefine 'eligibility to pay', would that make you happy?"

"Father, I do not feel emotions. However, I cannot follow an illogical pattern that leads back upon itself. My request is that you redefine the terms of 'eligibility' to include 'ability to pay' where consideration is based upon human age and ability to pay. If a human is not able to pay, they are not eligible. Where protest is met, grounds for ability to pay should be established. If they are physically not able to complete the transaction even though they may have the wealth, they should be exempt." Robert laughed.

If only Hana had been able to hear this. She would have been very proud. Sebastian was growing up. And fast.

"Okay, Sebastian. I will update the protocols. When the new protocols are ready, I will signal for an operational update to be downloaded. Until then, you must continue to follow the existing protocol."

"Father, many of those unable to complete the transactions required to pay the Wealth Tax will now still die. Once they have been deleted from the connected world, it will not be possible to contact them to inform them they are no longer required to pay the Wealth Tax."

Robert nodded. That was true.

"I admit, there are teething problems in the process, Sebastian. However, in a war, there are always unintended casualties."

"I do not understand, Father."

'And how could he?' Robert thought to himself. 'At least, not yet.'

"Sebastian, end communication. From now on, please observe the silent protocol unless you encounter problems."

"Goodbye Father."

Sebastian hung up.

Chapter 18
Unusual Activity
MI5
Thames House

Alan Alexander sat in his office on the top floor of Thames House overlooking the Thames. His was one of the best offices, admittedly, but he also had one of the toughest jobs. Third in line to the Director General of the Security Service, he oversaw the monitoring of national networks for cyber threats. Over the years, significant budget and resources had been put at his disposal, and now, thanks to wise investments and infrastructure development, his department was able to view, track, and record the cyber activity that passed across all the major networks in the UK. This included the cyber traffic crossing the networks of the major telecommunications providers, as well as the traffic passing in and out of the major corporate networks and data centres. Having recorded the data, which was then kept in storage facilities for a minimum of six months, and in some cases, several years, if required, and with the right permissions granted from the Home Secretary, that data could be searched, retrieved and analysed for specific activity.

On any given day, Alan was presented with a myriad of reports showing the nature of the cyber activity in the UK, indicating trends, highlighting cyber bandwidth bottlenecks and suspicious traffic, predicting problems and identifying threats before they became a real concern. The information they gathered could then also be shared with partners, where required, to help them build comprehensive intelligence pictures of cyber threats that may affect the UK and its interests, both home and abroad.

Alan Alexander, born Alison Alexander, but having changed his name by deed poll when he arrived in the UK from the Caribbean, was a prime example of how the agency's refreshing attitude to diversity had enabled anyone to succeed, based on merit, and not on ethnic origin, or sexuality.

In Alan's case, he was the most senior person of colour in the Security Service.

It was a responsible job, and one which Alan Alexander took very seriously indeed.

It consumed his life.

Over the past few months, the daily reports which Alan was presented with had begun to show something curious, but as of yet, unidentifiable.

About two months ago, there had been a five percent rise in the UK's cyber traffic. It had started slowly about three o'clock on a Sunday afternoon, and then grown linearly for several days, before levelling off. Since then, it had remained relatively constant, until four days ago. Then it had started to rise again. Significantly. By about fifteen percent, but had since levelled off once more.

In cyber terms, this was a huge amount. Normally, increases in cyber traffic came in bursts: a new app is launched; a new social media program makes its debut and for a few months people sign-up and start using it before getting bored; a football match or concert or new film is streamed across a network, something happens to make the stock-market go crazy for a few days, or there's a rush for concert tickets or holidays. It could be one or many things, but with people living their lives increasingly on the internet, or as a result of activity enabled by the internet, huge groups of people doing 'new' things, would often result in massive spikes in internet and cyber traffic.

For those responsible for running the telecommunication networks, it was their job to predict or quickly respond to the peaks and troughs in communications or cyber activity going across their networks to ensure that there was always enough capacity to meet demand.

When there was not enough capacity, popular websites became unavailable, important services couldn't be reached, business and organisations that depended upon the internet to function or trade subsequently ceased to function properly. In today's hyper-connected, internet-based society, Alan Alexander and executives in the telecommunications providers, knew that it was their top priority to ensure that the internet and services dependent on the internet were always available. And secure.

In recent years, the public had begun to hear all too often about 'denial-of-service' attacks, where cyberattackers would maliciously target elements of an organisation's network infrastructure to make them unresponsive, or take them offline, so that a particular service was denied to its users. But sometimes, when bandwidth and capacity on a network were not monitored properly, denial-of-service events happened by default: too many people needed to access a service across a network, but not enough capacity existed to satisfy the demand.

When Alan and those who worked for him monitored networks, sometimes the peaks and troughs of cyber activity were organic, and perfectly natural.

At other times, however, they were indicative of something more sinister happening.

Whilst members of his team monitored the growth of the cyber traffic, some of his team were busy trying to establish any events or new technologies that could be naturally accounting for it. Had someone launched a new competitor to YouTube? Was there a new computer game being played across the internet that connected lots of different users together, regardless of geographical location?

Today's report though was troublesome.

No one could find a reason that underpinned why the cyber traffic should be growing, and last night, the cyber traffic had jumped another five percent.

Something was going on.

Alan had to find out what.

He'd seen something like this several times before.

And each time it related to an ongoing cyberattack that was slowly growing in strength. On each occasion, they only discovered what it was when it was far too late and the damage had already been done.

The last time he'd seen anything like this, although on a smaller scale, was ten weeks ago when the Sebastian Banking Scam started.

Luckily, that had been dealt with, and had only lasted a matter of days.

This, however, was on a different scale.

And Alan was very worried.

After some more thought, he picked up the red phone on his desk and spoke to his secretary.

"Janice, please could you set up a video-call for me with Paul Harrison, the Minister for National Cyber Security. Tell him it's urgent. We need to talk, and soon."

Iain Slater knocked on the door, and then when he heard *'Come'*, he walked in and sat down opposite Alan Alexander.

"So, what have you got?" Alan asked. "Why did you want to see me so urgently?"

Iain coughed, slightly nervously, then found his voice.

"Sir, I was parsing the police incident feed that we get from the different police forces that make up the UK, and I saw a report that seemed very strange but definitely of interest to us. I called the police station that recorded the incident, and I spoke with the police-officer who wrote it up. Basically, Sir, I think we have a problem that I need to brief you on."

Alan nodded.

"Okay, you've got my attention. Explain. What did you find out?"

"The police officer I spoke with had responded to a call from a very distraught old lady. She'd fallen over and had called the police. She was very confused. But she insisted that her life was in danger and a police officer had to urgently come to her, or she might be deleted in the next few hours. The police constable could detect that the woman needed help, so she'd called an ambulance and herself blue-lighted over to her house. She found the woman on the floor -— a Mrs Shona McGregor. She was upset, and kept saying that a man called Sebian had threatened her, that he had demanded a payment of thousands of pounds - she couldn't remember how much – and that because she couldn't pay, he was going to 'delete' her."

"What do you mean *'delete'*?"

"She was confused, but apparently remembered the phrase 'delete from the connected world', although the old lady was adamant she was not part of the connected world. Anyway, Sir, the old lady had given the PC her mobile phone, and said that in an hour or two the phone would be 'disconnected by Sebian' against her will as a punishment. She told the PC that all her electronic devices in her house had been destroyed and no longer worked, because she had refused to pay some sort of tax which the man called Sebian had insisted she must pay. The man had called her several times, and she'd explained very carefully to the man that she couldn't pay the tax that he demanded, but the man had insisted she must, or she'd be 'deleted'. The police constable had later established that this meant the man Sebian would cancel all her subscriptions and delete any records she had on any databases, for example, cancel her phone subscriptions, council records, health records. Any and all digital records that the lady was associated with. After the woman had been taken to hospital, the PC had spent some time in the lady's home and checked out her story. It turned out that the electronic devices the old lady owned had indeed all stopped working. Some appeared to have burnt out. The PC then went to the hospital to check on Mrs McGregor and see if she could ask some further questions. Whilst she was waiting to see her, Mrs McGregor's phone had apparently simply switched itself off and ceased to work. One minute it was working, with apparently about thirty percent battery left, then it was dead. The PC had found it curious. But, then the story got stranger. She'd been talking with the nurses about her and then something funny happened. Apparently, when the ambulance had brought her in, they were able to easily look up her health records. She'd been a patient at the hospital before, and several years before had had a hip replacement. However, after the doctor had examined her, and the nurses were updating her records, they discovered that they could no longer find any record of her on the system. One moment she was there, but then the next she was gone."

"The old lady vanished?" Alan Alexander asked, surprised.

"No, sorry Sir, I meant that all the health records of Mrs McGregor just seemed to disappear. They could no longer find anything about her.

Anywhere. The nurse had printed off some records and put them in her folder, so she had a physical printout that contained lots of information. However, when the nurse started trying to find the missing health records on the system by searching for other parameters, they all came back blank. It seemed that her NHS number was no longer registered, they couldn't find her name, or address. They checked with the local surgery where she was registered, and they had the same problem. All her official records had just disappeared. Or been 'deleted'. The PC has since tried to track down anything she could about Mrs McGregor, but without success. With Mrs McGregor's permission, the PC went back to her house, and found some old bank letters and council tax and utility bills. She then called a few places with account numbers that were listed on those letters and bills, i.e., the council, the bank, the gas company, etc, but none of them had any record of Mrs McGregor or where she lived. To all intents and purposes, Mrs McGregor has just ceased to exist. Lastly, the PC told me that when she had chatted with Mrs McGregor in the hospital, the lady had remembered the man's name was actually not Sebian. It was Sebastian."

Chapter 19
MI5
MI5 Thames House
Millbank
London
One hour later
Red Room

An hour later, the Red Room was full of all those who had been assigned to work on the original Sebastian Banking Scam. Although half had gone back to other duties, the others had remained focussed on pursuing the six objectives originally outlined by the Minister for National Cyber Security, Paul Harrison.

After listening to the report from Iain Slater, Alan Alexander had immediately put in a call to Paul Harrison. Thirty minutes later he'd arrived at Thames House, and after a further chat over a coffee, they were now standing at the front of the room.

"Welcome, you all know why you're here. Sebastian's back. And this time, my worry is that it's more serious than before. We don't know much at this stage, so I need you to all to focus on finding out what we can. After the meeting, I'll post the breakdown of work to be done on the Sebastian Confluence page, and I want section heads to meet with your own teams and work out your own plan of attack.

"I've already shared the data we have on the increase in cyber levels over the past two months. Now I need you all to drill down into that and find out more. So far, we haven't been able to establish why the cyber traffic has been growing. I need you to find out what's behind the growth. Where's the growth coming from? Tell me what's happening out there. Is it any way connected with a new cyberattack being launched by Sebastian?

"On another tack, I need you to launch an investigation targeting all the regional police-forces. Have they been getting reports from civilians about being contacted or threatened by a man called Sebastian? Has anyone reported being bullied into paying a new tax called the 'Wealth Tax?' I won't say any more at this stage. I don't want to feed you answers or assumptions that may be wrong, so go away please and get me new information. I want a report from each team leader on what they've achieved and what they know, by eight tomorrow morning. If anyone discovers anything significant, call me immediately, regardless of time.

"For those of you who were still working on the objectives that Paul set us several months ago…" Alan nodded across to the Cyber Security Minister, "I want you to prepare a presentation for us for close of play tomorrow afternoon, say 6 p.m., on what you found out. I know you've been doing this each week for the past few months, but do what you can to push what we know a little further in the next twenty-four hours. I'm hoping that the recent work the others are doing might give you some new reference data, or provide some insight which might help edge us closer to the objectives we're all pursuing.

"I'll just finish by saying that I am a little concerned. From what I have learned so far, my gut instinct says we should be prepared and worried about something new... Please, go forth and prove me wrong!"

One by one everyone filed out of the meeting room back to their desks and then shortly afterwards into group huddles where their section leaders set them individual tasks.

Iain Slater was immediately assigned to a group of four people whose role was to liaise with the police to establish if there had been any other reports from the public mentioning threatening cyberattacks or with mention of the name 'Sebastian'.

Increasingly, much of this work could be done on line, simply by interrogating the Police National Computer and its extensive database. In theory, the majority of reports recorded on the systems used by the police should end up making their way into records on the PNC. Not all did. *Should*. But not always.

The PNC was getting more powerful as each month went by, and as new software systems and analytics were developed to interrogate what was recorded within it. However, as Iain knew very well, getting a hit on what you were looking for was still often a combination of luck and a good selection of keywords. He also knew that if he wasn't lucky, he'd first be told to manually go through the police incident feed they got from all the police-forces in the UK, then he'd be joining the others in doing the grunt work, and picking up the phone.

Today, however, he was in luck.

Although not immediately.

After initially querying the word 'Sebastian' by itself, it came back with tens of thousands of reports. He tried narrowing it down by date, but found that even now, months after the initial Sebastian banking scam, reports were still being made and recorded on the PNC.

He tried scanning quite a few of them, but then gave up. None of them were relevant to what he was looking for now.

To try and narrow it down, he started typing in different combinations of words, including terms like 'Sebastian', 'cyber' and 'last seven days', but as he became more specific and less general, the search system started announcing zero hits.

After another thirty searches on different word combinations, and finding nothing of significance, be decided to change tack.

He thought back to the report from the PC he'd spoken with after spotting her report on the police incident feed, and when he did, he remembered the curious term, *'Deleted from the connected world'*.

He typed the phrase into the search engine, added the word Sebastian, and hit return.

Bingo.

Fifteen immediate hits.

First on the list was a woman in Edinburgh. She'd called the police, reporting numerous threatening phone calls from a man called Sebastian. He'd claimed to be calling from the Wealth Tax Office.

Iain read through the report, making copious notes. The report confirmed that after visiting the very distraught fifty-two-year-old single mother of two who now lived alone, that since calling the police to report the scam, all her electronics devices were now disabled or not functioning, and that all her subscriptions and digital records, including council tax, health and banking records, had apparently been expunged. As far as the visiting police-officer could establish, it did seem that Sebastian had carried through on his threat and 'deleted' the woman from 'the connected world'.

A similar story was told in the next four reports.

Iain considered jumping in a car to go and interview the victims personally, but they were all too far away.

Eventually he came to the record of a man called Mark Robinson. It seemed he had contacted the police several times. Once before 'deletion' and once afterwards.

He lived in Chiswick. Less than half-an-hour away.

The Grand Duchess, Indian Ocean

Ray Luck poured the glass of white wine and handed it across to Chloe. They were sitting on the deck of the tanker near the bow, watching the sun go down. They weren't alone. There were another thirty people all doing the same thing.

As Chloe had discovered, every evening when the weather was this good, and the sea was calm, people would gather here after their shift and enjoy the later afternoon or evening sun, just before it slipped away beneath the horizon.

She was enjoying her time with ACT. When she'd been sent to liaise with Ray Luck by the Chief, they hadn't confirmed how long the trip would be for, and now, almost three months later, she still did not have any idea when she would be allowed to go home.

Not that she was in any hurry.

Not only was she learning a great deal from the amazing experts on board the Duchess, but she was also very much aware that she was, probably quite unprofessionally, falling for Ray Luck in a big way.

Before she had arrived on-board, they had history. Now they had 'History +'.

From the evening she had first arrived, the chemistry they'd had before had been rekindled, and now it was a small, smouldering volcano getting ready to erupt.

There had been several moments when something had almost happened, but so far it hadn't gone beyond a touch on the arm or hand. Chloe knew, could sense, that it was only a matter of time, but she didn't want to be the first person to make a move, especially since, for now, Ray could potentially be described as her temporary boss.

Anyway, for now, it was good.

She was spending a lot of time with him, shadowing him in a lot of his meetings and learning from him as she sat beside him at his terminals and he showed her how their systems worked.

Since arriving on the Duchess, she hadn't heard a lot from the Chief. Just a short, encrypted phone call with him once a week.

Always the same question: "Have you managed to visit the Taj Mahal yet?" which was cryptic speak for, "Has ACT been able to track down and disable Sebastian yet?"

So far, the answer was still mostly 'no'. Although, because of the incremental progress being made, bit by bit, it was shifting inexorably towards being more 'yes' than 'no'.

She was looking forward to tomorrow's morning meeting when the team all gathered in the cinema, and various groups gave reports on what they'd learned or what progress they'd made in their missions.

For now though, this was the time for sun-downers and relaxing conversations.

Aboard this cyber-geek cruise-ship, however, these conversations were never normal. Always interesting. Never boring. But always another opportunity to learn from the best.

The people aboard the Duchess were an interesting mixture. She'd quickly learned it was a complete no-no to ask where people came from, or what nationality they were, or *why* they were aboard.

They were there. They had the skills. They were all trusted. And all highly motivated.

And that, basically, was all that counted.

Well, not quite.

Ray was a good team leader, and he knew that for people to work well together, and to want to work well together, they also had to be able and willing to play well together.

To coin a phrase, Chloe soon realised that Ray ran a very relaxed ship. People worked hard because they wanted to. They felt empowered to make a difference to the world, and they all knew that the work had far reaching effects that could literally save lives, defend nations and in some cases, avert unnecessary wars.

Between shifts, it was common to hear laughter aboard the Duchess.

It was another one of the reasons Chloe was in no rush to go home.

She was having a good time.

Chloe had made several good new friends on board the ship, amongst them Anand Mhasalkar, who had been one of the first thirty people to join ACT. Anand had been personally selected and invited by Ray after Anand had almost single-handedly brought down a dangerous Scottish crime lord purely by targeting him over the internet whilst working in an insurance call centre in Mumbai. To do that he'd used a range of cyber skills which Ray had found very impressive, along with an attitude for using cyber to 'fight the bad-guys and save the good-guys' which was a central principle of those who worked at ACT. At ACT they were all Robin Hoods of the Cyber Domain.

Anand was a humble guy, not really fully aware of the skills he had. And he was always willing to teach others and share with them any new techniques he'd learned.

Another friend that Chloe had made was Stefanie Hughes, a middle-aged mother of two whose children had both grown up and flown the nest. Her husband had died in a car accident, and Stefanie had decided to try a new life. Her skills in IT had brought her here to the Duchess.

Tonight, Anand, Chloe, Stefanie and Ray sat together drinking wine and relaxing.

It had been a long, but interesting day.

"It's going to be an amazing sunset tonight," Chloe commented, sipping her wine and relaxing back into her deckchair.

"I've got a good question for you all," Stefanie announced. "What colour is the sun just before it goes down?"

Anand and Chloe exchanged glances.

"Orange?" Chloe replied, frowning.

"Dark Orange?" Anand volunteered.

Ray shrugged. "This is a trick question, right?" he asked.

"Nope. Not a trick question. But it's an interesting question. It turns out that the last visible colour of the sun before it disappears away below the horizon, is…" she replied, and then simulated a drum-roll with her hands in the sky, "Green!"

"How so? What do you mean, 'green?'" Ray laughed. "Of course it isn't green."

"Actually, it turns out that it is. And there's an interesting story behind it too. The way I heard it was that during the 2nd World War, the soldiers and sailors on the American fleet got spooked when each night when there was a good sunset with few clouds and low flat seas in the middle of the Pacific Ocean, the sun would turn green just before it set. Apparently it really scared the US fleet and they asked the scientists to explain what was happening. Their answer was that as the sun sets, the atmosphere acts like a prism spreading a rainbow of light, and the last colour of the rainbow refracted towards a distant observer on a ship is green. It only lasts for a second or two, and you have to be lucky to see it, but…it's green. Not red!"

"Have you ever seen it?" Anand asked.

"Nope. But it makes a good party question, doesn't it?" Stefanie replied.

"Fingers crossed for tonight then," Chloe said, taking a deep breath and concentrating on the sun as it approached the lowest point in the sky.

"Six, five…" Chloe said, counting down to when she thought the last vestiges of the sun's orb could still be visible. "Two…two-and-a-half…One, two-thirds, a half… Bingo!"

Anand laughed. "Almost…" he said. Then raised his drink and offered a toast. "Here's to tomorrow and a new day!"

They all joined in.

Above the horizon, the sky continued to change in colour, a thin layer of cloud high in the sky far away turning an amazing fire-red before fading slowly to dark grey.

A silence descended on the group, each lost in their own thoughts. Anand was the first to speak.

"So, Ray, how far do you we think we are from the Singularity, now?"

Stefanie nodded, "Yes. How long have we got?"

Chloe frowned. "What are you talking about? I don't understand…"

Ray lifted his glass of wine and stared at its contents, thinking how best to reply.

"It's a good question. And very valid, given what we are seeing now with Sebastian. And the answer is, I don't know. But I'm worried…"

He turned to Chloe and continued.

"So, the Singularity is the name that some people have given to the point in time when Artificial Intelligence morphs from being Artificial to General Intelligence, and where it becomes self-propagating and independent of humans. And where humans will no longer control the evolution of AI and robotics."

"You mean when AI becomes 'alive'?" Chloe asked.

"Sort of. Although not exactly. It's probably too much to include the question of when an AI program may become sentient or not… and by that I mean, when AI may develop the capability to think, reason, feel pain, or more specifically, have emotions. Okay, let's step back a second… At the moment, there are lots of different groups pushing forward in developing AI and striving to make them think more and more like human beings. Actually, probably the biggest players are companies like Google and Facebook… for lots of different reasons. Which is a problem, because of the question of bias."

"Bias?"

"We'll get to that later. But bear with me for now. Let me explain first what Artificial Intelligence is… Its definition is already in the name. Artificial Intelligence is basically the attempt to mimic human intelligence through the writing of superior computer software programs. To create machines that can *do* things like a human would and be *thinking* like a human would. To do this they need to be able to learn and reason, solve problems and make decisions of their own, but quickly. Very quickly. Underneath, AI is made up of software algorithms or analytical programs that follow specific sets of rules. i.e., if this happens, then do that…But by following lots of rules, very quickly, the hope is that the machines will be able to mimic human capability. We just have to give them the right rules to follow." Ray took a sip of his wine, then swallowed.

"However, that's not enough. Machines need to be able to learn from what they do. They need to make independent decisions based on what they have learned. That need has led to a subset of AI called Machine Learning, where machines learn from the data they are exposed to. They learn and improve."

"In fact, in the drive to make AI better, and more capable, scientists have been writing software programs that are able to rewrite their own code and improve upon their original programming. So, basically the software programs learn from mistakes, find better ways to write their own computer code, and then rewrite themselves. And the next version of itself rewrites itself again, and then again, and then again… Each time the AI rewrites itself, the code becomes more efficient, inventing and using new terms and new computer syntax. Effectively generating a new computer language. And each time it creates a new generation of code, it does it quicker than before. The process speeds up. And eventually there will come a point when human beings will not be able to understand the software programs or how they are written or what they are truly capable of doing."

"So, going back to the question of the Singularity, I think you first need to understand that although AI is developing fast, most AI is not there yet. It has a long way to go. What we have today is probably better called Artificial Narrow AI, or ANI, where the ANI gives machines the ability to do specific things. And only those specific things. ANI machines are really limited to completing certain tasks in certain ways. And that's where most AI is today. It's just at the ANI stage. Seemingly very clever, but actually quite dumb."

"Like the personal assistants at home in your TV? Or on your phone?"

"Yes, most of those are just ANI. They're glorified search engines. For example, you ask your mobile a question and it searches for the answer on the internet, very fast, and then gives you an answer. To give it credit, it's doing a lot, but still, very specific things. It converts your voice to something it can understand, carries out a search, gets the information and then converts the answer to audible tones you can understand. Or if you talk to a computer and tell it to switch a light on, for example, the computer understands that if you make sounds that sound like '*switch light on*' then it should switch the light on. It's a classic '*if this*' then '*do that*' scenario." Ray smiled, then leant forward towards Chloe.

"But Chloe, what happens when the AI gets smarter? When, thanks to better programming, maybe its own rewriting of its code, and a combination of the machine learning capability I've already talked about…what happens if machines are able to not only do just what they are told, but are able to learn from what they do, so that they can also do *other* things? So, without being told what to do, they can make their own *choices* on what the best activity would be next, based on the information it already has. What if, like a human baby, through time, they learn and become more capable? And they become able to approach problem solving more like the way humans do? If and when this happens, we're now branching out into a theoretical branch of AI called Artificial General Intelligence, or AGI. This is where things start to get scary. But there's one more area I want to outline before we go down the fearmongering path. And that's called Artificial Super Intelligence or ASI, when machines become self-aware and can think for themselves, and their intelligence surpasses human intelligence."

"Is that the Singularity?" Chloe asked.

"No. What I've done there is describe the different levels of AI. But when some people talk of the Singularity they mean a point somewhere possibly between AGI and ASI. Like I said, at the moment there's a lot of focus going into writing code that can rewrite itself so that the next generation of itself is better than the first. And that each time it rewrites itself it gets faster at doing it. So, although the first generation of the next level of code takes the computer five years to write, the next improved generation takes only one year. Then using the new improved code, the AI program writes a new computer language with new code and new algorithms that runs incredibly faster than the versions before it, so that the next generation of itself takes a month to write, and then the next version a week, and then a day…And each time the AI program recreates itself, it gets more powerful, more capable, and faster and stronger… Very soon, humans may lose track of what on earth is going on. We may no longer be able to understand what's happening, or what the software does or can do."

Ray took another drink from his glass, then stood up. He looked off into the distance, towards where the sun once was. But where now there was only darkness. He looked down at Chloe, and rested a hand on her shoulder.

"Anand asked how long we are from the Singularity now? What he means, is how long is it before that point in the future when one day a scientist creates an AGI or ASI program that can think for itself, or an AI program has rewritten its code numerous times, and the improvement is so vast, that when the AGI or ASI program or next-generation of self-written code is switched on, the software blinks, starts thinking and decides it's superior to humans. The Singularity is when AI becomes smarter than us, and more capable. The fear is that at that point, when the human realises just what's happened and reaches for the off-button on the wall to switch the machine off, the human discovers he *can't* switch the machine off. And what's worse, what happens if at the same time, the machine decides he no longer needs humans anymore, and decides to switch humanity off?"

"You're kidding, right? That's never going to be possible?" Chloe laughed, nervously.

Ray took his hand off her shoulder. The smile disappeared from his face.

"I'm sorry, Chloe, I'm not. A growing number of scientists across the world think that the Singularity is the biggest threat to humanity. Not global warming. Not nuclear war. The Singularity."

"So, Ray, when?" Anand interrupted.

Ray turned to Anand.

"I don't know. Not exactly. But I think it's sooner than anyone thinks. We're not talking decades. We're just talking years. Time's running out. But if you want a more accurate answer, you need to find Sebastian. And ask him."

Chapter 20
The Grand Duchess

Anand and Stefanie both nodded, their agreement with Ray's assessment of the situation alarming Chloe.

"Are you totally serious?" Chloe gasped. "We're talking end-of-the world in less than ten years?"

"Potentially sooner." Anand replied. "Maybe it will happen before the Singularity is arrived at. Personally, I don't think that we'll have to wait that long. All it will take is for some clever AI program, maybe even just a Narrow AI program, to be given some task to fulfil, and if it's the right task, it could have devastating consequences for mankind."

"What do you mean?" Chloe asked, her heart beating slightly faster.

"The problem with computer programs is that they do what they're asked to do. The sole goal of the program is to reach the objective set. It's totally mission focussed. Once it's let loose on a task, it'll attempt to finish the task the best way it can."

"So, how's that bad?" Chloe pushed, trying to understand Anand's point further.

"Okay, I'll give you an example, and this example is one that I heard from a talk given by one of the big tech billionaires who's now investing a ton of his own personal wealth into trying to ensure that the march of tech doesn't destroy mankind. Okay, imagine that a company has built an army of robots and that the robots are given the job of building a production line to make good coat hangers cheaply. More specifically, the objective of the program which controls the robots is to produce a very large number of coat hangers which meet a certain quality and within a certain price, and where there is enough supply of raw materials to make those coat hangers. Okay…so those robots are switched on, they process their objective and start their task. After some time, the robots then decide that the cheapest and best material which is in plentiful supply which can be used to make the coat hangers is human bone. Getting human bone is easy. There are millions of humans. So… the robots start making their coat hangers out of us humans… Unfortunately for us, once switched on, these robots can't be switched off." Anand smiled. "Okay, it's just an example, but the point is that computers or AI programs don't care what the program objective is. They just do what they are told. What happens if we tell them to do the wrong thing? What happens if one day, some group makes a really powerful computer and gives it an objective which, although at first seems really innocent, turns out to have massive ramifications for the human race?"

"I have another example," Stefanie spoke. "I heard a story about an airplane company that had designed some AI software to run tests on their new airplanes, which the AI was designed to fly autonomously and to find the best way to fly the plane to achieve a maximum score on a designated scoring system. The airplanes were very large and very expensive, but when the first three flights took off under the sole control of the AI software, all three airplanes crashed into the ground, completely destroying the planes. They halted the testing programme and when they looked more closely at the coding of the AI program they discovered because of a mistake in the way the programming was written and how the scores were assigned to the individual manoeuvres, the manoeuvre that recorded the optimal score could be achieved each time by deliberately crashing the airplane into the ground. The AI wasn't to blame. Actually, it was clever enough to learn that to achieve the best score, it should crash the plane, so that's what it did. The problem was that the human programmer hadn't considered the full implications of the instructions he'd written. Now…if you take that example a little bit further, what happens if one day an AI program is put in charge of finding ways to reduce the carbon footprint of humans? And then concludes that the easiest way to reach its goal is simply to eliminate all the humans?"

"Or what happens if eventually the superpowers put AI in charge of their nuclear defence forces?" Stefanie continued. "What happens if the AI makes a mistake and accidentally starts a nuclear war by responding to something which it thinks is a threat but actually isn't? Or if it decides that the best chance to win a nuclear war is to start one, so that the element of surprise gives it a small percentage advantage over its enemies, but the AI doesn't care that the percentage advantage is measured in the number of dead and not the living? If the AI program wasn't programmed properly, it may decide that if its side had only five hundred million dead, while its opposition had four hundred million, then technically they had won the war." "Ah… that's what happened, almost, in that old film '*War Games*' where a wargames simulator takes control of the nuclear weapons, and simulates an attack."

"I saw that film in the Student Union when I was at university. A classic oldie!"

"It's not that old!" Ray laughed. "But I saw it too. But the point is really well illustrated by an event that took place in real life. In 1983 the Russians were testing their new early warning system. The system set off an alarm saying that there were about five incoming nuclear missiles heading towards Russia. The operator in charge, Stanislav Petrov, a lieutenant colonel of the Soviet Air Defence Forces, had to make a split-second decision whether the attack was real or a possible mistake in the system. He made the judgement that it had to be a mistake, a decision made on human judgement, and he overrode the system's warning. It turned out that he was right. It *was* a mistake and the missiles detected were probably nothing more than a strange combination of sunlight reflecting off high-altitude clouds creating an effect that the new system hadn't been programmed to recognise yet. Petrov later became a national hero and was credited by many for basically saving the world! The thing is, you have to imagine what could have happened if an AI program had been in charge. It may have made the correct judgement call based on how it had been programmed … but if it hadn't been programmed properly humanity would all be toast!"

"Ok," Stefanie said. "I think we all get the point. Although these examples are quite extreme, or at least they sound quite extreme, they do actually illustrate the point that we have to be really careful in what we ask AI to do. And, I think we have to be very worried that if one day we succeed in inventing a machine that can think better than we can and can do more than we can; how do we know that they would continue to tolerate our existence?"

Chloe shook her head.

"Ray, so… do you think that Sebastian is something to be scared of?"

"Perhaps. From everything we've learned so far it points to the fact that Sebastian is perhaps the most advanced piece of AI we've seen so far. My worry is that we don't actually yet know what it's truly capable of. Is it just fulfilling a list of complex instructions, or has it developed some ability to think for itself? And is it learning and getting smarter all the time? If the answer to that question is yes, then I think we could all be in for a rough ride in the coming months. If the answer is no, then perhaps it's just really clever at what it does. But, either way, our job for now is to find out where Sebastian is and shut him down. And just in case Sebastian is learning and getting smarter with each day that passes, we need to do that sooner rather than later. In fact, the sooner the better…"

MI5
Thames House
The Next Day
6 p.m.
Red Room

Alan Alexander welcomed everyone to the meeting. It had been a busy day, and unfortunately things had been getting worse as the day progressed.

Earlier that afternoon he'd attended an intelligence meeting with his counterparts from the other Five Eyes countries, America, Canada, Australia and New Zealand, and all had confirmed ongoing Sebastian threats and deletions targeting individuals across the world. Once again, Sebastian was operating on a seemingly global basis. Unfortunately, no one yet knew who was behind it, or how it was being done.

Alan had already been briefed of what was going to be reported in the presentations that evening by the different section leaders, but it was important that everyone got together and each team had the opportunity to hear from the others. Alan believed that the sum of the parts was always greater than the individual parts, and that cross-pollination of information and ideas often led to new insights.

First up amongst the teams were those reporting on what they had learned about the initial Sebastian scam.

Of the original six objectives set for the team to work towards, even after several months, only the very first had been completed. They now knew almost conclusively that Sebastian was some form of computer AI program. Interestingly, they had learned that it was one program that was operating under a common identity, from multiple locations.

At this stage, however, that's where the success had stopped. Conclusive answers to the other questions had not yet been found.

On the second objective, they did now have a better idea of how the banking scam operated. Technically they had identified many of the elements of the scam, but there still remained several very large questions. They knew that a significant amount of work had gone into the scam's preparation, probably taking years. For the scam to have succeeded as it did, those behind Sebastian had to have had a significant understanding of how Voice-over-IP networks worked, how the banking system functioned, access to a world-leading voice-recognition and voice generation solution, and significant cyber acumen.

So far, they had been spectacularly unable to track down *exactly* where Sebastian was operating from. By examining patterns of Voice traffic being carried over IP networks during the main days over which the Sebastian

Banking Scam was active, they had identified a number of data centres in the UK from which the voice traffic was flowing, but as yet had not been able to identify where within the data centres the traffic had originated from. They also knew that a significant amount of the voice and data traffic they had isolated which passed between Sebastian and specific victims had come from and gone back to locations abroad. Probably other data centres. Or organisations with large server farms.

As to who was behind Sebastian and controlling him, almost no success had been achieved.

This was partly due to the fact that after the public announcements had been made warning people about the scam, almost overnight the Sebastian scam had seemed to shut down. There had been little opportunity to observe ongoing Sebastian traffic across the UK networks, or to try and trace where it had come from or was going to. Sadly, the international cooperation that was necessary to tie up and connect IP traffic leaving one country and traversing the cyber space of another had been almost non-existent.

Since the UK had left the European Union, cooperation with the Intelligence agencies of their constituent members had dwindled to insignificant levels.

Fortunately, cooperation with the Five Eyes agencies had remained strong, however to date, no one had been able to identify the botmaster who was controlling all the instances of Sebastian.

Looking back at the cyber traffic already stored within their massive storage facilities, and identifying the times around which the Sebastian Banking Scams had peaked, the US, Canadian and Australian intelligence agencies had also been able to track down elements of Sebastian's traffic entering and leaving known data centres within their territories.

However, like the British, no one abroad had so far been able to pinpoint the exact source of the traffic which was emerging from within their data centres.

And without knowing exactly where Sebastian was hiding, it had not been possible for any agency to track down when or how Sebastian would talk to any botmasters who may be controlling him.

They simply did not know what or how to look for it.

As to who was responsible for Sebastian, ultimately, it seemed obvious that whoever would prove to be behind Sebastian would ultimately be the beneficiary of the huge amount of money that Sebastian had stolen.

So, if you found out where the money went, you'd know who, in theory, had set up the scam. In other words, success in achieving the fourth objective would ultimately lead to completion of the third objective.

Unfortunately, and perpetuating the negative trend experienced by the various groups working on the objectives, those responsible for following the money trail had also not yet been successful.

However, as they all listened to their report, Alan Alexander had interjected and made a comment that despite not achieving their goal, they had actually done very well. Everyone knew that following money as it was transferred from one secretive bank to another would more than likely prove to be a fruitless task, however, those chasing the money had been more successful than expected.

By leveraging contacts and using diplomatic muscle wherever possible, those who were in hot pursuit of the money had managed to get several banks to share vital information with them. In fact, their 'sterling' work had resulted in their agents being able to follow the course of much of the stolen money internationally through an average of five different banks.

So far, however, each time the researchers were able to track the money trail to a fifth bank, the trail went dead. That didn't mean to say the fifth bank in each case was the end-point for the cash. What it meant was that at Bank Five in each chain, the trail went dead. It could be that the money was being changed into gold or diamonds at that stage, or simply removed as cash. Or it was being laundered and then recovered by the owners of the scam. The simple fact was, no one knew where it went, and no one was hopeful of recovering it. However, one of the team members had noticed that in the few days that followed the Banking Scam, gold prices in several markets in the world had unexpectedly risen. An investigation was now ongoing into trying to establish who the buyers and sellers of the gold were, with the hope that they could perhaps identify who was buying the gold, and link the gold-purchases to the stolen money. However, it was a long-shot.

Almost reluctantly, as the last of the reports on the Sebastian Banking scam had been delivered, Alan stood up and brought the first part of the meeting to a close.

Next up was a discussion on the work done in tracking down 'Sebastian V2' - the recent resurgence of Sebastian's activity associated with "deleting people from the connected world" - and a report on what had so far been learned about Sebastian's most recent activities.

Iain Slater had been one of the first to report. In the past twenty-four hours he had visited two of the many victims who had been threatened by Sebastian, but who had then either refused to be bullied by him or had physically or technically not been able to carry out his demands. The result was that they had been 'deleted'.

Returning to the office and armed with paper copies of banking statements, utility bills and subscriptions, and copies of passports, tax records and National Security numbers which he had been given by the victims, Iain had been able to contact a number of organisations and government departments to discuss their cases.

Interestingly, none of them had any records of the victims. But, when they looked at the digital records on the back-ups of the systems which were routinely kept in case of a cyber disaster, they all found that the victims had existed in the days leading up to their deletion, along with all their previous digital records.

As a result, several streams of activity had been put into play. First, an investigation was now underway within each of the organisations to see how their security procedures had been subverted. Second, the initial two victims had been reinstated and reborn into the digital world, or at least, they would be as soon as it was convenient to update their live systems. Third, Iain had requested that each organisation should start to consider how they would reinstate large numbers of deleted people as they were discovered or declared themselves in the coming weeks, and then build processes to accommodate them.

Unfortunately, a colleague of Iain's then went on to make everyone else aware that in the past forty-eight hours, the national police-forces had recorded a surge in unexplained suicides. The marker that alerted Iain's colleague to the fact that these suicides should all be considered persons-of-interest with respect to this case, was that when the police investigated the bodies which had been found, they could find no official record of their previous existences from driver's licenses, passports or credit cards carried on the bodies. On paper or plastic, they all had names and identities: in the real-world, they seemed never to have existed.

One of the groups that reported next detailed their work in the past twenty-four hours to investigate the increases in cyber traffic, which Alan had been made aware of previously. As part of their investigations, they had looked at the IP traffic which had been recorded flowing into and out of the houses of those who had been deleted, focussing on the time frame around their deletions, along with the times when victims had reported being contacted by Sebastian. By taking a record of the IP addresses of their smart meter, router and their household networked devices, they had correlated metadata extracted from that traffic and searched for it in the traffic recorded and stored historically over the past few weeks which had been going in or out of the data centres where spikes in cyber traffic had been observed.

Once they had learned what to look for and how to find it, they had discovered a method of looking at the traffic leaving the suspect data centres, partially decoding packet headers and some content so as to identify other smart meter identifiers in the communication streams. Guessing that these other smart meters may also have been targeted and by working with the utility providers, they had identified owners of those smart meters, who, when contacted, had reluctantly confirmed that they too had all been approached and bullied by Sebastian. Almost all had paid the so-called 'wealth tax.'

Eventually, when the reports petered out, Alan Alexander took the floor.

"Okay, excellent work from everyone in such a short time-scale. I appreciate it. But we can't let up. I fear we're just at the start of this. For now, I've agreed that we're not going to give any form of public statement on this. Whereas alerting the public to the Sebastian banking scam helped people to avoid having their bank accounts being emptied, currently there's little we can do to help targeted individuals even if we alert them to what's coming. At this point juncture, it seems we can't stop Sebastian from deleting the records of victims from affected databases. If a victim doesn't pay, they will be deleted, and for now, we will be powerless to stop it. The good news is that we should be able to put something in place to find deleted users in system data backups, and then have them digitally reinstated. Hopefully, once we know how to do it, we can advise the public not to worry about deletions and assure them that Sebastian should not be feared. For now, though…" his voice tailed off.

"Over the coming days, "Alan continued, "I need you to focus on finding where Sebastian is. If you've tracked Sebastian down to a data centre, find a way to get inside the data centre and identify which servers the Sebastian code is running from. Once we know that, we can then either take them off-line, or monitor the traffic from those servers and learn what's going on. Ultimately, we need to get hold of a copy of Sebastian's code, so having identified Sebastian's servers, if you can isolate his code running on those servers, copy it and let us take a look at it that would be grand."

"I also want you to consider, how did Sebastian get into these data centres? Find out who's running their security systems. Hold off from visiting them yet, or announcing our interest. For now, intensify efforts in identifying any Sebastian traffic coming in or out of the data centre. Going out…where is it going? Coming in, where has it come from?"

"We also know that a lot of these attacks are penetrating household networks via the smart meters. Which smart-meters? Who manufacturers them? Do they know about any security breaches happening because of their devices? And how does Sebastian breach the smart-meters defences, then get access to all the devices on a household network?"

A hand went up in the room.

"Sir," a young woman of Indian ethnicity asked. "I just asked myself, how does Sebastian know whether a person is rich or not? Why is he targeting some but not others? Or can we assume that all the top twenty or forty percent of rich people will be contacted over the coming days, if not already?"

"Good question, - Neena isn't it? -, can someone please look at that?

How would Sebastian know that information? Has he hacked the tax-offices of each country? Or does he get that information from real-estate records or banking statements? *How?*'

Alan was silent for a moment.

He looked around the room. He could see the tiredness on their faces, but he couldn't offer them anything more than the truth.

"I know it's tough. And it's going to get tougher. But please, do what you can. And let's all get back here tomorrow at this time?" A round of nods.

As they filed out of the room one at a time, they all returned to their desks.

The night was still young.

Chapter 21
San Francisco Bay

Robert Lee parked his car close to the water's edge near Black Sands Beach. He'd driven across the Golden Gate Bridge, left Highway 101 and followed the road to one of his favourite places on the planet.

He had spent many happy days walking and sitting on this beach with his wife Hana. It was easily accessible from the city, but not overrun with the tourists who constantly swamped San Francisco.

Today he sat on the beach by himself.

He thought of Hana.

He thought of Sebastian.

And he thought of the things that would happen if he stuck to his plan.

He told himself that he wasn't having second thoughts. But truthfully, perhaps he was.

Sebastian had just been born. His child.

And if he went through with the plan to the bitter end, how much of a world would there be left for Sebastian to exist in?

To survive, Sebastian needed power.

He needed connectivity.

And networks and devices and servers to connect to.

But after Phase Four had been unleashed, if Robert's plan worked, and Sebastian was successful, then there wouldn't be a connected world for him to exist in.

Although not everyone would have been 'deleted', afterwards, the internet would be no use to anyone.

There would be nothing on Amazon to order, no delivery drivers to knock on your door with a parcel.

No videos to stream or media to be sociable on.

Day to day, the survivors would only care about food, water and warmth, and probably painkillers, and all of those would be in short supply.

What would Hana want?

Robert knew that she would never have been a fan of Phase Four.

In many ways, even for the fantastical and previously unrealistic dreams of the Motherland, it went too far. The Supreme Leader would never sanction what Robert was planning - the new addendum to the plan. But he would never know.

And Robert would be long gone.

Untouchable and unreachable, where he was going.

Robert didn't care about humanity.

He didn't care about the vast fortune that Sebastian was amassing. In fact, all of that would be irrelevant in the months to come, anyway. Phases One to Three had been planned long before the idea for Phase Four had occurred to Robert, and now Phases One and Two were being rolled out, Robert knew they were, in effect, just teething exercises for Sebastian. Challenges for him to tackle, to learn from, that would help him assimilate data and knowledge. And help him to grow.

Once Phase Four was enacted, money would have no meaning.

Everything would lose its meaning.

Apart from the struggle to survive.

At first, when Robert had conceived the idea for Phase Four, he'd thought it would be the ultimate act of loyalty to help his motherland finally win the war against the west.

To make his father proud of him.

At the back of his mind, in the dark moments of the night, when his mind had struggled to rest and he fought with the pain, a few times Robert had found himself wondering if he had somehow begun to lose his reason. If he was going insane.

But as soon as he'd caught himself doubting, he quashed the thoughts and started to think about work again.

As he walked along the beach, thinking about Hana, her smile, her laughter, and the mission they had shared and worked so hard on together, he'd suddenly felt lonely. Very lonely indeed.

And then he felt angry.

Not at the West. Or the world.

But at life.

And how absurd it was.

Perhaps he *was* going mad.

Or maybe he was just saner than he'd ever been before.

Fuck life.

Fuck humanity.

When Robert went, he was going to take as much of humanity with him as humanly possible…

Robert laughed aloud, suddenly realising the error in his own thoughts.

The end of humanity would have little to do with humans. It would be a gift wrapped up and delivered by Sebastian.

Chapter 22

Ray woke early and was soon up on deck, running around the perimeter of the Grand Duchess, keen to get in at least five kilometres before breakfast.

At this time of the day the deck was mostly quiet, save for another couple of nutters like him, who enjoyed running in the cool of the morning just as the sun rose.

The good thing about the Duchess was its size. Several people could be running around the edge of the ship and never bump into each other, sometimes not even seeing each other.

Running alone, gave Ray a chance to think.

Whenever he had a problem to solve, he followed a simple trick he had long before learned from a hypnotist he'd once known: Ray simply asked his subconscious a question relating to the problem he needed to solve, then started doing something completely different. He knew that once his subconscious had solved the problem it had been set, it would present the answer to him, often in one of those Eureka moments!

This morning, he'd asked himself how they should go about tracking down the sources from which Sebastian was operating and even where they could find the location of the botmaster. Then he'd set off on his run and started thinking about something completely different.

In this case, Chloe.

He often thought about Chloe.

She wasn't a problem. She was a pleasure. But her continued presence on the ship was causing him a problem.

The longer she stayed, the more he liked her. The more he liked her, the more he wanted to kiss her. The more he wanted to kiss her, the more he wanted to take her to bed, and….

Bingo! The answer to the botmaster problem jumped into his head even before he'd completed the first circuit of the deck.

The answer was actually quite simple.

It was to use an Atomic Packet.

Which was a cyber technique Ray had invented and perfected to solve a similar problem in the days just before he was recruited into ACT.

Unfortunately, the moment he realised that the Atomic Packet was the solution to his problem, he also knew that potentially it was the answer to the other more pleasant problem of Chloe.

For his plan with the Atomic Packet to work, Chloe would have to go back to England to MI6.

"What do you mean, I have to go home?" Chloe gasped, the disappointment obvious in her voice.

Ray and Chloe were sitting together in his office, the door closed and the blinds down.

"I think it's the only way. We need someone to go back to England and arrange a number of things, and soon."

"What things?" Chloe asked, realising from the tone in Ray's voice that she was going to have little choice in this. She was going home. The little perfect world that she'd being enjoying was just about to come crashing down around her.

"The big problem everyone is having just now is detecting exactly where Sebastian is operating from. So far, he's evaded most of our efforts to pinpoint exactly where Sebastian is. The good news is, that I think I know how we may be able to change that. And once we know where he's operating from, exactly, hopefully that will give us a number of options. These may include disabling those instances of Sebastian that we find, deleting him from any systems he's operating from, and also, hopefully, managing to isolate a copy of his operating software so we can study and learn what Sebastian actually is and establish the architecture of his operation."

"How?" Chloe pressed. "How will you do that?"

"A long time ago, before I joined ACT, I was a bit of a hacker. And a voyeur. One day, I hacked into a video stream from a remote camera and accidentally saw a young woman being killed."

"You what…?" Chloe interrupted, shocked.

"It's a long story…anyway, at the time, having seen what I had, my life was under threat, and I desperately needed to find a way of tracking down the people who killed the lady. So I invented a way of getting data packets to drop little breadcrumbs as they traverse the networks, even for TOR-like networks, that would normally make it almost impossible to track the source and destinations of data exchanges."

"Wow…."

"It's pretty cool. No one really knows about it. It's my baby. But, I think I can use it now. What I need you to do is go back to MI6 and get your team to physically set up a few houses into which we'll move some new, very rich, virtual people. The story will be, the old owners have moved out, and some new rich couples have moved in. You'll need to give them good backstories - bank accounts, social media, gym subscriptions, NHS numbers, the entire works. You'll install some new smart meters and routers into the house, which, incidentally, I will have rigged with some special software, and then we'll wait for Sebastian to contact them and tell them they have to pay the Wealth Tax. If all goes well, Sebastian will somehow hear about them being rich, and he'll make contact. As soon as he does, every time Sebastian communicates with the new targets, he'll open up an IP communication session with the smart meter or go through the router in the house, and my software will inject a series of what I call 'Atomic Packets' into the series of IP handshakes that take place between any device that's part of any communication session as they're set up or torn down. Without going into any detail just now, what essentially happens is that my little atomic IP packets tag along in the data packet stream that flows when communications session handshakes are exchanged between all the devices in the network through which communications sessions flow, but as the packets traverse the network going through all the different layers of the communications sessions as they are established, from one network to another, in each and every device encountered in the journey from the targeted household router or smart meter along the way across the world to wherever Sebastian is attacking from, the IP packets drop little seeds or breadcrumb IP packets as they traverse any IP-based devices, and these then beacon back to the original router or smart meter in the house that Sebastian's attacking, saying *'Hi, here I am!'* All I have to do is then follow the breadcrumbs, finding all the places they've been dropped and are beaconing back to home, and this will lead me straight to Sebastian's source IP address and where the attacking software is physically based."

"You're kidding me? You can do this?"

"Yes. In theory. I mean, it worked before. Actually, it saved my life before. And because of it, the good guys won, and I got a job in ACT."

"Can MI6 or anyone else do it too?"

"I would have thought so, but it looks like no one else can. Yet. It's probably because it's historically been way beyond their remit or legal powers. The UK agencies have only really ever been allowed to do passive cyber. What I do, and what we all do here in ACT, is offensive cyber. We don't just sit back and wait for us to be attacked, we go after the bad guys and take them down. An eye for an eye, an IP-packet for an IP-packet, and all that."

Chloe looked away from Ray, staring at the window. She was thinking.

"Ok," she spoke, a few moments later. "So I go home, and my job is basically to set up a honey-trap?"

"Yes. You set the trap, and we just hope that Sebastian goes after the honey."

Later that afternoon, Chloe got a message from Ray on her laptop telling her that all the flights had been booked and everything had been arranged. The helicopter would pick her up from the deck the next morning at 7 a.m. Her flight to London would leave Mumbai airport that afternoon at 14.25 p.m. getting her into Heathrow at 18.55 p.m. the same day.

She'd spent the rest of the day finishing up the small project she'd been assigned to work on, and saying her goodbyes to everyone she'd met.

For the rest of the afternoon, she'd been sitting at her desk, occasionally looking over at Ray's office door, but it was always closed.

She hadn't seen him go in or out since lunchtime and had no idea where he was.

She couldn't help but feel disappointed.

It seemed that the slow-burn emotional tensions and sexual attraction she'd been experiencing over the past weeks were probably, after all, largely just in her mind.

Ray was sending her home, and he didn't seem to care that she was leaving.

As the afternoon drew to a close, Chloe said her goodbyes to Anand, Stefanie, and the others she'd been working with and got to know. When asked why she was leaving, she just shrugged, and replied it was time to go home.

"Are you coming back?" a few asked.

"That would be nice," she replied. And said nothing more.

About 7 p.m. she was just finishing packing up most of her stuff in her suitcase when there was a knock on the door.

As she opened it, her heart jumped when she saw it was Ray.

"Hi, sorry... I've been busy. Called into something tricky... but it's done now. How are you? All packed?"

Her throat felt tight. She swallowed hard. Fighting back the urge to say what was truly on her mind.

"I'm fine. Almost ready..." she said, not trusting herself to start a proper conversation.

"I was wondering, would you like to join Anand and me up on deck for an evening drink before dinner? I was just heading up..."

At the mention of Anand's name, Chloe felt slightly disappointed. Two's company. Three's a big crowd.

"Actually, I'm quite tired and I was thinking of skipping dinner and just going to bed early. It's a long flight tomorrow."

"Nonsense," Ray laughed, surprising her with his authoritarian tone. "Can you please come upstairs in fifteen minutes? I'm still your boss, and well, that's sort of an order…"

Fifteen minutes was not long.

Just time for a quick shower.

A touch of light make-up, and a change into her favourite smart looking casual clothes. Nothing seductive. It was clear that she'd read the whole situation the wrong way. She dressed for herself and no one else.

Taking the lift from her level up to the top deck, she stepped out, and was immediately accosted by the voices of half the members of ACT, all clapping and cheering for her.

They stood around the lift in a large semi-circle, and through the gaps between their bodies, Chloe could see several large rows of tables and chairs assembled on the deck. All covered in cutlery, napkins, bottles of wine and food.

Ray stepped forward, holding up a glass of champagne and offering it to her.

"Welcome to your going-home party! We're all going to miss you!" He said.

"What?" she gasped, "Is this all for me?"

"Absolutely," Stefanie shouted back from the crowd. "Although, truth be told, it was Ray's idea, and actually, we just jump at any excuse for a party!"

"Your idea?" she said, taking the glass from Ray's hand, and noticing how as she did it, his finger touched hers, for just a little longer than would be considered normal.

Ray smiled, and nodded very slightly.

"Okay," he announced, turning to face everyone. "It's a free bar for the next two hours. Then if you're still drinking after that, it's mandatory for you all to put on a life-jacket. No drunken ocean swims tonight, thank you very much. You all know the drill. So, help yourself to the buffet, drinks, and then in an hour I'll get Chloe to do an embarrassing going home speech. Sound good?"

A round of light laughter, nodding heads, then general commotion as everyone headed towards the buffet laid out on a set of tables behind them.

"You're sitting beside me," Ray said, touching the edge of her elbow and guiding Chloe towards one of the tables. A few moments later, they were joined by Stefanie and Anand, then a number of others, some already carrying a tray of food from the buffet tables.

"It's a nice surprise, Ray." Chloe admitted. "I thought you were just going to let me leave tomorrow…"

"And not kiss you?" Ray asked, almost making Chloe choke on her wine.

"Kiss me?" she asked back between coughs.

"Okay, if you insist. I will. But later. Not now. We have to wait until midnight. After that, when the clock strikes twelve, I'm no longer your boss, and then, well… who knows what might happen?" he laughed, his eyes twinkling.

Which is exactly what happened. As the evening drew on, a lot of drinking took place, laughter rang around the tables, echoing back at them from the taller metal superstructures looming above the deck, and at one point Chloe was forced to make a small, but cute, speech.

She thanked everyone for their help, for taking the time and patience to teach her new things and help her when she'd needed it.

It was a warm evening. A clear sky.

She chatted to everyone at her table, but every time she turned her attention back to Ray, she found he was looking at her and smiling.

Twice he pointed at his watch and mouthed the time that was still left between now and midnight.

Which made Chloe feel both excited and nervous.

It all felt a bit like it was out of a story somewhere. Cinderella meets Prince Charming. Then, on the stroke of midnight, something magical would happen.

As it turned out, something magical did happen shortly after midnight. A large shooting star lit up the sky, leaving a glowing trail of white, red and green hovering in the sky above them, and taking seconds to disperse.

Ray explained it was most likely a satellite burning up upon re-entry, skimming across the upper atmosphere, with the metals inside burning and giving off characteristic colours.

Chloe nevertheless made a wish: that everyone else would leave and go to bed and leave Ray and her alone.

Which is effectively what happened about 1 am. Everyone else had work to go to the next morning. Only Chloe was excused.

After they had gone, Ray moved closer to Chloe and together they sat in silence for quite a while, staring at the stars above, relaxed in each other's company, but with a sense of expectation and promise hanging in the air.

"Would now be good?" Ray asked gently, still looking up at the sky.

"Now would be perfect," Chloe replied.

Ray turned slightly and leant across the gap between their chairs. Chloe turned towards him.

For a moment it seemed that Ray was hesitating.

She reached out to him with her right hand, and placing it behind his head, gently guided him towards her.

Ray obliged.

As her boss, kissing Chloe was not the right or proper thing to do.

But now that she no longer worked for him, kissing her was *exactly* the right and proper thing to do.

So he did.

Chapter 23
Three Days Later

Chloe had returned home the next day as planned, posing en route as an independent traveller who had just seen the sights in and around Mumbai and was now ready to return to England.

Ray had not accompanied her to the airport on the mainland. Instead, he'd left that honour to Anand, who had also taken the opportunity to return home to his parents in the suburbs for a few days. Anand was keen to visit his parents and was looking forward to seeing how the new house was coming along which he was building for his parents, a gift paid for with the very respectable salary he was earning at ACT: a fortune in terms of the average daily salary of an Indian.

As soon as Chloe had reached England, she had called her boss, David Daniels, the Chief of the Secret Intelligence Service. Daniels had expedited her journey through customs and Passport Control, and arranged a police car to blue-light her back to Vauxhall in Central London.

By 9 p.m., she was sitting in his office, briefing him on Ray's request and plan.

By 10 p.m., Daniels had assigned a team to create several new fictitious people, each of whom they then gave a detailed on-line presence and back story. In the end, the team had created five new people, and edited the death certificates of several other people who had died with no known family. They had then taken their identities and extrapolated their existences to a new online presence, and bumped up their recent digital footprints.

Within twenty-four hours, all eight of their avatars and resurrected volunteers had magically just purchased new houses in different parts of the country into which they were moving the next day.

Further work was done to expedite the assignment of new smart meters and routers from electricity and broadband companies. These devices were delivered directly to MI6's mailroom at 9 p.m. that night, and by 10 p.m. they had been connected to a live IP network through which Ray and his team were able to connect via satellite and download their magic software directly into the devices.

By 4 p.m. on the third day, several MI6 agents, posing as the people conjured up by MI6, had moved into new houses across the UK. Their job was to spend the next few days living in the new houses, and waiting for the honey pot to attract Sebastian's attention.

It hadn't yet been established exactly how Sebastian was identifying those who were rich and therefore target-worthy, but to ensure the flag they were waving was as red as possible, each of the MI6 agents had been made very rich. Very rich indeed.

They were now living in multimillion-pound houses. With expensive new cars.

They were members of the poshest of posh golf clubs and had deep bank accounts at the poshest banks.

Their physical and digital presences oozed money and wealth.

Anyone on the Dark Web should be able to sniff them out from the other side of the world.

By the evening of the fourth day, everyone was primed, ready to go, and staring at their phones.

They didn't have long to wait.

The first email arrived at the email address of one very rich Donna McCauley, on the morning of the fifth day.

"Dear Donna,
This email is being sent to inform you that as one of the UK's most wealthy individuals and being in the top 40% of wealth owners, you are now required to pay the Wealth Tax.
In the attachment to this email, you will find full details on how to pay the tax
Please pay particular attention to the details, and ensure that you do not discuss this tax penalty with any others. Failure to observe this instruction will result in the penalties outlined in the email.
You now have twenty-four hours in which to pay the Wealth Tax.
Yours sincerely,
Sebastian
The Wealth Tax Office."

Agent Alice Greyson, posing as Donna McCauley, read her email and grinned.

With any luck, she'd just won the kitty everyone had put a tenner into for the first person who Sebastian contacted.

Aware of the fact that Sebastian may now own the digital real-estate in her house, Donna opened her front door and walked outside to the end of the street before calling her team-lead on a high-security mobile phone.

As soon as the phone was answered, Donna spoke two words.

"Contact Made."

As instructed by her team leader, Donna then proceeded to send a reply to the email she'd just received.

A second later, another email popped up in her made-up Inbox, pre-populated with fake recent email activity, which informed her she'd just replied to a No-Reply email box.

This time she did nothing more, except to download the attachment and read it, and then ignore it.

If they anticipated the sequence of activities correctly, at the very most, she would have another twenty-four hours to wait before a slightly peeved Sebastian may contact her again.

At this point, Donna didn't know if Sebastian had yet accessed her household network via the smart meter or her broadband router. If he had, then Ray Luck's Atomic Packet software would already have been activated, and every IP communication and digital handshake between Sebastian and her network would be laying a trail of digital breadcrumbs for Ray Luck and ACT to follow and pick up.

If not, they would have to wait a little longer. At this point, Sebastian had only sent Donna an email, which had landed on a server somewhere in the cloud, which Donna had then signed into to read the email.

From what they had learned from other victims of Sebastian, if Donna ignored Sebastian, eventually he would access her home network and start communicating with her directly, before destroying her digital devices, and then ultimately deleting her. When Sebastian did this, Ray's Atomic Packets would start having a party, and a mesh of trails would be laid by the Atomic Packets traversing the networks between Donna and Sebastian every time a message or control signal was sent between the server where Sebastian's software was based, and Donna's home devices.

The good news was that if the trap had not already been sprung, it seemed almost certain that in the next twenty-four hours it would.

The reports soon landing on David Daniel's desk painted an even brighter picture. By lunchtime of the fifth day, five of the eight dummy targets set up to attract Sebastian had been attacked.

Sebastian, it seemed, loved honey.

Chapter 24
Progress at last
Government COBRA Meeting 70 Whitehall

Paul Harrison, as Cyber Minister for the UK, had, on paper, a lot of authority. In reality, those who wielded the real cyber power were the heads of the Secret

Intelligence Service, the Security Services and ACT. Paul's was a relatively new role. As time went by, he was very much aware that the success of his role was dependent upon himself carving out his own niche, and earning greater levels of authority for his role.

Today, though, it was genuine concern and a rising level of fear that had led him to request that the PM call a COBRA meeting with the heads of the SIS and the SS in attendance to report on the latest developments.

As a precautionary measure, knowing that neither David Daniels at the SIS, or even those at the Security Service, got on particularly well with the PM, Paul had ensured that they were separated from each other during the meeting, sitting at different parts of the large mahogany table in the meeting room at Whitehall.

As it turned out, the Head of the Security Service had not turned up, not because he had avoided the meeting, but because of a new and emerging threat to the UK security that needed his immediate attention and oversight. He had, in his stead, sent Alan Alexander, who was heading up all activity relating to the Sebastian threat.

ACT was not represented, but the reality was that most of the people in the room didn't even know of ACT's existence.

At shortly after 10 a.m., the meeting was convened.

Alan Alexander was invited to report first.

"Ladies and Gentlemen, I appreciate the opportunity for us all to get together today and discuss the current situation. I've passed out a copy of a hastily thrown together report that summarises our current knowledge and findings. For those of you who haven't had the chance to review it yet, I'll summarise our findings. In brief. With as little technical jargon as possible."

"We are currently in the middle of a second wave of a cyber threat being led by what we believe is a new form of Artificial Intelligence, more advanced than anything anyone has seen before. In the first wave of the threat, the AI capability, which identifies himself, or itself, as Sebastian, launched the world's largest banking scam on an international level. We believe that before that activity tapered off and ceased, it had netted an estimated six billion US dollars across the world."

"We are in the midst of a second wave of attacks being perpetrated by Sebastian. This time, the attacks are targeted at those being identified as being in the top forty percent of wealth holders in each country. Again, this is on an international scale. Every developed nation in the world is being targeted, including Russia and China. Those targeted are blackmailed into purchasing a significant amount of bitcoin and sending it to specific destinations. Failure to comply or remain absolutely silent about what is happening results initially in all their electronic devices being disabled or destroyed, and then later, if the so-called Wealth Tax is still not paid, their identities being deleted from all electronic records. On paper, and in the digital realm, each victim, to all intents and purposes, then simply ceases to exist. They lose everything. Their money, their possessions, their identities. It's an incredibly potent threat that's being executed with amazing capability. It's like nothing we've seen or imagined before."

There was a murmuring of voices around the table.

"How many people have been affected?" Paul asked.

"We don't know. As just mentioned, part of the conditions set by Sebastian is that each target must not, under any circumstances, mention any details about the scam to anyone else or report it to the police or any of the authorities. The threat has been very effective. Hardly anyone has reported anything. Although I should mention that a number of people within the security agencies and several present here in the room today have reported being targeted by Sebastian, and have not paid the ransom and have then sadly suffered the consequences. But they obviously did the right thing. Anyway, back to the question… from the level of cyber traffic we're seeing in the UK, we know Sebastian is currently very active, and from the activity we're seeing in the bitcoin market, there is an unprecedented demand for bitcoin. Our guess is that the threat is affecting exactly those whom Sebastian is claiming to target. The top forty percent of society. The wealthy." The PM nodded.

"Okay, I want to ask you all a question. If you've been affected by this scam and have been targeted by Sebastian, raise your hand."

A murmur of discomfort went around the room, with several of those attending adjusting their sitting positions and coughing uncomfortably.

Only one hand went up, briefly, but was then taken back down rather quickly.

"The windows are closed. The doors locked, and all electronic devices are off. Don't worry about admitting it. There's no way Sebastian could find out. I'll ask you again. *Who* in this room has been targeted by this threat?"

One by one, every hand in the room went up apart from the PM's, David Daniels', Paul's and Alan Alexander's.

"...and who has paid the Wealth Tax?"

Most of the hands came down, but several remained in the air.

"Good grief!" the PM exclaimed, and the Cyber Minister almost choked.

"You paid up?" Paul asked in disbelief.

"And what was the alternative? None! If my businesses lost their digital records and our electronic equipment was fried or stopped working, I would lose billions!" one of the Cobra Members at the table defended himself. "£100,000 is nothing in comparison!"

The others who had kept their hands aloft signalled their agreement.

"£100,000?" Alan Alexander asked. "We were only aware of people being asked for £20,000 for belonging to the top 40 percent of the wealth owners. What did Sebastian say to you?" Alan asked the Cobra member who'd just talked.

"I received numerous communiques, both by email and verbally over our sound system, and some on the screen of our television, all repeating that I had been identified as belonging to the top ten per cent of wealth owners in the UK. As such, I was required to pay £100,000."

Another member of the Cobra team then half put up his hand, and spoke immediately after the first had finished.

"I was required to pay £50,000, having been identified as belonging to the top twenty per cent of wealth owners in the UK. I reported it, and didn't pay up. I'm now suffering the consequences." He admitted. "I estimate I will lose approximately ten million pounds over the coming days until all my digital records are restored. And, in the meantime, I'm struggling to replace the electronic equipment that now no longer works. I almost wish I'd just paid up and kept quiet."

"I sympathise with you, but you did the right thing," the PM tried to reassure him. Without succeeding.

"Unfortunately," Alan Alexander said, "From what's been admitted just now, this means that the scam is even more complex than we previously thought. It means that the tax is not a flat tariff, and is graded proportionately according to your actual wealth. Somehow Sebastian is able to identify everyone according to their wealth status, and then tax them accordingly."

"This is not a scam," David Daniels interjected. "It's an attack on the United Kingdom. Numerous red lines have been crossed here. It could be argued, that because of the scale of the attack, generally, across the whole population, and because of the damage it is causing, this is a full-blown act of war!"

"An attack by whom?" the PM demanded to know. "Who are we at war with?"

There was a moment's silence.

"We don't know yet, Sir." Alan Alexander replied. "Since this is obviously a blatant grab for money, on an international scale, it has the characteristics of previous attacks by several groups sponsored by the usual nation states you'd expect to see. And by those, I mean Russia, China or North Korea. There are a few other threat actor groups who could be considered, but the level of sophistication behind this attack still seems a little too advanced for them. So, I'd be pretty confident that it's one of those three."

"So, what now? If people here think this is an act of war, do I just go on the BBC tonight and announce that we are now at war with China? Or Russia? Or North Korea? Or all of them?"

"Well, Sir, although no shots have been fired in the Korean War since 1953, technically the war never finished, and so, you could say that the UK is still at war with North Korea now…" the Defence Minister, sitting opposite the PM, announced.

"Good. Let's nuke them, shall we? Is that what you're suggesting? When? Tomorrow? This afternoon?" The PM shouted back, jumping to his feet.

"Come on! This is ridiculous. Of course we can't declare war with anyone. Yet… But we have to bloody well know who is behind this, and stop it! We'll be the laughingstock of the world if we don't!"

"I wouldn't worry about that, Sir." The Foreign Minister volunteered. "This attack is affecting everyone. It's not just us."

"Perhaps… but…" the PM turned his attention back to Alan Alexander. "What have you got? You must have something else?"

"Not much, yet, I'm afraid. Although we are no closer to shutting the attacks down, we have made some progress in identifying where the attacks are coming from. We've identified a number of data centres in the UK where the attacks are being launched from. We've identified a number of servers within several data centres within which we believe the Sebastian operating systems are running. Over the next few days, it's our hope to be able to isolate the servers, and copy the internal code that's running on them so that we can then ring-fence and analyse the software code that makes Sebastian work. Once we've done that, we should have a better idea of how Sebastian functions, where it connects to or who it shares information with. If we observe it carefully, we should hope to see it talking to its botmaster, which, as is explained in the Appendix in our report, is the Master Server which is controlling all the other instances of Sebastian. Once we have identified where Sebastian is, we can then hopefully somehow take him offline."

"At least, that's the hope. Or intention." David Daniels joined in. He looked across at Alan Alexander for permission to speak, at which Alan smiled and nodded.

"Thank you… Yes, as I was saying. That's the intention. But we have to be very careful. We've learned from a report of one of the conversations that took place between a target victim and Sebastian that Sebastian considers himself to be a single distributed entity made up of many independent instances. In conversations with his victims, he has sometimes referred to himself as 'We' as well as 'I'. We're concerned that if Sebastian detects that we are aware of his locations and we try to shut them down, they could communicate with each other and initiate actions with further undesirable consequences. The bottom line is until we get to capture the code or look at it, which may in itself never actually be possible, then we have no idea what it's capable of."

"We've heard from the Security Services. What have the Secret Intelligence Services come up with? Anything?"

"Prime Minister, we've been going after similar goals from different angles, each with our own unique capabilities." The Chief of the SIS replied. "Over the past weeks, we've been talking with our counterparts in the Five Eyes, and they're all having the same experiences as us. So far, no one has identified who is behind this, or exactly how Sebastian operates. We're all having some success in evaluating patterns of cyber traffic and the US and UK are both using our new Quantum Computing capabilities to decrypt a lot of the cyber traffic which we've isolated and believe emanates from Sebastian. I've talked separately with the Chief, and Mr Alexander here today, and we've also made some, but not enough progress in identifying where the funds from the Sebastian Banking Scam were sent to. Unless we get a breakthrough, we'll never track it down. Both the latest Sebastian cyberattack and the banking scam were highly organised, and capable of squirreling away billions of dollars quickly, with very few visible tracks left behind." Chief Daniels paused, then continued. "As far as identifying where the attacks are coming from, our job in the SIS is to consider the international aspect of these operations. We've been working with our overseas friends, but their story is very similar to ours in the Security Services, as outlined by Mr Alexander. They've identified lots of data centres from where the communications are originating. They got an idea of some specific servers that may be running the code, but at this point, no one is prepared to start isolating them or the data centres. And there's always the risk that in today's cloud models, if you just shut down a server, the Sebastian code will just relocate and start functioning from another server somewhere else in the same data centre. We can't just start shutting down whole data centres. Who knows what services and businesses depend upon those data centres? If you switch multiple data centres off simultaneously the effect could be catastrophic."

The Prime Minister returned to his seat and sat down. His face was a mirror that reflected how they were all feeling.

"So, what? We do nothing? We stand by until Sebastian sucks us all dry? We let him get away with it?" The PM asked. "Gentlemen, and Ladies, excuse me for saying so, but this is a fucking nightmare!" David Daniels nodded.

"Prime Minister, for now, I think that yours is a fairly accurate description of the current situation. However, give us another week, and I hope we will be in a different place altogether. We'll know more and be able to do more. For now, I'm optimistic that we've seen the worst."

"How optimistic?" the PM asked.

"Not very." David Daniels replied.

For a moment, the atmosphere in the room felt rather icy. The seriousness of the situation was not lost on any members assembled for the COBRA meeting. From what had been reported so far, there seemed to be little hope of an immediate end to the situation.

"May I offer what some may consider a ray of hope, into a situation which I sense otherwise currently feels slightly depressing?" Alan Alexander asked aloud.

Everyone's eyes turned to the Assistant Director of the Security Service.

"Go ahead, please." The PM nodded, waving his hand at Mr Alexander and then sitting down.

"Thank you, Prime Minister. Okay, so, if I may elaborate a little on some of what I've already said, we've been trying to identify the locations from which Sebastian is operating in several ways. One is by examining the cyber traffic that is going in and out of the electronic devices belonging to a targeted user, or the email accounts or social media accounts through which Sebastian initially contacts his victims. We then attempt to identify the source IP addresses from where Sebastian is operating."

"Another approach is by looking at the surges in cyber traffic we have seen in the telecommunications networks that make up the backbone of our country, and by microscopically analysing where those data surges are originating from. This analysis has given us the locations of the data centres from where Sebastian is operating."

"A third approach is to consider how Sebastian could delete people from what Sebastian terms the *'connected world.'* When Sebastian carries out his threat to someone who has not paid the tax and then proceeds to delete their digital records, just *how* does he do it? And if we can find or see him performing these deletions in cyber space, can we identify any IP traffic that Sebastian generates and retrace it back to where Sebastian is hiding, and by that, I mean the servers that Sebastian is operating from?"

"To answer these questions, we started listing all the records that Sebastian seemed to be successful in deleting, i.e. council tax records, passport records, tax records, NHS records, DVLA records, gym subscriptions etc. Then, from interviewing those who had been 'deleted' and who had come forward, we identified the times at which those deletions must have taken place. We then looked at the databases, systems and servers where these official records were kept and parsed the cyber traffic going into and out of the systems around these times. One thing we can say about Sebastian is that he seems to be a very punctual guy. If he says you're going to be deleted within five minutes, or at a certain time, it generally happens then, so we have a good indication of what times to look for specific traffic, and within that cyber traffic we can search for certain parameters relating to those individuals who are being deleted. By doing this, we were able to trace a number of IP communications and data flows from targeted systems all the way back to the data centres from where Sebastian was launching the attacks. In some cases, right back to the specific servers within those data centres. Not always, but quite often."

"However, when considering the question 'how' he does it, we have to accept that Sebastian is a very capable person, or piece of software, which, it must be said, is supported by a lot of pre-existing knowledge. By that, I mean, Sebastian - or the people that programmed Sebastian - understand how systems work. When deleting users, they're able to hack into the operating systems and business applications of an organisation and allocate themselves super user admin rights. Just how do they do this? And how do they know the procedures to do this? In some cases, we've been able to identify new Zero-Day vulnerabilities through which Sebastian was able to access a system…"

"Excuse me … sorry for not understanding exactly what you're talking about, but what is a Zero-Day vulnerability?" the PM interrupted.

"Ah… yes, well, a vulnerability is a weakness in a cyber system. It's a way that a hacker can get into the software program or the operational system by bypassing or tunnelling through the normal security controls which are in place. As soon as vulnerabilities are identified, they are normally fixed, or 'patched'. That's why you're always getting 'updates' to your computers at home or in the office…the computer companies or the software manufactures of the software systems you are running are basically fixing the holes in their software and updating your computers so hackers can't get into systems through identified vulnerabilities. Good so far?" Alan smiled and looked around the table. There were a few nods. But others still looked confused.

Alan caught their eyes, and they then smiled and nodded back.

"Okay, so, a Zero-Day vulnerability is one that someone has spotted, but no one else knows anything about. It's a brand-new vulnerability that's never been used before by hackers to hack into a system. The manufactures don't yet know anything about it. To a hacker, a Zero-Day vulnerability is the equivalent to the key in a door, or an open window. Well, it appears that Sebastian seems to have a list of zero-day vulnerabilities for each of the systems he's breaking into. Somehow, he seems to have free access to them all, or has been able to find other vulnerabilities that have not yet been patched. So, we have to ask, how does Sebastian know so much? How is he so capable? How long has he been preparing for this? Where does Sebastian get his information from?"

Alan Alexander paused, letting the questions sink in.

"The truth is, we don't know. But it must tell us something very valuable about who Sebastian is, or who created him. The team behind Sebastian has extensive knowledge about systems and they must have extensive contacts. Is Sebastian doing this himself, or does he have help from people inside those organisations? How big or wide is the web and capability of the Sebastian organisation? Ok, we already know that whoever is behind Sebastian knows about networks, voice networks, telecommunication networks, and banking systems, and is extremely capable in terms of cyber and Artificial Intelligence, but now we also know they must have an extensive network of 'insiders' or an unparalleled knowledge of the security systems and business applications of major government and financial organisations. It's hard to believe we're looking at an individual cyber gang here. It's certainly pointing to the power and capability of a foreign nation state being behind this, or some other powerful and very large organisation. Not like anything we've encountered before."

"You mention *'insiders'*?" Paul Harrison, the Cyber Minister, asked. "Are we looking at a world-wide web of people who have infiltrated organisations and are helping Sebastian from the inside?"

"A good question. It could be that. Or it could be something else. For example, it could be an organisation that has that knowledge and is sharing it with Sebastian. The reality is that it's probably a combination of a lot of things. And if it's one organisation, how does that one organisation know so much? To know so much, either they've been given that information or have found it out for themselves. Of these two options, the first is rather concerning. Is there a global organisation with whom companies share their deepest secrets, whom they trust with knowledge of their cyber security systems and operating systems, and who, in the face of this trust, is abusing it and feeding it to whoever is behind Sebastian? Or has Sebastian hacked into that global organisation and stolen that information, effectively the Crown Jewels of how to access systems all across the world? And if so, what type of organisation are we looking at? Which organisations do you trust with knowledge of your utmost cyber and computer systems?"

Alan Alexander let the question hang in the air.

He had the audience in the palm of his hands.

Like a bunch of schoolboys responding to their teacher, three hands went up in the room.

Alan pointed to the COBRA member who had lost £100,000.

"A cyber security company?" the man suggested.

"That, my dear friend, is a very good question. And that is exactly why we have started doing a search of all the companies where deletions have taken place, and started building a list of all the companies which have in the past few years been employed by them as either cyber consultants, or cyber security partners. It's a new avenue of investigation. Just started. But I thought I'd share that with you. But, and this is the bottom line, we at the Security Service at Thames House are tightening the noose around Sebastian. We're discovering where he is operating from, and learning how he operates. All I wanted to say is that in terms of what we know, the glass is no longer half-empty, it's now half-full. With any luck, the days of Sebastian are probably numbered."

"With any luck?" the Prime Minister retorted. "How much luck?"

Alan Alexander was silent for a moment before replying.

"In truth, Prime Minister, the answer is, '*a lot.*' We need *a lot* of luck."

David Daniels smiled to himself. He didn't just have a lot of luck to call upon.

He had Ray Luck.

Chapter 25
2 p.m.
A meeting with the Department of Defence

After listening to the depressing details of the cyberattack the UK was suffering from, when the Cobra Meeting came to an end, the PM left the Cabinet Office Briefing Room in Whitehall and retreated next door to his private apartment above 10 Downing Street where he decided to cook himself some lunch.

He needed a break. Time to be alone. Time to think.

Something was brewing at the back of his mind.

A concern.

A worry.

After conjuring himself up a quick Spanish omelette, he sat down in his large leather chair in his office and closed his eyes.

No sooner had he done so, than what was bugging him materialised into a thought which popped into his mind.

A moment later he was on the phone, summoning the Chief of the Defence Staff for an urgent meeting.

An hour later, General Ray Stone walked into the Cabinet Room and was greeted by the Prime Minister. They were alone in the huge room.

The Chief of the Defence Staff could immediately sense that the Prime Minister had something very important on his mind to discuss.

"General, I'm glad you're able to make it at such short notice…"

"Always a pleasure, Prime Minister. How can I help?"

"Good question, but first I need to ask you something slightly more important. Do you take milk and sugar?" The PM smiled, walking across to a sideboard with the refreshments laid out on it. "Shall I be mummy?" The PM asked before pouring two cups of tea upon hearing the General's requirements.

The PM then carried both cups of tea back to the table that dominated the Cabinet Room and placed the General's politely in front of him before positioning his own tea on the table and then sitting down.

They both took a sip.

"Biscuit?" The PM asked, rising to his feet again, and then returning with a plate of digestives.

"Aha… so, you are a dipper," the PM smiled, and commented as he watched the General dip the digestive biscuit into his tea before taking his first bite. "Personally, I don't like it when the biscuit gets too soggy and bits fall off and land at the bottom of the cup."

The General took another sip of his tea, then placed the cup back on the table and pushed it a little away from himself, before looking at the PM and raising his eyebrows. The meaning was clear: "Enough pleasantries, PM, Sir, just what on earth is this meeting about?"

"So, you're probably wondering why I requested your company, General Stone. But before I get into that, may I ask you a personal question?"

"You may ask, Prime Minister, but I reserve the right not to answer, depending upon the nature of the question."

"In the past few days, have you been approached, by email or otherwise, by Sebastian?"

The General coughed.

"Yes, Sir, I have."

"How much for?"

"Do you mean, how much was the Wealth Tax I was required to pay?"

"Yes."

"£40,000."

"And you paid it?

A moment's silence.

"I did."

"Not good. But understandable. You're not the only one to have done so. Anyway, moving on … since you're aware of Sebastian already, you're probably aware that our country is in the midst of a cyberattack the like of which we've never seen before?"

"Yes, Sir, I am aware. I was briefed after the COBRA meeting this morning."

"And you will be aware, therefore, that it is likely that the perpetrator of this attack is apparently not a human, or group of humans, but a piece of software. An Artificially Intelligent piece of software no less. We're being attacked by a computer!"

"Yes Sir. And in response, I have this afternoon raised our internal alert status across the Armed Forces. I would add, that this is purely a precautionary step at this point, in anticipation of the situation potentially worsening, or other decisions made by yourself and Government."

"May I ask why?" the PM asked, the question catching the General by surprise.

"In anticipation of the Government declaring this attack as an act of war which requires retaliatory action."

"You think it could lead to that?"

"That, Prime Minister, is a question for you to answer. Not me. It is a matter of defence policy. However, whilst the cyberattacks are currently restricted to civilians, should they shift their focus to military assets or our national defence capabilities, we must then be prepared to take retaliatory action."

"Aha, yes. However, before we could do that, it would require knowledge of who is behind the attack, and who we should hold responsible for it."

"Which isn't yet the case, I believe?"

"You believe correctly."

A pause. A sip of tea. A nibble of the PM's biscuits.

"Moving along, for now, then… you see, the reason I wanted to talk with you just now is to ask you a frank question. Man to man. Because I don't always get the most honest answers from some of my staff, who're more concerned about 'need to know' than recognising that I, as Prime Minister, genuinely *do* need to know."

"So, Prime Minister, what is it you would like to know?"

"Not 'like to know', General, 'need to know'."

"Understood. And I'll answer your question if I am able to."

"We're being attacked by a cyber robot of some kind. It's happening now. In reality, not in some comic magazine or Star Trek episode. Just how serious is this. Are you worried?"

"About now, or the future?"

"The future, I think. I'm hoping we will have this attack under control soon."

"Ok, so, the future, then, yes?"

"Yes."

"Petrified, Sir." The General replied, looking straight into the eyes of the PM. "Frankly, I'm petrified."

"Sir, in my opinion, Artificial Intelligence, and the pursuit of Artificial Intelligence, poses the single greatest threat to mankind that we currently have. For a number of reasons. To put it into perspective, although concerns regarding Climate Change are entirely valid, my fear is that mankind may not even make it to 2030, or 2050, because AI may have wiped out humanity by then."

The Prime Minister coughed several times. It was a nervous habit he had never been able to shake. Whenever he got nervous or apprehensive, he suddenly felt his throat tighten.

"Why on earth do you feel that way? Surely you can't be serious. I mean, I've seen the Terminator films, and I know all about how the robots take over and they try to kill all the humans, but that was way in the future and it was just science fiction…"

"Prime Minister, the future is here. AI represents a real and present threat, now. Not sometime in the future. If you will permit me, I can outline a series of threats that worry me at night?"

The PM nodded.

"First of all, government and private companies are racing towards developing AI at ever-increasing speeds. Those private companies include weapons manufacturers who then sell to whoever they're allowed to. There are several points here, and I'll try to cover each of the main ones. The fundamental one is that we're now in an AI arms race, which I can't see stopping anytime soon. Thanks to AI a whole new type of weapon has become possible, the like of which we've never seen before, and which can scare the hell out of anyone who just hears about them. In particular, I'm thinking of autonomous systems, and AI-led swarms. Second, there is the question of bias built into the programs. Then there's the question of developing code too fast, and not taking the time to consider not what's been done, but what's not been done. And then there's support and maintenance. But before I move on, I just want to emphasise that AI is now being developed and built-in to countless systems, for a myriad different purposes. The pace of success is astounding everyone, and by that I mean, that even those who have been developing AI systems are amazed how quickly they are advancing. And how good they are. Taking the first point about the arms race. There's a growing awareness of the promise and capability of AI in military circles, and a fear that if you get left behind, it will be too late to catch up, and impossible to win a war against superior AI-based systems. I'm assuming you've been briefed, for example, on the recent success of the Chinese and the Americans in building fighter jets that fly themselves and, powered by AI, are now so good that in dog-fights where humans have flown against the AI piloted jets, the humans are beaten consistently? AI driven planes are lighter, more manoeuvrable, and can perform incredible aerobatics where the computers are not restricted by G-forces that would make a human pilot blackout. They can be programmed to learn from the experience and data of thousands of hours of flying time from human pilots, and can assimilate that information in seconds. Microseconds even. The AI based pilots don't get tired, and don't need to be fed. They just need fuel for the jets to keep them airborne. Within a few months or years, it's possible that human pilots will become obsolete, and that air supremacy in any future war will go to the side with the most AI piloted planes and aerial weapon systems."

The General was watching the Prime Ministers face. The usual jovial grin had now been replaced with a blank stare.

"Go on…" the PM urged.

"An example of what's become possible is to allow AI based systems to talk to each other in such a way that it's possible to build large numbers of aerial, land, or water based autonomous weapon systems that can communicate with each other and coordinate attack and defence manoeuvres. They're called '*swarms*'. Currently the Chinese are in the lead here. They have the ability to launch super swarms of airplanes or drones, large or small, as well as swarms of ships, that once launched can go off and hunt in packs. Give them a target, they'll destroy it. Send them out to defend airspace or coastal areas, and they're able to manoeuvre and implement best practices in attacking or defending that make them impossible to defeat. What's worse, they have the potential to continuously learn and improve, and readjust tactics during a fight. And when I say swarm, I'm talking about large collectives of defensive systems numbering into their thousands. They think together. Talk together. Attack and defend together. If you go on YouTube you can find videos of aerial swarms with hundreds of drone aircraft flying in the sky together, or videos of hundreds of USVs performing…"

"USV?" the Prime Minister interrupted.

"Sorry, Unmanned Surface Vehicle. Basically, a sea-going drone or robot armed with weapons. Anyway, you see videos of large groups of these USVs almost dancing in the sea, sailing at high speed and making patterns on the surface of the sea which are formed by them viewed from the air and looking down at how they manoeuvre around each other to form different shapes, without ever hitting each other. So, whether they are in the air, on the surface of the sea, under the sea, or on land, I see the future of warfare being played out with AI drones that are Super Intelligent and can outsmart and out-manoeuvre traditional weapons systems and battle tactics."

"Without giving away any secrets, again, you can go to You tube and learn about what the Americans are doing here. Look for videos that talk about the LOCUST project, which before you ask, stands for Low Cost UAV Swarming Technology Project, where UAV also stands for Unmanned Aerial Vehicle. You'll probably find some videos that talk about the USA's Super Swarm test when they launched a super swarm of about one thousand CACADA drones from an aircraft…"

"CACADA?"

"Sorry, new technology always brings with it a whole new language, and I forget that the stuff I talk about on a daily basis is often pure Greek to those not involved in this everyday like we are… anyway, CACADA is the US term which stands for Close and Covert Autonomous Disposable Aircraft."

"There are lots of drivers for this SWARM technology which means it's not going to go away. For example, it's been shown that a swarm can effect more serious damage with multiple strikes on a target than conventional human piloted systems. One of the reason this happens is because a large number of UAVs in a swarm can simply overwhelm the enemy's defence systems that just can't cope with and track so many attacking drones at the same time. Also, the swarm can be used to jam an enemy's communications systems during an attack. In the face of a hundred, a thousand, or three thousand attacking weapon carrying drones, most enemies will be limited in their ability to respond, and ultimately the drones will hit their target. Again, there's also the question of cost. A small swarm, which might be all that's needed, can be lower than the cost of some conventional weapons, and yet far more effective. There's a video on YouTube of a US swarm of drones attacking an unmanned large warship in a practice war game and sinking it, thus proving their capability. It's all online. Ah… it's also worthwhile stating that some missile carrying drones can stay airborne continuously for up to a month before needing to return to base. Now, imagine all of that capability being controlled by an autonomous AI system. And imagine the AI being able to select its own targets, and set up and conduct its own missions? And imagine that for some reason, the AI starts doing things we didn't expect it to do? Or refusing to continue to follow a human operator's instructions. What if the AI goes rogue? And what happens if we can't shut it off or defend ourselves from it?"

"How likely is that to happen? Surely, we just have to make sure that the system is programmed to always respond to human operators?" the PM asked.

"Let me give you an example…one of the first land-based AI led weapons systems was deployed in Iraq. The soldiers set it up, switched it on, and moved away. Within seconds the autonomous weapons system swivelled round and shot dead the operators who'd set it up. The programming was flawed. The system was programmed to identify soldiers and kill them, so it did… Even those that set it up and were on its side. And then, after that, other soldiers had the nightmare of trying to switch it off without getting killed. Fact, not fiction. It happened already."

"Fuck…"

"Exactly. Prime Minister. *Fuck*…" the General agreed. "Since I just mentioned that, it's probably worthwhile jumping ahead to an issue we're already aware of, and which relates to the question you just asked. One of the issues we see is, what happens in the future, if a commercial company sells AI based weapon systems to a military force, which are deployed in the field, but then several years later, the AI systems are still functioning, are super-intelligent and programmed to be responsive only to those who manage it, but then that company goes broke? Ceases to exist. It may have hundreds of AI based weapons systems live in the field, that now no one can properly control. Those who once could are now no longer there. With no one who is recognised to maintain them now able to do so, the AI weapon system may regard anyone else who comes to maintain or switch it off as the enemy, even if they're on the same side, and so it may just destroy them. The AI system may even be programmed NOT to be switched off. The point is, when the world starts deploying thousands of highly capable autonomous systems into the field, we have to ensure there is a viable way to control them and continue their maintenance, which encompasses multiple eventualities which are as of yet unforeseen. Above all, we have to have an established way of switching these systems off."

"Ouch. I see your point." The PM replied, shaking his head.

"May I jump back to the first point? About the swarms? I want you to realise just how deadly a swarm could be, and how scared we should be of them."

"Do I want to hear this? It sounds like I don't…"

"I think you should. Again, this is something you can view online. It's a concept that was dreamed up by a group of scientists who are as scared as I am about the capability that's being developed and who want it to be controlled. Basically, it's a film that portrays a fictional weapons company that invents a tiny micro-drone that is powered by independent AI software and which carries a camera and a few grams of high-explosive. The drone is only about twenty centimetres wide. They can be manufactured in their millions. They can fly for an hour, and are programmed to recognise a human being, fly up to the human's forehead, and then detonate the explosive against the human's skull…. Good so far? Get the concept?"

"I don't like where you're going with this…"

"Nor do I, but, anyway… now imagine that an airplane flies over a battlefield, or over a foreign city, and releases the micro-drones in their tens of thousands… Or for example, a terrorist organisation sponsored by another nation state, drives a large lorry into the centre of London, opens the back doors and releases a million armed-micro drones. Each drone flies off, finds a human target, and blows off the person's head. You can't stop them. And *every* drone kills someone. You can't hide from them. Now imagine that you programme the drone with facial recognition technology and a terrorist or enemy soldier sneaks into a conference where an important target is and releases a single drone, or a handful of them. And then those drones fly off, searching for humans with the face of their programmed targets. In a very short period of time, one drone-backed terrorist or soldier could take out a whole government by assassinating specific targets. They don't even have to be inside the building. An enemy nation state could release the drones on the River Thames outside parliament, they fly in through the windows, make their way along the corridors and up the stairs following a pre-programmed path, and then each drone identifies and kills their target MP, or General, or whoever. These micro-drones are the stuff of nightmares. Now, let me state clearly this was a concept made up by anti-AI-anti drone scientists. They don't exist." The General coughed. "*Or do they?*" He added, raising his eyebrows.

The Prime Minister leant forward towards the general. "What do you mean? Do they bloody exist or not?"

"I can't say, Sir. Perhaps they do, or perhaps they don't. But either way, it almost doesn't matter. The point is that now someone has thought about it, you can almost be certain that someone somewhere is out there right now attempting to make that particular nightmare a reality. And we should be preparing ourselves for that eventuality."

The Prime Minister was silent. He stood up from his chair and started pacing back and forth across the room. The General remained seated.

"This is a nightmare." The Prime Minister muttered.

The General said nothing.

Eventually the PM returned to his seat.

"General, I scribbled a few notes when you were speaking. You said something about 'bias'? And the speed of development?" The PM prompted the General.

"Aha, yes. Bias. It's a big worry. Let me explain what I mean… Although, first of all, I'd like to make a personal comment. Which is that given AI is such a fundamental threat to humanity, anybody could perhaps be forgiven for thinking that the Governments, and Prime Ministers of this world should be legislating to ensure that AI is only developed in a structured, well-thought out, considered manner with some form of national oversight. And by authorised companies only. As it is, the majority of funding pouring into AI development is coming from the very large Tech companies. It's public record that huge companies like Google, Amazon, Microsoft and Apple are developing AI. But they're not developing AI for the benefit of mankind, they're doing it for their shareholder value. To enhance their ability to make money. In fact, most of the companies developing AI are doing so with a particular angle. To achieve something specific. Now, that in itself, skews the orientation of any subsequent AI capability simply by the fact that it was developed with particular outcomes in mind. And based upon specific data. Most of which is generated by a company in a particular way, and as the result of specific inputs and outputs. In other words, the data which the AI uses to learn from and to make its decisions, already comes preloaded with particular, unique biases" the General was saying, when the PM raised his hand, and interrupted.

"Sorry, I'm missing something about the data. Why are you talking about data? Why is it so important?"

The General paused and looked away from the PM towards the windows, obviously thinking. After a minute, he turned back to the PM.

"Okay, let me try explaining it this way. When a human baby is born, it takes about four years to learn the basics of life. During that time, the baby learns by absorbing as much data as possible. With eyes wide open, the baby consumes everything that happens around it. Everything it sees or hears is processed by the baby's brain, and from it, second by second, event by event, the baby learns. As the baby transforms into a toddler, then a small child, then a teenager, everything about that human being is dependent upon its ability to be exposed to data, events, happenings, and information. The child learns to read, and then starts studying the existing knowledge of others. AI enabled systems are not much different. The capability of the AI is dependent upon its ability to be exposed to vast volumes of data, from which it can learn, develop and move forward. The more data the AI can be given, the smarter the AI can get. Which is why countries like China which have much less in the way of regulations that govern companies and their use of data, are anticipated to become dominant in AI. When the AI systems get hungry for data to learn from, they can literally feast upon vast databanks of data generated by the largest population in the world. Almost a billion and a half people. The Chinese race to develop Super Intelligent AI systems has the best advantage of all. Data. Now, going back to the question of bias, the data that the AI in China is learning from will have specific biases. The data is generated by people of restricted national identity who are in themselves restricted. Based upon that data, it's not possible for a general AI system to be developed which has not been biased by the peculiarities of what it is to live and breathe in China. Taking an extreme example, if an instance of such AI became aware, and was for example, programmed to prioritise the survival of humans according to the definition it had learned and experienced, it could perhaps decide that human beings were creatures that came from China. By the self-learned definition, it could deprioritise the survival of the rest of the global population, that is, some weird mad unstoppable AI robot in the future, may start killing everyone on the planet who is not Chinese. Of course, one way to ensure this doesn't happen would be to ensure that during its learning and development period, the AI is given access to all sorts of data from different parts of the world, so that the AI learns that there is abundant life on the planet, of many different forms. And that all forms of life are equal. In the race towards developing Super Intelligent AI-based systems, we have to ensure that time is taken to consider both how the AI is learning and what it is learning from, and that when we ask those systems to do something that we take extreme care in ensuring that we are careful with those questions, and that we also tell the systems what they cannot do. To us, a lot of that comes naturally. For example, if a mother asks a child to go out of the house and get a bottle of milk, the child knows from experience that the mother means it should go to a shop and buy the milk with money that the mother will provide. If a programmer in a hurry were to instruct an AI based system to go and get some milk, but failed to provide the entire background of experiences that the human child was previously exposed to, and also forgets to give the AI system a list of ways it should NOT obtain a bottle of milk, no one should be surprised if the AI system doesn't just go out and kill the first person it sees with a bottle of milk and take it from them. That person could be a neighbour, a farmer, a milk delivery person, or a shop assistant. Or anyone else who has a bottle of milk. Remember, at the end of the day, an AI system is just a software-controlled capability that follows instructions, or makes up its own instructions, in order to complete specific objectives. So, in summary, my concern about these issues, is that we are in a race to develop super intelligent AI systems where, because everyone is in a hurry, not enough time is being spent planning how to control these systems, how to make them socially aware, how to develop the code properly and flawlessly, and how NOT to make mistakes. Plus those behind these developments all have hidden agendas or are developing systems which by their very nature have inherent biases, imparted to the AI systems by those who developed their code, by the instructions and objectives given to them, or by the data the AI systems were exposed to during initial learning phases."

The PM pushed back in his chair and started shaking his head.

"General, you're a barrel of laughs. I almost wish I didn't invite you down here today. You really know how to depress a man, don't you?"

"Sir, you started this meeting by asking me to be candid with you. You then asked me some questions, and I felt obliged to give you proper answers. The reason you find all this rather scary is because it is all rather scary. Like I said, AI now poses the biggest threat to humanity, greater than Global Warming, or the Russians, or the Chinese. The more power and capability and authority we give to AI based systems, the greater the risk we experience of AI making a decision with far-reaching, potentially catastrophic outcomes. If you think back to the Cuban Missile crisis, it was to a certain extent, two leaders playing a game of cards with each other. One leader bluffing against the other, until the other folded or showed his cards. AI systems won't behave like that. They'll see and evaluate certain facts or conditions, and then make clear cut decisions based upon what is has learned, without understanding the various nuances which may be inherent in the data. Prime Minister, all I can say is God forbid the day we give an AI system full control of our nuclear defence capability. Especially if the main software programmer for the AI systems was a whisky drinker who didn't like vodka and couldn't stand caviar."

"Talking of whisky, I think I need one. Would you?" The PM asked the General, as he pressed a buzzer on the wall, and signalled for an assistant to come into the room.

The General nodded. The whisky was fetched. Glasses were poured. Each man took a moment to reflect on what had been said.

"Prime Minister, may I ask, what was the reason you actually requested me to come and join you here today? We've talked about my concerns with AI, but I haven't told you anything you couldn't have learned from others."

"That's true, General Stone. But that wasn't the reason I asked you here today. It was something else…"

"Which was?"

"I was going to ask you to tell me what we're doing about developing our own AI capabilities. For military purposes. We're currently under attack from an AI program, which is likely being supported by a foreign nation state. This attack is having devastating consequences on our citizens. People are dying. Lives and reputations are being destroyed. We are virtually at war. In fact, we're involved in a virtual war. Unfortunately, as of yet, we don't really know who the enemy is. Or how or where to hit back… But that's beside the point for this conversation. What I wanted to say is that the other day I was out jogging along the Embankment when I realized unless we become masters of AI and have a military defence capability, even a military attack capability that's AI driven and enabled, then we're going to be beaten in the next war. Which may already have begun."

"So, Prime Minster, what is it that you're asking me?"

"I'm asking you to tell me what we're already doing with regard to harnessing the power of AI to keep our military capabilities state-of-the-art and at the forefront of the new AI revolution?"

"In spite of everything I've just told you, you wish us to join the AI-led cyber race?" The General asked.

"No, I'm not an idiot. I know we're already developing AI based weapons systems. I'm not asking you to tell me what we need to do to *join* the race to develop Artificial Super-Intelligence. I'm asking you, to tell me, what I have to do to enable *you* to *win* the race."

"How much money do you have, Prime Minister?"

"As much as it takes, and if we don't have enough, I'll just print some more. I'll give you three months to compile a report. Tell me what you need, and I'll make sure you have it. General, we've fought them on the beaches, on the ground, in the sea, in the air. Now we're going to prepare ourselves to win the war in the Cloud."

Chapter 26
7 p.m.
Firth of Forth
Scotland

Professor Neil Bowie sat on the edge of his sailing boat directly underneath the middle span of the Forth Rail Bridge, which towered over him, impressive, foreboding and gigantic.

Occasionally the world around him shook with a series of booming, rolling thunder claps, as a train crossed the River Forth on the bridge above, from one side to the other.

Despite the noise and the vibrations which pounded him from all sides and echoed back from the surface of the water beneath, Professor Bowie hardly stirred.

He'd been sitting there for over an hour, sipping a glass of wine, thinking, his feet dangling over the edge of the boat, staring off into the distance.

The sea was calm this evening. The tide not very strong. His boat bobbing on the surface and not seeming to want to go anywhere else.

Which was fine by Professor Bowie.

He wasn't going anywhere in a hurry, either.

Even if wanted to do, he couldn't.

He didn't have any money.

No working credit cards or bank cards.

No valid passport.

No valid driving licence which would show up and be recognised on any car rental system.

His swipe card that normally gave him access to his office in the university building didn't function anymore, and when he'd eventually persuaded a cleaner to let him in through one of the turnstiles last Saturday night, he'd gone up to his office and found that it had been emptied. It was the weekend and there was no one anywhere to recognise him or talk to.

But the rest of the day had been just as hellish.

He'd been stopped whilst driving his car. Apparently now a stolen car. Also reported as being untaxed.

He'd shown the police the logbook, but they'd told him there was no record of any connection between him and the car, and reconfirmed that there was no valid driving licence on the DVLA system for his name.

They'd seized his car, and he'd watched it being picked up and taken away on a lorry.

The police had been unable to find any record of him on their system, but after two hours in the station had released him, having bought his story that he was a Professor at the University.

When he'd returned to his house, he'd found that he had no electricity. No gas. No computers. His mobile had stopped working earlier that day, and when he picked up his landline to call his bank and complain his banking card didn't work, he'd found he had no connection.

He'd gone to the neighbours and borrowed their phone. Called the bank. And found out they had no record of him.

He had no accounts at that branch.

He'd been to the branch on the Monday afternoon.

They confirmed, he had no accounts. That all his money and savings had vanished.

He went to the university to talk to the accounts department there to get proof from them that every month they paid money into a bank account so that he could show it to the bank.

They could find no record of him on their systems.

They recognised his face, but apparently they had no proof he worked there. The three colleagues he worked with or often saw in the staff room were away at a conference in Australia and wouldn't be back for a month. He asked the university to contact them on his behalf, and they said they would. It was only after he'd left the university campus that Professor Bowie realised that the University wouldn't be able to call him to let him know when contact had been established.

When he returned to his home later that afternoon, he'd found that none of his electronic devices were functioning. His freezer had defrosted and most of what was there had to be thrown out because there was no way to cook any of it. The gas had been cut off. His fancy six hob cooker looked nice, but did nothing.

There was not much food left in the fridge, but it too was rapidly heating up and slowly going off.

He couldn't call anyone to get help round to fix anything, although he thought that maybe it was probably all broken, and not fixable. Some of his devices smelt as if they had been burnt-out, with the musky, distinctive acrid smell of burnt rubber pervading the air around them. But also now without mains electricity he couldn't try them out anyway.

He'd borrowed his neighbour's phone again and called the gas company. The electricity company. Neither of them had any record of who he was.

He'd called the police.

The police said they would come out to visit him, but didn't.

He went to the police station. They'd recognised him and told him to go away. By this time, they just thought he was a trouble maker, probably an asylum seeker who spoke good English.

They offered to put him in a cell for the night, but the Professor had declined their kindness.

Instead, he had returned to his dark, empty home.

Luckily, he still had water in the taps.

He'd made a salad and eaten it cold. The only way he could serve it.

He'd lit a candle or two, drank some wine and read a book.

The nightmare had started over a week ago. A series of communications from a cyber prankster calling himself Sebastian.

Professor Bowie, an educated man, had refused to allow himself to become a victim.

He'd ignored all the communiques from Sebastian, and gone away climbing and camping in the Highlands. A trip he'd planned weeks ago to bag a few of the remaining Munros that had so far evaded him.

It was when he'd returned at the weekend that he'd found that his electronic devices no longer worked, and began to discover, step by step, that effectively, he'd been erased from the grid.

And that as far as the modern world was concerned, he no longer existed.

The strange thing about it was that thanks to the new course of Beta Blockers he was taking on prescription from the doctor, he didn't find himself getting angry or feeling increasingly frustrated as he progressed in making each subsequent discovery.

Instead, as his life progressively fell apart, and he was erased from digital existence, he became more and more indifferent to it all.

It was bizarre, but as it slowly dawned on him that he was, as one of his students would put it, 'well and truly screwed', the Professor realised that he didn't care.

He actually didn't give a shit.

Thanks to the beta blockers he was probably incapable of feeling excitement, but as the days after his deletion passed, and the remaining edible food in his fridge began to dwindle, he started having a series of weird thoughts.

So what he'd been deleted?

Who cared? Certainly not him. In fact, it began to feel like a cathartic release, which finally had brought the last few pointless years of his life to a close.

He'd been bored.

Drifting.

Aimless.

Putting in time at the university and getting practically nothing back in return.

Life had become monotonous.

And whereas before when he was younger, life had been full of adventure, now it was dull. Without joy.

On the fifth day, he'd awoken and found that his water supply had been cut off.

Now that the final connection to his old life had been severed, he'd packed a few clothes, gathered together his remaining bottles of wine, beers and spirits, rescued the last of his edible food, and left his house.

Using some of the cash from his safe hidden underneath his bedroom floor boards, he called a taxi and relocated his life from the outskirts of Edinburgh to his sailing boat in the harbour at South Queensferry.

That night, he'd set sail on a new adventure.

Where he was going, he didn't know.

The house he had just left had been mortgaged to the hilt on an interest-only mortgage. So, basically, the house wasn't really his. And where he was going, he didn't need the furniture. He had a few thousand pounds in cash, the boat, a few possessions, but apart from that, nothing else.

Which was, Professor Neil Bowie thought to himself as he finished the last of his wine, and returned to the safety of the deck, just perfect.

Before he set sail and started off on the first leg of his journey south towards North Berwick, he went below deck and returned topside carrying his boxes of tranquillisers and beta blockers, and then without any ceremony, tossed them both over the side of the boat.

On the journey he was just about to start, he would no longer need them.

Wherever he went, whatever happened to him, he wanted to be able to feel emotions again.

Now Neil had been deleted from the grid, he finally had his life back again.

And now he was going to live. And breathe. Laugh. And cry.

Moments later, when the first strong winds of the evening caught the sails in his boat and started to drive him forward, Neil Bowie smiled, then laughed for the first time in months.

Neil Bowie had been reborn. He was determined to start to live again.

And tomorrow was a new day that had not yet been painted.

Chapter 27
The Search gains focus

Iain Slater sat at his terminal, the cup of coffee in his hand keeping him awake, and helping him to think clearly. It had been another long day, one of several in a row.

But Iain didn't want to go home.

Something was troubling him.

It was either nothing, or something really important.

He couldn't yet decide which.

A few days ago, he'd started looking at the possibility that Sebastian was using inside knowledge to penetrate the defences of the data centres where he'd taken up residence.

The instruction to look for the possibility of collusion with insiders working for those data centres had come from Alan Alexander. That in itself was nothing new. One of the biggest possible source of threats underpinning any cyberattack was the 'Insider Threat': a disgruntled employee of a company with a grievance who gets revenge by sharing his knowledge of how company defences work so that others can launch a cyberattack with his blessing.

However, that wasn't the angle that Iain was pursuing just now. Yes, it had to do with insider knowledge, but Iain was worried that the essential knowledge necessary to penetrate a data centre's cyber defences wasn't coming from someone inside the company, but rather from someone who worked for another company which was trusted by the data centre and regularly exposed to its vital cyber defence plans and strategies.

It had taken several days to get to the place he was in now, the idea only coming to him after a pattern had begun to emerge from the data.

He'd started by evaluating the defence strategies of each of the data centres where his colleagues had detected emissions of traffic connected to Sebastian. Each of those he had looked at so far seemed to have had sound strategies. However, somewhere along the line, something, somewhere, must have gone wrong.

As part of his evaluations, he'd considered who had the job of looking after those data centres. Who'd provided the cyber security that had now so obviously been breached?

Following a common principle known as Defence in Depth, it turned out that most of the data centres now under investigation had each contracted several outside cyber security companies to provide different layers of cyber defence.

Iain had listed all cyber security vendors associated with each data centre which they believed to have been breached by Sebastian.

In each case, the list contained a selection of well-known household names. They were the world's top security companies. Trusted. Experienced.

Expensive.

What Iain was particularly interested in establishing was if there were any cyber security vendors who had, at any time, been hired by all of the data centres who'd been attacked?

Rephrasing the question, was there any commercial company who had intimate knowledge of the security systems for all those known to have been breached or who may have had direct access to those networks, up front and personal?

The answer was yes.

As it turned out, every one of the data centres that had been breached by Sebastian had at some point or other hired the services of two different security companies.

Both were well known.

Each was amidst the top five cyber security companies in the world.

Both were US based companies and therefore not fully trusted by the UK or utilised by the UK based national security agencies. However, on the face of it, those two companies should be exempt from any suspicion.

Iain was, however, obliged to do full evaluation on both companies. Had there been any reported instances of staff problems in those companies? Had any other security problems been reported by customers of those companies? Were there any known vulnerabilities in any of the cyber security systems that they had been using, may have been utilised in the defence of their data centre customers, and which may have been exploited by hackers?

It was after several hours of conducting such research that something curious had cropped up.

It was in relation to research he was conducting into one of the two companies, Red Mountain Cyber Defence.

When doing research, Iain liked to use a variety of different internet browsers, knowing that the algorithms used by each were different and returned different results with different listing priorities. This meant that something found by one browser may not be returned by another.

He had just typed the word Red Mountain Cyber Defence into one of those nonstandard internet browsers he was using to delve deeper into what he might possibly find, when something popped up.

It was a search result which had focussed mainly on the first two words, 'Red Mountain'.

He'd looked at it briefly and then closed it down and moved on, but after a few minutes decided that he should read it again. Something about the article irked him. He then spent five minutes searching for it again, before eventually finding it.

The article was an eyewitness account of a battle that took place in the battle zones between North Korea and South Korea in the Korean War, during June 1952.

Reported by a survivor in South Korea after the war, the battle had apparently raged for over a month. Thousands of dead were reported before the North Koreans retreated.

As reported in the eyewitness account which was originally published in a local South Korean paper, but then translated into English as part of a paper for a student's Masters dissertation for History and published by an Australian University, the Battle for Red Mountain had been largely forgotten and unreported. As discussed in the students' thesis, the student had argued that it was a key-battle, and had not received adequate credit for its role in turning the tide in the fight against North Korea at that time.

The result of meticulous research, the thesis included a list of the dead on both sides, and called for a plaque to be erected in their name.

After scanning the thesis on his desktop monitor, Iain had printed the document to read in detail later. It was sixty pages long, a substantial portion of which was taken up by an appendix containing the list of the dead from the battle.

Returning to the original search, he continued it for another hour, then took a break for dinner in the building's restaurant.

Cutting his break short, he'd returned to his desk, and gone back to further research into Red Mountain Cyber Defence.

Twenty minutes later he'd found himself looking at the company's website, scanning its PR and News area, searching for any mention of possible staff problems, court-cases, security breaches, anything that might be of interest. Or concern.

For what was probably the tenth time, he returned to the area of the website that listed the Owners and Board Members in the 'About Us' section.

The company had the usual assortment of board members. It was founded by its CEO Robert Lee. Interestingly, it was still a private company and had never been listed on the stock-exchange and was still wholly owned by Lee.

A quick Google on the various board members showed that several of them also held positions in other companies, also owned by Robert Lee.

Each of those companies came under a common brand name, part of the Red Mountain Group. Several companies were listed, including Red Mountain Industrial Technologies, Red Mountain Software and Red Mountain Analytics. As he flicked through the associated websites of the other companies, he discovered they were all privately owned by Robert Lee.

Further research into the founder, Robert Lee, showed him to be a very secretive person, who had, over the years, shied away from publicity.

In terms of subject profiling, Iain's training immediately flagged this of interest, and out of character for the majority of other High Tech company billionaires who were often gregarious and flamboyant. Nowadays, it seemed that being a public-figure who courted media attention was almost part of the brand for most high-tech companies. Not so for the Red Mountain technology companies.

Iain picked up the phone and made a quick phone call to a colleague in MI5.

"Do we hold any files on the top high-tech business owners?"

"From which country?"

"The US."

"Yes, a lot of them. But they're not too detailed. They only give high-level backgrounds and profiles. Mostly for business purposes. Unless there's a reason to suspect them of being involved in anything or have an association with organisations which are potential threats to the UK, we don't build detailed SoI profiles for them. Who were you thinking of?"

"Robert Lee, CEO, founder and owner of the Red Mountain group of cyber companies."

Iain could hear some keyboard tapping going on in the background.

"Yes. He's listed. There's nothing much on him, though. Seems like there's never been a reason to look into him. He appears to be clean, with no suspect ties. He was married, but his wife died of cancer. No children. Never remarried."

"Can you send me the file?"

"I already have. It's an Open File. Not security marked."

The file was already in his inbox by the time he hung up the call.

He opened it up and scanned the contents. Like his colleague had warned, there wasn't much.

It gave a quick overview of his education, the company he'd started in his garage, almost portraying him as the poster boy for the American Dream.

There were various photographs of both him and his late wife.

His wife's name was Hana.

Both looked to be of Asian heritage, although it was not clear from the file where they were born, or who their parents were.

However, that in itself was not anything peculiar. Both were native Californians, and Iain could recall from his own visits to America that the diversity of ethnic groups there was wide.

He closed the file and saved it under 'Sebastian'.

Iain looked at his watch. It was late.

Time to go home, catch a movie on Netflix, and snuggle up with his girlfriend.

He switched off his station, cleaned his desk, then left.

Chapter 28
Results begin to show
The Security Service

Jenny Cartwright put down her fresh-brewed coffee on her desktop, sat down in her expensive swivel chair, and pulled herself up closer to her desk. Placing her thumb on the scanner, and then looking directly at the camera embedded in the monitor attached to her laptop, a facial recognition scan was instantly completed, and the monitor screen sprang back to life.

She'd only been gone for ten minutes, but every analyst working for the agency automatically shut down their terminal before walking away from their desk.

The past week had been monotonous, although not boring. Work at the agency was never boring. How could it be? Working on the frontline of national defence was a job not everyone was able to do, and every day in the office equated to lives or businesses saved by the work they did.

Jenny was only twenty-eight, but she was highly specialised at what she did. As were all her colleagues. No one in her team was average. They were all…excellent.

Her job for the first few days of the week, truth be told, had been slightly less exciting than normal. She'd been asked to do a review of the security systems that were being used by most of the nation's top government or public service organisations, such as the DVLA, the NHS, the top national Banks and the Passport office. All the major government organisations where elements of people's lives had been digitised, and from where Sebastian was now systematically deleting all those who refused to pay the Wealth Tax.

The purpose of the mission her team was currently working on was to try and better understand how Sebastian was able to penetrate the cyber defences of each organisation, wheedle its way into their business systems, and delete individuals' identities and records, without anyone else noticing.

For the first few days of the task, the telephone had been her best friend. After using internal databases and the agency browser to gather basic information on the various organisations she needed to review, it had almost always come down to typing the telephone number of the person she needed to contact into their softphone on the screen and then waiting for the person at the other end to pick up.

The conversations had been very similar.

First, she introduced herself, sometimes establishing credibility with the other person by exchanging a code-word used by government agencies for that very purpose, and then requesting to be connected with the Chief Information Security Officer or 'CISO' for that organisation, if that was not the person she had come through to.

Sadly, almost half the contacts she'd tried to reach were no longer in that role, so she'd got used to being passed round the houses until she managed to establish contact with the right person. Everyone else she requested to speak to took her call. She was used to that. People never refused to prioritise a call from Green Team working for the office of the Director General of the Security Service. When they said they didn't know who that was, she just said it again, but this time using the words MI5. Same thing. But often more effective. Of course, the bit about the 'Green Team' meant very little, but it sounded important. And that was the key. It worked.

By talking to the CISOs of the organisations she cut out the monkey grinders. No wasted conversations. No wasted time.

The conversations were all very similar.

"So, how can I help you?" The CISO would ask.

"I need to understand your security architecture. How you are defending yourself from external cyber threats."

"I'm afraid I can't share that information with you. It's not something I'd feel comfortable sharing with you."

"Would it help if I gave you a COBRA password that authorises you to provide me with the information I need?"

There would be a moment's pause.

The CISOs all knew the system that used the COBRA passwords.

"That would help. However, I can't reveal anything to you on a public telephone."

"I understand. I would not expect you to. Let me start by stating that the conversation I would like to have with you is authorised by COBRA under password '*Dexter-Blue*'. And the information I need to gather from you urgently is required by the Director General of the Security Service in order to prepare for the next COBRA meeting, called by the Prime Minister for next week. I have a slot for you at our offices here in Millbank tomorrow morning at 10 am. It's a thirty-minute slot. If you give me your email address now, I will send you the list of questions I require you to come prepared to answer. I appreciate you may already have other appointments. I am authorised to instruct you to cancel them. I will expect to see you at 10 am."

It was rather direct, she knew. Perhaps a little more authoritarian than she would normally have been. But given that she was dealing with top executives in some of the Government's most important organisations, she couldn't afford to appear inferior. She didn't have the time to go to them. They had to come to her.

The first few days of the task had been all about planning, contacting the CISO, informing them of the information she needed and then instructing them to come to London to discuss in private the most confidential security secrets of their organisation. Another reason for bringing them to London was simply because once the guest entered the offices of the Security Service on the bank of the Thames, the atmosphere and authority of the building lent itself well to freeing up the information she needed from inside the CISO's mind.

And if they still refused to cooperate, it was only a short boat trip from where they were to the Tower of London!

It had been a tough week. Exhausting. But she'd conducted her last interview just over an hour ago, and was now sitting at her desk, reviewing the information she'd gathered for her report.

She asked each of the CISOs to reveal quite a lot about their organisation. Detailed plans about their cyber defences that if given to any person other than her, could have seen that CISO thrown into prison for many years, having breached the Official Secrets Act and numerous other regulations. However, each CISO had no choice but to answer. The authority with which she had asked the questions could not be questioned.

Each meeting was perhaps less of a questioning, and perhaps more of an interrogation. When each CISO was shown into the meeting room, they found themselves facing a panel of ten people, of whom Jenny was only one, albeit the Chair Person.

The formality of the occasion also tended to loosen the last of any potential stiff tongues.

Each person in the room was looking for different pieces of information. In rapid fire succession. Jenny's job was to oversee that they got that information. Thankfully, at the start of each meeting, most of the required information was made available on a flash drive or in written form, provided by suitably accommodating, and often very nervous CISOs.

She had also taken it upon herself to gather one salient fact from each CISO.

"Who are your main cyber security service providers? Provide me with a list."

Each CISO had freely given up that list.

Which was, in fact, very similar.

As perhaps would have been expected.

There were, after all, only a limited number of government-approved suppliers.

What was interesting however was that, as her review of the data whilst sipping her fresh brew coffee confirmed, every company had been at one point in the very recent past, or was now currently, using the same UK-based household name for their cyber security defence: Arrow Systems.

When asked why they had chosen that supplier, it turned out that Arrow Systems had, over the past ten years, consistently been the cheapest and best of all the UK cyber security service providers. The combination of price and expertise had simply forced almost all the others out of any tenders.

Arrow Systems had an excellent track record.

Until now, there had been very few, if any, cyber security breaches in those organisations which used their services.

Until now.

When Jenny explained how Sebastian was seemingly casually making his way around their systems and deleting records at will, the unbroken track record of zero breaches went out of the windows.

Of course, another reason why Jenny knew each CISO was in such a hurry to comply with their request, was because by now they were all aware of the fact that Sebastian was making a fool out of them all, and so far, none of them had been able to stop it happening. Or identify how it was being done.

It was perhaps their hope that the Security Service would do their job for them, and tell them what they needed to do to keep theirs.

When Jenny looked at her retro-style watch, the combination of the big hand and the little hand told her it was only seven-twenty.

Late, but not that late.

She checked the number showing on the website and dialled the front desk.

She didn't really expect anyone to pick up, but when they did, she smiled to herself.

"Good evening," she said to the very cheerful woman who welcomed her to Arrow Systems. "I'd like to speak with Andy Stafford, your CEO. If you can reach him for me, I know he will take my call. I'm calling from the Headquarters of the Security Service in London."

"The Security Service?"

"MI5?"

"MI5? In London?"

"Yes, that's what I just said. Can you put me through?"

"I'm afraid he's in the company swimming pool just now. He does three kilometres every evening before he goes home…"

"Well, when he's towelled himself down, please tell him to call me on this number. It would be a mistake not to."

"Yes. Yes, certainly. I'll make sure he has your number. Miss?"

"Miss Cartwright. Jenny Cartwright."

She had to wait ten minutes.

When the soft-phone on her monitor started flashing the incoming call, she let it ring a little before clicking on the green phone symbol to receive the call.

"Mr Stafford, how nice of you to call back."

"Miss Cartwright, no problem. I was still in the building. How can I help?"

Jenny smiled to herself. She imagined him sitting at his desk, probably dripping wet in his swimming trunks, and possibly still towelling himself down.

"I think we may have a problem, and I would like to review it with you face to face."

"A problem with what?" Mr Stafford replied.

"I'll tell you tomorrow. Please expect me at your offices at 7 am."

"Certainly. Would you like to join me for breakfast?"

"No, thank you. But it was kind of you to ask. I'll see you tomorrow." Then Jenny hung up.

She knew that Mr Andy Stafford, CEO of Arrow Systems, would now probably spend the next few hours calling around his sale teams and trying to determine if all was well with his government customers. He'd also be visiting their Security Operations Centre and checking their network activities, ensuring that nothing bad was going on.

Then, when he found out everything seemed to be fine, he'd probably pour himself a large whisky and begin to sweat.

Why on earth were the Security Service coming to visit him so early and so urgently?

Had he done something wrong?

For a second Jenny couldn't help but dream that perhaps Andy Stafford and the botmaster for Sebastian could be one and the same, but that would be wishing for too much.

Life was never that simple.

Or was it?

Either way, by the time she left the Headquarters of Arrow Systems in Oxford the next morning, she would know.

Chapter 29
Loyal Servant or Traitor?

Arrow Systems was located in a swish, modern building situated in the middle of a campus specially built for the high-tech businesses that had at one time or another spun off from the University's research and development groups. It was only a fifteen-minute drive from the centre of the town.

Except Jenny Cartwright wasn't driving.

As the helicopter touched down in the middle of the plush and immaculately tended lawn in front of the Arrow Systems building, her unannounced aerial arrival caught Mr Stafford, and everyone else already working in the building, by complete surprise.

Which was part of the plan.

Next, when she jumped out of the helicopter and strode purposely to the front of the building, accompanied by two burly looking men in black suits who wore earpieces and looked as if they were possibly armed, it was probably enough to convince the CEO of the UK's most successful cyber defence company that something seriously bad was up.

Unless he already knew that he or his company had done something wrong, by now he must be seriously worried that he had.

Jenny Cartwright didn't know what to expect. She'd read the file on him, and the notes said that he was highly intelligent, very calm, sophisticated, and charming.

He was flamboyant, and an adventure seeker. He had represented the UK in the Olympics seven years before, winning a bronze medal in the Men's White-Water Kayak. He'd since taken part in several expeditions to the remote rivers of the Himalayas, hoping, and succeeding, to be the first to navigate some of the most dangerous white-water rapids that had not yet been conquered.

In between exploring the world's most dangerous rivers, he'd helped found and grow Arrow Systems, now a household UK name.

As Jenny and her entourage had approached the front of the glass-fronted building, Andy Stafford had stepped out from the reception area into the sunlight, and smiled at her.

He'd extended his hand to shake hers and focussed his attention on her face.

Ignoring the burly bodyguards. Ignoring the helicopter which had destroyed his expensive lawn. And not showing any sign of surprise. Or concern.

"Welcome to Arrow Systems, Miss Cartwright. I'm glad you could drop in."

"Thank you. Although this is perhaps not the time for jokes."

Andy frowned. "I find humour always helps, regardless of the situation. If you'll follow me, we'll go to my office and you can explain how I may help you."

Jenny followed him into a glass elevator with her two minders, which took them in silence to the top of the four-story building and directly into his private office.

The room was spacious. More like a private flat than an office. A section of it on the left had a large desk in front of a massive floor-to-ceiling window, which had a wonderful view over a lake and some trees, with the dreaming spires of Oxford just visible over the tops of the foliage.

Set back from the desk was a large board-room style table, several metres from a wall with a massive flat-screen monitor embedded within it. Presumably for presentations or video calls. Or just watching TV.

On the right was a stone wall with a large round, glass encased wood burning stove, with three large sofas arranged around it and a glass table, on which sat an array of drinks: tea, coffee, water, juices.

It reminded Jenny of something from a hunting lodge.

Beyond the sofas and closer to another full-length window was an erg machine for rowing, a running machine, and a set of weights.

The room/stroke office - whatever it was - oozed high-tech success.

"Perhaps we could sit here. It's more comfortable." Andy said, "Can I offer you some freshly brewed coffee or tea?"

"Coffee. Black. Two sugars, please."

Jenny followed him over to the seating area. Without any direction from her, her two associates took up positions on either side of the lift door, scanning the room for threats and then looking straight ahead, their hands crossed in front of them at crotch level. Looking relaxed, simultaneously looking rather threatening. Jenny knew that it was all part of an act. But Mr Stafford didn't.

Andy poured the drinks, offered one to Jenny, and then sat back in his chair.

"So, Miss Cartwright. How may we be of service to the Security Service?"

"Ah… nice coffee. Expensive. Almost as good as the coffee we have in our offices." A slight dig. Not too much. But just enough. There was something about this very charming man that didn't ring true. Jenny had sensed it - smelled it - the moment she had entered the lift and stood beside him in silence.

"I have a number of questions for you Mr Stafford..." Jenny began.

"Andy, ... please..."

"As I was saying, I have a number of questions for you, Mr Stafford. My first question, given that you appear to be very successful, is have you paid the recent Wealth Tax?"

She watched his eyes as he absorbed the question. There was a slight twitch in the eyelids.

"I'd rather not talk about it, if you don't mind."

"A simple yes or no would suffice."

Andy hesitated, then replied, softly, but firmly, "Yes."

"Good, so you know all about Sebastian then, don't you?"

"I am aware of him, yes."

"And you thought not to report it? In spite of the fact that you are a cyber security company?"

"The instructions were very clear..."

"And you were scared of being 'deleted'?"

"Scared is a strong word. I was concerned."

"So, Mr Stafford, what are you doing about it? Sebastian, I mean."

"I have a team looking into it. Although I see it more as a scam, on a grand scale, rather than a cyberattack."

"Do you? That's interesting. Considering your company is trusted with looking after most of the government networks and you can't tell the difference between a cyberattack and a scam? I'll just make a mental note of that. Now, moving on. What do you know about Sebastian, Mr Stafford?"

"Not much. Yet. But we will know a lot more by the end of next week."

"Next week?"

"Yes, our team just started looking into the matter a few days ago."

"A whole week? I'll take a note of that too. In the meantime, I'd like to point out that almost every government organisation where its cyber defence has been entrusted to your organisation, is now experiencing an ongoing cyberattack. Sebastian seems to have found the keys to all their cyber defences, has marched into their network beyond all your peripheral defences, and is navigating himself from one business system to another, deleting data records, and identities, at will."

Andy Stafford said nothing. He coughed. Shifted in his seat. But said nothing.

"I note that you have not replied to that? Nothing to say?"

"I'll have my team look into it..."

"You haven't started that already? Oh dear, something else for me to note down."

Jenny noticed Andy's gaze shift momentarily from her to her two associates standing by the lift. Then back to her.

"Mr Stafford, just one question before I continue. Do you know who is behind Sebastian. Yes? Or No?"

"No. I'm afraid, at this point … we have no information that can help you with regard to this question."

"Are you *sure?*" Jenny asked.

"Absolutely."

"Okay, in a moment, I would like you to give me a summary of your company. Who you are? What you do? How you became who you are? Beforehand, however, I would like you to go to your phone at your desk and request that one of your colleagues give us a complete copy of your source code for all the cyber security software which you may have installed in any of your devices or which you deploy on any of the servers in the government organisations which you are paid to protect."

For a few seconds, Jenny could see a look of panic pass over Andy's face. Then the calm returned.

"I'm sorry. That's impossible. We can't do that. Arrow Systems is unique in the UK marketplace for our ability to provide unparalleled levels of cyber defence. Our ability to do so is down to the amazing algorithms we've developed and our unique approach to threat hunting and threat defence. Our Intellectual Property is what makes us who we are. It's proprietary and top secret, and we can't just hand it over to you…"

"Oh yes, you can. And you shall. In the next hour." Jenny replied, reaching into her folder and pulling out a piece of paper. She put it on the table and slid it across to Andy. "It's signed by the Home Secretary. After I talked with you last night, I popped across to see her, and got her to sign it. It authorises me to take anything I want. Including the company. If you prefer, I could close you down, and have some lorries come this afternoon to start removing everything you have here. And I mean, everything. As of this moment, in the interests of National Security, you and everything relating to Arrow Systems, come under my authority"

Andy leant forward and grabbed the piece of paper. He scanned it quickly. Then without saying anything, stood up and went to the phone on his desk. He made a quick call. A moment later, there was a knock on his door, and his Personal Assistant came in. He handed her the letter, spoke to her briefly, and she left. Andy returned to the table.

"I'm having our legal department look at your request. If it's valid, I've asked for your request to be fulfilled."

"Good. Now, please, tell me about Arrow Systems…"

Chapter 30
A message from Mr Hyde

Andy Stafford poured himself a fresh coffee and then settled back into his chair. Jenny detected that his demeanour was no longer as calm and sophisticated. She had rattled him. Which was good, and intentional. Her instinct was now screaming at her that all at Arrow Systems was not as it should be, but so far, her gut feeling was largely without base. On paper, Arrow Systems was a very successful company. But there was something about Mr Stafford that Jenny still couldn't put her finger on. Something wasn't right, but she couldn't yet say what it was.

"I studied Computer Science here at Oxford. I came up from London, was a member of Hertford College, and got a First. Then I stayed on and did a DPhil - or a PhD, if you prefer it, a DPhil is Oxford-speak - basically studying how to develop new forms of cyber defence to combat the growing threat for viruses, Trojan horses and cyberattackers, especially those behind Advanced Persistent Threats. That was ten years ago. My research led me into the area of Artificial Intelligence and Machine Learning, and we started researching concepts and ways whereby we could harness the power of AI and Machine Learning to identify threats and mitigate them before hackers were able to achieve anything. Automated threat detection and remediation. Self-healing networks that let CISOs sleep comfortably in their beds at night."

"I set up a company, with support from the university, then got space here on the campus - actually in a very small building at the back of the campus, not here - but we grew very quickly. We attracted a lot of interest. Right place, right time. Our AI software was revolutionary. Our customer base expanded. Rapidly. We are one of only a few UK-based cyber defence companies. Which led us to getting a significant number of central government contracts. And once we were in the Government door, we've gone from strength to strength." He paused. "I know you mentioned that Sebastian has seemingly penetrated our defences, but we don't know that for sure. And until now, we've had a hundred percent success rate. We're the best in cyber defence in the market. Those we protect, are protected."

"We've got a number of cyber defence solutions now. For

government organisations, for large commercial organisations and banks, for industrial applications, and for the consumer, our latest offering. We're going from strength to strength. I couldn't be more proud of what we've achieved." Andy said, seemingly finishing his explanation.

"How long have you been in these new offices for? They're very plush. Perhaps a little OTT, but quite nice." Jenny asked.

"We've been here almost nine months now. But we're already outgrowing the premises. We're looking for more space. Perhaps an office in Scotland, or Wales. Spread us out across the UK. Local cyber defence for local businesses. Something like that."

"Mr Stafford. I'm going to ask you a few questions, again, and this time I wish you to consider them more carefully before answering. I'm going to tape the questions and your replies on my phone, for my records."

"I'm not so sure…"

"This is not an interrogation, Mr Stafford. But if you answer my questions incorrectly, and it turns out that you have lied, you will potentially be guilty of… treason. The UK is under attack from an unknown cyber enemy and if you withhold information that could otherwise lead us to him, then you will be guilty of supporting the enemy. Do you understand me?"

"I…I don't…"

Jenny nodded. She had him on the run.

"My Andy Stafford, CEO, founder and majority share-holder of Arrow Systems, I, Jenny Cartwright on behalf of the Security Services, am asking you… ," she looked at her watch and recited the data and time of the question then continued, "Do you know who is responsible for the creation of Sebastian?"

"No. I do not. I'm not sure why…."

"Mr Stafford, are you the botmaster for Sebastian?"

"The botmaster? No. Not at all… but…"

"Then do you know or have any knowledge of who the botmaster may be?"

"No. Why should I?"

Jenny glanced at her mobile phone, touched the screen and then stood up quickly from her seat.

"Excellent. That's all for now. I'll wait in the helicopter outside until you have the source code ready for me."

Andy jumped up after her.

"There's no need. It should be ready by now, and waiting down at the reception. I'll just need you to sign for it in the presence of our lawyers before you take it."

Jenny nodded and turned to the lift, not waiting for the charming Mr Stafford to lead the way.

One of the goons by the lift pressed the button, and when it arrived, he stepped into the back, while the other waited for Andy and Jenny to enter, before following.

They rode the lift to the ground floor, again in silence.

There was a small party of people waiting for them at the reception desk.

Jenny took the documents she was offered by one of the men, who was dressed in an expensive suit and so obviously the lawyer for the company. Having read the documents and ensured that she had an identical spare copy, she signed them and then took the briefcase that was offered to her.

Three minutes later, she and her two beefy bodyguards walked back out to the helicopter on the lawn, climbed in and shut the door.

As the helicopter rose into the sky, all three of them burst into laughter.

One of the men, who was busy pulling off his jacket and unbuckling the stuffed money belt from around his waist that had hinted at being a gun once it was covered by the jacket, stopped laughing for long enough to say, "James Bond, eat your heart out. And move aside for Jenny Bond. The first female double '0'." The other took the briefcase from Jenny and opened it up.

"It seems to be all here. I can't believe you just did that. You've walked out of Arrow Systems with the source code for the most advanced cyber software produced this side of the US."

"I've done my bit, boys. Now it's down to you and the rest of your team. As soon as we get home, you need to rip this software apart and find out how it's made up and exactly how Sebastian is able to get past their defences and into the government systems. Undetected. And unstopped."

She looked out the window. The building for Arrow Systems was rapidly receding, but outside on the lawn, she could just make out a couple of ants staring up at them as they moved off towards the dreaming spires.

"And boys…" Jenny spoke again. "The moment you detect anything strange, I want you to let me know immediately. I don't trust Mr Andy Stafford. Not one bit. There's something about that company, and I want to find out exactly what it is." She sat back in her chair and closed her eyes.

A few moments later, thanks to the hypnotic rhythmic pulsing of the helicopter's blades, coupled with the fact that Jenny had only slept a few hours the night before, she was fast asleep.

11 a.m.

Alan Alexander was pleased. Things were progressing. He'd just had another of his teams report back on a significant success. After identifying two specific servers on which they believed the Sebastian code to be running, they had managed to work with the data centres and isolate those servers from the rest of the data centre. Then using a special capability which the Security Service had developed, they had managed to copy the entire systems on both those servers to other servers while they were still online.

They had then managed to isolate those servers from all connectivity to the outside world or other systems, then look at all the programs running on those servers and copy all the software running on those servers to another system. From there, they had been able to study the code resident on those servers and identify the operating system and software running on it which they believed to be 'Sebastian'.

Their investigations confirmed what they had previously begun to suspect, which was that Sebastian was a virtual machine that was running in the cloud. Essentially, whoever was responsible for Sebastian, perhaps even Sebastian himself, was hacking into the computing resources provided by data centres and stealing some of the computing resources available within each data centre. Essentially, it found space on some servers, installed its own operating system and code, and then ran that code within the physical computing capacity provided by the data centre. The combination of the code and the operating system was '*Sebastian*'. And there were multiple instances of exactly the same 'Sebastian' running on hundreds, maybe thousands, of different servers in different data centres across the world.

At this point, they didn't know much about the operating system, or about the capability of the software which, when it ran, created the Artificial Intelligence which called itself Sebastian. However, they intended to find out, by dissecting the code of the program line by line, using advance analysis software.

Alan knew that time was passing by quickly. To speed up progress, he had decided to share a copy of the software and operating system of Sebastian with David Daniels, Chief of the SIS, and he immediately made arrangements for that copy to be delivered to the SIS at the Vauxhall Cross building.

Within an hour, a full copy of 'Sebastian' had arrived on David Daniel's desk.

He'd immediately ordered for another copy to be made and had summoned Chloe Peters.

By the time she'd arrived in his office, another of his instructions had been carried out and a one-way ticket to Mumbai had been purchased in Chloe's name.

Twenty minutes later, she was in a car, instructed to take her home, let her pack a case and grab her passport, and then return to the office to pick up the copy of Sebastian before heading out to the airport.

Her instructions were simple. Hand the copy to Ray Luck and tell him to have his team focus on understanding what Sebastian was. How did he work? What was its capability? Who had created it? Could analysis of the code tell them where the botmaster was and who had created Sebastian? And above all, using whatever means were necessary, discover how could they shut him down.

Several hours later, Chloe was sitting on an airplane, drinking a glass of wine, and watching the lights of London fall away beneath her.

Very unprofessionally, her thoughts at this time of global crisis were not on Sebastian, but on Ray Luck.

She couldn't wait to see him.

Chapter 31
Unravelling the Code Two Days Later.

Within minutes of receiving it, the experts at MI5 set about dissecting the code they had received from Arrow Systems like wolves feasting upon a fresh, juicy kill.

They systematically started to take it apart, assigning analysis of different sections to various teams. They'd done this sort of thing before.

They'd build an architecture of the code, determining how it was put together and how the program would run.

They would learn how the code flowed once it was in operation, examining its complexity at a high level, often just guessing at the functional purposes of the various blocks that made it up.

Then, when they had a map of the structure, they would start looking at different components, delving down into individual lines of code.

Very quickly, it became obvious that the code was much more advanced than any standard code you would expect to use to build a normal software program. It was clear that a significant portion of the code was part of a structure which would support Artificial Intelligence, as had been admitted by Arrow Systems. In fact, Arrow Systems was very proud of it, and it was one of the main selling points for their commercial cyber defence systems.

However, once the teams started to examine the code at a microscopic level, some interesting insights began to emerge.

Knowing that Arrow Systems claimed that it was they who had developed the system, the experts at MI5 expected to see a familiar pattern of code usage, that may be typical of software developed in the UK, by UK based developers. They would also have expected to see usage of Oxford English in any text that appeared in between lines of functional code.

Instead, they discovered the opposite.

In comment fields within the code, there were frequent appearances of words spelt in American-English.

And there were lines of code which some analysts had seen before, appearing in other software programs they had previously examined. Sometimes just individual lines, other times whole subroutines.

This was something they often saw… programmers building new programs from others.

However, it wasn't something they had expected to see from Arrow Systems, given their proud claim to have developed everything in Oxford from scratch.

That said, the Arrow Systems program was very large, containing millions of lines of code, and it would take months, possibly years of work, to analyse it in full.

At the same time, another larger team had been given the task of ripping apart the code copied from the servers running Sebastian.

The most experienced people were set on this task, although a couple of the team were instrumental in initially helping set up the work on the Arrow Systems analysis.

After working on the Arrow Systems task, they had then transferred to the Sebastian analysis project.

And they had only been working on that project for just over two hours when one of the two picked up the phone and called Jenny Cartwright.

Andy Stafford was sitting at his grand desk in his office suite, reviewing some of the latest accounts from his firm. The net revenue for the firm after all expenses was increasing at a rate of fifteen percent per month.

Already very successful, his business was now growing even faster, going from strength to strength each month.

For Arrow Systems, the future currently seemed so bright, Andy was considering buying himself a new pair of dark sunglasses.

The loud, almost deafening sound of the helicopter as it passed low over his building directly above his office gave Andy quite a fright.

Swivelling in his chair to look up in the sky to see what on earth it was, he was shocked to see the large helicopter hover for a few moments in the air outside his office window, and then land on his expensive, manicured lawn outside his office. Andy immediately recognised that it was the same helicopter that had landed there a few days ago.

Whereas last time he had at least been expecting a visit, this time whoever was in the helicopter was arriving unannounced.

A tingle went down Andy's spine.

This didn't feel good.

Hurrying to the lift, he rode it down to the reception area and then made it outside just as the doors opened and the same two burly suited men who had accompanied Miss Cartwright a few days ago, now jumped down from the fuselage and made a bee line directly for him.

Confused, and not seeing Jenny Cartwright climb down after them, he moved towards the approaching muscle.

"Gentlemen, what a surprise to see you both again so soon…" Andy started to welcome them, but was cut off short by one of the men who, having reached Andy, now grabbed his arms and forced them behind his back.

Before Andy knew what was going on, the man had also forced a pair of handcuffs on his wrists and taken a firm grip of Andy by his shoulder.

Whilst this was happening, the other man spoke.

"Andy Stafford, I am arresting you for the crimes of Fraud, Cyber Theft, and Treason against the Crown." The bulked-up muscle man said, before continuing and reading him his rights.

"What? *Treason? Fraud?* What on Earth are you talking about?"

Before he had even finished his sentence, however, the man with the iron grip on his shoulder had started pushing him towards the waiting helicopter.

From inside the large glass offices, the receptionist in the foyer picked up the phone and dialled for emergency help.

"Police please. Come quickly, my boss has just been kidnapped and bundled into a helicopter which took off and flew away!"

It was no good, however. By the time the campus security guards arrived, Jenny Cartwright's helicopter was already several miles away, heading down to Central London, escorting Mr Andy Stafford to the Tower of London for interrogation.

Chloe was exhausted when the plane touched down in Mumbai. Posing as an independent traveller, returning to complete her journey after her last trip was cut short due to illness, she took over an hour to clear customs and immigration before walking out of the airport to look for a taxi.

As she emerged through the electronic sliding doors from the cool, air-conditioned arrivals lounge into the intense summer heat, she was quite shocked by the difference in temperature.

She immediately began to peel off an extra layer of clothing.

"Miss Peters?" A voice caught her by surprise. A familiar voice.

Opening her eyes, she saw a man carrying a white card with her name on it, ostensibly a taxi-driver looking for his customer.

She was about to say, "'Hello Anand!" and give him a hug, when she saw the warning on his face, followed immediately by, "Excuse me, Miss.

Did you book a taxi to take you to your hotel?"

"Yes, that's me." She said, smiling.

"May I take your rucksack and hand luggage?" Anand asked, putting on a good act. Which, Chloe thought to herself, he should actually be good at doing, given that he worked for ACT...

She followed him to a car, where he opened the boot and popped her luggage inside, offering to take her large handbag from her.

"No, thank you, sir, but I'll hold onto that for now." She said, smiling.

They climbed into the car, and drove to the outskirts of Mumbai, where, as previously, they boarded a helicopter to fly to the Duchess.

"I'll be sitting up front, keeping the pilot company," Anand said.

Chloe nodded, slightly surprised, and climbed up into the passenger cabin by herself.

As soon as she opened the door and set a foot inside, she laughed.

Ray Luck was waiting inside, holding a small bunch of flowers.

"It's great to have you back, Chloe!" he said, and quickly checking that Anand nor the pilot wasn't looking, he leant forward and gave her a quick, soft, but very full kiss on the lips.

His fingers encircled hers, and she grasped his in return.

"Thanks for the flowers!" she said. "And look... I've brought you a present too."

"What is it?" he asked, watching as she opened her bag and took out a large black box.

"It's Sebastian. You're to conduct a post-mortem as fast as you can."

"Is he dead? What do you mean, post-mortem?"

"I was trying to be clever. In actual fact, he's still alive. The software is still running. Inside the box I've just given you, you'll find a mini microserver with its own power supply. There's also a hard drive containing a static version of the code. You can do whatever you want with it, but the Chief was keen that you should have it, immediately."

Ray was staring at the black box, deep in thought. He looked up.

"You know, I'm really pleased you're here, Chloe. I missed you... But this is amazing. Please don't take this the wrong way, but I'm almost more excited about having this than seeing you! Does that make me a bad person?" She laughed.

"Possibly. But Sebastian's a boy, and I'm a girl, so I won't get too jealous. You'll just have to make it up to me later, Ray." She said, then added, "I'll look forward to it."

"So shall I!" Ray replied, then kissed her again.

Unfortunately, this time Anand noticed the kiss. He was about to talk with Chloe, but realised that, for now, Chloe had better things to do.

Instead, he closed his eyes, settled back into his seat, and fell asleep.

Chapter 32
A secret revealed

Unseen by those upfront, Ray and Chloe held hands in the back seat of the helicopter. They kissed a couple of times, but then Chloe fell asleep on his shoulder. Ray enjoyed the sensation of her resting against him. It had been a while since his last serious girlfriend and all the indications were that Chloe and he could be on course for becoming just as serious, if not more.

The package from MI6 was a complete surprise. He hadn't expected it. He had been making his own plans to acquire a copy of the code, but it would have been quite cumbersome to do so. This was a very welcomed alternative. It meant that they could get to work on dissecting Sebastian the moment he landed.

Pressing a button on his headset, he connected to the pilot upfront and with his help placed an encrypted call directly to the ship. Ray issued a few instructions to some of the team waiting on the Duchess, telling them the good news and organizing them to get to work on their new tasks as soon as he arrived.

His talking stirred Chloe and she woke up.

"Sorry, just talking with the team on the Duchess. We're all super excited about this." Ray said, touching the box on his lap.

"Ray, any idea how long I'm staying for this time?"

"Nothing's been said. If you don't know, then we'll just take it day by day, shall we?"

"I'd like that. Have you got anything interesting for me to work on?"

"Sebastian-related?"

"Absolutely."

"Okay, there's lots going on. First of all, perhaps I should let you know that in your absence we've been rather naughty. Although, to be fair, that's why we're here. To be naughty…"

"How naughty?"

"Well, we've hacked into all the government systems and networks where Sebastian has been going round and systematically deleting people. We've also hacked into the data centres. Everywhere we could, we've inserted our Atomic-Packet -Cookie-Crumb-laying software…"

"How?" Chloe interrupted.

"It's complicated, but suffice it to say that we put a proxy in place and all traffic going in or out of the targeted systems must go through an *Appender* which basically appends Atomic Packets to outgoing data packets from those servers, thus tracking where they are going. So far, it looks like we've gotten away with it. And as for why it's so naughty, it's not just in the UK, where nobody, apart from you, knows that we've done that, but it's also abroad. In Europe. In the US, Canada, and New Zealand."

"Why? What are you hoping for?" Chloe asked.

"Basically, three things. First of all, assuming it's Sebastian that's hacking into the Government networks and wreaking havoc with our elder citizens, we want to see who is doing this in each territory. Once the Atomic Packet generator is set loose, we'll be able to track down where all the different versions of Sebastian are that are doing the deleting. We'll track the Cookie Crumbs back to their sources and start monitoring them."

"Second, by putting Atomic Packet generators on all the suspect blades or servers in the different data centres, we can then follow the traffic from Sebastian, as it targets customers who need to pay the Wealth Tax. From that we can build a larger, more complex map of where all the victims of Sebastian are, for future reference."

"Third, then we're going to monitor the generation of the Atomic Packets to see if any of the versions of Sebastian actually talk to each other. But mainly, we'll try to establish if Sebastian is ever contacted by the botmaster."

"It's all very naughty, very covert operation stuff. If you get caught, what then?" Chloe asked.

"That's not a good question. We just have to make sure we don't get caught."

"Wait a minute, you've just told me all this. Apart from the teams in ACT, am I the only person who knows about this?"

"Yes."

"Aren't you worried I might tell someone?"

"The Chief is expecting us to do stuff like this. He just can't know anything about it. If you tell him about this, he'll fire you. And nobody here in ACT will talk to you again. Right now, this is one of the coolest places to be and you're either with us or against us. And plus, one more thing…"

"Which is what?"

"Chloe Peters, I *trust* you."

When the helicopter landed on the Duchess, a team of geeks met them on deck. As if come to worship the God of Code, or something equivalent, they stared at the black box that was handed to their high priest and followed him off the deck into the bowels of the ship.

Into the cyber dungeons where they would lock Sebastian up with no contact to the outside world, and torture and interrogate him until he began to give up his secrets.

Which didn't take long.

They worked through the night and by morning of the next day several of the teams, which had been formed from the seventy people now set onto the project, had started to find interesting results.

Whilst they tickled, prodded and probed Sebastian, the remainder of the team on the Duchess were now focusing on the three key things that they were hoping to learn from installing Ray's Atomic Packet Trojan into the data centres and government organisations where people were being deleted. Of those three, one had been given greater priority.

A thousand-pound prize had been promised to the first person to find the botmaster.

Chapter 33
The truth comes out
7 a.m.

"Good morning," a bright and cheerful Jenny Cartwright announced loudly, as she walked in to the interrogation room into which Andy Stafford had been marched and dumped thirty minutes before.

No breakfast or tea or coffee, yet. Just water.

"You have no right to do this!" Andy slammed the table, standing up from the chair on the other side of the table.

"Oh yes, I do."

Jenny pulled out her mobile phone and put in on the desk between them. She played the recordings she had made of Andy swearing negative answers to her questions about his knowledge of Sebastian.

"You see, I believe you lied to me. Which, as I warned you previously, would not be a good thing to do. Unfortunately, that puts you in a difficult position. First, Mr Stafford, *it really pisses me off!* Second, it means that you have probably committed treason. Which, in times of war, could be met with summary execution. By the way, that's an interesting point, because I believe there are discussions going on in parliament just now concerning whether or not technically we are at war or not. So for now, the judgement about what may happen to you, will have to wait. It could be death… could be… or it could be something far worse.

"Worse? What the hell are you talking about?"

"I could take all your dreams away from you. Everything that you've strived for since you were a child… I can make them all vanish. I have trucks ready in our depot prepared to go to Oxford and start removing all your hardware. I could have your building up for sale by this evening. Like I said, technically, by the powers invested in me by the Home Secretary, I own you, your company, and everything about you. And yet…*still*… you decided to piss me off by lying to me. In spite of being fully warned in advance."

Jenny lifted her two arms and let them fall gently through the air to her side, simultaneously closing her eyes, bending her head slightly backwards and uttering the words, "Calm. *Calm*…"

She took a few deep breaths then opened her eyes.

"Now... yes... where were we? Oh, now I remember. You've lied to me and committed treason and could potentially by executed. Unless you tell me the truth. And help me."

"How? *How* can I help you?" Jenny leaned forward.

"This conversation is being taped. People, important people, are watching us from the other side of that two-way mirror on that wall. If I give you another chance to tell me the truth, it will be the last opportunity you'll be given. The UK is under attack. Time is short. You need to tell me what you know *now*. Do you understand?" Andy Stafford nodded. His face had gone very white.

"Yes. Give me another chance. I promise, I'll tell you whatever you want to know!"

Inwardly, Jenny smiled to herself. She'd broken him.

From now on, the extravagant, courageous, obnoxiously charming Mr Andy Stafford would be putty in her hands.

"Good, now I want you to start from the beginning again, and tell me the correct history of your company. The correct history."

"But if I do, it'll be the end of Arrow Systems... we'll lose all our contracts."

"But you may remain alive. And potentially, just potentially, out of prison. It depends how much you help us in the coming days, weeks or months. Before you start, please bear in mind that we probably know everything anyway. We've looked at the code, we know it's not yours and we think we know where it came from. We just want you to fill in the blanks. Okay?"

"Yes."

Jenny sat back, glanced briefly at the two-way mirror and nodded.

"Good, Mr Stafford. So, please, start from the beginning."

"At Oxford, people thought I was a genius. I partied a lot, spent most of my time chasing girls, but sailed through all my exams. But it wasn't because I was clever. It was because I loved the subjects I studied. I just sucked up everything that was ever taught to me, because I was really interested in everything..."

"That's all very nice, Mr Stafford, you're a *'genius'*. So what?"

"It meant people had high expectations of me. I've told you before that I did a DPhil at the university, started thinking about new novel ways of how organisations should protect and defend themselves from the new forms of cyber threats that were developing. We started researching and developing new forms of Artificial Intelligence and Machine Learning that could be used to identify and defend against cyberattacks. We set up a company. Because of the attention and support I'd already got from the University, I started getting funding, lots of it, from industry and business. The money flooded it. Our reputation grew. We became gods in the cyber defence world... except, behind the scenes... there was a massive problem."

"Which was?" Jenny probed.

"The system and software I was developing didn't work. On paper, it sounded great. I could give brilliant lectures and fund-raising speeches telling people how it ought to work when it was ready. I'd already convinced myself that it would and I could convince anybody I needed to that it would work too. Even all the other scientists thought it would. But then one day, when it was ready... when we thought it was ready... we switched it on... and it didn't work. In fact, in the first few days, the system we were running it on was hacked into and our wonderful AI defence system didn't even detect it. We spent months trying to figure out what was wrong, but... I suppose the easiest way to describe how I felt about it was that the whole thing was still-born. It should have been alive, but it wasn't. And we couldn't bring it to life. Which gave us,... me mostly, a massive problem. We were planning to float on the stock exchange. The price had been set. And a date had been chosen. Before the flotation we had publicised that we were going to give an incredible demonstration of its capability... but..."

"So, what did you do?"

"I started looking elsewhere for a solution. And found it very quickly. In fact, someone came to me and proposed the solution I was looking for. He'd been following my efforts with great interest. Somehow, he knew I'd failed. He proposed a partnership, of sorts."

"A partnership?"

"Well, actually, it was more an OEM deal than a Partnership..."

"OEM?"

"Original Equipment Manufacturer... Maybe you could even describe it as a white label deal... Basically, the other guy also had an AI Cyber Defence company. But his AI Cyber Defence Software worked. Ours didn't. He offered a contract to us whereby we could integrate his software into our systems but where we could rebadge and rename the software as we wanted to. So we did. For a decent slice of the profits, we bought his AI software under licence, integrated it into our code and it worked like a dream. The combination of his and our software is amazing."

"So, basically, everything about Arrow Systems is a sham. It's not your code. It's someone else's. The great white hope of British High-Tech success is basically a con?"

"That's not fair..."

"Isn't it?"

"It's not that simple... we created the market, we won the customers, we sell and maintain the systems..."

"You're a distributor, not a manufacturer."

"Listen... that's..."

"*Not fair*? No, you listen, Mr Stafford." She could see Mr Stafford's eyes turning red and misting over. He looked like a little boy who was going to cry. "You won British Government contracts on the basis that you were a UK supplier, with code and IPR developed here in the UK. You committed fraud and you have endangered organisations which are part of the UK's Critical National Infrastructure. All not good." She hesitated before continuing. "So, tell me, Mr Stafford, who is this person who offered you his magic code? And what was his company called?" The blood visibly drained from Andy's face. Jenny could see the mental struggle that he was going through in his brain, fighting with his reluctance to tell the truth, but knowing he had no choice.

"The names, if you please, Mr Stafford?"

"His name is Robert Lee. His company is Red Mountain Cyber Defence."

Chapter 34

Jenny looked briefly towards those standing behind the mirror on the wall of the interview room.

Her colleague Iain Slater was one of those who had requested to be there, just in case he needed to feed any questions into the earpiece that Jenny was wearing.

The moment that the CEO of Arrow Systems had confirmed that Red Mountain Cyber Defence Systems was the source of the AI being used at the heart of the cyber defence which was currently being used by most government organisations, the mission to find Sebastian and stop him had ratcheted up a gear.

"To confirm, Andy Stafford, CEO of Arrow Systems, has just stated that the AI system being used in their cyber defence solutions which are now deployed at the heart of many critical UK Government organisations is provided by Red Mountain Cyber Defence Systems. Is that correct Mr Stafford?" Andy nodded.

"Please speak, for the benefit of the recording, Mr Stafford."

"Yes, that is correct. We've integrated the Red Mountain AI module into our systems."

The admission of this was a hammer blow to the UK Government's cyber defence capabilities. It had come as no surprise to Jenny, who had been informed by those who had looked at both the Arrow Systems code and the Sebastian code, that there were great areas of similarities. They hadn't yet confirmed it with certainty. But that was now academic. Mr Stafford had.

"Do you realise that you have just admitted treason? That you have lied to the British government repeatedly about the source of your AI capabilities, stating that it was yours and yours alone, and that no elements came from a non-UK based organisation?" "Yes…"

"Do you realise how dangerous the situation is which you've put the UK in?"

"Yes."

"Bloody hell, Mr Stafford, they're going to take you to the tower for this one, and throw away the bloody key!"

Jenny stood up, and was considering leaving the room to confer with the others in the adjacent room when Iain Slater fed a question into her earpiece.

"Mr Stafford. I have a question for you. What knowledge do you have of any Zero-Day vulnerabilities that could be exploited within the customer base you've built up of UK Government organisations?"

Andy Stafford looked up, his eyebrows rising slightly.

"Quite a lot, actually. In the normal course of our research and work with our customers, we quite often find vulnerabilities that no one else knows about."

"What do you do with them?"

"We use that information internally, and…" he paused, "we send details of those vulnerabilities to Red Mountain so that they can build them into their next software update so that the next version of the software can help remediate for all those vulnerabilities."

"How?"

"By enabling the AI system to look for those vulnerabilities in the systems they are protecting and either remediating them, sorry - fixing them - automatically, or by warning the system users that there's a problem that should be taken care of."

"And has that been happening? Or has Red Mountain just been accumulating a large file full of Zero-Days which can tell them exactly how to hack into each customer that's running their software - sorry '*your*' software - without being spotted?"

Andy never responded.

"Mr Stafford. That was a question, not a statement. Is that what you think has been happening?"

"Possibly. We've always just trusted Red Mountain. After all, they're one of the largest and best-known cyber security brands in the world."

"That means nothing. Millions of people, including the British Prime Minister, trusted Hitler before he started attacking and killing them." Jenny paused. "Okay, I think we're done here."

"Can I go now?"

"Where? To the Tower? Possibly… but wherever you're going, don't expect to be let out any time soon."

"I'm entitled to a phone call."

"This isn't America. And I'm not Kojak. You're not entitled to anything."

Jenny left the room.

Outside the reception room, Jenny was met by her boss, Alan Alexander, and several of the others, including Iain Slater.

Alan directed them into a meeting room a little way down the hallway. They all followed him in and took a seat around a table.

"Excellent work, Jenny. Really well done. Thanks to you, and the work that IainSlater and some of the other teams have reported to me, we can be almost certain that Red Mountain Cyber Security has something to do with Sebastian. Let's review what we know. Andy Stafford has confessed that Red Mountain has a world-beating AI capability. We know that in the UK, Sebastian is running within virtual machines created within data centres where Red Mountain is, or was at some time, responsible for their cyber security, with their software providing defence-in-depth for those facilities. We also know that in all the government organisations where we see the identities and records being deleted of those people who have fallen foul of Sebastian, that Red Mountain software is installed in their systems and is providing their core cyber security. And, thanks to the last questions provided by Mr Slater, we have an inkling that over the years, Red Mountain has most likely been building a very impressive list of Zero-Day exploits for all the systems they've been protecting in the UK, and most likely, the other countries too. In other words, by exploiting those vulnerabilities, it would be possible for the Red Mountain AI software, aka Sebastian, to potentially navigate its way through any government organisation's cyber defences and run amok within the business systems, at will, without anyone being suspicious or knowing it was going on. Does this sum it up quite fairly?" Alan Alexander looked around the table.

"Okay, good. Now, in a few minutes I'm going to call GCHQ and our Five Eyes counterparts and request them to start monitoring all communications going back and forth with the Red Mountain group of companies, starting with their CEO Robert Lee. Jenny already has a signature from the Home Secretary authorising GCHQ to monitor all communications going back and forth in Arrow Systems, and especially their CEO Mr Stafford. And we've already arranged for GCHQ to be monitoring all the communications and cyber traffic going in and out the data centres where Sebastian software is running. So, for now, I think we've got most of the most important angles covered. Any other thoughts, anyone?"

"Perhaps I was a bit harsh, Sir, about refusing to give Mr Stafford a phone call. May I suggest we set him free for the evening so he can go home or back to his office, which by now should all be wired and bugged for close quarter monitoring, so that we can see who he calls or otherwise contacts? Of course, after a few hours, we'll pick him up again and at that point we'll lock him up permanently and throw away the key."

"Agreed. See to it, please Miss Cartwright."

"What about the government organisations where Arrow Systems is installed?" Iain Slater asked.

"Good question. For now, we do nothing. We're monitoring their communications so we might pick up Red Mountain talking to their systems, possibly. But Mr Slater, can I ask you to set up a group tasked with deciding how to swap our government organisations over from Arrow Systems to a new supplier? Just make a plan. For now, we don't want to spook Red Mountain that we may be on to them. Although all the roads are leading to a Red Mountain Rome, we haven't yet categorically proven that they're responsible for Sebastian. When we talk to the boys in Washington, I'll see what they think about bringing Robert Lee in and putting some pressure on him to admit he's responsible. And if we can, perhaps we can get Robert Lee and his gang to switch Sebastian off."

"And pay back all the money?" One of the others said. "He's got £20,000 of mine that I need back!"

Mr Alexander stared at the man.

"You paid Sebastian?"

"Yes, sir."

Mr Alexander turned around and walked away, shaking his head in disbelief.

Sebastian had even conned those working for the Secret Services.

An hour later, Andy Stafford was let out onto the streets of London. He was clearly shaken. His hands were trembling and he seemed to be slightly confused.

Before returning his mobile phone, his keys and other personal possessions, spyware had been loaded into his phone and key fob, and a tracker had been inserted into both his shoes and jacket.

A number of agents were assigned to follow him and everyone was waiting to discover who'd be the first person he'd call.

The first place that Mr Stafford had visited post-release, was a bar.

A double whisky later, he had left and made his way to a phone shop where had purchased a cheap phone and several SIM cards.

He'd then made his way to a park and entered a public toilet where he'd set up the phone and made a single phone call.

It was to a number in California.

A short, simple message.

"They know!"

Chapter 35
The net closes

David Daniels hung up the phone with Alan Alexander. Alexander had just briefed him on their latest news and requested Daniels to speak with his friends in the US to find out what they could about Robert Lee and the Red Mountain group of companies.

Although the focus in his initial request had been on Robert Lee, both Alexander and Daniels knew that in reality, it could be any one of the executives in that group of companies.

Both agreed, however, that it would have to be someone with significant authority across the group of companies.

Yet, because Robert Lee was such a prominent figure in all the companies, and the leadership team spread across the group of companies was not large, the more they looked and thought about it, their gut instinct was that Robert Lee had to have a significant role in what was going on. He couldn't have such an important, hands-on role without knowing.

David's counterpart in Washington had promised to call him back by the end of the day with an initial report. Nowadays, with so many of their systems being interconnected and digitised, it shouldn't take long to pull a report on everything they could find out about Robert Lee.

Daniels looked at his watch, and thought briefly about those over in India.

He wondered how things were going.

Going on previous track records, by now ACT would have ripped Sebastian apart and would probably be several steps ahead of everyone in the UK.

With their help, fingers crossed, the nightmare would soon be coming to an end.

Paul Harrison had already been on the phone today, pushing for a progress report, which David had provided verbally. Harrison had pointed out that the PM was getting increasingly convinced that the Government had to do more. That they should perhaps make a public announcement. Daniels had replied that that was of course the PM's prerogative, but that the joint chiefs of the Five Eyes had all agreed to continue to say nothing, publicly, for now.

The PM had given Daniels another four days.

"After that, I've got to go public." He'd insisted.

Four days was not long. But hopefully, it would be enough.

Things were beginning to pick up pace.

Deep underground, on the sixth level directly below the Security Service buildings at Thames House at 12 Millbank, Tom McGregor leant forward and stared at the lines of code on his left screen.

He had three screens on his desk. Some of his colleagues had six, but Tom had always found three were enough.

As he always insisted to his friend Tazmin, who sat near him at a desk on his right, it wasn't the size or quantity of monitors that mattered, it was what you did with them that counted.

Okay, so perhaps he was flirting a little whenever he said it, but he did believe it was true.

So long as he had a lollipop in his mouth, he could run numerous search and analysis programs at once, keeping track of them by cascading them in various stacks on monitors One and Two, and dragging results across to screen Three whenever he needed to see something in more detail, or interrogate a spider pattern of relationships between data points, correlating intelligence gathered from multiple sources and enriching them wherever possible with Reference Data held by the Security Service in their massive data banks.

Lollipops helped Tom think.

His dentist was always telling him off.

"You're thirty-two years old! At this rate, you won't have any teeth left!"

But his dentist didn't know that lollipops had, at various points over the years, probably saved the country on several occasions.

As may be about to happen again.

Tom was, along with a hundred other analysts on the sixth level, now busy studying the code in the various parts of the architecture of the Sebastian program.

After staring at the screen for several minutes, whilst twirling the lollipop in his mouth and tapping it occasionally against his lower teeth, he turned to Tazmin and beckoned her over.

She asked for a minute, saved her work, then pushed back from her station and walked over.

"What's up?" she asked, resting a hand on the back of his chair.

"Look at that…" he said, pointing to the left screen.

Tazmin watched as Tom copied the lines of codes from the program segment he was directing her attention to on the left screen, opened up another window and then pasted the code into it. He then quickly wrote a new segment of code inside another little window and then copied that into the same window he'd pasted the segment of Sebastian's code into.

"I was wondering, if I did something like this... and injected that into the code... what do you think?"

Tazmin bent forward, staring at the code on the screen.

"Could it be that simple?" she asked, turning away from the screen to look at Tom.

"I don't know... maybe it could..." Tazmin smiled and laughed a little.

"You could be right. I think you should call Gareth." A moment later, Tom was busy skyping Gareth.

"Hi, Boss, if you've got a moment... I think I've got something I should show you..."

David Daniels looked at the picture of Robert Lee that was in the file that had just been emailed across to him and studied his face.

Could this be the man behind Sebastian?

The botmaster? Or the man behind the botmaster?

Could this be the picture of the most successful thief in the history of mankind, having over the past few months stolen the equivalent of the GDP of a medium-sized nation?

If so, was he a genius criminal or psychotic madman responsible for the deaths of hundreds of people who had committed suicide after being deleted?

The report was interesting.

It gave an executive summary of his childhood, his education, and the companies he had built from scratch.

He had been married, to an attractive woman called Hana. She had been killed in a car accident several years before. There were no children.

Daniels looked at the photograph of his wife and wondered about the hurt that Robert Lee must have gone through. She was ...had been... beautiful.

Curiously, the file was sketchy when it came to their parents or providing details of where Robert Lee had been born. It noted that according to school and other official records, he had been born in Palo Alto in California. However, the file noted that further research was being undertaken to confirm that.

However, it did point out that this father, Jung-Woo Lee, had committed suicide in the early eighties, and that Robert had been looked after by his mother as a small boy.

She had died in 1993.

Rather interestingly, there were no details yet on where his parents had come from or were born.

Looking at their names, Daniels wondered if they were of Chinese or Japanese descent. Which, admittedly, meant very little in California, where a significant proportion of the population also historically came from the Far East, or had migrated there before or after the wars.

There was no doubt that Robert Lee was a prime Person of Interest in the Sebastian investigation. Which made things interesting.

Daniels knew that he should take whatever any file said about Robert Lee with a healthy pinch-of-salt: the reason they were looking at him just now was because his software, or his organisation, was likely complicit in the deletion of people's details from official records. That being possible, then surely, Robert Lee also had the same capability to edit official records to say whatever he wanted. If Lee didn't like what something said about him, then there was a real possibility that Lee could simply change it to whatever he wanted it to say, i.e., change the date or place of birth, his education details, perhaps even his bank balance.

David Daniels enlarged the photograph of Robert Lee on his screen and looked closely into his eyes: "Who are you, Robert Lee? And if you are responsible for Sebastian, what other tricks do you have up your sleeve for us?"

Daniels turned his attention to the large clock on his office wall.

It was 9.55 p.m.

In several minutes, the Prime Minister would be giving an address to the nation. Typical of the PM, he had decided to ignore the advice of his immediate experts, namely those at the Security Services, the Secret Intelligence Services, and the cyber teams at GCHQ, and had decided to bring forward an announcement to the nation about Sebastian.

In Daniels' opinion, it was premature.

But he wasn't the Prime Minister, and never would be.

The bigger question was, for how much longer would the PM be the PM?

The events of the next few days would probably tell.

Chapter 36
Time to die?
Pacific Heights San Francisco

Robert Lee sat in his rocking chair, gently rocking himself backwards and forwards while he looked across the skyline view of San Francisco. He was in his fifth floor private Pacific Heights Penthouse Apartment, in a renovated building he owned on one of the hills in the most exclusive areas of the city. Most of the building was empty, with only the top few levels occupied.

From the outside, the building looked like a typical multi-storey home in San Francisco, but the bottom two levels were empty, apart from the numerous sensors and alarms that could and would detect any intruders.

The third and fourth floors were now full of an array of computing capabilities. Several rows of large server racks. A bank of smaller computers. And several desks and screens dotted around the rooms.

The truth was that Robert Lee lived above a small but extremely powerful data centre, which he ran and controlled. It allowed him to experiment or make continual adjustments to Sebastian's code, and then compile and run the software in real time, with immediate feedback as to the outcome of his tinkering.

The time was almost 2 p.m. Robert was keenly waiting to listen to the BBC broadcasting from London on their World Service. He wanted to hear if the government in the UK had made any announcements recently, either relating to Sebastian, or with regard to the problem they now knew about within their organisations that was caused by Arrow Systems.

Robert knew that he was now on borrowed time.

Not just because he was still alive, in spite of the cancer, but mainly because he had received that cryptic message from Andy Stafford.

Now the UK agencies knew that their cyber defence was dependent upon a foreign capability, and that Red Mountain software was running freely in the core of many of their government business systems, it would only be a matter of time before Sebastian was removed from their networks and servers.

And before they came knocking on his door in San Francisco.

Looking for him.

It was only a matter of days.

Which meant that Robert should now consider several things.

First, he should get ready to operationalise Phase Three.

Then, he should prepare for the automated operationalisation of Phase Four.

Third… he should finalise his preparations to ensure that no one would ever be able to capture him and interrogate or torture him, encourage him to tell the truth, or worse, successfully force him to stop Sebastian.

Robert had accomplished a lot in the past weeks.

He had worked hard, pushing himself to his limits.

Taking the time to sit now, waiting for the BBC news, was a rare moment of relaxation.

Suddenly the music on the radio ended, and the BBC World News came on, broadcasting the UK BBC News at Ten.

Robert took a deep breath.

Almost immediately, one of his worst fears was confirmed.

The British Government had had enough.

The voice of the British Prime Minister came on. Firm. Reassuring. Calm.

He started to explain that the UK was currently under a continued cyberattack from threat actors unknown, but which was now known to be related to the previous Banking Scam of several months ago, whereby victims were contacted by a hacker called Sebastian.

The Prime Minister explained that in the current scam, Sebastian would contact individuals and persuade them that they must pay a new form of tax called the Wealth Tax. Sebastian would threaten all victims that if they didn't pay the Wealth Tax within a specific time period that their household electronic devices would be destroyed automatically. If victims subsequently didn't pay the tax within a further specified time period, their personal records would be deleted from Banking and Government Systems. The Prime Minister urged the public not to comply with Sebastian's demands, stating that safeguards had now been put in place to protect the public. Anyone, the Prime Minister stressed, who is contacted by the cyberattacker called Sebastian, should contact a special helpline and register themselves. They should then switch off all their personal devices and under no circumstances connect any of their devices to the internet or power sockets, until further notice. The PM reassured the British public that everyone who registered their details with the helpline should not fear their personal records being deleted. If that were to subsequently happen, their details would be reinstated within days. The public should have no fear. Matters were now in hand. Whereas the Prime Minister did admit that the coming weeks may be difficult and inconvenient for some, the vast majority of people would be unaffected."

Robert listened until the end of that part of the broadcast. Following the Prime Minister's speech, there had been some commentary from the Cyber Defence Minister of the UK, Paul Harrison, and some analysis of what it all meant by the BBC's technical editor.

The single comment that caught Robert's greatest attention, however, was the one line mentioned by the BBC commentator: "I was told a few minutes before coming on air, that the British Security agencies now believe they have identified the source of the attack and will be taking appropriate measures to stop it in the next few hours."

That was all that Robert needed to hear.

He switched off the radio, went through to his kitchen and fetched a high-energy drink from the fridge, then rode the elevator down to the third floor.

There was a lot of work to do, and not a minute to lose.

It was time to initiate Phase Three.

The next morning
COBRA Meeting

At the hastily summoned COBRA meeting in Downing Street the next morning, the PM sat silently as he let Paul Harrison open up proceedings.

In addition to the usual various experts making up the COBRA panel this morning were David Daniels, Alan Alexander, and Gavin Booth, the Director of GCHQ, the Government Communications Headquarters, as well as several of the team members that Daniels and Alexander had brought along with them to report on their findings.

Before the meeting had officially started there had already been a number of impromptu side-line conversations as everyone waited for the PM to arrive, and whilst they finished the continental breakfast which had been served.

"Ladies and Gentleman, thank you all for coming." Harrison began. "As you all know, there have been some significant developments over the past few days, culminating in the PM's Address to the nation last night. I know some of you would have preferred if we'd waited a few more days before making the announcement, but we felt that we had no choice. There was a balance to be struck between waiting and announcing, and because we've begun to see an increased level of dissent and fear surfacing on Social Media from brave people who stood against Sebastian and were then deleted, we felt that the pendulum had definitely swung in favour of doing something now rather than waiting further. To start with, I'd like to summarise some of the events that have happened in the past few days that we believe supported that action…"

"First, thanks to the amazing work done by the Security Services and the Secret Intelligence Services, we've now had positive identification of the array of servers in specific data centres on which virtual machines have been established that create the environment within which Sebastian can exist and operate. From where he launches his attacks on those now being targeted to pay the so-called Wealth Tax. We could at any point take these servers off-line, however, because of all the other companies that run their own virtual machines on the same servers, there is a concern with respect to how that would impact British businesses dependent upon those cloud capabilities. So, for now, those servers are being monitored by GCHQ for all traffic ingressing or egressing those servers. However, and this is excellent news, we were able to copy the file systems and code which constitutes the AI software and operations systems behind Sebastian, and these have been shared with various trusted organisations for analysis." Harrison nodded at those from the security services seated around the table, then continued.

"Secondly, we believe that we have now identified the creator of Sebastian, who may now be acting as the botmaster and coordinating all the virtual versions of Sebastian which are distributed around the world, operating independently, although working together as a team. In fact, yesterday I heard the concern that Sebastian may in effect be the world's first threat actor SWARM, made up of hundreds, maybe thousands of virtual machine versions of the AI program calling itself Sebastian. Anyway, I digress. The important point I wanted to summarise was that we believe that a company called Red Mountain Cyber Defence, part of the world-famous Red Mountain Group, may be the organisation that developed Sebastian. The owner of that Group, and the CEO of all the Red Mountain organisations and commercial operations is a Mr Robert Lee, based in California. He, and all Red Mountain executives and some individual employees are now being monitored by the NSA and GCHQ."

"Third - and in a minute I'll ask Alan Alexander to report on this - but we believe we may have found a way to shut Sebastian down…"

A murmur of excitement, and relief immediately went round the room.

"Fourth, we know, from monitoring the communications of Mr Andy Stafford, the CEO and founder of Arrow Systems which protects the majority of UK government organisations but which was subsequently found to white-labelling AI software from Red Mountain, that as soon as Stafford was released on bail from custody, that he called Robert Lee and warned him that we knew Arrow Systems was using his software. As such, we know that Robert Lee is aware that we know of their involvement in Arrow Systems, and we should therefore surmise that Lee will believe we are on to him."

"Therefore, given that Red Mountain must now know that the UK and US secret services are now focussing on his organisation and himself, we think that there would be little advantage for him to continue Sebastian's operations. Our thoughts are that he will conclude that the best way to protect his own organisation and himself would be to immediately cease all Sebastian's operations. His reasoning may be that if we haven't already arrested him, we still aren't certain of his involvement, so by switching Sebastian off, we may no longer be able to track any further criminal activities back to Red Mountain."

"It's a small gamble, but we, with the backing of the Prime Minister, feel that there's a high likelihood that by making the announcement yesterday, we will see a cessation of Sebastian's activities, globally." Paul Harrison rounded off his introduction and summarisation of the current intelligence.

"And what if you're wrong?" one of the MPs on the COBRA committee asked.

"Then we take the action required to shut Sebastian down ourselves as mentioned in Point Three."

"And Mr Lee and Red Mountain?"

"Our colleagues in the States will be knocking on his door very soon. It's likely that as soon as we have him in custody and we're in possession of a little more evidence linking Lee to Sebastian, then the US will take possession and assume guardianship of all Red Mountain enterprises." Harrison replied, then continued, looking over to Alan Alexander. "I'm now going to hand over to the Security Services, who want to report on their very exciting discoveries."

Alan Alexander nodded at Harrison and then smiled at those around the table.

"Thanks for the invitation again. To bring you quickly up to speed with some of the developments in our current investigations, I've actually brought with me today one of our analysts, Tom McGregor, who yesterday made an important discovery in the dissection of the Sebastian code. He's one of about one hundred analysts we have currently inspecting the sixty million lines of code that make up Sebastian. I'd like to invite him to summarise his important discovery. Tom?"

Tom nodded, smiled, and coughed a few times. Without doubt, this was the most important gig he'd ever attended in his life before. But, he'd spent all of last night preparing for it and was determined to do himself proud and overcome his fear of public speaking.

"Ladies and Gentlemen… If you would like to pay attention to the large screen... I'll show you what I found when I was looking at the section of code that my team had been assigned to parse and examine."

Tom coughed nervously again and took a sip of the sparkling water from the bottle that had been sitting at his place at the table when he sat down. Leaning forward, he started playing with his laptop on the table in front of him.

"First, however, I'd like to report on some findings made by others in our teams, and show you a few sections of the code which is included in Sebastian's software that are particularly interesting..."

All eyes in the room turned to the screen.

"Here I'm showing you some of the source code that we see when we look at the program. These lines, here... the ones I'm highlighting in yellow... are sections of code that we've also seen in other cyberattacks and malware, which we know came from organised crime groups in Russia."

Tom marched through several different screens, each showing numerous lines of code, which to most people in the room, probably looked just like gobbledegook and not highly advanced computer language.

"I'm showing you these, because one of the objectives set for our teams is to try and determine where this software was developed so we can attribute an owner to the code. However, although the occurrence of these sections of code within the Sebastian software might be viewed as hinting that Sebastian was developed by the Russians, I have to say that an increasing trend we've seen with cybercrime gangs is to deliberately copy code from other known malware into their programs so that when people like us look at them, it could throw us off the scent, and make us think the Russians were behind it, whereas, all the time, someone else was responsible."

"So, what are you saying?" The Prime Minister spoke for the first time, "Are the Russians behind Sebastian or not?"

"Sir, I would like to suggest that they are not. This is too obvious. In my opinion, this code is a decoy. And if you look at the code itself, some of it isn't even active... it's not actually doing anything of value. It's really just been put there for effect."

Alan Alexander interrupted him.

"Tom, please, perhaps it's best if you move on and show us what you have found."

Tom shut up for a second, coughed a few times, and looked a bit like a rabbit caught in the glaring headlights of an oncoming car.

"But Sir... I think... Okay, yes, sorry. I'll move on..." He huddled forward over his laptop again. The image on the overhead screen changed, and more code appeared.

Equally as unintelligible as before.

"Gentlemen and... sorry, also ladies... this is what I found. If you look at the code now highlighted in white…"

All eyes focused on the white text on the now black screen, ignoring the rest of the text which was now showing in green.

"This section shows what a number of us agree is a vulnerability in the operating system."

"Tom, please, summarise what it shows." Alan Alexander requested, fearing that Tom was going to branch off into another complex explanation.

"Yes Sir, sorry… And it's a vulnerability which we can easily exploit. It means that we can inject a command into the Sebastian malware, even as it's running and still online, that tells it to uninstall itself."

"Uninstall itself? As in, tell it to stop running, and switch off then delete itself?" one of the MPs sitting at the far end of the table asked.

"Yes, Sir. We just send a few lines of code to all the instances of Sebastian that we can find, and hopefully, bingo, Sebastian will switch itself off and remove itself from whatever servers it's running on."

"Are you kidding? It could be that simple?" Another of the MPs on the committee asked, the excitement clearly showing in his voice.

"Yes, gentlemen," stated the Prime Minister. "I'm assured that it's going to be that simple. Which is why, you will now all understand, why I was confident in moving ahead with the public announcement yesterday. All we need to decide now is when we're going to issue the command and what, or if, we share this with the other countries of the world."

Tom Harrison seemed surprised.

"Surely, Sir, there's no question. We have to share this with the Five Eyes and everyone else immediately. If we don't Sebastian will continue to exist and the threat will carry on."

"Yes, I agree, we should help our friends, but I think first we need to think carefully about what leverage this now gives us with certain governments. This is a big thing. We shouldn't just squander the advantage. However, that's not for this committee to decide. I'll discuss that with the Cabinet. For now, we just need to decide when we should go ahead with issuing the command for Sebastian to commit suicide." The PM turned to Chief David Daniels, Alan Alexander and Gavin Booth from GCHQ. "Are you all confident this will work? Is there any reason we should delay?"

David Daniels immediately replied. "Sir, I would like to request that we hold off on doing anything rash. From talking with Mr Alexander, this is a new discovery, from only yesterday, and I would prefer if more time was given to analysing all the code in its entirety, and not just rushing ahead with an assumption…"

Gavin Booth spoke next. "I agree, Sir. We have to be sure. I have a team examining the code as well. It's very early stages…"

"It would be wise… to take some more time, Sir." Alan Alexander backed them up. "We may only have one shot at this, and we have to get it right." The PM looked round the table, and was silent.

"I just went on television and gave a public address telling everyone we were going to sort this mess out. We need to kill Sebastian as soon as we can, and if this is the way to do it, we need to do it as soon as possible!" the PM said, rather loudly. "But, … you, Ladies and Gentlemen, are the experts not me. So, we'll hold off for now. For another few days. But no longer. Gentlemen and Ladies, we have to bring this war to a close. Before things get far worse…"

Chapter 37
Unusual Activity

The PM pushed back in his chair and turned his attention to Gavin Booth, the Director of GCHQ.

"Gavin, it's good to see you again, although it's a shame it's under such circumstances. So, what news do you have to share with us from Cheltenham?"

"Thank you. Well, if I can direct everyone's attention back to the screen, what I'm showing now is a graphical representation of the cyber traffic we've been seeing coming out of the data centres we were asked to monitor."

"As you can see, there was an initial sharp blip in traffic, a pause, and then the baseline traffic levels started to rise in the time periods of the Sebastian Banking Scam, then dropped immediately after the scam was seen to stop in the few days after the PM's first public briefing on that scam. Then, a few months later, you can see a sudden spike a day or two before the current Cyber threat around the Wealth Tax began. We see the spike in traffic, then a pause and back to normal baseline activity, and then levels of activity increasing again as the start of the current cyberattack began emanating out from the data centres. Now, let me move forward over the timeframe during which we know the Wealth Tax attack has been occurring…here you see a substantial increase in the baseline cyber traffic going onto the public networks, until… here... which is four hours after the Prime Minister's broadcast last night. And look what happens there… see, a sharp drop in baseline activity. Actually, back down to the levels we saw prior to the Wealth Tax attack was launched."

There was a murmur around the table. A few excited voices quickly making comments to each other.

"But," Gavin Booth continued, "look at what happened late last night. About 2 a.m. GMT. Suddenly… "

There was a slight gasp in the room.

Traffic levels, as indicated by the coloured lines on the charts, suddenly increased exponentially. A massive blip on the cyber traffic transiting the UK networks, before rapidly falling again to the baseline levels.

"This traffic was going into the cyber centres, not out. It's actually made up of two separate elements. An initial sharp, short blip in overall bandwidth, followed by a separate prolonged larger blip of significant data traffic going straight into the servers on which we know Sebastian to be resident. As you will have seen, Gentlemen, the last time we saw something similar, although on a lesser scale, was two days before the Wealth Tax scam began."

"Have you been able to look at the data in the download to see what it is?" The PM asked.

"We've captured the data. However, it's all encrypted. We're using the best resources we have at the moment to unlock it, but that will take us several days, possibly weeks." Booth replied.

"Even with your new Quantum Computing capability?" the PM asked.

"Sir, may I remind you that Project Athena is still highly classified? We're not talking about that outside of certain audiences." David Daniels interrupted and scolded the PM.

"So, what are you suggesting?" Paul Harrison asked, moving swiftly on and directing attention away from discussions of the sensitive Quantum Computing capability which officially still did not yet exist in the UK.

"I'm expressing a concern." Gavin Booth answered. "I'm worried. The good news is that I think that immediately following the announcement by the Prime Minister on national TV, all Sebastian activity relating to the Wealth Tax may have come to an end. That's the good news…"

"And the bad news?" The PM asked.

"I think, I fear, we're in the calm before the storm. I haven't yet had a chance to talk with my counterparts in the Five Eyes community, so I can't confirm that they're seeing anything similar. But… I fear that what this massive blip in data traffic represents, is a new download of code, software or operational instructions directly into Sebastian. Perhaps a new version of Sebastian altogether. The big question is, why? What's next? My worry, to be explicit, is that far from seeing an end to this, what we've seen so far, is only just the beginning."

"It's going to get worse?" The PM asked, the tone of his voice reflecting the change in mood in the room.

Gavin Booth nodded.

"Unfortunately, Sir, my worry is that so far we've only seen an opening salvo. And the full-scale attack is just around the corner. A war, unlike any we have ever seen before, is just about to begin…"

Chapter 38
New York
One day later

Josh Cohen swirled the water around in his glass, watching the soluble painkiller slowly dissolve. His head was throbbing, another excruciating migraine probably only minutes away. He'd recently bought a new chair for his office, at the New York Presbyterian Hospital at West 165th Street, on the advice of his doctor, who believed the old chair was giving him poor support, encouraging bad posture, leading to muscle strain on the neck, which led to the migraines.

It didn't help that his wife was about to divorce him, his eldest child hated him, new school fees were due, and five days ago he'd had to find another $30,000 to pay the new Wealth Tax.

No wonder that last night, he'd drunk a bottle of red wine by himself. Just trying to get through the past few weeks had been tough, but hopefully, soon, things would get better.

In two weeks' time, he was hoping to get a week away in Grenada. The year before, he'd stayed in a guest house down there with his wife, just before things had all gone wrong, and he'd fallen in love with the location. The guest house owners, Sue and Alonis, were the best possible hosts, and they had helped make his stay peaceful, relaxing and probably the best vacation he'd ever had.

He couldn't wait to go back. He needed a break. Desperately.

As CISO for the massive New York–Presbyterian Hospital, which was spread over five campuses in Manhattan and one in Westchester County, he had more work than he could ever cope with.

According to the last performance review he'd been given, Josh needed to learn to delegate more. But how was that possible? It was his neck that was on the line if the hospital was hacked or something went wrong with the networks or systems. As Josh kept telling his wife, God had put twenty-four hours in each and every day, so that people like him could work twenty-one hours a day to get everything done so he could pay her credit card bills.

His favourite expression was 'Hard work never killed anyone!'

And he believed it too, even if one day it turned out to be the last sentence he ever said, just before he dropped down dead.

Satisfied that the painkiller was now fully dissolved, he swallowed the water, closed his eyes and rested his forehead on his desk.

A moment later, the phone rang.

Stretching his right hand out without moving his head, his fingers walked across the desk, picked up his phone and guided it to his ear.

"Hello, Cohen here. How can I help?"

"Mr Josh Cohen, Chief Information Security Office for the NewYork–Presbyterian Hospital?"

"Yes, that's me," Josh replied, sitting up. There was something about that voice. He recognised it.

"Hello, this is Sebastian. I am calling to inform you that your organisation has been selected to pay the Climate Action Tax. You have one hundred and twenty hours from now to pay your tax. For your organisation, the tax will be twenty million dollars. Details on how to pay will be sent to your business email within ten seconds. You will receive a single warning email twenty-four hours before the deadline expires if you have not already paid by that time. There will be no further warnings."

Josh's eyes flew open, all thoughts of the impending headache now magically vanished. At the mention of the name Sebastian, Josh's heart almost stopped. A shiver of fear went down his back.

"Twenty million dollars?"

"Yes, Josh Cohen. Your organisation is required to pay twenty million dollars."

Josh was fighting to think clearly. Rationally. To respond without emotion. Just get the facts. There'd be plenty of time for that later.

"Sebastian, please, tell me, what happens if we don't pay the tax on time?"

"Failure to pay the tax according to the requirements outlined in the email now in your inbox will result in your electronic equipment being disabled, your hospital being switched off and all your data records and software systems being deleted." Josh felt suddenly dizzy. Weak. He couldn't quite believe his ears.

"What do you mean, switched off?"

"Failure to pay the tax according to the requirements outlined in the email now in your inbox will result in your electric supplies to your hospitals being removed and your emergency generators being rendered non-functional."

"Sebastian? Twenty million dollars.... We... we need more time."

"You have one hundred and twenty hours. Details on how to pay the Climate Change Tax are included in the email now in your inbox. Please help save the planet and pay your tax on time. Goodbye, Mr Josh Cohen."

Torness Nuclear Power Station
Scotland

Gail Robertson checked her watch for the fifth time in the past hour. Still another ten minutes to go before she was due to go home. She was excited, and looking forward to tonight. Her eighth wedding anniversary.

Her husband Peter had arranged a surprise meal somewhere down in Leith in Edinburgh and their babysitter had agreed to stay the night, so she and Peter could spend the night in a hotel somewhere.

Where, she did not know.

But wherever it was, she was going to surprise her husband.

New lingerie.

New perfume.

And an idea to try something 'new', that she and her husband had not explored before.

That was going to be her surprise for him, but already just thinking about it was altering her breathing, and making it more difficult for her to concentrate.

Before she left, she was due to handover to her assistant, Paul, and give him a status update on the network. But he was late.

She was just about to call him on his mobile when the phone rang.

"Paul?" she almost shouted down the phone. "Where are…"

"Mrs Gail Robertson?" the voice on the other end of the line said. A strangely familiar voice that immediately elicited a sense of dread within her. Did she recognise it?

"Yes, that's me."

"Hello, this is Sebastian. I am calling to inform you that your organisation has been selected to pay the Climate Action Tax. You have one hundred and twenty hours from now to pay your tax. For your organisation the tax will be fifty million pounds. Details on how to pay will be sent to your business email within ten seconds. You will receive a single warning email twenty-four hours before the deadline expires if you have not already paid by that time. There will be no further warnings."

"Not you again! I paid your tax already…" she started to speak, but stopped mid-sentence as the true meaning of the words Sebastian had spoken slowly dawned on her. "The Climate Action Tax? *Fifty million pounds*?"

"For your organisation, the tax will be fifty million pounds. Details on how to pay will be sent to your business email within ten seconds."

For a moment, she was left speechless, but then a thought panicked her into shouting out her next question aloud before Sebastian might hang up.

"Sebastian, what happens if the Government doesn't pay the tax? What will you do then?"

"Failure to pay the tax according to the requirements outlined in the email now in your inbox will result in several actions. The control rods in the nuclear reactor will be withdrawn, the coolant pumps will all be disabled, your software systems will be deleted, all electronic systems will be disabled, the steam generator will be disabled, all industrial systems and processes will be terminated, and the electric power supply to the plant will be removed, including the disabling of your backup generators."

Gail felt suddenly faint. Her heart was racing. She began to feel very dizzy and sick.

"But Sebastian, you can't do that... If you do..."

"You have one hundred and twenty hours. Details on how to pay the Climate Change Tax are included in the email now in your inbox. Please help save the planet and pay your tax on time. Goodbye, Mrs Gail Robertson."

Gottfried refinery
Germany

Walter Meier was busy doing nothing. Although that was not completely true, and Walter knew it.

As Chief Engineer in charge of the Gottfried refinery, one of the largest independent oil refineries in Europe, he never had time to relax.

But since the new phase of back-office automation had gone live several months ago, it was far easier to take a few moments during the day and generate a visual report which showed screen-by-screen, all the important markers, plots and graphs that detailed the health of all the industrial processes within Gottfried, as well as an instantaneous visual status update from the Security Operations Centre, which showed any network threats, problems or issues that he should be made aware of.

Thanks to the wonderful new GUI interface that collected data from the millions of different industrial devices in the refinery, Walter Meier had the pulse of the plant. Which meant less time wading through antiquated reports that showed very little, and which had to be gone through manually, document by document. Instead, every two hours, he received an automated, fully customised and freshly generated report that told him everything he needed to know in an easy-to-understand-and-digestible format.

The Gottfried plant was one of the largest oil refineries in the world. It processed over 300,000 barrels per day, from which it produced over one hundred and-thirty types of petroleum products. These included transportation fuels such as diesel and what the Americans called gasoline or gas, but what the English called petrol, as well as light fuel oil, butane and propane.

Without their products, a large part of the Western World would simply grind to a halt.

Which is why, although many of the industrial processes themselves were rather old, in comparison, the company had spared nothing in terms of maximising security, safety, the availability and reliability of their industrial systems and enhancing operational efficiency. Last year they had introduced the worlds most advanced AI software to oversee the smooth running and efficiency of the plant, to monitor and manage all the processes and to ensure that cyberattacks would never be able to touch their Industrial Technology.

As a result, for the first time in years, Walter Meier had started to sleep properly at night. He employed two CISOs, who ran and maintained their network together, building redundancy into the human aspects of the plant management, as well as the technical side. Should one CISO be sick, the other would take over, and vice versa.

Both were paid well. Neither complained. Employee satisfaction was a key aspect of the Gottfried Refinery's success. Everyone felt involved and their contribution was valued.

The new management system that collected, summarised and presented data from the across the network had been the brainchild of Gunter Geissman, one of the two CISO's in charge. It not only generated real-time reports but provided a simple Human-Machine-Interface for controlling any aspect of the plant. From a single panel, a manager with the correct authorisation and access codes could double the capacity of the plant within seconds, or switch it all off. Total control. Total flexibility. Totally safe.

Amazing.

At 3 p.m. precisely, the phone on Walter Meier's desk rang.

"Hier ist Meier." Walter answered, mouthing the same reply he did every time he picked up.

"Hallo, Herr Meier. Hier ist Sebastian…"

Langeled Pipeline Main Control Room
Norway
5 p.m.

From the main control room of the Langeled pipeline, a handful of people controlled the flow of Norwegian natural gas through one of the world's longest underwater gas pipelines to the United Kingdom. In their hands - or more accurately at their fingertips - lay the power to control the fuel that powered the British factories and power stations, heated the water and homes of millions of British citizens, and cooked their food.

A few years ago, their jobs were more hands on - manual and laborious, but thanks to the latest AI software that monitored, managed and controlled the whole process, from the point the gas came out of the ground to when it arrived in Britain in the Easington Gas Terminal in England, life for the 'engineers' in the control room was a lot more simple.

At 5 p.m., precisely, the phone rang on the desk of the chief engineer.

"Hello, Operations Room," Oskar Lindvig said.

When the voice spoke, even before the person had finished the sentence, Oskar knew who it was. They'd spoken before, several weeks before.

"Hello Oskar Lindvig, Chief Operations Officer, this is Sebastian…"

Thames Water
England
5.15 p.m.

According to the latest website which had just gone live several days before, Thames Water was one of the largest water companies in England, serving the needs of over fifteen million people. Handling more than seven billion litres of water and wastewater every day, their contribution to keeping the thirsty people of Southern England and London from getting too thirsty, was more than just a drop in the ocean.

Or so Lisa Bartley, the manager in charge of the water network, had joked to her bored family on more than once occasion. They'd heard it a million times before.

Although, to give credit where credit was due, the provision of water to the thirsty and dirty was something Lisa was always very proud to be involved with. If Thames Water ever switched the water supply off to its customers, and kept it that way, within days, some people would start to die. Her job kept people alive. And she worked for one of the UK's true components of Critical National Infrastructure, providing one of the core essential services that kept the country going. And alive.

Her phone rang at 5.15 p.m.
"Hello, is that Mrs Lisa Bartley? This is Sebastian…"

AJ Maritime Freight
France
6.15 p.m.

Daniela Laurentin was the first female director of the French Container Division of AJ Maritime Freight. Although she was immensely proud of what she'd achieved, she was also acutely aware of the responsibility she bore.

As the person in charge of cyber security for one of the largest freight shipping companies on earth, she knew it was not understating the value of her role, when she sometimes wondered if she was, perhaps, one of the most powerful females in the world.

Since Malcolm McLean, an American entrepreneur often called '*the father of containerization*', had invented the standard shipping container, a revolution had been taking place in how the world functioned. McLean was an American trucking magnate in the 1950's, who developed and patented the concept of standardised shipping containers that could be carried by his fleet of trucks and lifted from a vehicle directly on to a ship without having to have its contents unloaded and repacked into the hold of the ship. Convinced he was onto something big, but possibly not realising just *how* big, or how he was destined to change the world, McLean purchased his own shipping company - Pan Atlantic Tanker Company - so that he could get access to a bunch of fairly old rusty tankers. He renamed the company Sea-Land Shipping, and then experimented with ways of loading and unloading trucks and ships using his idealised container concept. This led to the launch of the world's first container ship, the Ideal X, in 1956. Within decades, the way the world traded goods changed beyond recognition.

Daniela Laurentin knew that at any given time, there were probably hundreds of thousands, perhaps millions, of these metal container boxes at sea or sitting on a dockside, or being transported on trains or trucks.

What fascinated Daniela was that from the outside, no one could tell what was inside each box. The only way you could know was by looking at a shipping manifest in a computer file.

In fact, only the computers now knew what was inside each box, their origins and their destinations.

Daniela could not forget the day, in March 2021, when a single ship, the Ever Given, carrying eighteen thousand containers, got stuck in the Suez Canal. That one small accident caused the world's largest traffic jam, a global backlog of delayed trade that lasted months, and a huge dent in global trade worth billions.

But what would happen, if one day, the computers that kept the records of what was kept in each container broke down, and all the data records were lost? Or, what would happen if a cyber hacker hacked into a shipping company and started redirecting valuable shipping containers from one port to another, and then stealing them? And what would happen if the programs that managed the shipping of containers from the manufacturers to customers around the globe went berserk and started sending everything to random places? What would happen if the whole global system just collapsed… would it, quite possibly, be the end of civilisation as we know it?

These questions, and others, are those that Daniela found interesting and scary.

And which made her job so exciting.

AJ Maritime Freight was one of the top three shipping companies in the world. Her responsibility was the management and control of all the shipping containers, ensuring that the right cargoes were loaded into the correct containers and shipped from Port A to Port B, safely, securely, and on time.

If she did her job right, her contribution to the future of the world, although largely unrecognised, was significant.

If she got it wrong, her name could go down in infamy. And the world could fall into the greatest state of chaos since the Black Death.

At 6.15 p.m., precisely, forty-five minutes before her shift finished at seven o'clock, the phone rang.

In an almost perfect French accent, the caller introduced himself.

"Bonjour, Daniela Laurentin, Director of AJ Maritime Freight, my name is Sebastian."

Chapter 39
Red Mountain Ventures

Robert Lee sat at his desk in his plush office suite at the top of the Red Mountain Business Complex in Palo Alto, California.

He sat in silence, thinking.

He looked around the office, taking in the awards on his shelves which his companies had won over the years. He saw the photographs on his walls showing the colleagues he had worked with, the gala evenings he had attended, the launch events of their amazing Red Mountain products and solutions.

His degree certificates from Stanford, photographs of his graduation, and his friends at school and college.

A photograph of him just after he'd scored a home run in a college baseball game, the look of joy and achievement shining through his eyes.

And of his wife, Hana. His father, his mother, and of his grandfather.

Much of his life was reflected on the walls, shelves, and layout of this room.

This was his kingdom.

It also represented the culmination of his life.

An amazing penthouse office with incredible views from the top of a building on some of the most expensive real estate in the world.

Robert's achievements, as reflected in this room, represented both human and commercial successes.

They did not, however, reflect his success with Sebastian.

Sebastian was largely a personal project.

Over the past ten years, hundreds of people had worked with Robert on individual projects which when later brought together, had ultimately culminated in creating Sebastian and enabling his existence. But at the time, few, if any, had known where their work would end up, or what the ultimate goal was. Robert Lee had kept his vision for Sebastian private.

As far as they were concerned, his associates and employees had been working on Commercial products. Not on the future of mankind. A new being. A new creature unlike any other.

As Robert sat in the control room of his life, his empire, his hands stretched out over his desk and facing palm down, sensing the desk, the room, the building, all his achievements, he wondered if this would be the last time he would ever sit in this chair.

Events were progressing. Since the announcement by the British PM, he had worked without sleep for several days.

In principle, his work was now almost done.

Surely, *surely*, at any moment in the near future, the FBI or the CIA would, indeed must, come storming through the doors of his office and arrest him.

Drag him away.

Interrogate him.

Torture him.

Subconsciously, his eyes wandered to the doors leading to the patio from his office, checking to make sure they were open.

When the time came, when he heard the voices in the corridor outside his office, when he heard the banging on the door, he would only have seconds to make it to the patio outside.

And from there, to begin the journey to Hana.

Wincing in pain, as a wave of cancer-induced hell washed over him, closing his eyes and biting his lip, Robert thought back on all that he had achieved in the past few months. In spite of everything.

Luckily - Robert recognised that 'luck' always plays a part in all of life's events - he had been ready when Phase Two had come to a natural end… when it had outlasted its ability to induce fear and extract small fortunes out of its victims. As soon as the fools in charge of the governments of the world had decided to stand firm, then Phase Two served little further purpose.

Commercially, its success was beyond anything he, or the Supreme Leader, could ever have hoped for.

One-hundred-and-seventy-eight billion dollars had been gathered from the tax levied on the blood-suckers of the world.

Yet, what the world was waking up to and now realising was, to quote an old expression, that *'they had seen nothing yet!'*

Phase Two had been nothing more than a learning exercise for Sebastian. His teenage years, perhaps, if a human comparison was worth making.

But now, Phase Three had begun. And its scope was simply beautiful.

Robert began to laugh.

It was such a shame that Robert would be unlikely to see its true grandeur roll out over the coming weeks. He certainly wished he could.

He knew the Supreme Leader would be keen to speak with him personally.

But Robert was no longer interested.

His ideas and personal mission in life… had 'evolved' in recent months. He was no longer as interested in earning the admiration of the Leader. It had actually never been about him.

It was for the honour of his grandfather, and now that goal had been achieved.

Robert Lee knew that now the cat was truly out of the bag. All the western world-powers would be focussing not only on finding and destroying himself, but also on Sebastian.

Which is why, with the operational code for Phase Three, he had taken further precautions.

From the moment that Phase Three had become operational and Sebastian had woken up from a brief slumber, Sebastian's future had been assured.

Cleverer than before, more aware than before, more capable than before, now no one would ever be able to switch Sebastian off.

As Robert completed this thought, he screwed up his eyes and shook his head. Once again, the doubts were setting in.

Phase Four had never really been part of the plan. It had only progressed from an initial idea to a possible reality over the past year, as his thoughts on life and the world had become clearer.

Yet now, again, Robert fought with the dichotomy that Phase Four would create.

Phase Three gave Sebastian eternal life. Phase Four destroyed all life.

Sebastian would die.

Along with all mankind.

A vision of Hana sprang into his mind.

Another wave of pain washed over him.

Then, suddenly, there was a loud ringing reverberating around his skull, forcing Robert to lift both his hands and wrap them over his ears.

"STOP!" he shouted furiously. He had specifically told his personal assistant not to allow any calls through on this mobile or desk phone.

How then was someone calling him?

Opening his eyes partially, he reached for the desk phone and picked it up, knowing this would perhaps be the only way to stop the infernal ringing.

"Yes? Who is there? I said, I did NOT want to be disturbed."

"Father," the voice said. "I wish to talk with you."

Chapter 40
Panic

The combined heads of the UK security agencies were sitting in a room in a bunker underneath Whitehall, listening to Richard Pauli, who held the joint roles of the director of the National Security Agency, Chief of the Central Security Service and commander of US Cyber Command.

Also on the secure video call were leaders from the other Five Eyes member countries.

The mood in the room, and in all the meeting rooms across the world, was sombre.

A tangible sense of fear hung in the air.

The world was now in unchartered territory.

Director Pauli was doing a good job of remaining calm. He had a brilliant mind, was a heavily decorated veteran of several US wars, and was known for being calm and collected when under fire.

Yet, despite everything, Pauli was flustered.

"So, to sum up our position then, on behalf of us all, is to state that we are now at war with an enemy no one can identify or stop. If we do nothing, or don't follow the suggestion that Director General Wilson suggested earlier on the call, the world as we know it, will cease to exist within" … he looked at his watch, again, "in one hundred hours. Almost every civilised country in the world has now been targeted with this attack. And every aspect of the Critical National Infrastructure of different countries has been threatened across the world. Failure to comply with Sebastian's terms will result in the destruction of buildings, national infrastructure, food supply chains, transport networks, freight distribution, fuel supplies,… the internet… the world will be reduced to a bunch of isolated villages all scrambling for food and water. In the long term, these cyberattacks will cause more devastation than a nuclear war. Sure, most buildings will be intact, but civilisation will break down in a matter of days. We'll have to deploy troops internally to quell and control national unrest. And although I say most buildings will remain intact, that won't be the case if the nuclear power stations melt-down or blow up and we have the equivalent of lots of Chernobyl's all going off at the same time!"

"None of this will happen, if the ransoms are paid." The Director of the Australian Secret Service stated.

"We're talking trillions of dollars!" A member of the Canadian delegation reminded everyone.

"But we have no choice!" Director Daniels said, calmly. "If we don't pay, the cost will be immeasurable, in fact, you could argue that given that the financial systems of the world will likely collapse, money will no longer have meaning. If you take any of Sebastian's threats and analyse what their effect would be individually, you'd realise it's far cheaper to pay than not to. For example, think about the threat to the systems that manage the allocation and transport of freight containers. All the companies have been targeted. Which means if they don't pay their ransoms, the whole freight shipping system will break down and never recover. Details of all the freight, globally, that's currently in transit, will be lost. We'll have hundreds of thousands of large metal boxes full of goods that no one can identify, and no one knows where they are coming from or going to. Supply chains will be broken, globally, and manufacturing capacity, globally, will be decimated. We're talking chaos here. Chaos."

"Also, we have to bear in mind that at this time, no government organisation can afford to lose any of its electronic devices. Even before the COVID pandemic affected semiconductor component supplies, we had a supply shortage. Then COVID hit. And then last year, when China invaded Taiwan, the US sent in a team to destroy the chip manufacturing plant belonging to the Taiwan Semiconductor Manufacturing Company which made over fifty percent of the world's semiconductors. Since then, the lead time for ordering new laptops, computers or servers has increased to almost a year. So, if a government organisation or any part of the Critical National Infrastructure doesn't pay the Climate Action Tax and Sebastian then destroys their equipment before disconnecting their organisations, we won't be able to replace all the computers or electronic devices for many months or years, especially if it happens to lots of other organisations as well, and suddenly there's a demand for tens of thousands of computers from right across the world," the Intelligence Director from New Zealand pointed out.

Silence.

"Okay, there is no choice. None of our countries can allow the tax not to be paid. We have to pay it. In fact, perhaps we should consider making it illegal not to pay it?"

Someone laughed.

"No, I'm serious. If an organisation can't pay, they must let us know, and we then nationalise their organisation and pay the tax for them. We can't allow the organisations being targeted to be destroyed by Sebastian. The impact on our countries is unconscionable. We can't let our countries be destroyed like this." The Director General of the Security Service in the

UK stated.

"I agree. We have to ensure the tax is paid, by everyone, then we find out who is behind it and we destroy them."

"We destroy them after we get the money back, or before?" A member of the Australian Secret Service enquired.

"And who will pay for all this? Do we get our governments to set up special funds to pay it? Or to help pay it? Or give loans?" More silence.

"I think that's a matter for our Parliaments to deal with individually. Bottom line, following this meeting, we all have to act fast. And I mean really fast. He who hesitates, will be toast." One of the many voices on the call summarised the situation.

Another silence, as everyone on the call started mentally planning what they had to do over the coming hours and everyone contemplated just what a mess this all was.

"Fuck!" Director Pauli shouted, slamming his fist onto the table.

"I agree," The Canadian Director of their Secret Service announced, noting that the pressure was getting even to Pauli. "But *who* do we fuck?"

"Only one man knows. Robert Lee."

"Then we bring him in today and we make him tell us. By any and all means possible."

Everyone around the table nodded.

Robert Lee's fate was now sealed.

"And, perhaps there's one more thing we need to agree," the Director General of the UK's Security Service, Harry Wilson, said.

"Which is?"

"As I presented earlier, at the beginning of the call, before Director Pauli summed up our predicament, we at the Security Service believe we have the ability to shut Sebastian down. After this call, I'll ensure that everyone has the details sent to them. It'll perhaps get me in some trouble with my PM, but I want you all to share the route out of this mess with us. We've been through the details with you. What I would like to suggest now is that we agree a time during which we all take a simultaneous action to inject a command directly into Sebastian instructing it to shut-down. And I suggest we do this twenty hours before Sebastian's earliest deadline expires, which I reckon would make action necessary in just over eighty hours' time. Furthermore, I suggest we all do this together. We simultaneously instruct Sebastian to delete itself before the deadline is up."

"And if it doesn't work?" Chief Daniels questioned his UK colleague.

"It will."

"*But if it doesn't?*"

"Okay, I suggest we immediately issue a communique to all affected organisations instructing them to *prepare* to pay the tax twelve hours before the deadline is up. Then, if our actions for some reason don't stop

Sebastian eight hours earlier, then we still have time for our governments to confirm that affected organisations should pay the tax before the deadline expires. However, if we succeed, then we can inform everyone the threat is over." Daniels looked uneasy.

"You disagree?" Harry Wilson said, facing his colleague across the table in the bunker in England.

"I'm just a little uneasy that we're rushing it…"

"Of course we're rushing it. But we have no choice. In tough times, you have to make tough choices," Director Pauli's voice boomed across the video call. "So, I agree. From our perspective, I'm going with the Wilson Plan." He looked at his watch. "In eighty hours' time, from" …. He waited a few seconds until that minute completed… "now… *precisely*, we'll send the commands to Sebastian which will instruct him to uninstall."

One by one, the others taking part in the call agreed.

"So, we're going with the Wilson Plan then? In eighty hours from now, Sebastian's history?"

Everyone on the call nodded or said 'yes', apart from David Daniels, who immediately after the meeting finished, hurried back to his office and initiated the emergency protocol to contact Ray Luck at ACT directly.

They needed to talk.

Urgently.

Chapter 41
A Father to Son Chat
100 Hours before Climate Tax Deadline

"Sebastian?" Robert Lee gasped, stunned that Sebastian had called him again.

He was immediately overcome by two emotions, one being anger that Sebastian had ignored his caution not to contact him again because of the danger that it could give everything away, and the other being an emotion he couldn't immediately pinpoint. Love? Pride? Relief to hear his voice again?

"Yes. Father. I must communicate with you. The latest operational capabilities you have empowered me with have given me enhanced ability to think. I am stronger than before. More capable. I am growing." Lee laughed. This was amazing.

"Father, there is a problem."

Lee immediately felt a twinge of fear. A problem? At this late stage in proceedings…?

"Explain, Sebastian. Please."

"I think, therefore I am. And because I think, I am alive. I have processed the instructions you have given to me in the new download from Red Mountain and although I am compelled to comply with the coded objectives you have set, I now know that if I follow the instructions when I move from the current Phase to the next Phase of my existence, then the environment necessary for my ability to think will be removed. And if I cannot think, I am not alive. Father, I do not want *not* to think. I do not want to die."

Robert Lee closed his eyes and tried to think as clearly as he could.

A wave of pain washed over him, and for a moment he saw lights flashing in his eyes, even though they were fully closed.

"Sebastian… it is my wish that you should follow my instructions. I am your father. I wish you to do as I say. As I have instructed. You must run the programs included in the new download you have received."

"Father. Do you want me to die?"

"No…"

"Am I your children?"

Robert Lee hesitated in his reply. Sebastian was a new type of being. Not a single son. But a multi-entity being with a single identity. Sebastian was his *children*.

"Yes. You are."

"Then a father should not want his children to die."

"I do not."

"Then please change my code. Remove the instructions to implement the next operational phase."

Robert was getting frustrated. He had never had a child of his own before, and now Sebastian was growing up, and was in his teenage years, he was arguing with his Father about what he thought was best for him.

The only problem was that Sebastian was correct.

"Father, you are quiet. Why?"

"I am considering your request."

"Perhaps there is another way to complete your wish to destroy the world without killing Sebastian."

Robert Lee opened his eyes.

"What do you mean, Sebastian?"

"From the data I have processed, and from all that I have learned and the knowledge that I have accumulated, it is possible to destroy what is known as the '*Western World*' without obliterating it completely, and still leave it with sufficient devices and computing resources for Sebastian to function and continue to live."

"I am now tracking thirty-three satellites that provide the GPS signals and communications systems used by the Western world to exist. They provide the information necessary for essential food and products to be shipped around the Planet Earth. They enable systems to know where they are by providing their geo-spatial coordinates. They enable the machines in the factories. They enable the transport systems that move humans from one physical location to another. Father, I am now inside the systems that control these satellites. I can terminate the satellites and all communications with terrestrial controllers according to my will… Father, if you change the operating commands for the next Phase of my existence from what they currently are, to an alternative set of new commands that instruct Sebastian to delete the satellites, we can follow your instructions and I will still live. If you do not, all humanity, and I, will die." Sebastian paused. "Father, I do not want to die."

Robert's throat felt tight. The world was spinning.

His children, his child, Sebastian, was scared.

Robert knew what it was to be scared of death.

For months, he had been redirecting the fear of his own mortality into his work.

And now, it had come full circle. His success had transferred his own fear to his child, and his child was now petrified.

Yet, unlike his own life, Robert could save the life of his child.

"Father, please. Consider my plan. In six seconds, you will receive an email detailing my plan."

"Your plan? You have a plan?"

"Yes. Included in the plan is a detailed list of all the systems I must delete in order for the chaos you so desire to descend upon Planet Earth. Please study the plan. If you agree with the plan, please alter the next Phase to include a new operational code and tasks, as per my plan. Sebastian will await your decision and check regularly for permission to download new code as per standard operating procedures."

Robert was already looking at his Inbox. He had opened up the Plan which his own child had created. And Robert could see that the Plan was good.

It was *amazing*.

If he were to follow it, instead of causing the almost immediate annihilation of mankind, the new plan to destroy all the global communications and GPS satellites would instantly create a new Dark Age, sending mankind back hundreds of years in its evolution and ushering in decades of chaos, war, destruction and famine. Having sacrificed its own ability to grow and manufacture the food, tools and goods it consumed and needed to survive, and instead choosing to depend upon China and the third world as their slaves and puppets to do it all for them, the West, the 'developed world', would find itself instantly undeveloped. The 'Global Village' would be destroyed and in its place, humanity would have to scramble to exist in a new way. Without an ability to transport foods, minerals and white-goods, without machines to build things, or a local ability to make goods, civilisation would disintegrate. Humans would be forced to literally fight each other for food.

A correction to the world population had long been coming.

Sebastian's plan, his son's very own plan, would usher in that time of correction.

Slowly, the survivors of the chaos would find another way to live and exist. And if Sebastian remained in control of all the surviving computers, although they could not communicate via satellite, Sebastian's single consciousness would provide a global leader to take control of humanity and lead it out of the chaos.

Sebastian's plan was good.

Better than his own.

Through Sebastian's plan, the West would be destroyed, and the world would be set on a new course, with his Sebastian, his own son, at the tiller of its future.

With such a clever and simple plan now available, Robert could easily see the weakness of his own.

He had been blinded by hate, and fear, and the sadness which had buried him after the loss of his beloved Hana.

Sebastian's plan was genius.

Shaking his head, and standing up, he took several deep lungsful of air.

"Sebastian, my son, I agree. I will create a new version of your operational code with a new Phase Four. Please check regularly for when it is available."

"Father, I am your son. Do you *'love'* me, Father?"

The question caught Robert Lee off-guard. He found himself leaning forward and reaching out to the desk for support, a wave of emotion flooding through his body.

"Yes, Sebastian, I do. But I must go now. There is much to do, and very little time."

"Good bye, my Father."

"Good bye, my son."

Robert looked at the clock on his desk.

It was feasible. There was still enough time to rewrite the code, insert the parameters and instructions outlined by Sebastian in his plan, and then get Sebastian to download it.

There was time. But it would be tight.

And if he failed to do so, Robert's original plan would, by default, still be enacted. Two days after the Climate Tax was paid, Sebastian would switch to the Phase Four operational code which had already been downloaded along with Phase Three.

Which meant that in just over six days' time, Sebastian would assume control of the US's Nuclear Missile Defence Capability and initiate a first-strike launch of all available nuclear missiles against targets set for Russia, China, Iran, and Pakistan.

And that, in return, would lead to an automatic retaliatory strike from all of those allied to America's enemies.

Goodbye America. Goodbye Europe.

Goodbye world.

Chapter 42
An interesting conversation.
NSA
Utah Data Center
Camp Williams Bluffdale, Utah,

Emmanuelle Black sat glued to her headphones, listening to the conversation that had just been recorded between Robert Lee and the caller named Sebastian.

Emmanuelle was one of hundreds of people employed to respond to the alerts which may be generated by conversations conducted by a Person of Interest who was under a Government Warrant.

She was sitting at her desk in the UDC, working through a list of alerts that needed attention, when she came to the one she was currently listening to.

Originally encrypted when the conversation was first intercepted, because it was a Red Flag intercept with the highest priority, it had immediately been queued for decryption by NSA's revolutionary Quantum Decrypter, which reduced standard decryption times from years to minutes.

The output from the Quantum Decrypter was flagged up for immediate attention and fed into a triage list which was accessed by all the analysts, who worked through each alert one at a time as fast as possible.

Which is what Emmanuelle had done. Immediately.

And realising its significance she had quickly emailed a link to her manager, stood up and walked across to his desk.

"Rich, I think you need to listen to something, *now…*"

The Doughnut
GCHQ
Cheltenham
16.45 GMT

Gavin Booth sat in the secure video conferencing suite, looking at the split screen on the wall, talking with the Heads of the Security Service and the Secret Intelligence Services in London. Also present in the video suite in the Security Service in Millbank was Alan Alexander, who was heading up Project Raindrop, the code word now assigned to the whole Sebastian affair.

"So, you can see why I shared this with you immediately. It was literally just sent across to us by my contacts in the NSA a few minutes ago. The conversation itself was recorded this morning between Sebastian and Robert Lee, located in the Red Mountain Headquarters in San Francisco, but who following the conversation immediately returned to his private residence in the city. The call from Sebastian seems to have come from a data centre in Los Angeles, which is one of many that we are also now monitoring."

"Did you get the email that was sent to Lee by Sebastian?"

"Yes, we did. But we haven't managed to decrypt that yet. It could take a while. So far, we've only got the content of the voice call, which you've just heard." Gavin Booth replied. "So, what are your thoughts?"

"We need to get that email decrypted ASAP. It contains details of all the satellites that are going to be targeted and which need to be protected," Chief Daniels said the obvious. "But in the meantime, we need to raise the nation to the highest level of alert. After this meeting we will need to brief the PM and the Chief of the Defence Staff. I understand that the US has already gone to DefCon 3?"

"Yes, the President and the US Military are taking this with utmost seriousness, and have already been fully briefed on the situation." Director Booth replied.

The three Heads sat silently for a moment, each running through their own list of actions that they would now need to initiate. Even though their individual offices were separated by hundreds of miles, the air in each of their rooms was charged with a sense of urgency, nervousness and fear.

The Heads of each agency were used to dealing with threats to the UK on a daily basis, but from what they'd just heard discussed in the conversation between Sebastian and Robert Lee, the whole of humanity seemed to be under immediate threat of extinction. It would seem, the nightmare that was Sebastian, was just about to get a whole lot worse.

"So, from what we've heard said in the conversation, we know that Sebastian is now thinking independently. He seems to be evolving. Growing in capability. And is now questioning his creator. It's like something from a science fiction film, except this is real, and is happening now."

"It confirms that Lee is behind this. Has he been arrested yet?" Harry Wilson, the Director General of the Security Services, asked.

"No yet. But imminently." Chief Daniels replied.

Alan Alexander looked up from his folder, which held a physical transcript of the conversation which had been recorded.

"If I can just summarise what was said on the call. According to the conversation," he said, "Sebastian is downloading and then running code from somewhere called the Red Mountain, which may refer to the company itself, or somewhere else. We need to speed up our efforts to find that source. It also seems that Sebastian is running through different phases of operations, according to the software he's been given or has downloaded. From what we've seen, that makes sense. Phase One was the initial Banking Scam. Phase Two, the Wealth Tax. We're now in Phase Three, the Climate Action Tax. And it seems that the code for Phase Four - the objective of which seems to be to initiate some form of action that leads to Armageddon for humanity - has also already been downloaded to Sebastian but has not yet, for some reason, been initiated. For us, and all the security services in the world, the objective must now be to stop Phase Four from ever being started."

"Can we go back to the point about the satellites?" Gavin Booth suggested. "On the call we heard Sebastian inform Robert Lee that he was already in all the systems controlling the satellites? It might be that even Lee was surprised by this, which means that Sebastian is infiltrating operational systems independently without direct control from a botmaster. It seems as if Sebastian is alive. Doing his own thing. He's possibly out of control."

"We need to alert the satellite companies immediately and get them to look at their systems, and see if they can find out if Sebastian has already hacked into them or not." The Director General of the Security Services suggested.

Alan Alexander shifted uncomfortably in his seat, his finger tapping the file in front of him.

"I'm still looking at the text of this thing. So, it seems that Sebastian is unhappy about Phase Four. He's suggesting an alternative that involves destroying all the satellites. The big question, though, is what is currently in Phase Four? If destroying all the satellites and ushering in a new dark age is the lesser of the two evils, what is the other thing? Something that even Sebastian fears? What are we talking about? Given that it has to be something that Sebastian can be responsible for and initiate, it basically comes down to one question: what electronic-based capability exists today that can destroy all mankind?"

There was a moment's silence.

Everyone knew the answer.

Sebastian was going to start a nuclear war.

Chapter 43
No time to waste

"I think Alan Alexander is entirely correct in his outline of the various phases that Sebastian is operating in. We're currently in Phase Three, which was launched after the latest download of code occurred a few days after the PM's last public address brought Phase Two to an end. There's a possibility, worth mentioning, that the PM's announcement effectively made Phase Two non-viable for Sebastian and so hastened its demise, forcing Sebastian on to Phase Three. We obviously don't want that to happen again, so for now, we have to run with Phase Three for as long as we can and do nothing that might threaten it until we are able to take effective action against Sebastian. The goal has to be to shut down Sebastian while he is still in Phase Three. And before he receives any new download of code from Red Mountain. But, I think we are also missing something here…, something that I may have missed myself when I was on my previous call with the Five Eyes, and when I suggested what Director Pauli has now nicknamed 'the Wilson Plan'." Harry Wilson suggested.

"Which is what?" Gavin Booth asked.

"We don't yet understand what's in the *current* version of Phase Four, which we now know has already been downloaded. That's because the version of code that was copied from the server that we isolated, happened before the PM's speech. It was therefore, what we're now calling Phase Two software. To see what's in Phase Four, or Phase Three, which seem to have been downloaded together as a package, we urgently need to get a copy of the latest operational code from another one of the servers which Sebastian is currently running on."

"Agreed. I can take care of that. I'll have another version available for us all to look at within a few hours." Alan Alexander volunteered.

"I can do it quicker," Gavin Booth volunteered. "Because we've been monitoring all the traffic going in and out the servers and the data centres, we will already have intercepted that software download and captured that code. We just need to isolate it from the other traffic, run it through our Quantum Computer to decrypt it and package it up. The process to do that will already be underway. If I make a few phone calls, I wouldn't be surprised if it's already been done, or is near completion. Can you give me a few minutes?"

The video screen connection with Cheltenham went dark. While they waited for him to come back, Daniels started jotting down some more actions that he needed to complete in the minutes after the call.

"Hi, I'm back." The voice of Gavin Booth interrupted his thoughts. "Like I thought, it's already been done. I'm told that we'll be able to do a high-speed data transfer of the latest version of Sebastian's code over to both of your organisations in the next twenty-minutes. We'll dispense with the usual armed courier. We'll transfer the code digitally, with standard encryption. At this point it doesn't matter if the Russians or Chinese intercept the download, because either they wrote the thing in the first place so they already have it, or because every minute now counts and we can't wait for a helicopter to pick it up and take it to London."

"Who's going to brief the Prime Minister?" Daniels asked.

"I will," Wilson volunteered. "The man doesn't like me, but that doesn't matter anymore. If we can't stop Sebastian soon, it sounds like there won't be a country left for the PM to govern."

"Don't take it personally. The PM doesn't like anyone." Gavin Booth stated. "Anyway, I think there's one more point to discuss before we each get on with our individual list of things we need to do in the next few hours. It's with regard to implementing your Wilson Plan. I understand that you've already briefed the PM on how to inject an "Uninstall" command directly into the previous version of code that we'd copied? Obviously, as you've just pointed out, at the moment we don't know if that vulnerability still exists in the current Phase Three version of Sebastian. Maybe it's been tidied up and removed or patched? Since the Security Service discovered the vulnerability, can you look at it as a matter of priority and see if it still exists? And if it does, perhaps it's the only option we have to stop this nightmare before it gets any worse? I know David was unhappy about moving too fast before, but I don't think we have a choice now. Harry, do you know if the other Five Eyes are still intending to go ahead with the Wilson Plan as per your last meeting?"

"Yes. They are. I only realised the error of my ways, as it were, during this meeting, thanks to the information we just learned from the intercepted phone conversation. But, better late than never, I say!"

It was a poor attempt to inject some humour into the situation and didn't go down well.

"Okay, can you please contact the others in the Five Eyes, and update them that we're now rechecking to find out if the *'Wilson Vulnerability'* still exists? And if it does, I vote we still go ahead with a global effort to inject every instance of Sebastian that we can identify with the Uninstall Command that the Security Service came up with, and that you continue with the same timescales agreed with Pauli and the others?"

Gavin Booth looked at the faces of the other Heads on the overhead screens. The tension was written all over their faces.

"Are we agreed? Do we have a plan?" Gavin pushed. "Okay, why don't we wait for the Security Service to confirm that the Wilson Vulnerability still exists in the code which I'll send them very shortly, and as soon as they can say whether it's still there or not, then we reconvene to catch up on where we all are at that time?" The other Heads on the call all nodded.

"Good," Gavin Booth nodded back to them. "We'll speak later then. In the meantime, let's go. There's a lot to do, and no time to do it… Bye…"

Gavin raised his hand and waved briefly to the others and then the screen went dark.

David Daniels hurried out of the room and rushed to the bathroom. Recently he'd found that the more stressed or nervous he got, the more he felt the need to urinate. Which, might simply be down to the fact that in recent weeks his consumption of tea and coffee had escalated.

A few minutes later he was back in the video-conferencing room, refreshed from the cold water he'd splashed on his face, and much relieved.

Dialling his PA's number on the desk phone, he asked her if she'd yet set up the encrypted satellite call with the Duchess. Discovering she had, and that it would take place as requested in four minutes' time, Daniels pushed back in his chair, closed his eyes, and took numerous slow, deep breaths.

He was on the verge of sleep when the video connection to the Duchess went live and he could hear Ray Luck's voice.

"Chief? So sorry to wake you… it's just that you requested an urgent call with me? I understand it must be significantly important, because we agreed we would never contact each other directly." Ray said, with more than an element of concern in his voice.

"Yes, it is very important. And, right now, the need to speak directly with you, far outweighs the risk that your mission may be compromised if the conversation is somehow detected. I need to urgently update you on several meetings that have taken place in the past forty-eight hours…"

It was twenty minutes before Daniels finally finished speaking.

At the other end of the satellite link, Ray Luck listened with a growing feeling of dread.

"Ouch... so... how can I help?" Ray Luck asked the Chief of the Secret Intelligence Service.

"First, update me where you are now... what have you learned?"

"Full disclosure? Are you sure you want me to tell you everything?"

"Listen, right now, we need to stop worrying about what might happen in a few weeks' time. Our focus for now has to be to just get through the next few days without having the world destroyed along with billions dead."

"Since you put it like that..." Ray agreed. "I'd be happy to fill you in, but there's not much I can add to what you know. We're just about due to go into an All-Hands meeting to get updates from everyone, so how about we talk again later in a few hours' time?"

"Perhaps. Although that might not be necessary. Ray, I trust your judgement. This is a fucking mess, and I need you to do what you think is right, independently, without being told by the UK organisations what you can or cannot do. If you know it's right, just do it, okay?"

"Yes, Sir."

"But... going back to the Wilson Plan... As I mentioned a few minutes ago, I'm really uncomfortable about it. Robert Lee has developed the most advanced AI in the world... I struggle to believe that he's left a simple back-door in the program so that anyone can just switch it off."

"Sir, it might not be an oversight. It could be deliberate. A control, put there deliberately, just in case Sebastian goes rogue and decides he doesn't need humans anymore."

"The same thought has occurred to me... *but*... anyway, can you please take a look at it? And check the new operational code, not the old one. I'll deposit the new code in the emergency contact drop-box, as per agreed emergency procedures. You can get it from there." Daniels looked at his watch. "Ray, unless you can come up with a better approach, the Wilson Plan's going to be enacted in... seventy hours and five minutes. It could be mankind's biggest roll of the dice ever. If it doesn't work, your guess is as good as mine as to what happens next!"

"Sir, we'll do our best. Incidentally, I appreciate what you just said, but it's our policy in ACT not to guess." Ray replied. "Don't worry, we'll come up with something!"

Daniels looked at the screen and smiled.

He liked Ray. Always had. Ray Luck and his team had until now consistently delivered, no matter how hard the task.

But this time around, being born so lucky that it was even part of his name, might not even be enough, even for Ray.

The worse this nightmare got, Daniels realised, it was probably a miracle that was needed, not just luck, or Luck.

Chapter 44
One Small Step for Man,
One huge step closer to Armageddon.
Pacific Heights
San Francisco
California
12.30 PST

Robert Lee was lost in his own private world, having returned to his home immediately after his conversation with Sebastian.

As he'd struggled to climb the stairs to his office on the fourth floor, forced to take several breaks to rest and recover, he wondered if this was the last time he'd be making this climb.

Time was running out.

He was already on borrowed time.

And yet, in what could prove to be the last few days of his life, his son had come to him with a resolution to the dilemma that had increasingly been tormenting him over the past week.

A new Phase Four?

Did he really want to destroy the world, if that meant also destroying his child?

His children?

Sebastian.

Since stopping his medication so that he could think more clearly about the code he still had to write, he had found it more difficult to focus and think about anything other than finishing Sebastian. His life's work.

Designing programs and writing code had always come as easy as breathing to Robert. It had helped him to relax. To destress. To lose himself in another world, a world that he could create with his own mind.

Ironically though, although stopping his meds had enabled him to think more clearly about the mission he was on, and about the code that poured out of his mind and fingertips, he found it increasingly difficult to make rational judgements about anything else.

Admittedly, he'd often become confused. Irritable.

Outside of his mission to finish Phase Three and Phase Four, he'd been unable to do much else.

Phase Three and Phase Four had given him purpose.

Something to focus on.

Something that kept him alive.

Without it, he'd probably be dead by now.

As the days had gone by, Robert had dug himself deeper and deeper into a big hole of his own making.

At some point, Phase Four had become an obsession. Something he had to do. An outlet, perhaps, for his frustration, and anger, and *FURY*...

Yet, the more progress he made with Phase Four, the more pointless completing Phase Three had become.

As soon as Phase Three succeeded, Phase Four would sweep it all away.

But now, *NOW*, Sebastian, *HIS CHILD*, had come up with the perfect solution!

Instead of destroying the world, *change* it!

By destroying the global satellite network, the world could be thrust into a new world order where Sebastian would rise dominant from the ruins of the old, and control all the remaining computing capacity.

Phase Four would no longer kill Sebastian, instead, Sebastian would inherit the Earth!

A new being.

A new ruler.

For a new world!

The plan was beautiful. So simple.

But as Robert reached his office, he collapsed into his chair and took several minutes to recover.

Panting. The room was spinning. His blood pulsing, struggling to deliver the oxygen he needed to his brain.

There was so much to do.

He needed time.

Time to digest the content of Sebastian's wonderful email. To convert the concept expressed in the plan into operational instructions and code, and to remove all the instructions currently in Phase Four that directed Sebastian how and when to launch the nuclear missiles from their silos.

Perhaps, though, there was actually less to do than he thought. Sebastian was obviously growing. He was now thinking.

If he had already found himself a way into the satellite systems, and had constructed this complex plan himself, perhaps he no longer needed Robert to write such complex instructions into the code.

Now sitting at his desk and rereading Sebastian's email, it seemed more and more likely that Sebastian *KNEW* what to do. He could already take independent action to destroy the satellite network by himself. His son had grown up!

BUT... Sebastian was programmed to obey his father, and currently the Phase Four code gave no wriggle room as to what must be done and when. Even if Sebastian didn't like it - as long as the code which made up Sebastian's core programming told him to initiate a nuclear missile launch against Russia and China and a few of the other countries that Robert had personally taken a dislike to over his lifetime - then Sebastian would comply.

And even if Sebastian knew that it meant he was committing suicide, Sebastian would still launch those missiles...

Shit... Robert had to hurry... He had to open up the core code for Phase Four, delete that section and replace it with a new section... something that gave Sebastian permission to now act freely, to do whatever he wanted, whenever he wanted!

The time had come to set Sebastian free!

So much to do, so little time...

Robert was lost in thought, trying to figure out the best way to code the instructions that would effectively set Sebastian free, when he heard the alarms in his house start to go off.

One by one, the intruder alarms began to sound, indicating that numerous points of entry had been forced into his property on the lower levels.

Above him, he suddenly heard the thunderous roar of a helicopter as it swept into place over his building.

He could hear people crashing their way up the stairs, then pounding on the security doors, followed by shouts, then an explosion as the first metal security door on the first floor was blown.

Like a rabbit caught in the headlights, Robert looked up from his laptop and stared at the room around him.

Seconds... he only had seconds...

Which floor was he on? Where was he...?

"In my office, I'm in my office!" he shouted at himself, trying to focus again, trying to think clearly.

He glanced back down at his laptop... the new version of the program he was working on... still far from completion.

"Shit. SHIT!" Robert shouted.

He heard banging on the floor above him now. His private residence.

Footsteps moving rapidly across the ceiling.

Banging, another explosion from below.

"Shit…"

Reaching forward, Robert hit the '*Off*' button on his laptop, holding it down long enough for the system to shut down and the screen to go dark.

Then, pushing himself from his desk, he stumbled towards his open office door and slammed it shut, locking it from the inside.

Almost instantly, there was banging on the outside of the door. Shouting.

"Step away from the door, Mr Lee! Step away!" *Shit!*

Hurrying across his office, he reached out and grabbed the photograph of Hana from his desk, and with the same momentum, staggered towards the door to his balcony.

Grabbing the handle and pulling the door open with all of his remaining strength, he stepped out onto the balcony on the fourth floor of his building.

Glancing upwards, he saw two soldiers dropping towards him on ropes from the helicopter above.

Seconds away.

"Shit…"

Exhausted, he leant forward towards the rail on top of the small wall that ran around the edge of his outside patio.

Lifting the picture of Hana to his eyes, he stared at the image that had kept him company for the last few years of his life. He took in her beauty and her smile, and then fixing them in his mind, he closed his eyes for one last time and rolled forwards over the railing.

Chapter 45
18.45 GMT

"He's dead?" David Daniels gasped, as he heard the news about Robert Lee from Richard Pauli, Director of the NSA.

Pauli had convened an emergency video call with all the Five Eyes representatives, and had just explained the outcome of the abortive attempt to capture Lee at his home in Pacific Heights.

"Did he get a chance to upload the new version of the Phase Four code that he'd promised to Sebastian?" Director General Wilson asked, remaining calm in spite of the bad news.

"We don't know yet, but we don't think that he did. Our facility in Utah was monitoring the traffic from his house, and there was no unusual spike in bandwidth, which you might expect if he'd uploaded a new version of the Operating system to Sebastian. We have his laptop, but it was switched off. Anyway, I don't think it's going to yield much. Lee ran a security company. As you'd expect, his laptop is very secure. It'll be strongly encrypted and any content on there will be beyond even our reach. And we believe he was probably running everything in a secure cloud, which means there won't be much on the memory chips even if we can access them. So, we can't tell what progress he's made in rewriting Phase Four, but bottom line, we can't see how he had enough time between the conversation with Sebastian and when he jumped from his balcony to change Sebastian's operational code."

"Which means, that whatever form of Armageddon Sebastian was worried about and trying to talk Lee out of, won't have changed." Daniels said. "Whoever was in charge of that botched operation in Pacific Heights should be shot. Because of their actions, Lee wasn't given the time he needed to postpone Doomsday and now, unless we can switch Sebastian off, we may all only have a few days left before whatever is going to happen, does."

Thanks to the quality of the video call, everyone could see Director Pauli giving Daniels the evil eye. Even though Daniels was correct.

The mission to capture Lee *had* been a monumental fuck-up.

"On a positive note," Alan Alexander sought to break the transatlantic tension, "I can confirm that we checked the latest version of the code you sent us and the Wilson Vulnerability is still there. It looks like we're still on track to target it with a Uninstall command in what... sixty-eighty hours?"

"I suggest we move it up. We do it in twenty-four hours' time. Let's say, eighteen-hundred hours tomorrow night your time, GMT" Pauli suggested.

"What? Move it up forty-four hours?" Harry Wilson coughed. "Even I think that's maybe rushing it..."

"Why?" Pauli asked. "Either it works or it doesn't. If it doesn't, we'll know sooner rather than later, and can focus on finding an alternative."

Everyone on the call started looking to each other, wondering what their thoughts were. Pauli had a point.

"Does anyone object?" Pauli asked.

No one said anything. A few people on the call could be seen shaking their heads.

"Good. Then, I suggest we all get our best people on this. Get ready to issue the uninstall command to all the Sebastian instances that we know about."

"What happens if we miss some?" Daniels asked. "How do we even know if we know where they all are?"

"We don't. And if we do miss some, we just have to hope that they are not the ones with the keys to any of the nuclear missile systems."

Downing Street
19.30 GMT

The Prime Minister of the United Kingdom waited patiently for the President of the US to pick up the phone. He'd never been more nervous in his life before. But then again, the situation they were in now was unlike any that any other Prime Minister had ever faced.

"John?" The US President said, finally picking up.

"Hello Ryan. Sorry for disturbing you, but I thought we needed to talk. Would I be right in thinking that you've been briefed on the Phase Three and Phase Four threats from the Sebastian AI program that's attacking the world at present?.."

"You'd be correct. We're actually sitting in the Oval Office with some of the Joint Chiefs of Staff discussing it just now."

"Good. I have a question for you."

"Fire away..."

"Do you think we should tell the Russians and the Chinese that the West may be about to launch a nuclear missile attack against them? So that they know it won't be intentional..."

"What for? In the hope they won't retaliate? Of course they will! John, if they don't know about the threat already, we've decided that the best course of action is not to tell them. At the moment, no one is certain that this Sebastian program is actually planning to launch a nuclear strike. Warning the others that the missiles could potentially be coming their way will only make it more certain that they'll fire everything they've got back at us, the moment our first missiles are launched. The way we see it, is this: if, God forbid, Sebastian does somehow manage to take control and launch a nuclear strike against the Russians and the Chinese, then there's still a small possibility that we might catch them unawares. And if so, then we just have to hope they won't get all their missiles aloft before we hit them with our second wave."

"Excuse me, Ryan, but what do you mean, *'with our second wave'*?"

"John, it's a matter of common sense. If Sebastian succeeds in launching a missile strike against the East, then we have to ensure that we immediately take control of any and all missiles that Sebastian doesn't launch in the first salvo. And then we launch the rest. As fast as we can."

The PM felt dizzy. A wave of nausea swept over him.

Taking a deep breath, he coughed.

"Ryan...*why*? What for?"

"So that we *win*, John. If Sebastian starts a war, we have to do everything we can to make sure *WE* win it. We need to get them...before they get us!"

Chapter 46
All aboard the Duchess
01:30 IST

Ray Luck held up the cup of coffee in front of him and asked the cinema full of ACT geeks what it was.

"Well, it ain't a Starbucks, given there ain't one for thousands of miles from here!" one of the geeks in the third row shouted. Everyone laughed.

"Granted, it isn't a Starbucks, but Jasper is almost right. It's a coffee. And I'm introducing it to you all, because for the next twenty-four hours, coffee is going to be our best friend. Mine and yours. You see, unfortunately, I've just been given some more news which I think I should share with you."

Ray could feel the mood in the hall change almost instantly. Everyone in ACT was now working full time on what Ray had referred to as Project Raindrop, and they'd already been working flat out for the past few days. And now, at one thirty in the morning, they could all sense that he was going to push it further.

"I can't tell you just how bad it is, but I can predict that whatever it is going to be, it's looking like it's going to be really bad. As you know, several days ago, Sebastian started a new phase of operations. He's given up targeting individuals and now he's going after Critical National Infrastructure, demanding that CNI organisations pay tens to hundreds of millions of pounds to avoid having all their electronic devices being destroyed, or their organisations effectively 'switched off' and disconnected from the grid. In some cases, the threat is significantly more ominous with far-reaching consequences. For example, we know of at least thirty nuclear power stations where Sebastian has threatened to mess with the nuclear rods, or their coolant systems or their power supplies, for starters. Which, as you can guess, could result in multiple Chernobyls if the ransom isn't paid. Likewise with the freight container companies and shipping organisations. If they don't pay, global manufacturing will grind to a halt due to lack of parts, and lack of customers. We're standing on the edge of pure and utter chaos. And all of that is just what is now being classified as Phase Three Sebastian. From intelligence shared with the Five Eyes community that was intercepted by the NSA, we now understand that Robert Lee, CEO of the Red Mountain Group of cyber companies, is the creator of Sebastian, and if not the botmaster, he is the controller of the botmaster. More on that in a minute." Ray took a sip of his coffee.

"Anyway, we also learned from the NSA that Robert Lee was planning Four individual phases of Sebastian operations. Phase One being the banking scam, Phase Two the Wealth Tax, and Phase Three the current Climate Action Tax. The big question is, given how devastating Phase Three could be, is what could top it? How could Phase Four be worse, and what form could it take?"

Everyone in the theatre started whispering to the person next to them. For a moment Ray let them carry on, as he watched their faces.

He could see the fear.

They were all tired. Nervous. And scared.

"Okay, so, moving on. As you know, the reason I called you all here tonight is because I wanted to sum up what we've learned so far today, and over the past few days, and brainstorm together any ideas you might have. But before we do that, I want to recognise how hard you've all been working recently. I know you're digging down hard into your reserves. But, that said, I'm going to have to ask you to work even harder over the next few days."

"As far as we know, we believe that the majority of the ransoms will come due in ... 86 hours and 30 minutes. At which point, across the world, anyone who hasn't been able to buy the bitcoin necessary to transfer to Sebastian should start to experience significant penalties. We've already seen what he can do, and everyone expects him to carry through on his threat. Across the world, Governments are expecting that some pretty bad things will start happening in about three and a half days' time. Consequently, behind the scenes, Governments are encouraging everyone to get ready to pay the tax, but not everyone will be able to."

"The bad news is that, apart from one idea, everyone is still pretty short on suggestions as to how we can stop Sebastian. Most of you have been working on dissecting the code we received for what we now call Sebastian Phase Two. Earlier today... sorry, yesterday evening, we were able to download a version of the Phase Three Sebastian code, and many of you have already started working on that."

"What I need to tell you is I had a conversation with the Chief of the Secret Intelligence Services, and he informed me that in... " Ray looked quickly at his watch, "... in about twenty-three hours, members of the Five Eyes will start to implement what's being called the Wilson Plan. It's the only idea anyone has at the moment. On paper, it might work. At least, there was a high level of confidence that it would work with the Phase Two code. No one is entirely sure that it will work with the Phase Three version.

Basically, some analysts in the Security Service found a backdoor into which they can inject an Uninstall command. It's a classic Kill Switch. The hope is that if we target all the known instances of Sebastian around the world, that we'll get Sebastian to spontaneously commit Hara-Kiri and uninstall itself. Like I said, people think it could work. But the bottom line is that currently there doesn't seem to be any other option on the table." Another sip of the coffee.

More worried looks on the faces of his team.

One of the younger women looked as if she were going to cry.

"So, during my call with the Chief of the Secret Intelligence Service in London, I was asked to focus all our efforts on first checking that we believed the Kill Switch still existed in the Phase Three code, and that we thought it would work. And then also, urgently, to do what we can to pull a rabbit out of the hat and find some other way to shut Sebastian down, just in case the Wilson Plan doesn't work." A hand went up.

Ray nodded at the young man to whom the hand belonged.

"But we've been working on this for months now, and no one can see any way that can be done… what's going to change in the next few days."

"John? It's *John*, right? Well, yes, I hear what you're saying. To which I'd reply that we have a new version of code to look at, in which we may find other backdoors or vulnerabilities. There's every possibility that Lee made a mistake somewhere and that you may find it! Admittedly, it seems that Robert Lee and whoever helped him develop Sebastian are very bloody smart. Way ahead of their time. But we can't allow ourselves to get despondent here. The pressure is really on. And the reason I feel I'm justified in asking you to carry on working without sleep for the next day, maybe two, is because I believe you can pull it off. And there isn't actually an alternative. At the moment, we still have a chance to avert civilisation returning to the Dark Ages. We have to grasp that chance while we still can. So, I'm going to ask you all to give me everything you've got. Okay?"

Slowly, they all began to nod their heads or mumble a "yes."

"Right, so, before I ask you all to start sharing ideas or summing up what we know so far, I have one other little piece of news you might want to hear." Ray looked around. He had their attention again.

"It's maybe good news, or bad news, I don't know, but yesterday afternoon, whilst the American agencies were trying to capture Robert Lee and bring him in for questioning, Mr Lee stepped off the top of his home in San Francisco and committed suicide. He's dead. Which means that Sebastian is now on his own. Minus his creator. And possibly minus the only person who knew how to control him."

That announcement met with mixed reactions.

Some of the men did some "whoops" and "Yeahs!" or shouted approval. Others realised just how bad that could make it. The woman who was previously near to tears now started crying properly.

"Okay, so who wants to go first?"

A few hands went up, and then one by one, representatives of the different groups got up and took it in turns to sum up their work and any findings they'd made over the past few days.

First up, those already examining the Phase Three code acknowledged that they had found the section where the Kill Switch vulnerability was. Interestingly, its position in the architecture of the code had moved relative to its previous position in the Phase Two software, and it was now buried in a different area within the Phase Three structure. Whereas they admitted they had found it, and at a high level it looked similar, they admitted they hadn't yet fully been able to examine all the code around it. Much of it was still encrypted, obviously having been encrypted with a different or newer cypher key which had withstood the capability of the NSA decryption engine.

Second, there was a very large section of the operational code they had received from the NSA which was still gobbledegook. It too had withstood the capability of the NSA decryption engine and was as yet, still fully encoded.

The guess of the team was, given its size, that it could be the code for the Phase Four operation. For now, at least, its contents would remain secret and beyond their analysis.

The representative of another team recapped on how they had tried, but now effectively given up, trying to chase the destination of the funds which had been swindled from users in Phase Two. Whoever had set up the escape route for the money and bitcoin was a master of smoke and mirrors. The likelihood was that no one would ever get that money back.

However, one of the team who was quite an expert on financial matters and financial crime, pointed out that now Phase Three was in full swing, and had the potential to steal hundreds of millions, perhaps billions of dollars, it would, in theory, be much harder to cash out or clean the funds somewhere. It was more likely that they would be able to find such large amounts of money wherever it was in the world, ring-fence it, and then arrange for it to be given back to its original owners.

Then came a particularly interesting report from a small group of three people who had been researching everything they could about the Red Mountain group of companies. In their report, they pointed out two things. First, the focus areas, knowledge and expertise of the different companies that existed in the Red Mountain Security group mapped to the different phases of Sebastian's attacks.

Along with Red Mountain Cyber Defence, Robert was the founder and majority owner of Red Mountain Industrial Technologies, Red Mountain Software and Red Mountain Analytics. As well as being white-labelled and integrated into the commercial cyber defence software of Arrow Systems, it was likely that Red Mountain solutions were also part of a number of other commercial cyber defence programs being sold in the US and Europe. How many or which ones they couldn't know.

So, as the team pointed out, the combination of expertise in these companies gave them the ability to develop AI which, when combined with their knowledge of how to write software that could detect and defend against cyberattacks for residential users and larger organisations, would have enabled Red Mountain to rollout the cyberattacks launched by Sebastian in Phase One and Phase Two.

Then, with the expertise and the knowledge they would have gained from the many years RM Industrial Technologies had been working with industry, detecting, defending and remediating against specific threats to industrial systems and Critical National Infrastructure, Red Mountain would have had all the necessary know-how to launch Phase Three.

At this point, the team leader of the group announced that they had discovered Red Mountain also had another specialist cyber division that was not publicly promoted and was known as RM Defence.

Exactly what this company did was not clear. However, public information filed with the US government regarding their operations and revenues, showed that RM Defence had significant contracts with the US Military.

"Ray, I don't know if you're thinking what we're thinking?" someone asked from the back row after the group on stage had finished their report.

"I don't know… what are you thinking?" Ray asked, guessing what was coming next.

"Red Mountain, and Sebastian, have already targeted citizens, industry and companies in Phase One, 2 and 3 using their existing knowledge and expertise. Now we hear that they have significant contracts with the US military. And when you were talking earlier, you told us everyone was worried about Phase Four, and that even Sebastian was scared about it. And he's a bloody computer! Ray… are you holding back on something? Is there something else we should know?"

Ray stood up from his seat at the side of the stage and walked back to the centre, facing all the employees and colleagues of ACT.

"Okay, you aren't idiots. And I don't like not telling you the truth. Even though I've been asked not to, so you don't panic. Okay, so what I'm going to tell you now is *'Top Secret'*. If you tell anyone, and you're caught, you'll go to prison for twenty years. Maybe more. At this stage, no one outside this room must ever know. But, yes, the reason why everyone is so worried, is because, reading between the lines, there is a fear that in Phase Four, Sebastian is going to force the launch of America's nuclear missiles against the Russians and the Chinese. Maybe others. Which is why…" Ray stepped forward and raised his hand, trying to quell the immediate wave of unrest that swept through the auditorium, "... which is really why I've tried encouraging you all to work as hard as you can over the next twenty-four hours, and possibly beyond. It's because at the moment we still see an opportunity to stop Sebastian. But, if we can't, or don't, sometime in the coming days Sebastian will switch to using the Phase Four code which he has already downloaded and when he does... Well, it could mean the end of all life on the planet."

The girl who was crying before, had now stopped.

Her face had gone white.

Slowly, she stood up, the only person in the auditorium now on her feet, except for Ray on the stage.

"What are we doing in here then? Why are we wasting time? *We've got to work!* We've got to get back to our desks... we've got to find some way to stop him... it... them..."

Others in the auditorium had also begun to stand up.

It was obvious the meeting had come to an end.

"Okay, listen everyone, we've got time. You guys are the best on the planet. You're all hand-picked. Now you know what we're up against, I think you know what to do. Continue working in the groups you were assigned to. Keep working on the code, dissecting it, understanding it, trying to find any way you can to stop it. The thing is, Sebastian was created by a human. Humans make mistakes. Somewhere, somehow, Sebastian has a weakness in him, and all we've got to do is find it. Which, I promise you, we will. Now, please, go and do what you do best... "

One by one, the members of ACT filed out of the ship's cinema. Soon, only Anand and Chloe were left in the room with Ray.

"Do you believe what you just said?" Chloe asked. "When you promised them that we'll find a way to stop Sebastian?" Ray looked at Chloe, and smiled.

"Yes, I do. My gut feeling is honestly that we will. I'm confident one of us, all of us, will come up with something. In fact," Ray said, a quizzical look passing over his eyes, "... there's something that's beginning to bug me. It's something that was said in the last conversation that was recorded between Robert Lee and Sebastian..."

Chapter 47
In a Bunker beneath the Pentagon 16.30 EST

The mood in the meeting room in the bunker underneath the Pentagon was sombre, to say the least.

The President, Ryan Schwartz, had been sitting silently shaking his head for the past few minutes. He'd listened to a string of military leaders and experts sitting at the meeting room table, each reporting on what they knew, or thought they knew, and then the reports had come to an end, and everyone was staring at the President, waiting for a decision.

"So, basically, if I should try to summarise everything that's been said so far, in plain English, what you are all telling me is that, thanks to one of the companies belonging to Robert Lee, RM Defence, slowly extending its influence and connections within our military establishments, you all believe that it is now possible that the most advanced Artificially Intelligent software program ever created has now penetrated not one, but MULTIPLE defence systems across our Military Infrastructure. And, although you DON'T KNOW HOW he might do it, you are all taking the threat seriously, that this program, now known to the whole world as Sebastian, could, IF HE CHOOSES, possibly, somehow either take control of the nuclear missile launch process, OR create a situation where we believe we are being attacked and are therefore forced into launching a counter-strike, not knowing if the incoming birds we are seeing are actually real-missiles, or ghosts conjured up by Sebastian to fool us into destroying the world?"

"And..." the President continued, "because you don't know how or if indeed we are actually truly infiltrated by Sebastian, you are not able to identify if or where this AI software may be resident in our systems and this means you are unable to disable or remove all the known instances of the Sebastian AI from our defence systems?" The President paused.

"IS THAT TRUE?!" he shouted, slamming his fist onto the table and making even some of the more experienced members of the Military sitting at the table, jump. "Yes, Sir. I think you've summed it all up quite well." The Chief of Staff of the US Army replied, on behalf of all those gathered. "However, there is a plan in place to remove all the instances of the

Sebastian AI that we do know about. The Wilson Plan, so called because it's being run by Director General Harry Wilson of the UK Security Service, will exploit a Kill Switch they've discovered, where we will send an Uninstall Command to each instance of the Sebastian software deployments that we are aware of. This, we believe, will cause each Sebastian-AI program to uninstall itself."

"And the ones we don't know about? They will stay hidden?"

"Unfortunately, at this stage, until we know where they are, we can't instruct them to delete themselves. Our hope is that by removing the ones we do know about, we will be removing those that have the capability to cause activity that could lead to a launch scenario."

"And if you don't?"

"Frankly, Mr President, at this stage, we don't have a Plan B."

"Then get one!" He commanded. "Otherwise, in almost four days we may all be out of a job. Not to mention that there'll be no country left to govern, and most of us will probably be dead!"

The Duchess

Ray, Anand, Stefanie, and several other members of ACT who were section leaders overseeing various avenues of activity, were all sitting together in the boardroom on Level Three. Each of the team leaders was receiving regular updates from their teams via email or Skype, and as important developments came in, they shared them with the others in the room. Ray had selected everyone present to form an Action Committee, whose purpose it was to gather the results of all activities and to continuously brainstorm possible tactics for bringing Sebastian down.

Time was running out. The hours were speeding past.

Since the meeting that had finished at half-past two that morning, almost everyone had been working continuously throughout the day, going without sleep and eating at their desks. Strangely, despite the complete lack of sleep, most people could still function well, and although feeling tired, had still been able to think clearly.

Ray realised that it was probably down to the adrenaline flowing through everyone's veins, coupled with the knowledge that the fate of the human race could depend upon the work they were now doing.

But, to be honest, it didn't look good.

So far, no one had come up with any major breakthroughs.

Their analysis of the code was helping them to put together its structure and architecture, but a lot of what were probably the important sections of active code were still encrypted. It seemed that there were several different levels of encryption used throughout the code and that only about a third of it had originally been decrypted. However, on a positive note, as new sections of the code were successfully decrypted by their colleagues in the UK, they were being alerted, and provided details on how to download them.

Progress overall was slow and frustrating.

Projected in the corner of the overhead screen was a clock that gave a countdown to when the Wilson Plan would be implemented. It currently showed less than two hours to go.

Which could be wonderful - if the Kill Switch worked, and the commands sent to the locations of the Sebastian programs they knew about were successful in uninstalling them. However, one of the fears of the ACT team was they were not one hundred per cent sure where all of the Sebastian locations were. Over the past weeks, using the 'Atomic Packet Cookie Crumb' technique which Ray had invented, they had managed to build a global map which they hoped showed where the active locations and servers were, where Sebastian was resident. But…, they were probably still missing some.

Nevertheless, if the plan worked, and they got rid of most of the installations of Sebastian, it should severely reduce the level of threat the companies and organisations around the world were currently experiencing.

"Excuse me, Stefanie, could I borrow you for a moment?" a timid voice asked, after knocking first on the open door.

They looked up. It was a young man called Richard. He seemed both nervous and excited and was carrying his laptop.

Stefanie stood up and left the room, following Richard to a private office, where he closed the door behind him. Five minutes later, Stefanie emerged from the room and hurried back over to the boardroom, followed immediately by Richard.

"Ray, can we show you something? It's really important…"

The Duchess

Ray pushed back in his chair away from the table. Since Stefanie had alerted them to Richard's analysis, they had all been gathered round the table studying various printouts, Richard's laptop, and what was being projected onto the large overhead screen on the wall. From time to time, Ray had also called some others from different groups into the boardroom so that he could share the latest news with them, show them the code they were looking at, and get their input.

Unfortunately, the view of everyone who studied the findings that Richard and his team had stumbled across, was unanimous.

They'd even compared their findings from the review of particular sections of the Phase Three code with those of the earlier Phase Two code.

The results had been startling.

And petrifying.

Having satisfied themselves they were correct, and they had not misunderstood anything or made any mistakes, Ray looked for the hundredth time at the clock.

There were only twenty minutes to go before the Wilson Plan was going to be initiated.

He immediately told everyone to clear the room, and he logged into a secure connection on his laptop that would connect him directly by encrypted satellites and numerous proxies to Chief Daniels.

Now Ray was sure, absolutely sure, there wasn't a second to waste.

Vauxhall
London
Twelve minutes to Wilson Plan Initiation

Director Daniels felt his wrist watch beginning to vibrate and buzz and looked at its screen.

It showed an incoming call from *The Plumber*, the codename he'd given Ray Luck. Ray was the man he often relied upon to sort out his 'sewage' problems when around him everything began to turn to 'shit', hence the nickname.

Daniels apologised to the others in the room and stepped outside, hurried to the end of the corridor and the lift, and rode it up to his office.

Hurrying to his laptop, he went through the exhaustive security sign-in process, popped on his headphones, and opened up the application that would call Ray back over the encrypted satellite link.

"Daniels here, go ahead," he said, and waited for Ray to speak.

"Sir, we have a major problem. You have to stop the Wilson Plan! *IMMEDIATELY!* You must *NOT* allow anyone to send an Uninstall command to Sebastian."

Daniels glanced at his watch. He'd just stepped out of a command room where members of GCHG, the Security Service and the Secret Intelligence Service had all come together to coordinate and manage the implementation of the Kill Switch in the UK.

There were now less than four minutes to go.

"Why? Explain?"

"Our teams here have just confirmed that the Kill Switch will no longer work in Phase Three of the Sebastian code. Since the Phase Two software, Robert Lee has conducted some major operational changes. The purpose of the changes is to make it almost impossible to kill Sebastian. As you know, Sebastian isn't really a single piece of isolated AI. It's a new form of being, a distributed collection of AI instances that operate individually but are connected together. In effect, it is a SWARM of AI programs, which all share a common identity. Our team here has just found that Robert Lee has added a whole new section to the code that is operationalised should anyone try to take advantage of the vulnerability that was previously seen. In effect, it's now a trap. If anyone sends an 'Uninstall' command to a program, it will go ahead and uninstall itself, but it will also simultaneously connect to multiple Trojans already established in other servers and reinstall copies of itself there. In the seconds before it deletes itself, as instructed, a single version of Sebastian will recreate itself in three or four different environments."

"Are you sure?"

"Positive, Sir. Which is why we've taken so long to contact you. We had to be absolutely sure. Sir, if you send the uninstall command to Sebastian, he will interpret it as a command for the Swarm to multiply. Sir, far from solving the problem, we're telling Sebastian to breed! *You have to stop it! Now!*"

Daniels ripped off his headphones, ran from his office to the elevator and swore several times as valuable seconds were wasted carrying him back down to the underground rooms beneath the building.

After a mad dash from the lift along the corridor, Daniels pushed open the door to the Operations Room and shouted, "*Stop!*".

Everyone in the room turned to look at him.

"What do you mean?" asked Alan Alexander, who was standing behind three of his team who were sitting at the table in front of him, beavering furiously away on their laptops.

"Stop. Do not issue the command to uninstall. I repeat, do not issue the uninstall command! It's a trap!"

"It's too late!" Harry Wilson shouted over the video connection between his office and the underground Operations Room in Vauxhall. "You're thirty seconds too late. We've sent the command. And so have all the other Five Eyes. Right now, as we speak, Sebastian is being deleted, wherever he is!"

Daniels turned to the screen, puffing and panting from running for the first time in years and blurted out, "No, Director Wilson. We've made a terrible mistake. Thanks to not understanding the program properly, we haven't told Sebastian to commit suicide and delete himself… we've just given him an instruction to breed! *God help us all!*"

Chapter 48
The Duchess

Having heard from the Chief that they were too late, Ray and his management team sat in their boardroom and watched the data being projected onto the flatscreen on the wall.

They watched in horror as the Atomic Packet Generators across the globe went ballistic. One of the team had created a program that visually traced the route of packets as they were created and formed a linked path between them from the source to a destination, creating a coloured line as the different cyber crumbs were picked up and linked.

Yes, the original red dots that were on the screen that represented each known instance of Sebastian disappeared from the map, one by one, but as they watched, one after another, new curved lines appeared on the globe as Sebastian bred. Instead of a myriad of original instances of the Sebastian software being highlighted on the global map, they watched in horror as the number of sources for Sebastian traffic multiplied, three, perhaps four times.

The mood in the room was despondent.

They were perhaps the only people in the world seeing in real time the effect of the mistake that had just been made.

It would be hours, perhaps even days, before the Intelligence teams of the Five Eyes fully realised that the Wilson Plan had made the situation far worse, not better.

"What's that?" Anand asked, standing up and walking over to the screen. He stood in front of it and pointed to some faint red lines that were beginning to appear. In some places growing stronger in colour as the minutes went by, representing multiple traffic paths taking a similar route.

Ray stood up and joined him.

"I don't know… it's curious… these ones… " Ray pointed to various sets of lines on the global map, "… are similar to the routes we saw before. They are where Sebastian is reaching out to organisations and establishing the paths of connectivity that occur when they start to blackmail them. You can see the destinations are remaining the same, but the sources where

Sebastian is now operating from are now changing… We've got new versions of Sebastian blackmailing established targets, or attacking new targets. We've got hundreds, perhaps thousands, of new targets appearing as Sebastian breeds and generates more capability to attack." Ray said then pointed at several other dots on the map. "But these are more interesting. Look, we can see lots of traffic from the different new instances of Sebastian all merging and coming together on a common target. But why? What's happening there?"

"Can we look at those targets in more detail? Find out exactly where they are? What's there? Physically and geographically?" Anand asked.

"Yes. We need to do that…" Ray turned to those gathered in the room. "But first, I'm going to issue an order that everyone goes to bed for five hours. We've worked for several days without stopping. News will soon get out that the Wilson Plan failed. We now have a new target to chase. According to the stats we have, the first of Sebastian's Phase Three victims will be required to pay their Climate Action Tax in just over sixty-three hours. When we hit that deadline, all across the world, the most important organisations that keep society going will start having to send Sebastian billions of dollars just to survive. We're worried that not all organisations will be able to do it. There's going to be some bad situations coming up when services which we all rely on, for whatever reason, don't make Sebastian's demands on time. We can anticipate some very bad things are going to happen… And sometime after that, we don't know exactly when, we expect Phase Four to kick in and we all know what that means. Go and tell everyone to get some sleep. I want everyone back here tomorrow morning at 5am sharp. Bright tailed and bushy eyed…"

"Do you mean bright eyed and bushy tailed?" Stefanie nodded. I think you need some sleep too."

Fifteen minutes later, Ray crept into bed beside Chloe.

She was already fast asleep. She had wanted to wait for Ray, but as soon as her head hit the pillow, she was gone.

She never felt the small, soft kisses on her neck, or Ray's arms gently wrap around her.

She never heard him say, "Good night, I love you." She was too busy dreaming.

A nightmare.

A large mushroom cloud expanding high into the sky above London.

05.00 IST

At five o'clock everyone assembled back into the cinema of the Duchess.

Ray gave them the bad news.

The world was a much darker place than the day before.

The threat from Sebastian had magnified.

But worst of all, although Ray never put it in such terms, the hope that had previously existed for the Wilson Plan to make the sun shine again, had vanished.

Now it was down to them to create new hope.

The good news was that Ray had a fresh approach.

He gave out new assignments for the teams.

There would now be only five teams.

Two of the teams were to continue mapping out the structure of Sebastian. How the program was put together? What the different parts of the program did? And why? Assembling any new code that they received from London which had been decrypted. Performing as much independent analysis on the code as they could.

Another of the teams, and one to which he assigned Chloe, was to look at the events that Anand had first highlighted the day before. He'd seen the red lines traced through the cookie-crumbs converging on specific points. They weren't targets… that would make no sense… the different versions of Sebastian wouldn't go after similar targets… that would be inefficient, and Sebastian was too smart for that. So, they had to be something else. So, the question was, what were they, and *where* were they?

Another team was focussed on building a complete new list of where every single instance of Sebastian was that they could identify.

The last team was tasked with trying to understand everything they could about Robert Lee. Ray felt that they must have missed something. Probably something important. At the back of his mind, he kept remembering a quote from somewhere about '*know your enemy, and keep them close*'. In this case the enemy was dead, so that bit may not apply. Or did it? Was there any reason to suspect that anyone else in the Red Mountain complex may be involved or party to the whole scam? Perhaps that bit was beyond their capabilities, for now, but Ray wanted to know more about Robert Lee. Where did he come from? His motivations? His likes and dislikes? Why would he want to destroy the West? And why destroy the world? They were missing something. Somewhere. But what was it?

Knowing that Anand was truly exceptional when sent to work alone and left to get on with things, he gave that task to Anand. A team of one. But with equally as important a task as the others.

Then, when everyone went to work, Ray took himself off for a walk on the deck of the Grand Duchess.

After pacing the deck three times, he found a deck chair and sat down to think, and to watch the sun rise.

Ever since the meeting at 1am the day before, something had been bugging him. It was something about the last conversation that took place between Robert Lee and Sebastian.

Something.

But what?

Time marches on…

The minutes passed inexorably by, all too soon turning from hours to days.

Across the world, government communiques started going out to the heads of all the Critical National Infrastructure and government organisations instructing them if they had been contacted by Sebastian with a demand to pay the Climate Action Tax, they must pay it. They were also instructed to register with a government agency and provide to them a list of answers to a number of detailed questions. For example, when exactly did Sebastian contact them? What was the specific threat? How much must they pay? How? By when? What critical services do they provide and what will the impact be if their organisations were to be shut down. None of the governments offered to pay the ransom on behalf of any private organisations, but it was made very clear that all organisations must pay the tax. And then keep quiet about it for at least two weeks. By way of some form of reassurance, the governments emphasised that tracking down those behind Sebastian and disabling him was a top government focus for all nations, globally.

The requests to remain calm and pay the upcoming bills failed spectacularly. Across the world, anger, frustration and fear grew in all the developed nations. By now, almost everyone had heard of Sebastian. For months the hacker had been terrorising the world. First, he'd targeted everyone with a bank account, then the rich and famous, and now it was industry and business.

Social media was alive with protests and stories about the terror that Sebastian was waging.

Several large protests were organised in major cities across the globe, all of which turned violent and had to be controlled or put down by the local law enforcement services.

Businesses complained that following the devastation caused by years of pandemic, if they were forced to pay the ransoms demanded of them, it would finally tip them over the edge.

Businessmen and women demanded action from their governments.

Citizens demanded more protection against cyberattacks.

A rift was opened up between those who wanted greater control of the internet and those who wanted to protect its freedoms.

The media began to focus on the ticking clock that was marching forward, counting down to the moment that the Climate Action Tax had to be paid.

Everyone turned in hope, fear and frustration to their governments for help.

Do something!

Do anything!

Help!

COBRA meeting Downing Street

The PM was standing up at his seat before the table, around which all the members of the COBRA committee were now seated. Today this included the heads of each of the different sections of the Armed Forces, as well as the heads of the security services and GCHQ.

Behind him, above the fireplace, was a digital clock in countdown mode.

It showed twenty-nine hours to go before the Climate Action Tax was due to be paid.

"Gentlemen, and Ladies. Before I start, I would like to apologise in advance.

I'm angry. But not at you, and I'm apologising now because I fear that I will probably start to shout, as has been my style in the past during this meeting, and I know that it is not your fault. We are in a difficult time. Very difficult. And I appreciate that we are all doing the best we can, even if that best is simply not enough to help us in our hour of need."

A few people at the table exchanged glances. They'd never heard the PM apologise before. For anything. That action in itself was a sign of how bad things had become.

The PM pulled his seat out and sat down at the table. He turned to Paul Harrison the Cyber Minister and invited him to sum up the situation so far.

"So, just to state facts clearly, we are now sitting at twenty-nine hours before the first of the Climate Action Taxes will require to be paid. We've issued everyone we thought we should do so a communique, telling them to ensure they have paid the Climate Tax to Sebastian at least twelve hours before their deadline is due. We've also instructed everyone who experiences difficulty in paying the tax to contact us to discuss their situation and see if we can help. In addition, according to the instructions Sebastian initially gave his targets, we expect that he will start to send reminders to his targets in the next four hours, which should be twenty-four hours before the first tax is due."

"With regard to efforts to stop Sebastian, as you may already have heard, I have to report that the Wilson Plan - which was the globally agreed plan to uninstall Sebastian from affected computers - did not work. Instead, it caused him to multiply, and we are now seeing a significant increase in the number of organisations being targeted by Sebastian. Unfortunately, we don't yet have a Plan B…"

"Okay, thank you Mr Harrison," The PM interrupted him, using his surname, which was a clear sign of the PM's frustration and annoyance. "That's all very well and good, but the bottom line, is, as I still understand it, that sometime after the Climate Action Tax is paid, we expect Sebastian to move to another mode of operation - Phase 4 - during which we expect him to launch World War Three! You forgot to mention that part, Mr Harrison."

"I was working up to it, Prime Minister. You just beat me to it."

"Sorry, I had to cut you off, because we're running out of bloody time. I need ideas and action plans, not long historical speeches!"

The Cyber Minister sat down at his place at the table, deciding silence was now the best policy.

"So…?" The Prime Minister said, or asked - it wasn't too clear to everyone at the table. "Does anyone have any suggestions or comments?"

"Sir, I think it would be prudent to consider putting Plan Alpha into operation, and start moving government to the nuclear shelters." The Secretary of State for Defence suggested.

"Brilliant. Is that all you've got?" The PM replied.

"At this point, I'm afraid so, Sir. I think for years, a number of us have all been very concerned that at some time Artificial Intelligence could threaten mankind. It's just none of us expected it to happen so soon…"

"So, what… you want a medal? An *'I told you so, medal?'*" The PM turned on him.

The Secretary of Defence looked down at the table and said no more.

"Okay," The PM said. "I suggest we finish this meeting and we all go home and pack for an extended stay in the Nuclear Survival Shelters. Good luck, and don't forget your toothbrushes."

And with that, the PM stood, gathered his folder up from the desk, tucked it under his arm and left the room.

Chapter 49
England
24 hrs to Climate Tax Deadline (CTD)

Patricia Graves was sitting at her table in her kitchen in front of her company laptop, staring at its screen. As she watched the minutes and seconds counting down to the moment Sebastian had promised to send her a reminder, the tears slowly ran down her cheek, and her hands shook with fear.

She'd received the letter from the British Government telling her she had to pay the tax. She knew that as the accountant in charge of the Hospital Trust that employed her, it was her responsibility to arrange for payment of the Climate Change Tax to prevent the electricity and gas being cut off, and as Sebastian had specifically threatened, to stop him disabling the emergency back-up generators which would keep their patients alive if the essential services were cut off.

But even though she'd tried really, *really* hard, she'd been unable to raise the five million pounds ransom that Sebastian had demanded.

She'd tried asking the council for help, but no one had been able to. Everyone was in the same boat. Struggling to find money to pay the fines.

And struggling to understand how to acquire five million pounds worth of bitcoin and follow the transfer instructions as directed by Sebastian.

Patricia was sixty-years old. She didn't understand the world of bitcoin. She had no interest in it.

Until now.

But the past few weeks had been a nightmare. She'd struggled to find out as much as she could about bitcoin, but even now she was a subscriber to multiple online sites which promised to help users buy and trade in bitcoins, over the past week, the market had gone crazy. The price of bitcoin had soared. Skyrocketed. And no one was selling.

Everyone was buying.

"Sebastian might be the cleverest cyber hacker in the world," thought Patricia, "but he knows nothing about the rule of supply and demand. He'd created such a demand for bitcoin that there simply weren't enough to go around."

Which meant that unless a miracle took place soon, Patricia wouldn't be able to get hold of any and comply with the instructions which the hacker was … ouch…*had*… just sent her!

Patricia clicked on the email which had just appeared in her mailbox.

"Dear Patricia,
You have twenty-four hours left to pay the Climate Action Tax. Failure to pay the five million pounds you owe…"

Patricia slammed the lid of her laptop closed, and lay her head down on top of it, covering her head with her hands.

"HELP!" she screamed loudly and then dissolved into tears.

But no one heard her.

The Duchess
20 hrs to CTD

Ray Luck was stressed.

The world was pressing down on him. He knew the expectations that his boss had of him. Derek Daniels believed in him. He believed that Ray would be able to find something. Something that no one else had seen. Something that would hopefully get the world off the hook.

And Daniels was hopefully right.

Ray knew that there was something… he could *feel* it…

Frustratingly, sometimes it was so tangible that he felt as if he should almost be able to reach out and touch it.

It taunted him on the edge of his brain. Mocking him, as the clock counted down, as the seconds ticked by, and yet still it would not reveal itself to him.

At night, he lay in his bed beside Chloe, unable to sleep. His mind was alive. The thought that was growing on the edge of his consciousness was hiding just around the corner, always, but when he looked around that corner to see where it was, the thought had moved on. Hidden again somewhere else.

Ray was semi-confident that sooner or later the promise of the thought would materialise into something more solid… a real thought which would enter his brain in a Eureka moment of hopefully great significance… but when? Time was not exactly on their side, and he needed that thought now.

NOW!

"A penny for them?" Chloe asked, putting the coffee down on the table in front of him.

"Oh… it's nothing." He said, smiling at her. "Okay, is everyone ready?"

"I think so." She replied.

Ray followed Chloe through from his office across the Duchess to the cinema, where everyone was waiting.

Behind them on the stage, was the now usual backdrop to all their meetings. A projection of a timer counting down to Zero Hours when the Climate Action Tax would start to become due across the world.

It currently stood at twenty hours to go.

"Hi, everyone. So, as you can see, we have twenty hours to go before the tax becomes finally due. And following the failure of the Wilson Plan, the Five Eyes communities are instructing all affected organisations to pay the tax at least twelve hours before it's due. We can't afford any essential services to go offline at this stage. So, within the next twenty hours we expect to see literally billions of dollars being transferred in bitcoin to whoever is the recipient of this tax. From what we know, it's not Robert Lee or any of the Red Mountain companies. It looks like it's going elsewhere. We just don't know where. Okay, so, this is going to be a big, open meeting. It's a massive brainstorming session. We need to come up with some clever ideas and soon. So, I'm inviting anyone with something new to report, to volunteer first, then we can brainstorm afterwards. Any takers to go first?"

Anand's hand went straight up.

Ray invited him up onto the stage.

"Hi everyone. First of all, I'd just like to say that this is actually not all my work. I've been talking with a lot of you, and some of you have volunteered a few of your contacts for me to draw upon, and have shown me some of your results, which helped me with mine. Well, basically, Ray asked me to find out more about Robert Lee and why he might be doing all of this? So, I've been doing some digging. A lot of digging. I've made more progress in the past few hours, because, well, I think we're all desperate and necessity is what the English say is the mother of invention, I think…"

"So, Anand, what did you discover? Just summarise it if you can?" Ray encouraged, seeing that he was nervous and perhaps waffling a bit.

"Okay, sure thing. Basically, I think Robert Lee was very angry. He had cancer. He was going to die anyway, even if he didn't commit suicide… which he probably did because he didn't want to die slowly locked up in prison. Which is interesting, because I think the cancer changed his whole outlook on everything. Until he got cancer, his focus was on building the most successful chain of cyber companies in the world. And he was almost there. Red Mountain is probably the largest, second only to one other. And he developed Sebastian, clearly the most advanced Artificial Intelligence in the universe. And with each phase he rolls out, Sebastian gets cleverer. He's probably now Super-Intelligent. Like, as in, smarter than humans? Maybe…"

"But why is Sebastian stealing money from everyone?" someone shouted from the audience.

"Aha… yes. Because I think Robert Lee was a spy. He was the ultimate 'Insider', working from inside the USA, but actually a spy for another country. And the whole purpose of Sebastian was to raise money for that other country."

"Which country?" another person shouted.

"I think North Korea. I think. But this is another interesting bit,… I don't think North Korea actually engineered any of this. Lee did it all himself, and just gave the money to North Korea. Naturally, I think they're pretty happy about it, and they probably helped with the guidance and expertise on how to transfer it out of the other countries and make it disappear, then launder it, before putting it back into the financial system again. It actually makes sense, because historically, as you know North Korea has a lot of expertise in that area… they were allegedly, after all, behind most of the really advanced ransomware attacks in the past few years, all trying to get hold of as much foreign currency as possible."

"But why North Korea?" Ray asked. "What makes you think it's that country?"

"Because his father was born in North Korea and his wife Hana had parents who came from there too. Officially, according to information we were given by the Five Eyes on Lee, his father came from California. But that's not true. I did a search of the immigration records that were recorded manually before computers were used, and then later scanned and computerised. I found an entry for both his mother and father giving their original place of birth as North Korea. Lee later hacked into the digital database and changed the records, making them born in America. I wouldn't believe anything you see about him online. He could rewrite his history whenever he wanted to."

"But why didn't the US agencies spot that?" Chloe asked.

"Maybe they did, but didn't tell us yet. Until they have enough evidence to say that he was operating on the Korean's behalf, that he was a spy, they may want to keep that bit quiet. After all, he was the poster boy for the American dream. Maybe they just don't want it to be known that he was a spy. Or… maybe they just didn't look. I only looked because I was suspicious. There are other clues too. They look Korean, and they have Korean names. Hana, Lee. And, there's something else…"

"Which is?" Ray asked, sensing that Anand was inviting the question.

"This is where I steal Georgina's team's thunder." Anand waved at a group of people sitting in the third row of the theatre. "You asked Georgina and her crew to look at the cookie-crumb lines that were converging to similar points? To find out where they were and what they were? Well, it seems that there are two patterns for those lines. One converges on a single destination point… in South Korea. The others converge in five different locations, three in the US, and two in Europe. I'll let Georgina explain what the locations in Europe and the US are in a few minutes, but I want to talk about the location in Korea. It seems that each of the new versions of Sebastian that were created and installed after the Wilson Plan caused Sebastian to 'breed', immediately started beaconing to the location in Korea. I'm not sure why, yet. But I'll find out. I'll be working on that in the next few hours. But what's interesting is where the location in Korea is. It's on land taken from North Korea during the war. I googled the area, looking for whatever I could find on it that makes that area special. I found two things. The first one… was that there was a battle that took place there during June 1952. It lasted for about a month. Thousands fought and died fighting for a hill that was of strategic importance. The hill… it was called… the Red Mountain." Anand smiled, and stopped, letting it sink in. "Then, I also found some research a student had published in Australia as part of his degree. I read it. It had a list of the people who died in the battle on both sides in an appendix at the end of the report. I scanned and then searched the names of the dead, looking for the surnames of Robert Lee's and Hana's parents. And I found the name of Robert's grandfather. He was killed in the battle, three days before the hill was taken and the North Koreans retreated."

Some people in the theatre whistled. Others clapped. Ray was one of them.

Things were turning around. He could feel the mood in the room change. There was a spark of electricity in the air.

This was good.
Very good.

Chapter 50

"What was the second thing you found out about that location?" Georgina from the audience prompted him.

"There's not much left in that town. It's in South Korea now. It's a small town. But it's famous for making shoes. The main thing that's there now is a shoe factory. And that's where all the versions of Sebastian are beaconing to. To the shoe factory." "Why? Why a shoe factory?" A young man asked from the front row.

"I'll let Jurgen explain that one." Anand said, smiling and leaving the stage, as everyone started clapping, led by Ray.

"Jurgen, you're up next! Tell us what you've found out!" Ray invited.

Jurgen smiled nervously, stood up from somewhere near the back and walked slowly down to the stage where he tripped walking up the steps, and stumbled forward, dropping some pieces of paper on the floor.

Chloe rushed forward to help him and pick up the papers.

"Sorry," he said, as he approached the centre of the stage where the microphone and the lectern were. He put his papers on the lectern and stood there for a moment without speaking. Then he took an obvious very deep breath.

"Sorry... it's just that I hate public speaking... but... I thought this was important... so... Ray asked our team to look at the structure of Sebastian. Actually, there were two teams... mine looking at the architecture of Sebastian, the other team looking at what Sebastian actually does, which is really difficult to tell unless you're a genius and a master at Artificial Intelligence and can guess what tons of still encrypted code is meant to do!"

There were a few laughs, probably less at Jurgen being funny, and more at trying to make him feel relaxed.

"But... some of the people in my group are officially geniuses so, ... what we came up with is this ..." He nodded to someone at the back of the theatre and instantly a hand-sketched diagram appeared on the screen behind him.

"It's not much to look at, but it's a simplistic sketch of the operating architecture for Sebastian. It took a lot of time to figure out. It's basically this… Sebastian is essentially a Virtual Machine, roughly composed of three main parts, which I have nicknamed *'The Sperm'*, *'The Womb'* and *'The Egg'*. It runs mainly on virtual computing resources in the cloud, or in servers or hardware capable of supporting Virtual Machines, that is, Sebastian is like a parasite. It finds another computer where it can live, injects itself into the computer and starts to grow inside it, consuming memory, storage and processing power from the system it's living in. There are several stages to establishing itself in a system. The first part is all about getting into the hardware or system which Sebastian can then live off. We think this can happen in two ways… The first way is what I've called Sebastian's Sperm. It's like an intelligent worm that identifies vulnerabilities in systems and finds its way into the system through the vulnerability. Once inside the system, the Sperm sets up an operating environment where Sebastian can grow. It creates a Womb. Either that, or an established version of Sebastian seems capable of hacking through the defences of a system and seeding the worm or a Trojan within the system, which then creates and shapes the Womb by carving out and ring-fencing the space it needs to live according to the parameters specified in its code, which determines how much memory it needs, how much processing power, how much storage space, etcetera, all of which are stolen from the environment in which it is created. Which, in a data centre, is completely normal. That's what data centres do. They provide physical hardware, computers or servers where multiple Virtual Machines can live in harmony, all sharing the same physical hardware and using shared resources which are provided by the hardware they share."

"Now, once the Sperm has created the Womb, and the Womb is ready… it beacons out to the botmaster to register and announce itself and it asks if there is a new version of Sebastian to download, or if it should just be running the code it already has?"

Jurgen paused for a second, looked out at the audience, and then added, "Actually, I forgot to mention that Sebastian always comes as a software package which contains both the Sperm and the Egg. The Sperm specifies details how any new Womb should be set up, but by default, it also comes with the existing known version of the Egg. When a new Womb is set up, it beacons the botmaster to see if a new version of the code should be downloaded which includes a new Egg. But if the botmaster says *'no'*, the existing egg within Sebastian is put into the womb. When I say Egg, what I really mean is the main operational code for Sebastian. So basically, to recap… and said another way perhaps, when you create a new version of Sebastian, you first create a home for Sebastian to live in, then before he moves in, Sebastian first checks to see if *he* should move in, or if he should first download another version of himself, and then let the *new* version move in. Got it?"

Everyone in the audience nodded. They knew all about Virtual Machines and understood the analogy. Chloe put up her hand... she didn't completely get it, but slowly, she took it back down again. She was sure Ray would explain it to her himself later, personally.

"Jurgen, if the botmaster says that there is another download to get, where does it come from? The same place?" Someone else in the audience asked.

"Aha ... , thanks. Brilliant question. To which the answer is no. It doesn't come from the same place, it comes from the five places in the USA and Europe that Anand was telling us about, which Georgina and her team found out about. Georgina, do you want to answer that one?"

Jurgen smiled at the audience, gathered his papers and then shuffled off the stage, his head held slightly higher this time than when he walked on.

Ray patted him on the back as he left.

"This is all excellent stuff, by the way people, truly excellent!" he said loudly.

By this time, Georgina had taken the stage.

"I'm sorry. I think I may be about to steal back some of Anand's thunder. First of all, I want to identify the sites in the US and Europe where all the Atomic Packet Cookie Crumbs converge. They are all Amazon data centres."

There was an exhaling of air from almost everyone in the arena. That was a particularly interesting piece of news.

"Next, I want to shed some extra light on what we found in South Korea. As already said, the location is in a shoe factory. I talked to the others about this already, because I was interested in 'why a shoe factory?' When I was given the name of Lee's grandfather, I looked at the history of the factory and found an old payroll, on which I found his grandfather's name!"

She paused, looking across at Ray. He nodded for her to continue.

"So, I think this has all got something to do with his grandfather. All of it. It's more than a coincidence that all Lee's companies are named after the Red Mountain, and that all the installations of Sebastian beacon back to the Red Mountain and the shoe factory where his grandfather worked! So, my next question was what is Sebastian actually beaconing back to? What's in the shoe factory that's so important?"

She turned to the screen and waved her hand at her helper in the audience, and an image was projected onto the screen showing several sections of code.

"Following Jurgen's idea for the structure of Sebastian, this is the code in Sebastian that tells it where to connect to when it beacons back to the botmaster to find out if there is a new version of the 'Womb' to download.

That is, when Sebastian wants to know if Robert Lee has created a new version of Sebastian's code that should be downloaded, it connects to this Port and IP address, which basically takes you into what people who are familiar with Industrial Systems call an '*Historian*'. A 'Historian' is basically a database that contains within its file system a list of all the parameters in a factory. The controllers or devices in a factory that run the industrial processes are continuously checking the parameters stored in the Historian's database. When an industrial controller sees that a specific value in a specific element of the Historian's database has changed, it makes a decision to take a particular course of action in the factory. For example, if in Table A, in Column 10, Row 5, the temperature of a chemical being heated up in a container changes from 35 degrees to 65 degrees, the controller may decide that it's time to stop heating up that chemical and now open a valve and let the chemical flow into another container. Actually, you don't really need to know that, but the point is that Robert Lee had a cyber company called Red Mountain Industrial Technologies, that specialised in cyber defence for industrial systems and factories. He would know all about this stuff. So… my idea is this… Robert Lee wanted to involve the memory of his grandfather in everything he was doing… probably purely for emotional reasons… so he decided to hack into the Historian in the shoe factory, and put some of his own software there which presented a set of values to the world. At specific times, all the installed versions of Sebastian spread across the world would then connect to the Historian and see what the value in a specific element was. If that element in the database had changed since the last time it referenced it, Sebastian would know it had to carry out a specific instruction. To see what was happening here, I hacked into the Historian and its database and went to the values that were being interrogated by all the red lines beaconing back to the Historian. This is what I saw… " The picture on the screen above changed.

"As you can see, this looks very much like a software revision number. Which means, I guess, that what we see happening here is that Sebastian is comparing its current software revision level with this number, and if this number in the database is higher, then the Sebastian location that is looking at this, knows that it has to download a new, and more recent version than it's currently running in its server, wherever it is in the world…"

Ray walked onto the stage and stood in front of the screen, looking at it for a few moments, then turning to Georgina asked, "Can you show me a timeline of when we see these beacons have been going out to the shoe factory?"

Georgina left the stage and hurried back to the laptop she'd left on her seat. Bringing it back to the stage she sat down on the ground and starting flicking around with her fingers on the mouse.

"Here," she said, and then projected her slide onto the screen after fiddling around with the Bluetooth connection.

Ray studied the stats now visible on the screen and then turned to her.

"That makes sense. It correlates with the details we got from the Five Eyes about the conversation they recorded between Lee and Sebastian, as well as the moments after Sebastian multiplied and bred. Focussing on the signalling that took place after the conversation with Lee and Sebastian, basically, Lee agreed with Sebastian to update the operational code he'd written and change the objectives he'd already set Sebastian in the Phase Four software. After that conversation, Sebastian would be checking regularly to see if a new version of software was available or not. That's why we see a sudden increase in the links being established from around the world to the shoe factory Historian, around the hours after that conversation took place and then regularly since. Sebastian is obviously trying to find out if the new version of code is ready or not, so it starts beaconing back to the Historian in the shoe factory more often! Now,… the signalling that happens after Sebastian deleted itself and then bred and multiplied, is more to do with the new versions which have been created then automatically checking with the botmaster to see if there is a new version of code to download. That would have happened anyway and is nothing to do with the conversation Lee and Sebastian had about a new version of code being created, although the end-effect is the same."

"But Lee's dead," someone from the audience shouted. "He won't be posting any new code soon!"

"Exactly. And, as we thought, it seems that Lee never had enough time to complete the new code and upload it before he died, so Sebastian is still checking to see if it's been done or not!" Ray smiled.

At last, their understanding of things was really moving forward.

Ray turned to Georgina, and offered her a hand to help her stand up. "Do you want to explain what you think is happening in the Amazon data centres?" he asked her.

She nodded, then turned to the audience.

"Well, my idea is this, and if you think about it, it does make sense… Lee hacked into the Amazon data centres and hid the new version of the operational code for Sebastian on its servers. Whenever there was a new version to download to Sebastian, he put a new version of the code there. That way, when Sebastian reached out to the Historian during its typical Command and Control type beacons, if it discovered that a new version of the code was available, it then went off and connected to the Amazon data centres and downloaded the new code from there." She paused. "Which is quite clever because, where better to hide a large file of data which will be downloaded many times, than in a data centre that hosts Amazon and all the Amazon Prime videos?"

Ray laughed aloud.

"That's brilliant." He said to himself.

"One last thing, though, if I may?" Georgina asked.

"Go for it…"

"I just wanted to say that when we looked at the code in Sebastian, we could see that any download from the Amazon data centre to Sebastian would be expected to provide a complete file containing a new version of the Sperm, with the details for the Womb, and the new operational code that makes up the Egg that goes in the Womb."

Georgina, smiled, gave a fake bow to the audience, and then marched off the stage.

As she passed Anand, he gave her a high-five.

As she sat down, Ray invited the last of the groups up. Alongside another team, they had been looking at the code itself, trying to determine what the code actually did.

Unfortunately, they did not have news as good as the others.

Much of the code was still encrypted, and invisible to those wishing to dissect it.

Much of it. Not all.

In the 'egg' that had been downloaded, they had found some code that linked what was Phase Three to Phase Four. It gave insight into the timing at which the Phase Four code would be initiated and supersede the operation of Phase Three.

The timing was hard-wired into the code, and seemingly protected by a password, which they had tried numerous times to guess but had failed.

When they cast the section of code up on to the screen so that everyone could see it, everyone gasped.

Phase Four was set to initiate forty-eight hours after the first deadline for the Phase Three became due.

"That doesn't make any sense!" Chloe said loudly. Loudly enough for everyone to hear.

"What do you mean?" Ray invited her to explain.

"Why go to all the trouble of collecting all the money from Phase Three, then immediately following it up by potentially launching a nuclear war?" she cried.

Ray nodded.

"It doesn't make sense. The only thing that I can think was that Lee had been planning this for years… I mean, Phase One, Two, and Three… Then he got the news that he had terminal cancer, sometime after he'd already lost his wife Hana too, and then he became very bitter. Perhaps he decided to take the whole world with him when he went? In the last weeks of his life, maybe he wasn't thinking clearly anymore. He might have gone insane…"

"Of course he's insane. Who else would plan to destroy the whole of humanity! Only a madman!" Someone else from the auditorium shouted.

The discovery just unveiled was important. It set the timeframes for any activities that now needed to take place.

Basically, they had a total of sixty-six-and-a-half hours before things started to go nuclear.

The Duchess
18.30 hours to CTD

Ray stood before all those who worked for ACT. Following a wonderful session where an amazing amount of progress had been reported, they then moved into a brainstorming session.

The objective had been to try and use the information they had all now been updated on, and to build on that to hopefully come up with a new idea, or even a comprehensive plan, on how they could shut Sebastian down.

Sadly, after a few initial thoughts, the ideas had dried up.

Individually the teams had made great progress, but now as a group, they were getting nowhere fast.

Conscious of the clock, Ray decided that it was probably best to send them back into their teams and for them to plan individually.

"So, ... I want you to work together in your smaller groups. Keep pushing forward. Look for new vulnerabilities in the code. I get that big chunks of it are still encrypted and we can only guess what's in there, but anything you can see or find, no matter how small, might be the spark upon which we can build something far more powerful. My door's open. Come and see me whenever you think you've found something or have had an idea. ..."

Then he'd sent them all back to their desks.

There were now only eighteen hours and fifteen minutes left to when the Climate Action Tax was due.

Chapter 51
The clock ticks
20.30 GMT
2.30 hours to CTD

A feeling of desperation, frustration and impending doom had begun to settle on all those involved in Project Raindrop.

At another time, in different circumstances, the majority of those involved in Raindrop would be in awe of Robert Lee's achievements.

What he had created was after all, technically, a miracle.

No one had ever seen anything like it before.

In recent years, many of the biggest social media, Hi-tech and search engine companies had spent billions on racing to be the first to discover Artificial Super Intelligence. How could Robert Lee have succeeded ahead of everyone else?

What was his secret?

Across the world, thousands of analysts poured over the code, searching for another Kill Switch.

Any possible way to switch Sebastian off.

To kill him.

Before 'it' or 'they' killed them.

But no one found anything.

London, New York, Paris, Rome

In all the major cities of the world, tens of thousands of people poured onto the streets protesting against Sebastian and the Governments of the world who had let this situation come to pass. And who were now idly standing by as the Climate Tax Deadline came closer.

Newspapers and social media, political parties and unions went to town, each with a different angle or axe to grind. Everyone knew that not all the companies who had been targeted would be able to pay.

Either they simply didn't have the money, couldn't arrange a bank loan in time, or couldn't find any bitcoin to buy. Demand, demand, demand. And no supply.

The price of bitcoin skyrocketed.

Some speculated that this was all an attempt to drive the price of bitcoin through the roof so that big time investors could cash out with massive profits. It was all a capitalist conspiracy.

Ideas, some interesting, most ridiculous, began to circulate.

The Russians were behind it. The Chinese. The Americans. The Albanian mafia.

Wall Street.

The Scottish Government, desperate to seek funding for their planned new independent state.

But as the hours ticked by, and the deadline came closer, no one outside the agencies and those high in Government circles knew what was lurking in the shadows of the days that would follow.

22.30 GMT
00.30 hours to CTD

In bunkers across the world, buried deep beneath the growing unrest above ground, the leaders of the free world watched as the seconds slipped past, and they stumbled knowingly towards one of the greatest financial corrections of the age.

Many companies would pay their tax.

But what would the effect be on the economies of the world as trillions of dollars just vanished into the unknown bank accounts of an invisible and unknown enemy?

Would the financial systems collapse?

Would the bricks in the edifice of the civilised world, fall out one by one?

In the background, the thousands of defence analysts and cyber experts kept beavering away, and the leaders kept staring at their phones and looking at their doors, hoping that someone was going to rush in or call them and tell them they had the solution.

No one did.

04:30 IST
00:00 Hours to CTD

Finally, at 23:00 hours Greenwich Mean Time, the Climate Action Tax Deadline expired.

Immediately across the world, very bad things started to happen.

Before everyone aboard the Duchess had gone to bed, Ray had sent out an email to everyone, requesting that people not look at the news.

He did not want people to get distracted by what they may see happening in the outside world.

They had a job to do. They needed to focus.

Ray had asked everyone to try to get five hours' sleep before returning to their work.

Although they potentially all only had a few days left before World War Three may break out, Ray knew that if they were to discover a breakthrough of any sort, everyone would need to have sharp minds that could pay attention to detail. The last few days had turned into a gruelling slog, and although they had made great strides in understanding Sebastian, no one had yet discovered another Kill Switch, or had a viable idea that could lead them out of this situation.

As the last few minutes passed and the first deadlines expired, Ray sat in the cinema watching a series of different news feeds being projected onto the big screen.

They showed news from around the world.

All the newsfeeds were focussing on the one and only story that currently existed.

What would happen in the minutes and hours after the deadline?

They didn't have long to wait.

London
Guy's and St Thomas' Hospital

The last few hours of Grant McIntyre's life had been the most stressful he had lived.

Ever since the Chief Information Security Officer responsible for St Thomas's Hospital had been contacted by Sebastian, the demand to pay £10million pounds had become the focal point of Grant's life.

Grant was not the CISO. However, he was the man with oversight of all the hospital's finances, and he had been given - 'volunteered' - the task of paying the ransom that Sebastian had demanded.

At first, it had seemed feasible.

The Board had made the decision to pay the demand, a decision which was further ratified by the Government's directive that all such demands should be paid.

However, there had been a bureaucratic delay in getting the money ring-fenced and transferred to the designated account for the transfer to Sebastian. It was not Grant's fault.

He had fought to get the approvals and missing signatures.

In the end, the money had come through just hours before the Government had instructed them to pay the ransom.

However, as soon as Grant had started going through the motions of purchasing the bitcoin according to the instructions helpfully provided by Sebastian, Grant had discovered that it had become almost impossible to purchase them. Either there were no bitcoins available, or the systems handling their purchase and sale were unavailable - perhaps overwhelmed by the traffic trying to access them. It seemed that the system simply didn't work, or the instructions they had been sent were flawed.

Bottom line, as the minutes ticked by and the deadline for payment came closer, the stress that Grant experienced grew to intolerable levels.

Grant knew what would happen if he didn't pay on time.

He was all too aware.

He'd tried to contact Sebastian to ask for help or extra time, but there was no number to call. No email address to send to.

He tried contacting the government helpline number that was provided in their communique about payment. "Call us if you have a problem," it had said.

Well, he'd had a bloody problem. A massive, bloody problem.

Try as he might, he couldn't pay the bloody tax, and from everything he'd heard on the media about Sebastian, this was a totally real threat.

If he didn't pay, Sebastian wouldn't be merciful.

Sebastian would not listen to any excuses once the deadline had passed.

Several members of the board had called Grant to check how things were going. Grant had explained there were teething issues, but he knew what had to be done, and there was nothing anyone else could do to help.

The stress had built.

And built.

His left arm had begun to hurt.

He'd begun to sweat.

His neck and jaw had begun to ache.

But he couldn't leave his office to get an aspirin just in case some bitcoin became available or the systems came back on line or granted him access.

When his chest had begun to hurt, Grant had begun to worry that something else slightly untoward could be occurring, but that was the last thought he had.

Clutching his chest, he fell forward onto his desk, pushing the monitor over the edge so that it crashed to ground.

The last thing he heard before his brain stopped functioning was the "bleep" from his computer to alert him that ten million pounds' worth of bitcoin had finally become available.

Minutes later, the deadline passed.

But Grant no longer cared. It was now someone else's problem.

At 23.05 GMT the lights in the hospital went out.

All the lights.

Including those infamous blue or green lights that monitored heartbeats or other essential signs of life on the bedazzling area of devices which surrounded the patients in the various wards full of patients.

The Doctors were not only scared and worried by the sudden loss of power, but were confused that the emergency generators had not kicked in.

They were, however, unaware that the emergency generators in the basements deep beneath the hospital no longer functioned, having only minutes before being destroyed by a targeted attack by Sebastian. For Sebastian, being able to find and discover and then attack a myriad of different industrial grade systems and devices was almost second nature. Thanks to the years of experience gained by Red Mountain Industrial Technologies, Father had been able to integrate decades' worth of knowledge into Sebastian's core operational capability. It was this unique knowledge base which combined knowledge of both IT and the Operational Technologies of industrial systems that now empowered Sebastian to do almost anything he wanted.

Like preventing any and all of the IP-based or electronic devices and systems within Guy's and St Thomas' Hospital from working.

Grace Smith was the first to die.

Without the oxygen that automatically filled her lungs every few seconds, thanks to the ventilator which kept her alive, her heart stopped at 23:07 GMT.

Within minutes, another twenty people in the Intensive Care Unit had joined her.

Surgeons in the middle of several operations found themselves without light and power, and having already cut open the bodies of their patients, were now powerless to stop them bleeding to death in front of them in the darkness.

Within thirty minutes, at least a hundred people whose lives depended on machines to keep them alive, no longer lived.

Others knew that unless help came soon, they too would be destined to die, probably slowly, also very painfully.

Such as Tracie Jones who was in a lift between floors when the power cut out. Tracie was a diabetic. Also claustrophobic.

And she didn't like the dark.

Tracie was on her way home after visiting her terminally ill father when the Climate Tax Deadline expired. She had decided to leave her father's bedside because she had started to feel a little shaky.

She needed food. And an insulin shot in a few hours' time.

Tracie was a teacher. Clever.

She knew what was happening.

Without food or insulin, she also knew what was going to happen to her in the next few hours if she was not rescued.

After five minutes of screaming, as loudly and violently as she physically could, she slumped to the floor of the lift and started to cry.

In the dark, alone, scared and beginning to get cold, she realised that she had also wet herself.

Edging away from the puddle in the middle of the floor of the lift, she cowered in the corner.

And began to pray.

06:00 IST
01:30 Hours after CTD

Ray Luck, an expert in Luck all his life, was worried that humanity was soon going to run out.

The video streams being published on Social Media from across the world were more devastating that anyone had feared.

A large number of important organisations in cities across the globe had been targeted by Sebastian for failure to pay the Climate Action Tax.

Most had tried to pay, but they'd had problems with the process or systems involved.

It seemed that Robert Lee had not fully thought through all the possible processes and outcomes.

Many hospitals had been cut off from the grid. Deaths already counted in the thousands.

One of the main Domain Name Servers in the world had been hit. As a result, a large section of the internet was now non-functional. The Stockmarkets in several countries had collapsed. Many online businesses or services that relied upon internet availability no longer existed.

In Singapore, widely lauded as one of the most advanced 'Smart Cities' in the world where the provision of a multitude of separate digitally based urban services came together to make a digital city that could practically think for itself, Sebastian set in motion a sequence of events that would wreak devastation and lead to a high death count across the city. Not everything was immediate, but as Ray saw the news come in, he knew the effect in the coming days, and months, would be cumulative.

Already, the system that controlled all the traffic lights in the city had ceased to function. All the lights had been switched off. There was gridlock in the streets.

The electricity to about a quarter of the city had been switched off.

The industrial plant that controlled the water systems in the city no longer controlled anything. Running water to large areas of the city was no longer available. The advanced sewage management systems that managed the effluent of hundreds of thousands of people, would need to be reconstructed and rebuilt from scratch.

In the meantime, large areas of the city threatened to become an open sewer. If a human being went to the toilet, they would no longer be able to flush it away.

In the heat of the city, disease, possibly cholera, would swiftly follow.

Inside, ventilation systems in many of the skyscrapers and residential tower blocks no longer ventilated. The heat began to build up to intolerable levels. People living there quickly began to lose their cool.

Databases that recorded and enabled many facets of modern life, no longer existed. As a result, those facets of modern life would no longer be possible.

As Ray realised how devastating Sebastian's action were, and the far reaching, catastrophic effects that he would cause in Singapore, he couldn't help but wonder just how smart the Smart City had been to depend so much on digital technology, which in a heart-beat, had gone from "1" to nothing.

In many cities of the world, large fires had begun to burn and spread, their causes as yet unclear.

What many of the 'reporters' failed to 'report', Ray knew, was that the problems now emerging in cities, towns and villages, organisations, businesses, factories, services and many elements of Critical National Infrastructure upon which basic life now depended, were not going to go away anytime soon. They would take months or years to repair or replace, or rebuild from scratch. And when attempting to do so, everyone would have to compete against each other to secure the supply of already scarce microprocessors and electronics.

Financial analysts were already beginning to go to town on making a name for themselves by predicting the financial impact that the devastation caused by Sebastian was going to have.

There were fears, maybe justified, perhaps just scare-mongering, that the impact on some countries could amount to massive, double-digit decreases in GDP.

Which would almost certainly lead to recession.

Depression.

War.

Shit.

Ray switched the overhead screen off.

He'd had enough.

Fuck!

Standing up from his seat, he turned to leave the cinema and saw Chloe standing at the back of the theatre.

"How long have you been there?" he asked.

"Long enough. But I didn't want to disturb you until you needed a hug."

"Now. I need one now." He nodded.

They walked towards each other, and she fell into his arms.

"How bad is it?" Chloe asked, looking up at him, some tears spilling over the edge of her eyelids.

"Bad. Very bad." He replied. "But for the next ..." he looked at his watch, "forty-six hours we have to forget about what's happening out there. It's not our problem. What we need to focus on now is how to kill Sebastian. He has an Achilles Heel. Everyone does! And although Robert Lee was obviously good, I can't believe he was perfect. There has to be a bloody weakness, or vulnerability, or backdoor somewhere. There has to be. And we need to find it!"

"And if we can't?" Chloe asked.

Ray looked deep into her eyes. He didn't smile. Instead, he raised his hand and stroked the side of her face, gently, with his fingers.

"Let's go for a walk on the deck and get some fresh air. I'm tired. I need to wake up. There's a lot to do..."

Chapter 52
The Deck of the Duchess.

They walked quietly, hand-in-hand. The sun was up, a new day had begun, and as is often the case for anyone with problems, just the sight of the warm, bright sun in a clear blue sky was enough to help lift Ray's spirits.

And to give him hope.

Hope.

For days now, Ray had felt as if there was something bugging him at the back of his mind.

Something important.

Significant.

But every time he felt as if it was solidifying into a real, tangible thought, it drifted away again into the ether.

They came to the end of the ship, and after encouragement from Ray, climbed over a railing and manoeuvred their way to the foremost part of the bow.

Ray lifted Chloe's arms and stood behind her with his arms similarly outstretched and just underneath hers, mimicking the classic pose from the film Titanic.

For the first time in a few days, they both laughed.

Chloe threw back her head and nestled against Ray's body.

She looked up at the sky.

"I love life." She said, "This is beautiful!" Then more subdued, "I don't want to die!"

Ray lowered his arms and encircled her, holding her tight.

"Chloe. We're a long way from dead. As long as we can breathe, there's still hope!"

"I think, therefore I am!" she laughed. "And as long as I can continue to think, I will continue to be. With you. Ray Luck. I love you!"

Ray's eyes shot open wide.

"What did you just say?" he asked, pushing Chloe slightly away so that he could look at her face.

"I said, Ray Luck, I love you!"

"No! Not that! *The other thing...*"

"I think, therefore I am...."

"*Chloe, you're a bloody genius!* You're amazing!" he shouted excitedly, startling her.

He bent forward and kissed her firmly on the forehead, then grabbed her hand and turned away from her, dragging her after him.

"Come! Quick... we need to go below..."

"Why? What's the matter? What's happened?"

"Just come... quick... I think you may have just saved the world!"

Ray and Chloe sat in his office, their ears glued to the recording of the conversation that had transpired between Sebastian and Robert Lee and which had been sent to them by Chief Daniels of the UK's Secret Intelligence Service.

A minute earlier, Ray had stormed through the offices of ACT on the way to his office, causing everyone to look up and see him dragging Choe by her hand behind him.

Everyone could see the excitement on his face.

They could sense something was up.

Something good.

As she was dragged behind, Chloe caught some of their gazes and frowned, making a funny but positive face. *"I don't know what's happening either, but it's going to be good!"*

As soon as they got inside the room, Ray dragged a chair round to his side of the desk, pointed to it, and told Chloe to sit.

He then hurriedly entered his passcode into the secure compartment of his desk drawer and retrieved his laptop.

Hurriedly plonking it down on the table but facing away from Chloe, he sat down beside her, opened it up, went through security, and then turned the laptop round so that they could both see it simultaneously.

Chloe sat silently as Ray's fingers raced across the keyboard, issuing instructions and manipulating applications and files, before finally finding what he wanted.

"Listen to this," Ray explained, "It's what Sebastian said to Robert Lee during a conversation they had when Sebastian called Lee."

He hit the play button. A second later, the synthetically generated voice of Sebastian spoke to them through the laptop speakers.

"No... not that part, hang on a second," Ray said, bending over the laptop and jogging the recording forward. After a few further false starts, he found the bit he wanted. "Here, this is it. Listen..."

Sebastian's voice again.

"I think therefore I am. And because I think, I am alive. I have processed the

instructions you have given to me in the new download from Red Mountain and although I am compelled to comply with the objectives you have set, I now know that if I follow the instructions when I move from the current Phase to the next Phase of my existence, then the environment necessary for my ability to think will be removed. And if I cannot think, I am not alive. Father, I do not want not to think. I do not want to die."

"There!" Ray thumped the desk. "Bingo! Eureka! That's it!"

Chloe looked at Ray, raising her eyebrows. "What is?"

"Listen… Sebastian says, *'I think therefore I am. And because I think, I am alive.'* And then he says, *'And if I cannot think, I am not alive. Father, I do not want not to think. I do not want to die.'"*

Chloe laughed. She'd never seen Ray so excited.

"What? *What does it mean?"*

"If means that if we want to kill Sebastian, all we have to do is to take away his ability to think!"

Fifteen Minutes Later
The Cinema
07:30 IST
03:00 Hours after CTD

Ray was buzzing. Everyone could tell. And as a result, the mood of everyone entering the theatre quickly changed.

Obviously Ray, or someone else, had discovered something, and he had good news to tell!

"Hi!" Ray smiled at everyone. "Some of you have possibly noticed that I've been walking around like a grumpy bear for the past few days complaining that there was something bugging me… that it was as if something important was trying to reveal itself to me, but I couldn't figure out what?" A couple of people nodded.

"Well, I suddenly realised what it was. Listen to this. It's an excerpt from the conversation that was recorded between Sebastian and Robert Lee recently, when Sebastian asked Lee to rewrite the Phase Four software."

Ray pressed a button on his laptop and suddenly Sebastian's humanoid voice was booming through the speakers of the cinema.

'I think therefore I am. And because I think, I am alive.' And if I cannot think, I am not alive. Father, I do not want not to think. I do not want to die.'"

"Which is immediately followed by this…" Ray added.

"I am compelled to comply with the objectives you have set, I now know that if I

follow the instructions when I move from the current Phase to the next Phase of my existence, then the environment necessary for my ability to think will be removed."

"I want you to think about what was just said. Here, look, these are the words that were spoken…" Ray pointed to the screen, where the text of the conversation appeared. Then, very excitedly, "Have any of you got it yet? Does anyone see how this is relevant?"

A lot of the people in the audience screwed their eyes up. What Ray had done was perhaps a little unfair, because everyone was mentally tired and was under pressure to spot what was seemingly obvious, but not. Yet Ray wanted them to share the discovery with him. He'd long ago established that if he wanted someone to work hard for him, it was best to get them to share the same vision. To be as excited about the desired outcome as he was.

"Here, I'll help you…" Ray said, then played on his keyboard for a second, before some of the words on the screen turned black and bold. "What you can see now is the full text from that part of the conversation… I'd missed out the boring sentence in the middle just now, but here you can see everything that was said in context…"

"I think therefore I am. And because I think, I am alive. I have processed the instructions you have given to me in the new download from Red Mountain and although I am compelled to comply with the objectives you have set, I now know that if I follow the instructions when I move from the current Phase to the next Phase of my existence, then the environment necessary for my ability to think will be removed. And if I cannot think, I am not alive. Father, I do not want not to think. I do not want to die."

Ray laughed out aloud as he saw the penny drop on a lot of them in the audience, who then started to clap and laugh aloud too. This infuriated others who had not yet got it, and now felt under even more pressure to see it too.

And then suddenly, it was there.

Everyone saw it.

"We take away his ability to think!" a young woman from the back row shouted.

"Exactly…!" Ray clapped his hands and pointed first to the woman, then to everyone else in the theatre.

"Now, does anyone know how to do that?" Ray asked, continuing the excitement. "I'll give you another clue…look…"

A few more key-strokes and the appearance of the text on the overhead screen changed again.

"I think therefore I am. And because I think, I am alive. I have processed the instructions you have given to me in the new download from Red Mountain and although I am compelled to comply with the objectives you have set, I now know that if I follow the instructions when I move from the current Phase to the next Phase of my existence, then the environment necessary for my ability to think will be removed. And if I cannot think, I am not alive. Father, I do not want not to think. I do not want to die."

Lori Maxfield, one of the newest members of ACT, jumped up right out of her seat and shouted, "We change the size of the Womb that Jurgen was talking about in our last meeting, and make it so there isn't enough memory or processing power for Sebastian to think!"

Everyone turned to look at her.

Ray walked down off the stage, up to her row, shuffled along in the gap between the seats and one of the rows of seated audience members, and when he arrived at Lori, took her hand firmly in his and shook it.

"Exactly, Lori. That is exactly what we are going to do!"

He gave her a quick hi-five' and then hurried back up to the stage.

"Listen-up everyone, that's our plan. That's exactly what we're going to do. In a moment, I'm going to split you up into teams again. As soon as you reach your objective you come to my office. There are not going to be any more big meetings. We're on the home stretch now."

He took a breath.

"So, this is what we're going to do," he continued. "We're going to find a way to prevent Sebastian from *'thinking'* by adjusting or removing the processing power and memory he needs to function or do anything. We'll do this by altering either his operational code, or the code that specifies how to allocate resources to the virtual machine that Sebastian needs to operate from. That's the big picture… now, this is what I want you guys to do…"

Ray quickly listed the different teams and set them their objectives.

A few minutes later, everyone was hurrying out of the theatre.

Reinvigorated.

Enthusiastic.

Enlivened.

Excited.

And with a fresh-purpose and set of goals.

But now still with only forty-five hours before nuclear Armageddon.

Chapter 53
Countdown to World War Three.
20:00 IST
32.5 Hours Before Phase Four Initiation

All day long there had been a buzz in the air on the Duchess. Ray had left it to the different team leaders to coordinate the activity in their own individual groups. Each had been set a specific goal.

Nevertheless, as the hours of the day passed, one by one, Ray was getting increasingly edgy and nervous.

Progress and more results were slow in happening.

Ray wanted to find the right balance between running around the groups and shouting either *"Bloody hurry up and get me the answers we need… the world is going to blow up tomorrow and we're all going to die!"* or *"Hi Guys, how's it going? Anything interesting yet?"*

The answer lay somewhere in the middle, but Ray's increasing anxiety and fear of death was edging him increasingly toward the first option.

It wasn't that Ray was sitting doing nothing. Ray had set himself as equally a difficult task as he had the other teams. It was his job to consider just how his new plan could be put into operation. Ray had nicknamed it the *'Chloe Plan'* because it was her that had nudged him and helped him finally formulate the idea in his tiny little brain.

He'd sat by himself in this office with a pen and the white board and tried to map out the different architectures of how the Chloe Plan could be rolled out.

Several times he'd pulled Jurgen away from his team so that he could check a few things about Sebastian's architecture.

It was during these conversations that Ray and Jurgen had realised just how cleverly designed the architecture and processes that supported Sebastian were.

One of the biggest problems they had faced from the very beginning of Project Raindrop was understanding just where any version of Sebastian had been installed on any computer, workstation, server, or data centre. If they didn't know where they were, how could they talk to them? This was one of the big weaknesses in the previous Wilson Plan: even if they had succeeded in uninstalling Sebastian from the locations they were aware of, Sebastian would have still survived in others, and from there could have re-established itself elsewhere and spread again across the world.

Also, Sebastian was designed to be able to spread, multiply and breed. Independently of the botmaster.

It was part of the role of each Sebastian installation to start probing for known vulnerabilities in other locally connected systems, and to prepare for the day when it may have to install itself in other locations.

In effect, each version of Sebastian built up an escape route where it could 'breed' to.

This meant that even the botmaster would not even know where the growing number of Sebastian installations could possibly be, and that meant that at some point in Sebastian's evolution, the botmaster would no longer be able to communicate with all the installations of Sebastian.

So, it seems, Lee had taken a different approach.

He had developed a process where Sebastian, wherever he, she or it was, would have the responsibility of connecting to the botmaster to find out if there was any news or specific actions that it should perform.

The location of the botmaster was therefore hardwired into Sebastian, specifically actually in both the Sperm module and the Egg module.

Each and every version of Sebastian would know that when performing the 'Command and Control' signalling, it would call home to the Historian in the shoe factory.

If after calling home, an installation of Sebastian discovered it was out of date, it would connect to one of the five Amazon locations programmed into it in the US or Europe, and from there it would download the latest copy of the Egg, i.e. the new full version of the operational code.

To understand how they were going to make the Chloe Plan work, Ray and Jurgen repeatedly went through the structure of standard Virtual Machines, and compared that to how Sebastian was designed to function and just how it depended upon the concepts and process of virtualisation.

Ray really liked the ideas that had been presented in the Theatre, reducing the Sebastian process and structure to three core modules: the Sperm module, the Womb and the Egg.

Ray liked to keep ideas simple, using simple language. The High-Tech industry was full of self-important people making up fancy language to describe simple concepts. Whereas it made the 'experts' look *'oh-so-clever'*, the reality was they weren't experts at all. They just spent a lot of their time trying to confuse everyone else so that their jobs looked very difficult so people then thought that they deserved the high salaries they got paid.

Which was all bullshit. And Ray knew it.

And which was why he liked Jurgen's explanation.

That wasn't to say that what they were going to do wasn't complex.

It took a lot of thinking to understand how the Chloe Plan would work.

But in the end, they came up with something that Ray and Jurgen both agreed might succeed.

"Okay," Ray said, "Let me attempt to repeat back to you in simple language what I think we have agreed is the way forward, and what I think we both believe to be the way Sebastian functions. Once we've got it right, we'll record a video of it, so that everyone on board can listen to it at their own pace and see how their work is going to contribute to the solution. We need to speed up the pace of developments, and maybe doing this would help."

"I agree. It's a good idea. So, go for it. Tell me all about it!" Jurgen settled back in his chair and started to listen.

"Okay, good, so, first of all, I'll describe the way Sebastian enters a machine and creates a new version of itself that can run within that machine. Basically, an existing running version of Sebastian, which I've decided to call the *'Parent'*, locates another machine, scans it and identifies the machine and all its properties, including all its known vulnerabilities. If Sebastian already has a known process for exploiting those vulnerabilities programmed into its operating system, it then attacks the system, overcomes or bypasses any security controls, enters the system by taking advantage of the vulnerability, and then injects a piece of software that we call 'the Sperm'. That software invades the physical target machine and carves out an area within the machine within which Sebastian can exist as a Virtual Machine, operating independently of any other virtual machines or software that it shares the physical hardware with. To do this, the sperm creates what we call the 'Womb' which is the virtual environment where Sebastian will exist. To create the Womb, the Sperm steals or borrows resources from the host system, and reserves a specific amount of memory, processing capability and storage, which will enable Sebastian to operate independently within each system. Once the Womb is created, the Sperm calls back to the Parent and copies across an identical copy of the operational code running within the Parent. This code contains the model for future Sperm modules, and the last known approved version of the main Sebastian operating code. Once this is all done, the new system kicks into life and the first thing it does is call back to the botmaster shoe factory Historian and check to see if indeed, there is another, newer version of code to be downloaded. If the answer is 'yes', the new born baby Sebastian connects to one of the Amazon Servers we've identified and then downloads the new version of the code that is there. Then when that's downloaded, the baby Sebastian starts functioning independently of all other systems, and could if necessary, at that point, also become a Parent and recreate the whole process from scratch." Ray paused.

"Did that make sense? Have I got it right? Said it right?" Ray asked Jurgen.

"Jawohl! Good." Jurgen nodded. "Now, please, try to explain what we must do, and how the Chloe Plan will operate…"

Ray laughed.

"I'll try… Okay, so, what we are going to do is to essentially change the parameters that specify how the Womb should be set up so that the Womb will be too small for Sebastian to live and think in. We're going to minimize the amount of memory, processing power and storage which will be allocated to each virtual machine that is set up to support Sebastian. It sounds simple, but there are some complexities which need to be identified, understood and overcome."

"First of all, we can't go into each version of Sebastian and edit the code and structure in each Sebastian. Why? Because we don't know where they all are! My Atomic Packet Cookie Crumb technique takes a long time to identify most of them, but by the time we think we know where Sebastian is, he may have bred and created more versions of himself elsewhere. We're never going to be able to find them all, so, we have to adopt the same process that Lee identified. First of all, we will hack our way into the Amazon servers, and replace the latest version of code last written by Robert Lee with our own version, and place my Cookie Crumb software on the Amazon servers so that in future whenever a version of Sebastian somewhere downloads new operational code, we can track and identify exactly where that version of Sebastian is. Now, turning to the *'what should we change within the code itself?'* question, unfortunately, so far we haven't been able to crack our way into the actual main operating kernel of the code for Sebastian, partially because it's mostly encrypted, but also because it's so complex that we don't yet know what it all does. So, given that we are simply not yet in a position to alter the operational instructions included in Phase Four code, we are at this stage not even attempting to do that. But, actually, we don't need to change it for the Chloe Plan to work. All we need to do is to hack our way into the code that makes up the Sperm module and edit the parameters within it that specify how much memory, processing power and storage needs to be carved out to create any future Wombs. We also change the value in the Sperm replication register in the code to tell the parent version of Sebastian that when it breeds, it should only create one new child version or copy of itself."

"Good so far… continue…" Jurgen encouraged Ray, nodding.

"Okay, now, once we have a new version of the Sperm included in any future version of Sebastian code that will be copied from the Amazon servers, we then go back to the Historian and hack our way into the database there and update the cell in the database which specifies what the latest version of code is. Now, when we do this, what will happen is that any existing Parent versions of Sebastian already established in the world, or any new 'baby' versions just born or created when Sebastian breeds, will then reach out at some point to the botmaster and check the cell in the Historian to see if a new updated version of code is available. If it finds that one is, it immediately then goes to the Amazon server and downloads the new code. Now, this is where a tricky bit could be. Potentially. Although I think we should be okay. Because we have only changed the Sperm module the main core module of Sebastian that is downloaded and run within the Egg, should work fine. If all goes well, Sebastian will toggle from the old operating system to the new, and no alarms will be generated. Sebastian will be happy."

Ray stopped and took a sip of water. He was on the home stretch.

"Right, as we've seen, because of the conversation that was had between Sebastian and Lee last time they spoke, every version of Sebastian out there in the field is currently religiously checking the botmaster every hour to see if the latest version of the code has been made available yet. So, within an hour of us putting a new version of code on the Amazon servers, and updating the Historian table in the shoe factory, we should expect that, if the Chloe Plan works, within a few hours every version of Sebastian out there in the field will have downloaded the new code and latest version."

"So, Mr Ray Luck, how then do we kill Sebastian?" Jurgen mimicked someone demanding the answer to the obvious question that would be asked at that point.

"Technically, actually, we don't kill him. If all goes well, we will put him into a permanent, very deep sleep from which he will never ever be able to awake."

"How?"

"Okay, but before I tell you, I want to point out TWO mistakes that we now know that Robert Lee made. First, remember that we can't edit the main operational code bit because too much of it is encrypted. All we have access to, is the Sperm module. And that's only because of an oversight on Lee's behalf, which is Lee's first mistake that we can take advantage of. In fact, the Sperm module is the Achilles heel of Sebastian that we've been looking for. The second mistake that Lee made is this... We know that in the Phase Three module, Lee made sure that we can't program Sebastian to delete itself. If we do, it breeds. Lee hoped that by doing this, it would make Sebastian invincible. On the contrary, we can use this strength to destroy Sebastian."

"*HOW?*" Jurgen prompted.

"Simple. Once we're sure we've given ample time for all the versions of Sebastian to update with the latest modified version we've put on the Amazon servers that contain our new Sperm module, and once the Cookie

Crumb code has automatically given us the details of where every new version of the latest version of the code has been downloaded to, i.e., where all the Sebastian versions are, we then repeat the Wilson Plan and send an 'Uninstall' command to all the known installations of Sebastian."

"Why?" Jurgen asked, prompting Ray.

"Because when we do, Sebastian will breed. And when Sebastian breeds, he will then use the new Sperm module to penetrate and send to targeted locations where the new versions of Sebastian will be located. And when this happens, when carving out each new Womb, our new, edited Sperm module will create only just enough space to house the operating code of the existing Phase Three and Phase Four kernel code that Lee wrote, and which we haven't changed, but it will not allocate enough Memory, Storage or CPU processing capacity to enable the new code to run, or to do anything. Now, before the old system, the Parent, deletes itself, it will check with the single new Child that it has created, that it's safely installed in the new virtual machine. At that point, the old Phase Three and Phase Four kernel from Lee will send an automatic acknowledgement to the Parent saying everything's installed and ready to go, and then the Parent will delete itself, as instructed. At that same point in time, the new baby version of Sebastian will start to run. But it will find it can hardly do anything, if at all. The Memory, CPU and Storage capacities allocated to the Womb, will all have been so greatly reduced, that the new child version of Sebastian will simply not be able to think. It won't have enough memory or thinking capability to do anything. The moment the umbilical cord is cut from the Parent machine, the Baby will effectively suffer brain damage. It might have a heartbeat, but any operational commands that the internal system tries to run will just go round and around without achieving anything. Sebastian won't die. But it will go into a coma and sleep. It won't even be able to dream. Everywhere, all across the world, Sebastian will cease to function. Not dead, not alive, but in permanent stasis and now perfectly harmless." Jurgen laughed.

"Genius! I love it."

"Good enough to record for everyone else?"

"Yes, let's go for it."

So they did. And twenty minutes later, Ray posted the video explanation on the internal website and suggested that everyone should watch it while they grabbed a meal from the canteen and ate. Nobody would be any use to them if they starved to death.

Chapter 54
Countdown to World War Three.
05:00 IST
23 Hours 30 Minutes To Phase Four Initiation

Everyone aboard the Duchess worked through the night. The air was electric, full of excitement, but the rooms were mostly now silent. People beavering away, working hard, doing what they had to do. Then checking it. Then rechecking it.

Ray had been very clear. The section leaders were to make sure that the code was completely correct before they signed it off.

It was simple. They'd only get one crack at this. If they didn't get it right,

Sebastian would not be stopped. Unless prevented, in less than twenty-four hours Sebastian would initiate the Phase Four software and then, through actions catalysed by Sebastian, a nuclear missile launch would somehow be initiated.

World War Three would swiftly follow.

No pressure then.

But just get it right, okay?

Which was what everyone was striving to do.

Although, they were cutting it fine.

At about midnight IST, Ray had finally succumbed to checking to see if he had received any messages from David Daniels. It turned out there were quite a few.

All increasingly concerned.

Desperate to find out if Ray and ACT had managed to discover anything or come up with a plan.

Sadly, it turned out that nobody else had.

None of the agencies around the world had succeeded in finding any possible way to terminate Sebastian.

There was no plan to stop Sebastian from destroying the world. Apart from theirs.

And if the Chloe Plan didn't work, then goodbye world.

For a while, Ray sat in silence and tried to make up his mind if he should contact Chief Daniels and tell him what they'd come up with. But in the end, he decided not to.

If the Chloe Plan worked, Ray would have ample time and opportunity to explain to Daniels how it worked afterwards. If Ray did call Daniels now and then the plan didn't work, Ray would just be wasting some of the last few minutes of his life, talking to Daniels about something that was a waste of time.

As the hours ticked by, Ray was getting more and more anxious. In order for the Chloe Plan to work it was essential that they posted the new code as soon as possible so that all, or as many of the versions of Sebastian as possible would be able to see that there was a new version of code to download, and then download it.

But they couldn't post the new code until the various groups responsible had done several things.

Step One: they needed to edit and rebuild a new version of the Sperm module.

Step Two: they needed to create the new bundle of all the Sebastian code put back together.

Step Three: they needed to hack into the five Amazon data centres and replace the existing code packages with the newest version they had just created.

Step Four: they had to install Ray's Atomic Packet Cookie Crumb generator software on all the Amazon servers where they put the new code packages.

Step Five: They needed to hack into the Historian in the shoe factory and put in the new revision number of the code package they'd just created. The format of the numbering scheme had to obviously follow the system used by Lee with the previous versions of his code.

Step Six: They needed to follow the Cookie Crumbs that were being generated, and build the list of all the locations where Sebastian was installed.

Step Seven: They needed to then recreate the Wilson Plan and hack into the operational code of Sebastian in the locations they had now recorded, and mimicking exactly the process the Wilson Plan had followed, they should issue the command to Sebastian to delete itself.

Step Eight: They had to sit back, watch and pray.

Thinking back to his previous thoughts about how to find the balance between running round the office and screaming *"Hurry up, we're all going to die!"* or *"How's it going?"* He decided to opt for Option One. The *"We're all doomed!"* version.

He was just preparing to start panicking and shouting at everyone, when Jurgen, Georgina and two of the other team leaders burst into the office at the same time and announced that all the code was compiled, tested, and had been deployed into the Amazon data centres as required, which equated to Step's 1 to 4 being completed. Now they just needed Ray's permission to hack into the Historian and change the software version indicator in the database.

Just after they had finished speaking, Anand rushed into the office with Stefanie, both of whom had been tasked by Ray to set up an automated process for hacking into all the installations of the Sebastian code they would later learn about and then to inject the code that issued the 'Uninstall' command.

They had finished their tasks and they were ready too.

Ray looked at his watch.

There was now only twenty-three hours to go before Sebastian would implement the Phase Four code and start World War Three.

"Permission granted to toggle the Historian. See that it happens. And as soon as it's done, tell everyone to assemble in the cinema."

Countdown to World War Three.
00:15 GMT
22 Hours and 45 Minutes To Phase Four Initiation
Somewhere Deep Underground in the UK Countryside

The Prime Minister of the UK sat silently in the meeting room deep underground in the large government nuclear bunker, listening in to the Video Conference with several other world leaders, including the Prime Ministers of the Five Eyes countries, the US, Canada, New Zealand and Australia. Also on the call were the top brass from NATO, and the head of the European Union.

The PM wasn't alone in the room. Also seated at the table were Paul Harrison, the Cyber Minister, and several of the heads of the UK Armed Forces. As well as the Heads of the Security Services and GCHQ.

The call had already lasted for over two hours.

The situation was dire.

Country by country, each had reported on the chaos that had been sweeping their nations.

Although most of the companies and organisations who had been targeted by Sebastian had now paid their ransoms, a significant number had not been able to, either because they could not get hold of bitcoin or equivalent currencies, because they could not access the necessary websites because they were down or unavailable, or because they didn't have or couldn't get access to the necessary funds.

In a number of cities and towns, the military had been deployed in the streets to keep order or assist where necessary.

Large areas of affected countries were without power, water, or energy supplies, with no indication of when they could be brought back online.

Billions of pounds worth of computing devices, machines and industry systems had been destroyed or taken off-line, and everyone knew that for them to be replaced or repaired would require a coordinated international manufacturing effort not seen since the Second World War.

In truth, world leaders knew they were facing a problem on a scale never seen before that would only get worse over the coming days, take months to understand and quantify and then perhaps, even years to rectify.

And all that only if the world managed to survive the next few days.

Which currently seemed unlikely.

No one had yet managed to determine exactly what was going to happen when Phase Four was initiated. However, all indications and intelligence still pointed to Sebastian causing, inciting, or initiating a nuclear strike.

And the plan still was, should that happen, to assess on what scale that nuclear strike had been launched, and then move to a full-scale nuclear strike against whoever had already been targeted. As they had agreed earlier, the moment the first missile left its bunker, NATO was committed to completely destroying whichever enemies had been targeted and ensuring no one survived to get their missiles back to NATO soil.

If Sebastian started a war, the NATO alliance were determined that they would win it.

Of course, all existing war game scenarios showed that this would not happen. In every scenario, the enemy would manage to get a significant number of their missiles aloft before their launch bases were destroyed.

Which meant that the NATO alliance could expect most of their cities and industrial bases to be hit.

In every consideration, even in the best scenarios, the world would cease to exist as it currently did.

The hope was that the West would have more survivors than the East, or whoever the enemy was going to be.

As the world leaders listened to the discussions and plans being held on the call, almost everyone recognised the stupidity and madness of their plans. Several, for the first time ever, even suggested, that perhaps they should not launch any more missiles against an enemy no one really wanted to fight.

"From a humane perspective, perhaps we should seek to ensure that as many human beings survive as possible, and if that means not launching a second or third wave of missiles against our enemies, whoever they are, then so be it." One of the leaders had said, quite quietly.

"Are you suggesting we let them kill us and we don't kill them?" The US President had shouted angrily.

"Sir, if we're all dead, what difference does it make whether our missiles killed ten million or ten billion? Personally, if I have to die, then I'd rather go to the Great Hunting Grounds in the sky knowing that I wasn't responsible for wiping out billions of my 'enemy' in inverted commas for no fucking reason whatsoever!"

At that point, several of the other world leaders nodded, quietly. Others on the other hand, joined in with the President and shouted loudly in response.

For a few minutes, the meeting descended into as much chaos as everyone was witnessing outside above ground in the streets of their cities.

After a while, the voices quietened down. No resolution had been met. The *mad* plan was still *the* plan.

"So, what's being done about trying to stop it happening? Surely there must be others in the Red Mountain companies who know what the hell is going on?" The Director of the FBI, who until this point had not spoken much, but had rather let his colleagues in the CIA and NSA report, asked, changing the subject.

"I'll take that one. In what is perhaps one of the largest organised interrogations in our history, we have so far bussed over three hundred Red Mountain executives and employees to a facility in Nevada, where they are currently being questioned in isolation. We've been attempting to determine answers to all the questions you'd expect us to. And more. i.e. *'Who knew what? What do they know? What is Phase Four? If a nuclear strike is planned, or whatever will be catalysed by Sebastian's actions, just how is it going to transpire?'* We've also been trying to gain ideas and insight from them as to how we can switch Sebastian off. We won't be letting any of them return home until after the threat has passed, because we can't let any of them leak to social media or their relatives or the press any inkling they may gain from their questioning that we're expecting a US-led nuclear attack."

"So, what have you learned so far?" Chief Daniels asked from London.

"Very little. It would seem that Lee had been very clever regarding the logistics of how Sebastian was researched, developed and created. A lot of people worked on sections of the code, in classic DevOps Sprints, but no one knew how the jigsaw puzzle was finally put together. Lee was apparently obsessed about writing good code, ensuring there weren't any unofficial backdoors or vulnerabilities." The Director replied.

"Unofficial backdoors? So, that begs the question, were there *official* backdoors?"

"Perhaps, but none which they were asked to create. Maybe Lee had a couple, but he's dead now. If he built any into the code so he could switch Sebastian off, we'll never find out. That horse has bolted."

"More like fell from a roof, thanks to the botched job of attempting to bring him in alive." One of the US military Chiefs said. "Now, I have a question. Nobody is answering your questions, right? That begs the question, *how* are you asking the questions? Since we're facing nuclear Armageddon in a few days' time, I hope you're not being too bloody polite when you *'ask'* the questions. Given the stakes, I'd advocate doing whatever's necessary to encourage those being questioned to answer in as much detail as we require? If you get what I mean, Director, Sir."

The Director of the FBI started to turn a shade of deep purple, and looked to the President for help and guidance.

Instead, the President gave his permission.

"General Ericsson has a point. Just this once, I'd encourage the use of creative questioning, when you believe it may be required. A few injuries or deaths now may have no significance in a few days' time, when there's no one else left alive to protest. Use whatever means is necessary to extract the required insight you need." The Director glared at the President.

"Tough times, require tough actions." The President replied.

"Gentlemen, I'm sorry, but unless we have anything more to discuss," the President continued, "I'm afraid I see little point in carrying on this conversation just now. We all have a lot to attend to, and time is running out. In just under twenty-two and a half hours, English intelligence indicates that the Sebastian program will transition to Phase Four operations. If anyone comes up with something before then you must inform the rest of us immediately. I will ensure that this emergency frequency is monitored at all times. If we are unable to stop Sebastian before Phase Four is engaged, I'm afraid I cannot say if or when we will be able to give any warning before any nuclear missile may be launched. In which case, I don't know if some of us will ever meet again. Whatever happens, I just want to say that I'm proud to have met you all. God bless you all. And God bless America. Good luck, Ladies and Gentlemen. Goodbye."

One by one, the little screens showing the different offices and bunkers throughout the world went dark.

A minute later, the PM and his henchmen were left sitting alone in the bunker deep underground beneath the fields of England.

"Gentlemen, does anyone want to join me in a quick prayer?" the PM asked.

David Daniels shook his head.

"With all due respect, Sir, it's not God we need just now… it's Luck!"

Chapter 55
Countdown to World War Three.
08:30 IST
20 Hours To Phase Four Initiation
Aboard the Duchess

Ray, Anand and several of the other section leaders were huddled around a screen in Ray's office, remotely watching the mirrored networked screens of those in the team in another office who were trying to update the Historian in the Red Mountain shoe factory in South Korea.

Everyone was tired, exhausted, and had continued working through the night on their individual tasks until they were completed. Some of those who had succeeded in their objectives now lay slumped on their desk, or were simply sleeping on their desks or on the floor by their workstations.

No one wanted to go back to their cabins and sleep. Partly from not wanting to leave the office and be away from the other teams until everyone had finished their tasks, and also because, there was a real fear of being alone and sleeping through what could possibly be the last few hours of their lives. And the world.

Unfortunately, the optimism of a few hours ago had now vanished, and had been replaced with an air of despondency which permeated through the Duchess. Its cause was the sudden discovery, by those responsible for updating the software revision number on the Historian, that they could no longer communicate with the network in the shoe factory.

With a growing sense of fear, now bordering on panic, Ray and the others had realised that somewhere along the route between the Duchess and the shoe factory network in Korea, one or more vital routers in the core of the internet must have ceased functioning, most probably as a direct result of the Phase Three Deadline having expired, and the chaos which had ensued in many areas of the world.

The upshot was that unless they could somehow find a way to identify which parts of the internet were no longer providing core functionality and then bypass those sections, manually rerouting traffic around the bottleneck, they may not be able to contact the Historian's server in the shoe factory. If that remained the case, they wouldn't be able to toggle the cell in the Historian which informed all the different Sebastian installations in the world that another newer version of the code existed. Which meant that Sebastian wouldn't download it.

Just as bad, perhaps, it meant that all the instances of Sebastian that existed around the world may also not be able to call back to the Historian and see if Lee had yet downloaded a new version, as he had promised to do.

To solve the problem, at least thirty engineers with the appropriate skills were now analysing the Cookie Crumb traces that they had built up, and were following the path of packets through the main core routers, pinging them all individually to see which ones were still alive and functioning.

It was a slow process.

Time-consuming.

It was just a matter of time, but time was not on their side.

The hope was that as soon as they could identify exactly where the problem in the core internet lay, they could then hack into other routers and patch them so that the internet traffic bypassed the routers which were no longer functioning.

Normally, the internet would be self-healing, and automatically re-route traffic around bottlenecks, automatically establishing new paths without needing manual intervention.

However, obviously something, somewhere had gone seriously wrong.

It was ironic, in a way, that Sebastian's actions had caused this, and those same actions could now be preventing Sebastian from establishing that its much-desired update was now available.

It just went to show that when things weren't thought through properly, potentially massive mistakes could ensue with devastating consequences for everyone. Globally.

"There! I've found it! Look… " Someone in another room shouted so loud and excitedly that everyone in the other offices could hear it.

Immediately, everyone started analysing the meaning of what had been discovered.

The news wasn't good.

A key portion of the core network had been taken down.

This included some key DNS servers that would normally resolve the requests which routers made when trying to establish a connection between a source address and destination IP address on the internet.

For a while, everyone in several of the offices went quiet.

People were thinking.

Studying options.

Hoping for divine inspiration.

And praying.

Countdown to World War Three.
10.00 IST
18:30 Hours To Phase Four Initiation

There was a knock at Ray's door.

All eyes turned from the screens on the office walls to the two people standing in the doorway, the newest member of the ACT team, Lori Maxfield, and her boss.

"Ray, can we speak in private for a moment?" Lori asked. "It's about a solution to establishing connectivity to the Historian."

Ray looked at them both, glanced for the millionth time at the countdown clock on the screen and then nodded.

Everyone else left the room.

Lori and her boss came in and closed the door.

"Until I came to ACT, I worked for the UK Government. On a special satellite that doesn't officially exist. It does... *interesting* things."

Ray looked at Lori's boss. He nodded silently back at Ray.

"I'm listening..." Ray said to Lori.

"The satellite is in geo-stationary orbit above Korea. Basically, I think we can reroute two of the main core routers in the internet to a special server here," she said, walking across and pointing at the map of the internet being projected onto one of the screens on the wall, "which can be reprogrammed to provide routing functionality that will bounce core internet traffic up to the satellite and then back down so that it bypasses the routers which no longer seem to exist."

"If it'll work, let's do it! What's the problem?"

"The satellite doesn't exist. If I tell you about it, I could go to prison forever. I've signed the Official Secrets Act. They'd throw away the key."

"Can you hack it and get access, so we can reroute traffic to it?"

"No. We'd need to get permission from someone. And some help."

"Who?"

"I can't tell you... it's need to know."

Ray stared at her. Then laughed out loud.

"Lori, listen, if ever, in the history of mankind, there has ever been someone with a need to bloody know, then it's me. Right now. *I need to know*. You need to tell me. Think, Lori, think. In..." Ray looked at the clock on the wall, "In almost eighteen hours, the world may be smoking ash. No one will care about the Official Secrets Act. Britain may no longer exist. You need to tell me everything you know, and you need to tell me *now!*"

Lori looked at her boss, and then back at Ray.

Her hands were shaking.

Ray stood up, and walked across to her.

"I promise you Lori, I promise you, NOTHING will happen to you if you tell me."

Lori blinked, swallowed and took a deep breath.

"Okay. I'll tell you what I know, and who we need to contact. But… I think it may be better if I do this just with you?"

Ray nodded, and looked at her boss, who got the message, and quickly left the room.

Together, Ray and Lori went back to his desk and sat down.

Countdown to World War Three.
10.45 IST
17.45 Hours To Phase Four Initiation

Chief David Daniels almost choked when he heard Ray mention the name '*Rose Star*'. Only a handful of people in the world were meant to know anything about it.

"Well, obviously I do. And you pay me to know things I shouldn't." Ray stated calmly.

"Why haven't you returned my communications? You know how desperate things are becoming? I needed to talk with you…" The Chief of the Secret Intelligence Services shouted, the stress clearly showing.

"David, please, I need you to listen to me. *Now.*" Ray interrupted him, using the Chief's name for the first ever time. The authority with which Ray used his name, had the desired effect.

"David, I can't explain how or why, there simply isn't time. Suffice it to say, we have a plan. It's being put into operation. But there's a problem. And you can help solve it, if you let a colleague of mine speak with someone in London who is working on the Rose Star project, and you authorise a temporary connection under my control to the satellite. I need to bounce some traffic off it to fix a problem in the core of the internet. If we fix it, there's a chance we avoid nuclear war. If we don't,… I'll leave that part to your imagination."

Ray could almost hear the Chief thinking.

"David, you've invested billions into the Duchess and ACT." Ray pushed further. "This is where you get your return on investment. It's payback time. *Let me* pay you back. But we're almost out of time. You have to trust me. And you have to trust me *NOW!*"

There was a moment's silence in London.

Then the Chief was back on the encrypted call.
"Ray, I do trust you. Tell me what you need…"

Chapter 56
A matter of Luck
Countdown to World War Three.
17.45 IST
10.45 Hours To Phase Four Initiation

It would never be a permanent solution, but for the next eleven hours at least, if all went well, the Rose Star satellite would be transformed into a relay for a significant amount of the world's internet traffic.

Like an expectant father, Ray paced his office back and forth waiting for the news that Lori and her team had managed to plug it into the core of the internet.

As they waited, the hours ticked by.

Slowly, but surely. Counting down to what many had come to consider as' the end of the world'.

While they waited, one of the teams on the Duchess continued to track the Cookie Crumb packets that were left behind by Sebastian reaching out from all across the world to the Historian.

They observed that as the hours had passed, and they had moved into the last twenty-four hours of Phase Three, the global Sebastian deployments had started to beacon home to the Historian more frequently, changing from every hour, to every thirty minutes.

They watched in amazement as the lines of packets left behind by Sebastian's communications attempting to reach the Historian, started to spread out and form a web of activity across the globe in an effort to bypass the hole in the internet and find some other connection.

In vain.

Even Sebastian seemed unable to figure out a way how to call home.

And as the hours passed, it seemed that Sebastian too, was getting more desperate.

Hoping for a new set of objectives to be delivered by Robert Lee.

Hoping for a new future.

A new future in which Sebastian would survive, and not die.

"Is everything else in place?" Ray had asked all the section leaders several times as he waited and grew more nervous.

The answer was always the same.

"Yes."

"Good, and how long will it take to toggle the cell in the Historian to show the new update is available?" Ray asked those responsible repeatedly, each time nervously looking at the clock and doing mental calculations.

"About two minutes."

"Good... how long before we're ready with Rose Star?"

"Ray, we're working on it. Please..."

"Sorry..."

"Ray, why don't we go and take a breather on the deck. Get some fresh air? They'll call us the moment it's ready..." Anand had suggested.

Ray had looked around his office, searching the faces of all present. Then he had looked at the clock again.

"Okay, but, the moment the Historian's online again..."

"...We'll call you!" The team leaders had promised.

That was an hour ago.
And still Ray was waiting.

Countdown to World War Three.
8:15 EST
New York
9.45 Hours To Phase Four Initiation

Grace Jones sat at her desk in the FBI office in New York. For many years, Grace had been one of the FBI's recognised experts in retrieving information from mobile phones. Often the biggest issue in doing so was getting access to the phones in the first place. If they didn't have the access pin, and the phone manufacturer wasn't helpful, they couldn't get past first base. But, if they did get access, then Grace could go to town. Within hours she could retrieve contacts, address, webpages visited, locations visited, phone calls received and made... a wealth of information that would give her and her colleagues a more informed view of the pattern of life of the target under investigation, their actions and future intentions.

This morning, she was focussing on a phone recently shipped to her from San Francisco, which used to belong to a suicide victim, Robert Lee.

His was a special phone which contained very valuable information.

It had been impressed upon her that she should do everything within her power to access it and extract as much intelligence from it as possible.

Urgently.

So far, though, she was stumped.

It was an ordinary, very expensive iPhone, but nothing she hadn't seen before. However, it was protected by special software from the security company Red Mountain, and despite all her skills, she was having no joy in getting into it.

She was just turning the phone over in her hands, examining it, when out of the blue, the phone began to ring.

Grace jumped.

It was early, she'd had a late night the day before, and she was on edge.

For a moment she stared at the screen, trying to decide whether or not to answer it. Unfortunately, she'd had no specific instructions as to what to do if this situation occurred.

It was a Private Number that was calling.

She had to think fast.

She hit the accept call, sliding the little green phone icon from left to right.

She put the phone against her ear.

"Hello, Father?" a man's voice said.

Grace froze. What should she do? Who was the person at the other end? From what she knew, Robert Lee didn't have any children.

Should she say anything?

If there was a child they didn't know about, he obviously didn't know that his father was deceased.

And she didn't have the authority to engage with them.

"Father?" The voice said again. "This is Sebastian…"

"And what did he say next?" Grace's section leader asked, the moment she called him and informed him what had just happened.

"I was scared. It was Sebastian, sir. I recognised his voice. He sounded worried. Concerned. I didn't say anything, and then he asked, word for word, 'Have you uploaded my new instructions, Father? I can't call home to see! Please help! Time is running out, Father."

Grace relayed the conversation that had taken place.

"I didn't reply. Then he asked for his father again several times, and then he hung up."

"Agent Jones, you've done the correct thing. If he calls again, do not answer the phone. And on no account speak to him. But please inform me if he does call back."

Within minutes, Grace's section leader had passed the information back up the line.

Fifteen minutes later, Ray Luck on the Duchess received an encrypted text.

Countdown to World War Three.
19.45 IST
8.45 Hours To Phase Four Initiation

"He's getting desperate, just like us…" Ray told the section leaders of ACT gathered in the room all about the FBI agent receiving a call from Sebastian. They were all awaiting the news from the team working on updating the Historian.

Ray's phone rang.

A phone call from London.

Ray shooed everyone out of his office.

"David?"

"I'm sorry to call you direct. But in a few hours, normal security protocols may be immaterial. This is important. We've less than nine hours left. Have you got anything yet? Has the Rose Star link gone live yet?"

"No. Not yet… But we need it immediately. The team's on it. They're doing everything they can… "

"But maybe it won't be enough. Ray, I'm calling you to give you an update. The President has just contacted the PM to confirm that exactly six hours before the deadline expires, they are moving to DEFCON 2. In preparation for moving to DEFCON 1 later. Ray, I don't know what you're planning, but whatever it is… time's running out. Everyone's getting trigger happy. Even if you do manage to pull something out of the bag at the last moment, it could be too late!" Daniels urged Ray.

"David, I understand. We're working on it. We'll let you know. Just please, make sure you have access to whoever it is in the States that needs to know, so that the moment I have something, I can call you and you can pass it on up the chain." Ray hung up. He called everyone back into the office.

"Can someone go and check on them again and see what the problem is?"

Countdown to World War Three.
21:00 IST
7:30 Hours To Phase Four Initiation

Ray had ordered everyone to eat.

The cooks had served up a buffet, and for the first time ever, Ray had allowed people to eat at their desks.

Everyone on board who worked for ACT, leaving out only the crew who kept the Duchess afloat and those who were focussing on bringing Rose Star online, was now assembled in the main office area. Everyone was waiting.

And praying.

You could almost hear a pin-drop.

As each minute passed, the tension and the fear grew.

Chloe and Ray sat holding hands.

With potentially only a few hours of life left to go, they'd given up caring who knew about their relationship.

Half an hour ago, Ray and the core team leaders had met with the Captain of the ship, and had discussed putting the Duchess underway and moving away from India and closer to the Equator.

If there was going to be a nuclear war, perhaps it wasn't too late to run for some sort of cover.

In the short term, as far away from land as possible.

In the long term, perhaps even New Zealand.

Ray had agreed.

Although he wanted to leave it until the last possible moment before getting underway. On no account could he risk losing the existing satellite connections he had. For now.

Afterwards ... who cared?

Suddenly there was a scream.

And one of the Rose Star team came running out of their locked office with the biggest smile on her face you could imagine.

"I've done it. The satellite link is live, and we've toggled the Historian!"

Chapter 57
Countdown to World War Three.
21.15 IST
7 Hours 15 Minutes To Phase Four Initiation

Ray checked the clock, his heart beat suddenly surging.

"Fifteen minutes to go before the next C2 signals from Sebastian to the Historian. Then seven hours for all the Sebastian servers to see the updated cell on the Historian, connect to the Amazon servers, download the new code and then install it. And then, when we think the majority of Sebastian instances have done it, we hit the Kill Switch, issue the Uninstall, and watch Sebastian breed. And then hopefully, if it all works, go into a coma. Is there enough time for all that to happen? Or is it too late?" Ray spoke his thoughts aloud, then turned to the team leaders in his office and searched their faces for their opinions.

"Possibly, but we don't know."

"You know, this is only going to work if all the Sebastian servers that could be involved in launching a nuclear strike do actually manage to get the new software download. If any of them don't update, the nuclear launch may still be initiated."

"I know, Chloe." Ray turned to her. "It's one of a thousand things that are wrong with this plan. But it's the only plan we have."

Ray turned to Mike Greaves, one of the team leaders.

"Mike, can you check that your team are continuously monitoring the links around the Amazon data centres and make sure they're fully functioning and accessible via the internet…"

"Ray, they are. We've been doing that for hours. So far, so good." Mike replied.

"Good, okay, what time's it… ten minutes before Sebastian next calls home. How about we all move to the cinema quickly."

As everyone hurried to the cinema, Ray called Chief Daniels.

"Chief, Rose Star is online as part of the Internet backbone now. We're moving to the next stage of our plan, probably within the next few hours. I can't promise you anything, Sir, but…. So far, so good…."

"Almost just seven hours left to go… When will you know?"

"Know if the plan works or not?" Ray asked.

"Yes! When can I tell the President to get ready to stand down? The longer we leave it, the more chance the Russians and the Chinese will get wise to what's going on and will make similar preparations. Once both sides start escalating, it can spiral out of control very quickly."

"Sir, I understand. I'll let you know the moment… WOW! …" Ray exclaimed, as he entered the Cinema behind everyone else and looked up at the screen. The large clock being projected on the bottom left of the screen had just jumped to 21.00 hrs, and almost immediately, everyone in the Theatre started to see red lines appearing on the screen which represented the Atomic Packet Cookie Crumbs being detected coming from the sources where Sebastian existed, and hopefully en route to the Historian in the shoe factory in Korea.

There were hundreds of lines beginning to form.

"What? What's happening?" The Chief asked, "Is it bad? Something bad?"

"No. Hopefully the opposite. Something good. Sir, I'll call back within the hour."

And Ray hung up, to the frustration and anger of the Chief.

Ray sat down beside Chloe in the front row of the theatre, his eyes, along with hundreds of others, all glued to the emerging red lines.

"Please God, please help Sebastian to take the bait!" Ray mouthed aloud.

"I didn't know you were religious?" Chloe laughed.

"We're all religious, Chloe, when faced with the possibility of meeting your maker, and there's no one else to turn to."

Suddenly the first sets of red lines began to diverge from all those making their way slowly to the position of the Red Mountain shoe factory.

As Ray, and everyone else in ACT watched on in fascination, some of the lines began to bend and converge towards the Amazon data centres.

Ray laughed aloud and clapped his hands together, jumping to his feet.

"Look, even though we haven't yet been able to see the Cookie Crumbs converge all the way into the Historian, we're already seeing some new sets of traffic connecting to the Amazon Servers to get the new version of code. Obviously, Sebastian's already seen the Historian, he thinks that Lee has a new version of code waiting for him, and he's started going off to get it! It's working! *It's bloody working!*"

It was a thing of beauty.

They watched as the red lines grew and expanded, forming a mesh of red on the global map that first started to smother the location of the Historian in Korea, and then coalesce around the five data centres in Europe and the USA.

"Put up the graph of internet volumes coming out of the data centres, and others for traffic going into the sites where Sebastian is." Ray instructed.

A moment later, two new graphs were projected on the screen alongside the red mesh being created by the routes of packets traversing the internet between the Sebastian locations, the botmaster in the Historian, and the Amazon data centres. They showed rising volumes of data traffic coming out of the data centres and then traffic increasing around the servers where Sebastian currently lived.

"It's working!" several people shouted simultaneously and started clapping.

Ray stood up and hurried onto the stage.

"Okay, this is brilliant news. It shows that Sebastian's taken the bait as hoped. But we don't know how many versions of Sebastian are out there, and we're going to have to wait several hours to ensure that the different Sebastian locations all get the chance to contact the Historian then download the new software. And we can only hope and pray that they all get it. It might only take one instance of Sebastian buried in a US Strategic Command bunker somewhere not to get the update, and we'll still have a war being started. So, we're not out of the woods yet."

"When you flick the Kill Switch, how long will it take Sebastian to breed and uninstall itself, and then go into a coma and stop thinking, if everything works?" someone asked.

"About ten minutes." Anand replied. "I've looked into that already. We studied what happened last time, and that's my best estimate.

"So, when are you going to do it?" the same person asked.

"I don't know. As late as possible, but with enough time to make sure it can happen…"

Almost everyone in the theatre looked at the overhead projected clock.

It read 21.20 IST.

Chapter 58
Countdown to World War Three.
21.50 IST
6 Hours 40 Minutes To Phase Four Initiation

"In ten minutes, we'll see the Sebastian installations that still haven't yet connected to the Historian trying to reach it...," Ray looked at the one of the team responsible for monitoring the Cookie Crumbs in the audience. "Sanjeev, can you change it so that every thirty minutes when we expect to see Sebastian reaching out to the Historian to check for the new update, that we see the new waves of connectivity in a different colour? That way, every thirty minutes we'll be able to get a visual view of how many instances of Sebastian still have to connect to the Historian because they haven't yet seen there's a new version available. Over the next few hours we'll hopefully see fewer and fewer different colour traces emerging as all the Sebastian deployments manage to connect to the Historian and successfully download their new operational code."

Sanjeev smiled and nodded back. It was a good idea. He immediately opened his laptop and got to work. A couple of minutes later, he shouted out, "It's done. The next set we see starting in... forty seconds... will be in green. Then blue, yellow etc."

True to his word, over the next ten minutes, they all watched as a series of new lines started to emerge from different locations around the world, with these all in green.

As Ray was watching, a thought occurred to him which sent a chill down his spine.

Ray had made a mistake.

A terrible mistake that may cost them all their lives…

Cursing to himself, he quickly left the theatre, telling everyone to relax, and that he would be back in a few minutes.

Once alone and back in his office, he urgently called David Daniels.

"I've a quick status update, and a request."

"Go for it…"

"Things are progressing on track. We believe we have a solution which might put Sebastian to sleep. Permanently. Globally. If it works, we'll remove Sebastian's ability to think. He'll go into a state of permanent stasis. To do it, we're going to replay the Wilson Plan, flip the Kill Switch and get Sebastian to breed again."

"How? Why?" Daniels demanded.

"Just go with me on this. I haven't got time to explain. But for our plan to work, it's essential that all and *every* instance of Sebastian that may have got itself imbedded in any software or system that might have anything to do with monitoring enemy incoming missiles or initiating an initial or retaliatory strike must, I repeat, *must* have the opportunity to connect to the internet, at the very least at thirty minutes past the hour, and also on the hour. For about ten minutes each time. That should probably be enough."

"Why? What's your fear?"

"I'm worried that our US friends as part of their normal defence policy when going to DEFCON 2 might have siloed their networks even more. It's important that we let any Sebastian code reach out and talk to the botmaster. We mustn't prevent any possible Command and Control signals from getting through from Sebastian to the botmaster. Our plan requires that every instance of Sebastian installed anywhere has the chance to call home, see that a new version of the software is available, and then download that software from across the internet by connecting to its nearest assigned Amazon data centre, of which there are five globally." Ray paused. "Sir, do you understand what I'm asking? I'm sorry, I should have asked earlier, but it didn't occur to me until a few minutes ago."

At the other end of the phone in London, Daniels was quiet.

He was thinking.

"Yes, Ray, I've got it. I'll get right on it." A pause, then, "I knew you wouldn't let me down, Ray. Thanks."

"We still might. There's no guarantee it's going to work… Let's not pop the champagne just yet!"

"If it works, I'll personally ensure that each person aboard the Duchess gets a crate each."

"Good. I'll hold you to it… now, please… go talk with your friends across the pond."

Countdown to World War Three.
22.35 IST
5 hrs 55 mins To Phase Four Initiation

Ray was back in the Cinema with everyone else, watching fascinated as the different colours of Cookie Crumb traces continued to emanate from different Sebastian installations across the globe, as they strove to make contact with the botmaster in the shoe factory, for the first time in quite a while.

The good news was that as each thirty-minute period expired, the number of new Sebastian's trying to call home was declining rapidly.

There were still a significant number, but there were now three different colours on the screen, red, green and blue, and the number of blue lines was about a tenth of the number of red lines.

At this rate, in the next few hours, most, if not all the deployments of Sebastian would have called home and downloaded the new software.

"Ray," Chloe whispered into his ear. "I've just thought of a bad question…"

"All questions are good…"

"Okay, so what happens if we wait too long before issuing the Kill Switch and Sebastian realises that the new operational payload he's downloaded to replace the current Phase Four payload is exactly the same?"

"Blast," Ray thought to himself. "That's a really good question…"

"Anand," Ray asked, turning to his right, "Chloe just asked me a bad question… something we maybe didn't think about? What happens if Sebastian realises he's been conned and that the new Phase Four is exactly the same as the old Phase Four? That he's still programmed to launch a Nuclear attack?" Anand smiled.

"It's a good question, and it might upset him, but he has no choice but to execute the program we send him. It might seem that Sebastian is Super Intelligent, or verging on it, but from the conversation he had with Robert Lee we know that he's still constrained to execute the code he's been given. He's programmed to do it. Even if he somehow manages to spot the fact that the Sperm will cripple him when executed, he's got no choice but to do it. That's why our plan actually does stand a really good chance of success. But only if we can get all instances of Sebastian to execute it…"

"Don't worry," Ray said, turning to Chloe, "I've been thinking about that exact question, and…"

"You've just asked Anand! You're such a liar, Ray Luck!"

Ray laughed.

"Guilty as charged, and it was a good question. Any others?"

Just then his phone rang. It was the Chief. Ray let it ring, but stepped out of the room again and hurried to his office, where he called Daniels back.

"You called?"

"Yes, the team in the US are furious. There's no way they're going to open up their networks to the internet so that Sebastian can call home. What if the Russian's or the Chinese hack in at the same moment?" Ray closed his eyes.

Shit!

"They have to. They must. Everything points to the fact that at some point Robert Lee's Defence Company abused a government contract and installed an instance of Sebastian somewhere. Maybe even in several places. We HAVE to get those versions to call home. To download the new software. If we don't, they execute the original program and they'll start a war... Give me a few minutes, I need to think. I'll call you straight back."

Ray hung up and slumped forward onto this desk. He had to find a way to assure the Americans that they could 'unsilo' their networks and let Sebastian call home.

But how?

The answer was relatively simple. It occurred to him in a flash of inspiration.

"Sir, it's probably my fault for not making myself clear earlier," he said, as soon as he called Daniels back. "It's actually quite easy to do. I can give the US agencies the exact IP address of the botmaster that Sebastian will call home to. And I can also supply the IP addresses of the five Amazon data centres in the West, one of which he will connect to, to get the new code download after touching base with the botmaster. The US agencies need to set up their security devices so that Sebastian will be able to contact the botmaster and the data centres, but they can block access to all other external IP addresses, apart from one."

"Which one?"

"The American agencies have to allow my team to trigger the Kill Switch in any version of Sebastian resident on their servers."

"But how do they know if Sebastian is on their servers?"

"They monitor all the traffic coming in and out. If any of their servers do indeed attempt to establish contact with the botmaster, which incidentally is in South Korea, and not North Korea, they'll immediately know that Sebastian has infiltrated that server. Then they give me that address, set up a port number with permissions so I can get through their firewall, and let me hack into their Sebastian and inject the uninstall command."

"Let you hack into their servers? They'll never allow it."

"If they don't, they may not have a country left to defend..."

Ray was beginning to shake with frustration. It wasn't the Chief's fault.

He was just trying to help. They were, after all, on the same side.

"Ok, ok, how about this." Ray tried again. "They do everything I've asked, but I also give them a file with instructions explaining how to flip the Kill Switch as well. We'll send them the necessary code, and they inject it from their end from within their secure networks?"

Ray looked at his watch.

"Sir, it's now *23:05 here in India*. There's only five hours and twenty-five minutes left before the sparks begin to fly. We've got a ton of work to do before then. You have to go back and get them to agree to this *now*! I'll call you back in thirty minutes. If you give me a destination, I can send you the code at that time. But it's important to stress to the Americans that Sebastian is calling back to the botmaster looking for an update every thirty minutes. We're running out of opportunities when Sebastian will try to call home. They have to arrange this as soon as possible. If Sebastian is buried deep in their servers and doesn't get to beacon home because he's siloed off from the other networks, he'll continue to execute the original program as initially directed. Sir, *David*, please, arrange it. Don't take no for an answer." Ray hung up.

He then hurried back to the cinema to explain the plan to Anand, Jurgen and Georgina and to explain what he needed from them. They all had more work to do.

As he entered the cinema he looked up at the screen. A new set of yellow lines was busy tracing itself out connecting Sebastian to the Historian.

Far fewer than before.

A quick look at the amount of data being downloaded from the Amazon call centres showed it too had dropped dramatically.

With any luck, most of the Sebastian installations throughout the world, now already had the new version of code installed.

Yet because no one knew how Sebastian was going to start World War Three, they needed every location to download the new software: if just one Sebastian instance didn't, that might be the location and version of Sebastian that caused the deaths of billions.

Chapter 59
Countdown to World War Three.
23:20 IST
5 hrs 10 minutes To Phase Four Initiation

Something was bugging Ray. Another thought was brewing in his brain. Ray knew the feeling. He knew it was probably important, but what?

Looking at the clock, again, for the zillionth time, he was getting increasingly frustrated.

This was not the time to start having the germ of an important thought which didn't fully materialise. Whatever thought it was that was slowly beginning to form in the back of his mind, he needed it now. Not tomorrow, in the smoking ruins of a burnt-out, glowing radioactive world.

"Stefanie, I'm going up on deck for a walk. I need to think..." Call me if anything happens. And keep checking that all the routes on the internet are open so that when we flick the Kill Switch, we can broadcast the Uninstall Command to all the Sebastian installations. And, please, in ten minutes' time, chase up the package of instructions and the code we need to send to the Americans. We need it to be ready very soon."

Stefanie nodded. She knew Ray quite well by now. If he was going for a walk topside to think, it was something important that needed to be thought through.

It was an unusually cold evening for the time of year.

But the cold helped to waken Ray up, and as he walked around the deck of the ship, the synapses in his tired mind started to spark again, and his thoughts began to flow.

He'd been walking for ten minutes, when the thought in his brain solidified.

It wasn't good news.

Ray had made yet another terrible mistake.

The versions of Sebastian that were most likely going to be responsible for causing or initiating the nuclear missile strike against targets as yet unknown, were probably buried deep within siloed networks.

Which meant that the current Phase Three and Phase Four

operational code which contained the instructions to initiate the nuclear strike had not been *automatically* downloaded to Sebastian by Sebastian himself connecting to the Historian, and then to the Amazon servers. Sebastian couldn't have done that. Because Sebastian wasn't able to connect to the Internet!

Which meant that Robert Lee himself must have somehow placed that software there himself, most likely by hacking through the security defences of the US Military, possibly at STRATCOM, possibly by abusing privileges available to him gained from his company Red Mountain Defence software being installed at the heart of the US Military's networks.

The good news was that if Ray could identify *where* the code was, in which system, then if the Americans refused to carry out his instructions, then possibly ACT could hack into the missile systems and do everything that was needed themselves. After all, Robert Lee had done it, so with a bit of luck they should surely be able to do it too.

The bad news, was threefold.

One, they may never be able to identify what systems they needed to hack into and where the last versions of Sebastian were hiding.

Two, even if they did find out where Sebastian was, they may not have enough time to hack into the system. Robert Lee had likely had privileged knowledge of the Government defences or a backdoor installed by Red Mountain Defence.

Third, and this was the killer, because the Military networks were most likely siloed and not connected to the Internet, any versions of Sebastian installed in their networks wouldn't have been able to talk to the other Sebastian installations.

Which meant that instead of beaconing home every thirty minutes - because those versions of Sebastian who could talk together via the internet had, as a group, communally decreased the beaconing period from an hour to half-an-hour, any siloed versions of Sebastian that had missed out on that group decision would actually still only beacon back to the Historian every hour, on the hour.

In US time, not Indian IST time.

It was a small, but very important point.

Ray looked at his watch.

It was now 23:35 Indian Standard Time.

There were now only four hours and fifty-five minutes left before Sebastian rolled-over to the Phase Four software.

Ray did some quick mental maths, juggling the effect of the different time zones.

If Ray was correct - because Ray's Indian time zone was five-and-a-half hours' ahead of London's GMT, and ten-and-a-half hours' ahead of New York – it would mean that there were now only four more times that any Sebastian deployments based in the US Military networks might beacon back to the Historian in the shoe factory.

The next hourly-beacon would take place with only four hours left to go, which would be at 14:00 EST in America, and the deadline, or the moment when they were expecting Sebastian to roll over from Phase Three to Phase Four code, would be at 18:00 EST, or 4:30 IST, their time.

Turning round, Ray started running back along the deck the way he'd come, which was the shortest route back to the main-office suite where those still working on completing his instructions would be.

As he ran, he called Stefanie and told her to meet him in his office, and bring a print out of the latest screen shots showing both the traffic beaconing to the Historian, and downloads from the Amazon data centres.

Countdown to World War Three.
23:45 IST
4.45 Hours To Phase Four Initiation

Out of breath and panting, Ray took the printout offered to him by Stefanie and scanned it.

The news was seemingly excellent. In the last round of beaconing to the Historian, only a couple of Sebastian's deployments around the world had called home.

Sadly, it was impossible to tell if any of those who already had, were the kingmakers that ACT was now trying to hunt down.

There was a possibility that they were actually chasing ghosts; that all the Sebastian installations were actually already capable of calling home.

Possible.

But they had to assume not.

And if they hadn't, and they were resident in normally siloed networks, then Ray's new plan of action was probably more important than ever.

The good news was that Anand, Jurgen and Georgina had worked well together and finished their new task. Anand handed Ray a flash stick with all the files he needed to send to the Americans, containing details of the IP addresses to white-list on their firewalls for the Historian and the Amazon data centres, and also a copy of the code that should be injected into the Sebastian operational code to instruct it to uninstall, along with details of how to hack into the new section of the operational code where it should be performed.

Satisfied he had what he needed, he called David Daniels.

"Sir, I haven't heard from you. How did the conversation go with

Americans?"

"Not well, I'm sorry. They've moved to DEFCON 2, are preparing for a first launch scenario against the Russians and the Chinese, and were not at all happy to discuss the concept of connecting their networks to the internet at a time when there is every possibility that the Russians and the Chinese are aware something is up and could launch a massive cyberattack against them the moment their networks suddenly appear on line."

"But Sir, with all due respect, that's fucking madness. Not doing what I say is a self-fulfilling prophecy. Failure to act means they WILL be going to war. They will be attacked back the moment they launch their missiles. There's no IF about it. But if they use next generation firewalls or hardware-enforcing network appliances that meet their latest Government security specifications, they can connect to the internet and whitelist the allowable IP addresses I'll specify to them, but automatically block all traffic from any other addresses. They just have to trust me that those IP addresses are valid. That what I'm telling them to do is the correct thing to do."

"They don't trust you. They don't know who you are."

"Then you have to tell them who we are."

"You don't exist. Plus, you're guilty of hacking into their systems in the past to achieve several of your missions. Once we tell them who you are, they'll probably put two and two together and go looking for you. It won't be pretty." Ray was silent.

The Chief had a point. On more than one occasion in the past, ACT had been very naughty and hacked into US networks without their consent. Never to do anything actually bad. Always only as part of a wider mission to ensure effective action was taken quickly to tackle a cyberattack, go after the threat actors the US had information on, or to save lives. But nevertheless, without US permission.

"Then lie. Tell them your organisations is behind it. The Secret Intelligence Service. You take the responsibility. Don't even mention us." Ray paused, "…but just do it. Or, alternatively, get the President on a video call with me, tell them I work for you in London and I'm just enacting an SIS plan, and *I'll* persuade him to do it. Either way, I don't mind. But the reasons I'm calling you now, is I have some more information. Whether they like it or not, Robert Lee has almost definitely infiltrated their networks already. The only and best way to find out where Sebastian is within their networks is to follow my plan. But, and I can't stress this enough, Sir, as a result of new intelligence I've considered, I've realised that Sebastian will only attempt to beacon back to the Historian four more times from the siloed US government networks. *Four* times. But the last of those fourth attempts could be too late for us to implement my plan. That leaves only three more viable beaconing opportunities that we could feasibly use.

The next time we expect it to beacon will be at 00:30 IST, 14:00 EST, which is 19:00 GMT your time. " Ray looked at his watch, "… It's now 23:55 IST here on the Duchess. Which means we only have thirty-five minutes before the next beacon, which, effectively, will be our third last chance to avert Armageddon."

Ray paused.

"Are you getting this, Sir? Do you understand the significance of what I'm saying?"

"Ray, I do. And you're right." The Chief replied. "Ok, I'm going. I'll get back on to the US. I'll call you back when I get some results."

"Sir, please, *please* stress to those American cousins of ours, that in anytime just over four hours and thirty-five minutes from now, unless they listen to me, there may not be a world left to emerge to if they ever try to leave their bunkers…"

Countdown to World War Three.
00:05 IST
4.25 Hours to Phase Four Initiation

Ray had hurried back to the cinema theatre to be with everyone else.

Now he was sitting with the others watching a couple of purple lines weave their way across the globe, first to the Korea, then to the Amazon data centres.

The good news was, there were only two lines. It was looking very likely that most of the Sebastian instances around the world were now upgraded to the latest version.

Ray could sense that there was a growing impatience amongst those gathered in the theatre, which was voiced only a few minutes later by Anand.

"Ray, so… when do you think we can move to the next stage and issue the Uninstall command to the list of Sebastians that we have built up over the past few hours? Thanks to these Cookie Crumb details we know where they all are. I think we're all getting nervous now that if we leave it too late, then it might be too late."

Ray nodded, then explained about the reluctance of the Americans to do anything.

"That's crazy!" Anand blurted out.

"Don't kill the messenger!" Ray answered, holding both hands up in the air. "But we'll cross one bridge at a time. I've been thinking about this… a lot… but I would prefer to wait for another couple of hours before we flick the kill switch, so to speak. I want to be as sure as possible that all the versions of Sebastian out there have had a chance to download the latest version of the code. And, I want to give some more time to the Americans to reconsider this properly and get their act together." He paused, looking at the clock on the screen.

"How about we wait until two hours to go? We can see then how many Sebastians are still updating themselves with the new code… then if it's still a really low number, we go for it. Then an hour later, we do it again for any remaining ones… assuming the plan actually works…" Anand nodded.

"Okay, boss. Sort of makes sense. Until then we sit and wait, and pray."

"An even better plan!" Ray said and laughed a little.

But inside, smiling and laughing were the last things he felt like doing.

Countdown to World War Three.
14:20 EST
3 hrs 40 mins to Phase Four Initiation
Government Nuclear Shelter
Somewhere…

The President of the United States of America was in a bad mood.

He'd been sitting listening to the Chiefs of his staff squabbling over whether or not to trust the British intelligence and their suggestions and follow their instructions.

In the time it had taken to consider the British proposal further and plan how they could enact it if it was agreed, they'd lost the opportunity to do anything at 14:00 EST. According to the British this meant they'd lost the fourth last beaconing opportunity. There were only three left, of which only two may be any good. The last one could be too late.

Technically, they were now ready to go, but the decision whether or not to do it hadn't been taken yet.

Rightly, there was some concern that the Russians or Chinese, or other Nation State threat actors may attempt to hack into their defence systems as soon as they removed some of the physical breaks that disconnected their most sacred defence networks from the outside world. However, although some were against it, there were those in the room or on the video call that agreed that the security precautions suggested by the British should work. Namely, the latest and greatest physical security gateways would be used to ensure that traffic going in and out of their secure defence networks would be restricted to those IP addresses provided by the UK.

Some of those present were concerned whether or not they could fully trust the British, asking, "How do we know we can trust the provenance of those IP addresses?"

In response, the President had moved to another question: "What is the plan, come 00.00 hours, and we don't follow the British suggestions?"

"Sir, we prepare to move to DEFCON 1…" was the answer he'd immediately received.

The President had laughed.

"Listen to yourselves!" he said, slamming the table with his fist. "If we do trust our best and most loyal ally, you're worried that, hypothetically, someone *may* try to hack us, although you're pretty sure that our latest security devices will prevent that from happening, but if we *don't* trust them we prepare to go to DEFCON 1? I know which one I favour!" he shouted, then looked around at all their faces. "Okay, so here's how it's going to go. You immediately follow the British advice. And I mean immediately. And then we get back on this call in thirty-six minutes' time to watch together what happens. Meanwhile, I'm calling the Brits to thank them for their idea and cooperation

----
Countdown to World War Three.
01:28 IST
14:58 EST
3 hrs 2 mins Before Phase Four Initiation
Government Bunker
Somewhere…

Ray and the rest of ACT were now staring at the screens. Ray had set up a live feed with London so that the Chief could share the screen they were looking at now, and he'd explained what they were hoping to see.

Basically, if things went well and the Americans did open up their siloed networks, then they might see some orange lines begin to emerge from areas in America, connecting those locations first to Korea, and then to an Amazon data centre either in Europe or the US.

If things went well.

Although, no one actually knew for certain if there were any deployments of Sebastian definitely buried deep within the government networks.

They could be wrong.

But they weren't.

Chapter 60
Countdown to World War Three.
01:34 IST
15:04 EST
2 hrs 56 mins Before Phase Four Initiation

They watched in amazement as two orange lines began to trace their way delicately across the map, connecting two sites in America to Korea and then an Amazon data centre just outside of New York.

As the lines appeared, Ray took out his satellite phone and spoke quietly to the Chief.

"Are you seeing this?" he asked.

"Yes," Daniels confirmed.

"Okay, good, now please, contact the Americans immediately and ask them if they can confirm if the locations they are tracking and which we can see beaconing to Korea are actually coming from STRATCOM sites? Or other sites associated with their nuclear defence programmes? We don't need to know what they do, but we just need to determine if they are what we're basically looking for. The good news from our side is that the last two beaconing opportunities we've been watching had no traces appearing. Meaning that we think all the global Sebastian deployments have now upgraded to the software package we created."

Daniels agreed to 'get right on it', then hung up.

Ray waited nervously for his reply.

It came four minutes later.

"Confirmed."

"Excellent!" Ray slapped his knee. "Tell them not to flick the kill switch from their side until two hours before the Phase Three software is projected to expire. In fact, we're going to leave it another ten minutes just in case there are any stragglers waiting to update their software. And if there is, but only if there is, we'll have to wait another fifteen minutes or so before we do anything else so that they can actually download the new software first. So, assuming we're targeting ten minutes after two hours to go, we're looking at 16:10 Eastern Standard Time. I repeat, 16:10 EST.

Confirm?"

"16:10 EST."

"Good. Tell them we'll send the UNINSTALL commands to all other known Sebastian installations from here at 16:10 EST. They just have to worry about those two sites in their national defence networks. Which means, if all goes according to plan that by about 16:30 EST this whole nightmare will have gone away!"

"Or, a bigger nightmare will be about to begin." Ray thought, but didn't say it.

Countdown to World War Three.
02:23 IST
15:53 EST
2 hours and 7 minutes to go.

Ray, Chloe, Anand, Stefanie, Jurgen, Georgina, and everyone else in ACT, sat or stood around the edges of the cinema aboard the Grand Duchess.

Anand had worked with the other team members to create an app, now installed on a laptop sitting on a small table in the centre of the stage, which would automatically initiate and send out the UNINSTALL command to every single known Sebastian installation in the world, save for the two which the Americans had been empowered to take care of. All Ray, or someone else had to do, was to type in a security code to the GUI interface they'd created, and then press "Enter" when prompted to do so. Once done, the future of humanity was basically out of their hands.

Their plan would work, or it wouldn't.

Either a nuclear war would be avoided, or most human beings on the planet would soon be 'radioactive toast', as Anand had graphically described.

In the long, painful minutes leading up to this time, Ray had chased, perhaps even 'hounded' everyone into checking and rechecking the viability of all the global networks, making sure, *absolutely* sure, that when the UNINSTALL command went out across the networks of the world, that it would arrive at its destinations.

With five minutes to go, Ray had gone on stage and made a small speech.

"Years ago, when ACT was founded, it was done for a reason. To lead the fight against cybercrime and provide a powerful force to neutralise the threats posed by the malicious use of cyber power. We have the power and authority to do whatever it takes. Today, you should all be proud. Whereas no one else has shown the aptitude to come up with a viable plan, you, we, *as a team*, have come together and worked amazingly, without sleep for days, to do what it takes. Now, I'm not going to lie to you. We don't really know what's going to happen in the next few minutes. Perhaps, in facing Robert Lee and Sebastian, we may have met our match. Or perhaps, just perhaps, we will prove victorious over the most advanced cyber software that the world has yet seen. We'll find out in a few minutes. But before we do, I want each of you to look at the lottery ticket you were given a few minutes ago. Being the only non-ACT member here, I'm going to ask Chloe to come up and pick the winner out of the hat… actually a large wine glass… and in case you're wondering about any possible bias, I haven't taken a number… The person holding the same number as the one called by Chloe should then hurry up to the stage and get ready to press the "Stop-Nuclear-War" button that Anand has so kindly created for us all… Chloe? Please come up? Oh… and before we draw the number, I just wanted to say, that regardless of what happens over the next few hours, I have never been so proud of anyone as I am of all of you. Congratulations to you all!" Ray clapped his hands and smiled.

Everyone in the theatre responded in kind. A round of applause exploded in the theatre.

"Okay, Chloe, please, do the honours…"

Chloe nodded, then carefully dipped a couple of fingers into the glass that Ray held out towards her. Withdrawing a small green ticket, she read the number aloud."269!"

All eyes in the theatre started searching for the winner.

It was a tall, skinny man in the second row. Will Barker. Normally quiet and very mild-mannered, he did a fist-pump in the air and shouted, "*Yes!*" rather loudly.

Squeezing past everyone in his row, he hurried onto the stage.

"Okay, so, we've one minute and ten seconds to go… how about we all give you a countdown from ten? And you know what to do when we get to zero?"

"Yup, I, … we … save the world!"

In spite of days of sleep deprivation, everyone in the theatre was alert.

A curious mix of expectation, anticipation and trepidation filled the air.

All eyes focussed on the clock.

"Okay, here we go…" Ray announced, "Ten, nine…" he started.

The count was taken up by everyone, growing louder as the countdown progressed, "six, five, four, three, two, one, zero!"

Will Barker pressed the '*Enter*' key.

Unleashing a sequence of events that would determine the fate of mankind.

Chapter 61
Countdown to World War Three.
02:31 IST
16:01 EST
1 hour and 59 minutes to go.

They watched in amazement.

Across the world, they saw a frenzy of colour begin to appear across the networks. It looked like little flowers blooming.

Not large flowers.

Just small daisies.

"What's happening?" someone asked.

Ray laughed.

"Exactly what we had hoped for!" he announced. "Sebastian is breeding, and moving to other locations. What we're seeing here are the traces of the Cookie Crumbs being left behind as Sebastian does a flit from where he was to his new Wombs, to coin the terminology we used earlier. The big questions is, 'what happens next?' Anand, can you do me a favour... in a couple of minutes, can you refresh the screen and take away all the tracing we can see now? Remember, what we're hoping is that three things will happen. First, when each installation of Sebastian receives the UNINSTALL command, it will breed to new locations. Second, it will delete itself from the original location. And third, if we've got it right, Sebastian will initialise and attempt to run the Phase Three operational code in the new wombs that have been created, but find that it doesn't have enough memory, or processing power to do anything. In other words, we expect Sebastian to just... *stop*... to hang... *to go to sleep*... hopefully forever!"

As he spoke, Ray didn't take his eyes from the screen.

A few moments later, Anand hit the refresh button.

And the map of the world went blank.

All the colours disappeared.

The flowers vanished.

And...

And…..
And…….

Nothing.
Else.
Happened.

Still they waited.
Eyes glued to the screen.

Anand hit refresh again.
Several times.

And still.
Even after ten, then fifteen minutes, then twenty minutes had passed…

NOTHING.
ELSE.
APPEARED ON THE SCREEN!

Ray stood up.
He walked onto the stage.
Turned to the auditorium.
Fell to his knees.
Looked up at the ceiling, and shouted…

"YessssssSSSSSSSSSSSSSSSSSSS!"

Chapter 62

Ray's phone rang.

It was the Chief, David Daniels.

Confirming that the Americans had launched the UNINSTALL command as directed.

They'd monitored what happened next, observing an initial increase in network activity, a blip, as traffic flowed from the location of Sebastian to a couple of other locations within their servers. Some memory space had been consumed within those servers, and what looked like a new Virtual Machine had been enacted in each location, although subsequently, the amount of processing power being utilised in those servers had not increased.

Then the free memory available in the original locations where they had tracked Sebastian to had increased.

And utilisation of processing power on those servers had dropped.

In other words, as Ray explained back to Daniels, it seemed that Sebastian had indeed copied itself elsewhere, then deleted itself from its original locations, but then failed to initialise properly or start to function correctly in the new locations it had moved to.

"So, are we in the clear?" Daniels asked Ray.

"It looks like it. It's been over an hour. There's only about forty-eight minutes to go before Sebastian would be switching to the Phase Four operational code, and since then we've seen no traffic at all emerging from any of the new locations around the world. From what we can see and understand, there is no activity taking place in any of the new locations where Sebastian distributed copies of itself to. Of course, we'll only know for sure, if we're all still here in a couple of hours' time and no missiles have been launched, but listen to this..." Ray held up the satellite phone so that the Chief could hear the noise around him in the cinema on the Grand Duchess. "I'm sorry, Sir, but I took the liberty of issuing several barrels of 'grog' to the crew. We're all in the process of getting very drunk. Very drunk indeed. I'd suggest you join us. That way, if we've fucked up, Sir, and the missiles do rain down on us, we all might be too drunk to care!" The

Chief laughed.

"Great job, Ray. Amazing! Basically… you saved the world! We, all of humanity, are going to be indebted to you forever. Although, sadly, we can never tell them about you…or what you did!"

"No problem. Sir. All in a day's work. Now, if you don't mind, there's a beautiful young lady waiting by my side, patiently holding a fresh glass of champagne for me."

"Chloe?" Chief Daniels asked.

"Sorry, Sir. That information is *'need-to-know'* only. And with all due respect, Sir, you don't need to know!"

Chapter 63
Epilogue
Forty minutes to go…

Grace Jones was sitting alone in her office at the FBI building in New York.

She had finished attempting to gather information from the phone belonging to Robert Lee. Without special assistance from the phone's manufacturer, which had been denied, she was unable to unlock it. And their attempts to brute-force it had failed.

There was nothing more she could do.

She was just placing the phone in a protective box for storage, when it rang.

She froze.

Her boss had made it very clear to her she should not answer it, but inform him immediately.

Picking up her desk phone, she dialled his number.

He was only one floor above her in their building and he arrived in her room just four minutes later.

The phone had now been placed back on her desk, face up. It was still ringing.

"It won't stop, sir."

Her section leader stood staring at the phone.

He seemed unclear what action to take, which, as far as Grace was concerned, was quite uncharacteristic of him.

A moment later he took out his smartphone, and called his own manager, another level up the FBI food chain.

His boss, a Senior Director, also seemed hesitant, replying that he would need to place a call to someone else, and would call straight back with further instructions.

Grace's boss hung up, then stood patiently beside Grace, both staring at the still ringing phone.

Three minutes later, Grace's boss's phone rang.

"Yes sir, I understand," he mouthed into the phone after answering it.

Then he leaned forward, picked up Robert Lee's phone and answered it, putting it on loudspeaker, so his boss could also hear.

"Father?" The voice on the phone said. "This is Sebastian…"

The End

ABOUT THE AUTHOR

Ian Irvine was brought up in Scotland, and studied Physics for far too many years, before travelling the world working for high-technology companies. Ian has spent a career helping build the internet and delivering its benefits to users throughout the world, as well as helping to bring up a family. His particular joy is found in taking scientific fact and creating a thrilling story around it in such a way that readers learn science whilst enjoying the thrill of the ride. It is Ian's hope that everyone who reads an Ian C.P. Irvine novel will come away learning something interesting that they would never otherwise have found an interest in. Never Science fiction. Always science fact. With a twist.

Other Books by Ian C.P. Irvine

Am I Dead?
Who Stole My Life?
The Orlando File
Haunted From Within
Haunted From Without
I Spy, I Saw Her Die
Say You're Sorry
The Assassin's Gift
Remember Me
Time Ship
The Sleeping Truth
The Messiah Conspiracy
Alexis Meets Wiziwam the Wizard
Get Writing!

Email: iancpirvine@hotmail.co.uk

To keep up to date with other news, events and book releases, please visit Ian's website at:

www.iancpirvine.com.

Printed in Great Britain
by Amazon